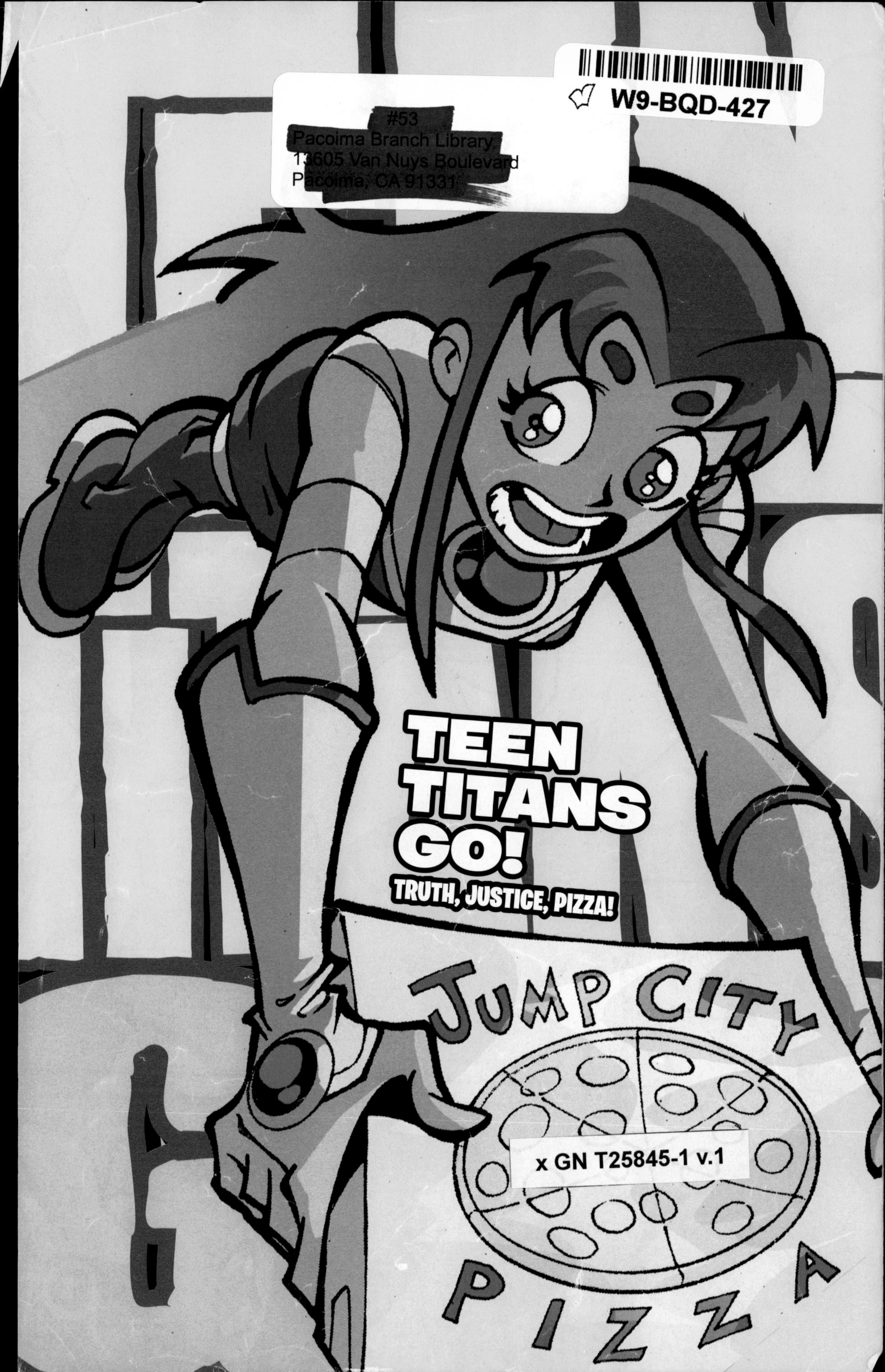
TEEN TITANS GO!
TRUTH, JUSTICE, PIZZA!
JUMP CITY PIZZA

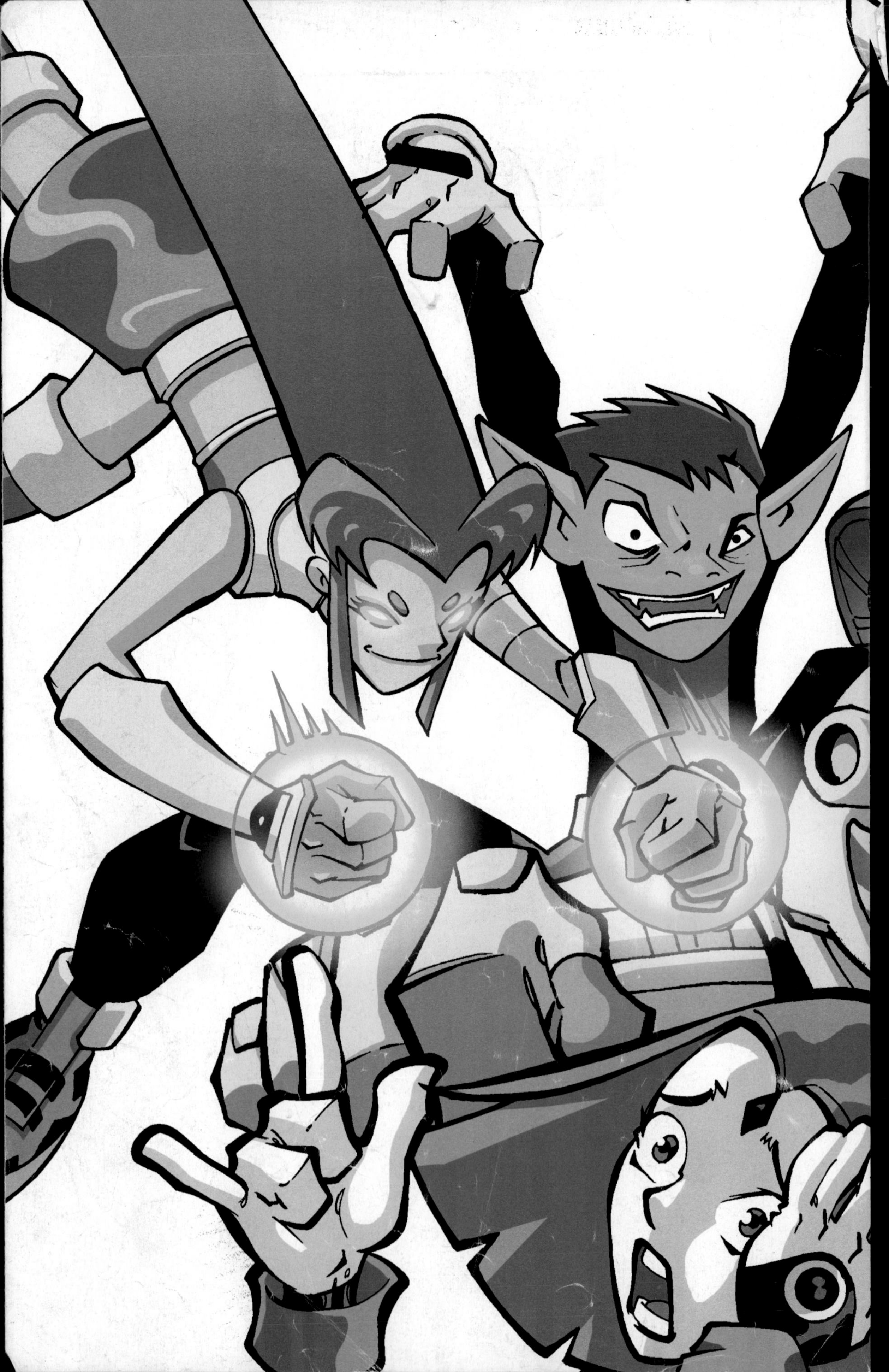

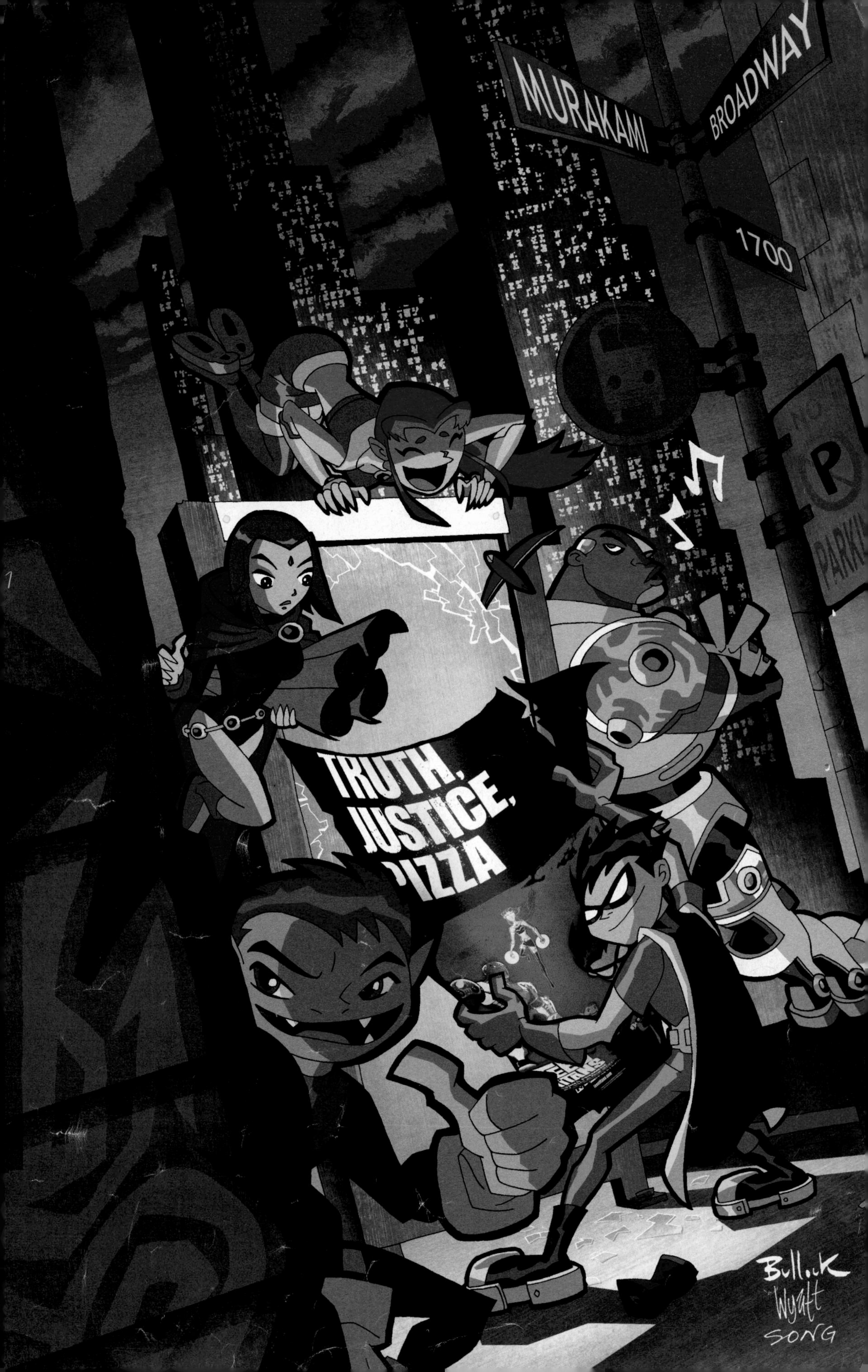
MURAKAMI
BROADWAY
1700
P
PARKI
TRUTH, JUSTICE, PIZZA
Bullock
Wyatt
SONG

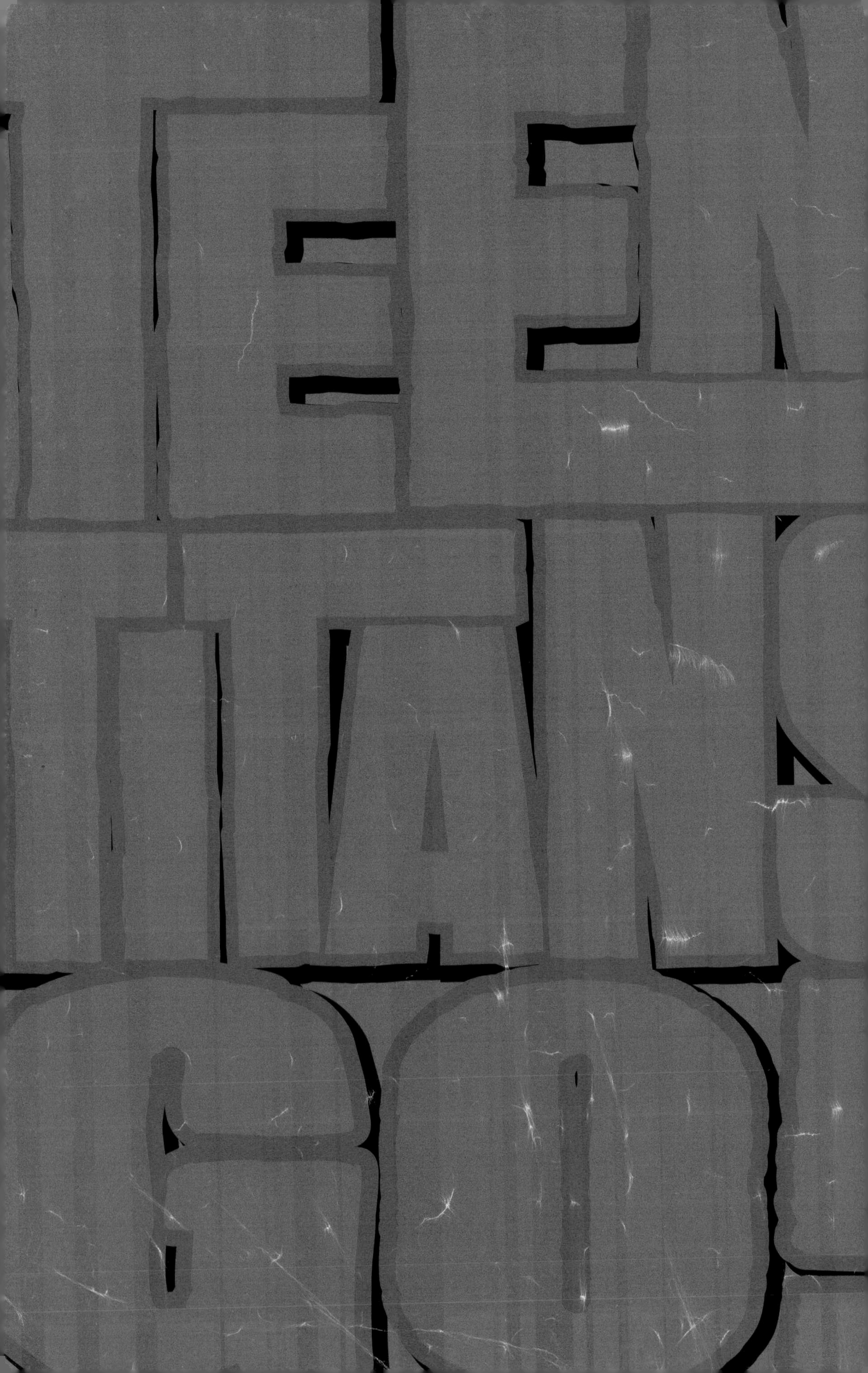

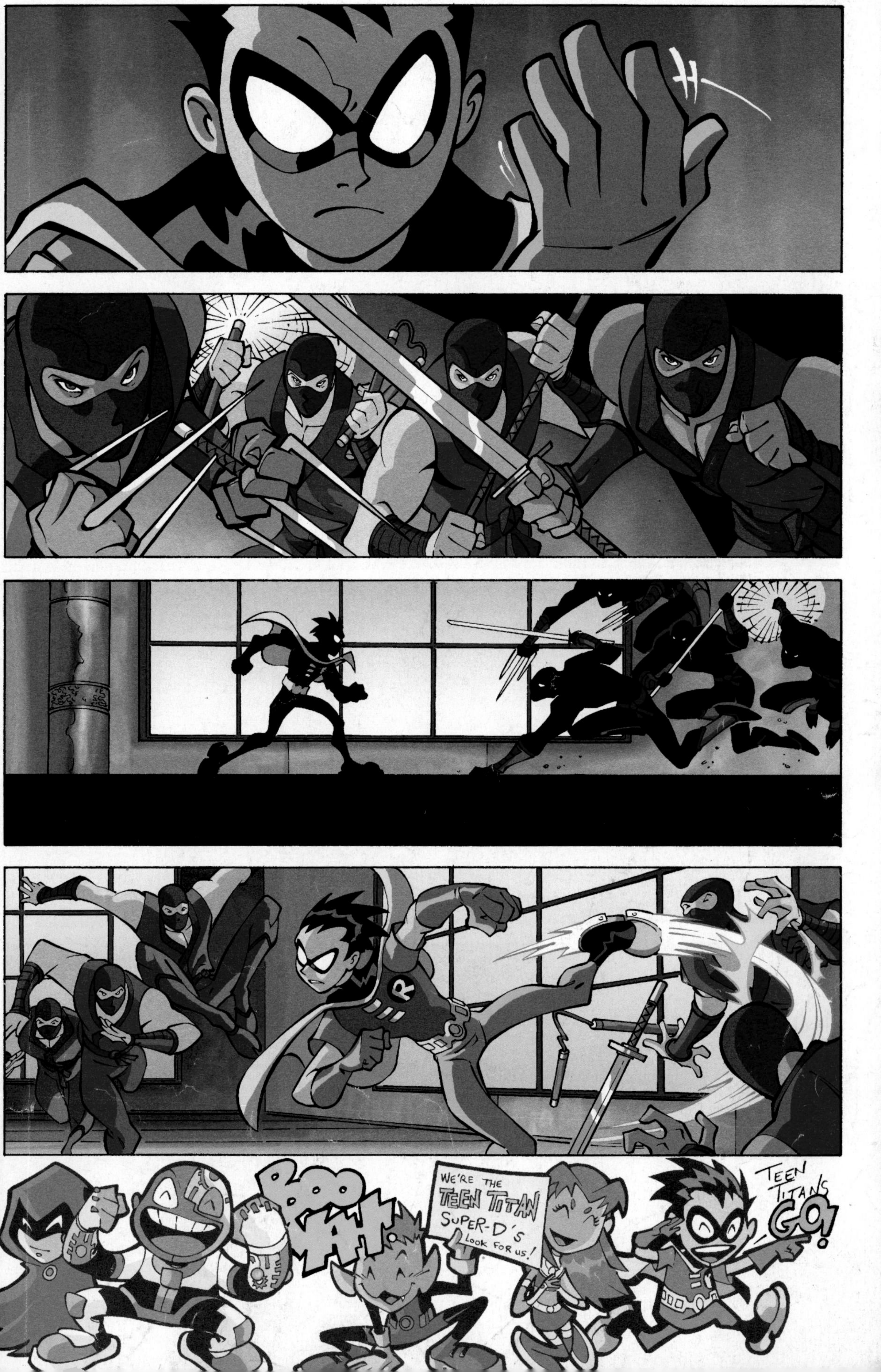
BOO YAH!
WE'RE THE TEEN TITAN SUPER-D'S LOOK FOR US!
TEEN TITANS GO!

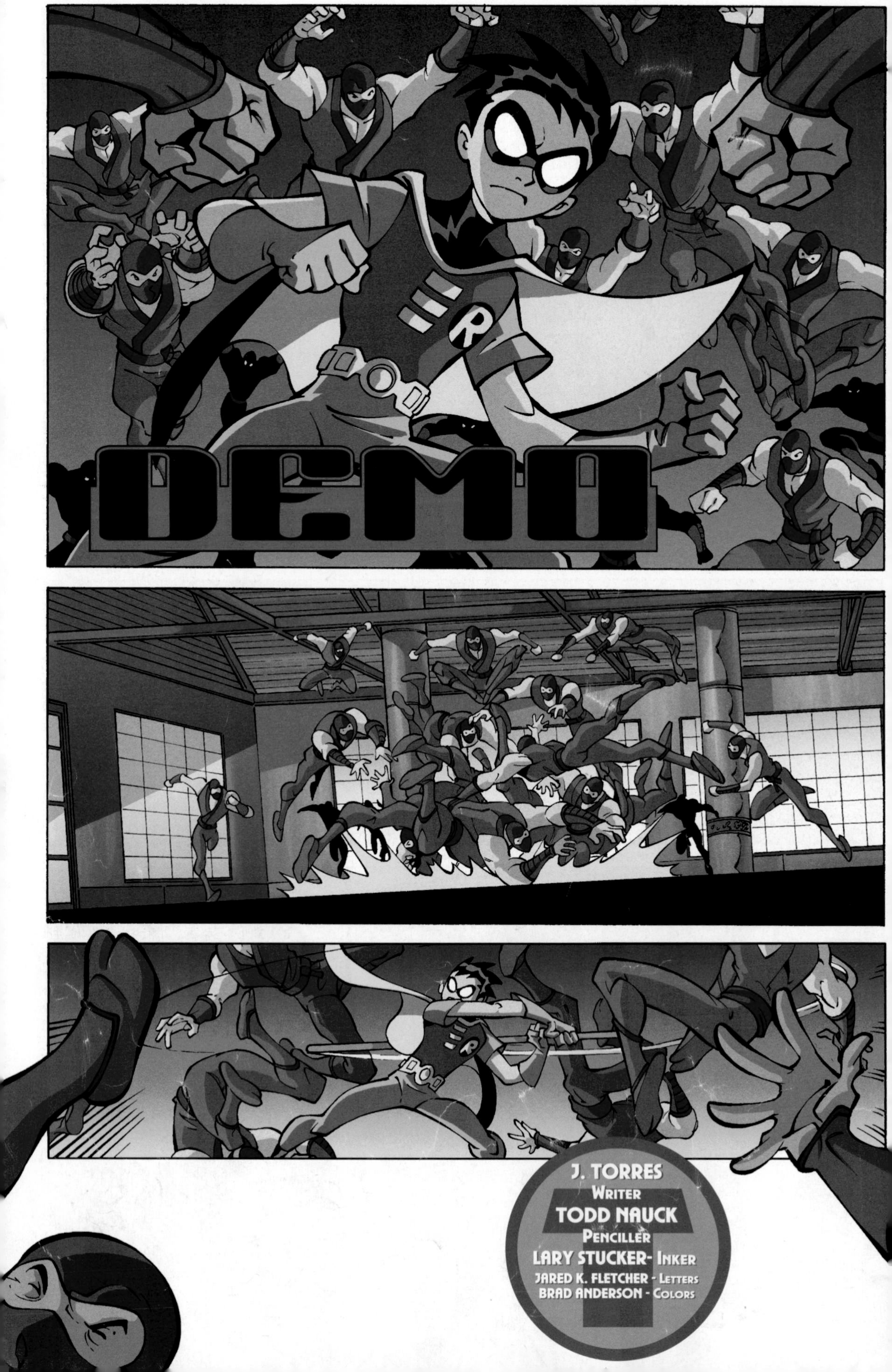
DEMO
J. TORRES
WRITER
TODD NAUCK
PENCILLER
LARY STUCKER- INKER
JARED K. FLETCHER - LETTERS
BRAD ANDERSON - COLORS

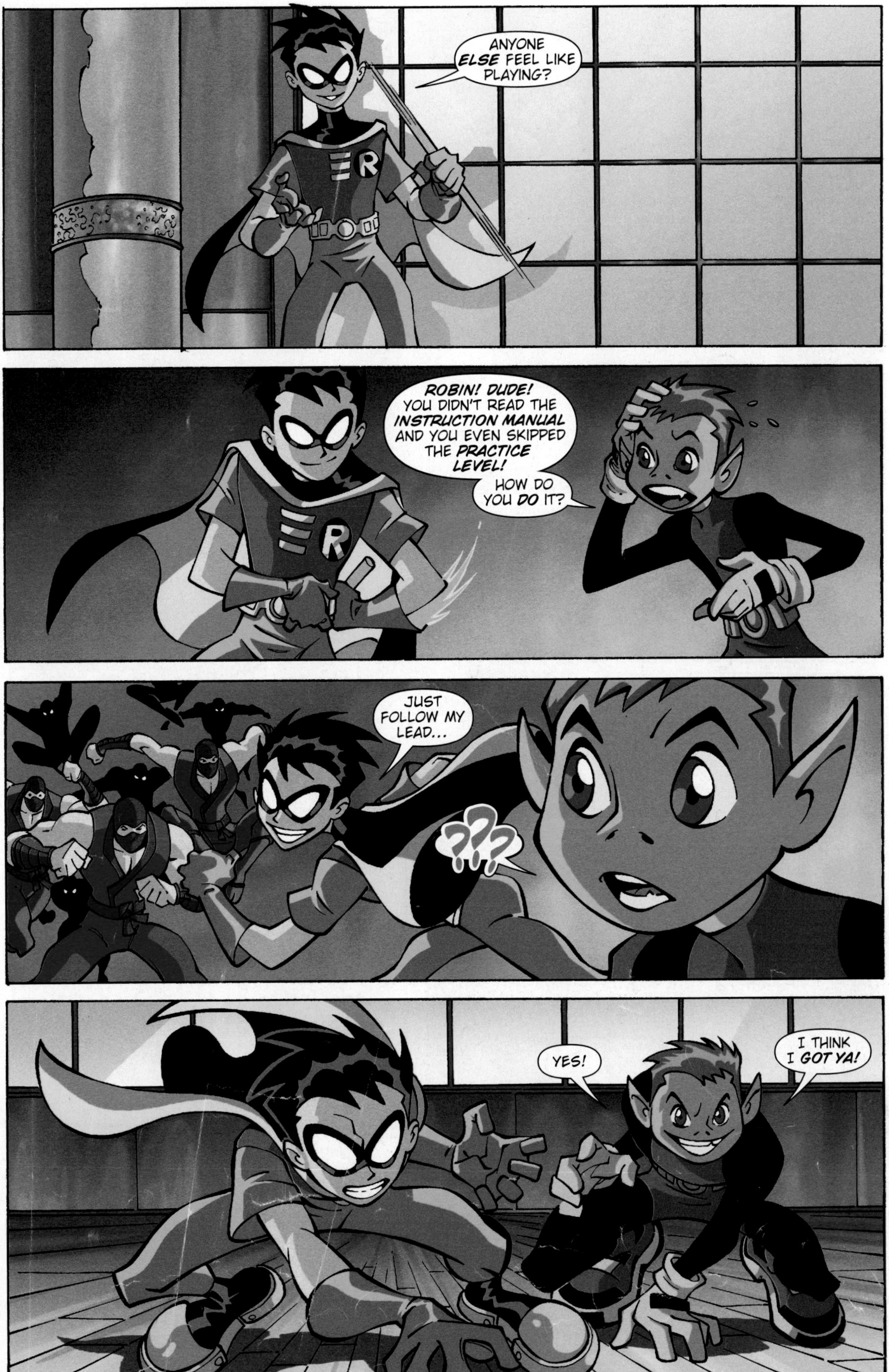
ANYONE ELSE FEEL LIKE PLAYING?
ROBIN! DUDE! YOU DIDN'T READ THE INSTRUCTION MANUAL AND YOU EVEN SKIPPED THE PRACTICE LEVEL!
HOW DO YOU DO IT?
JUST FOLLOW MY LEAD...
???
YES!
I THINK I GOT YA!

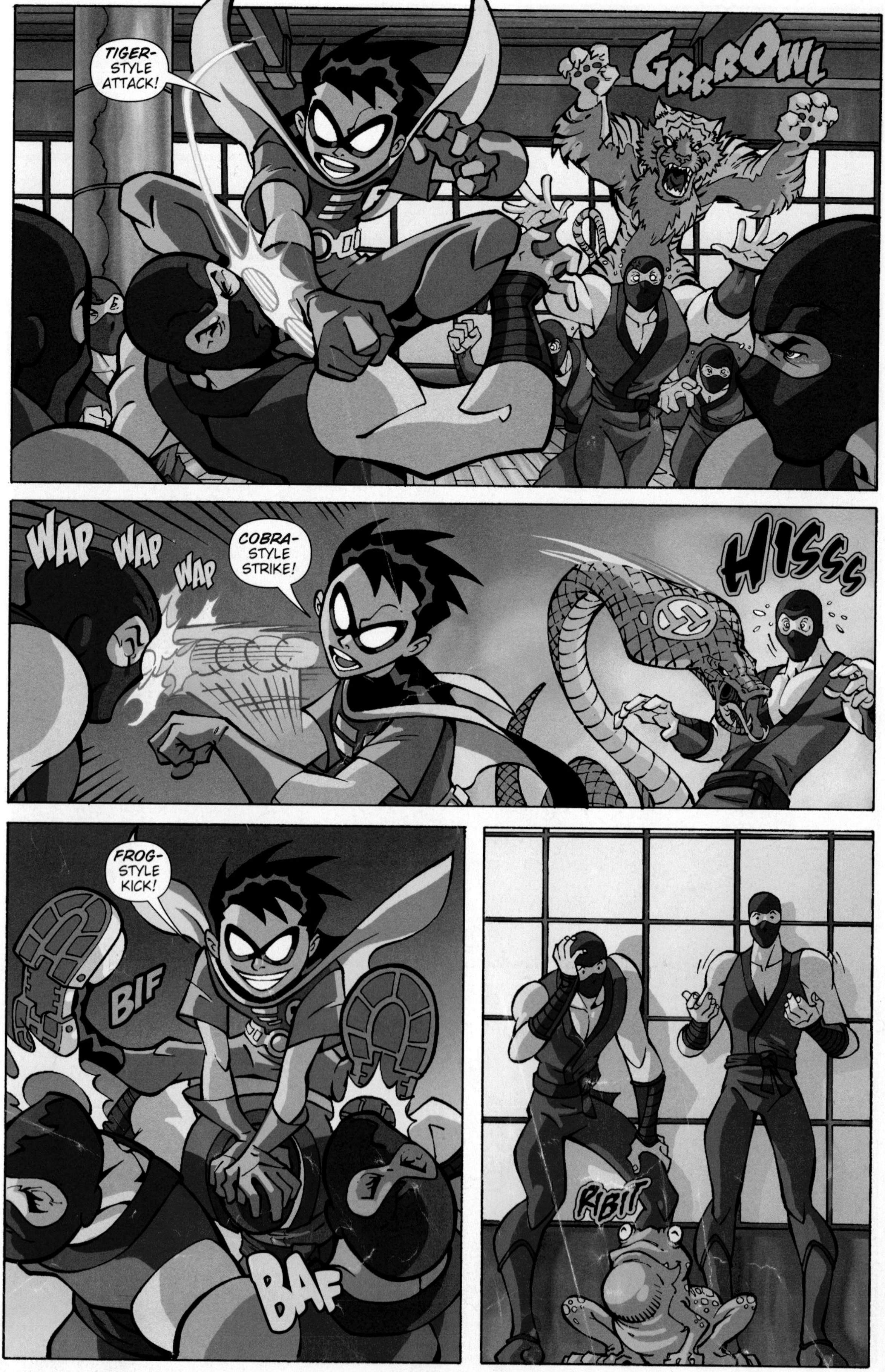
TIGER-STYLE ATTACK!
GRRROWL
WAP
WAP
WAP
COBRA-STYLE STRIKE!
HISSS
FROG-STYLE KICK!
BIF
BAF
RIBIT

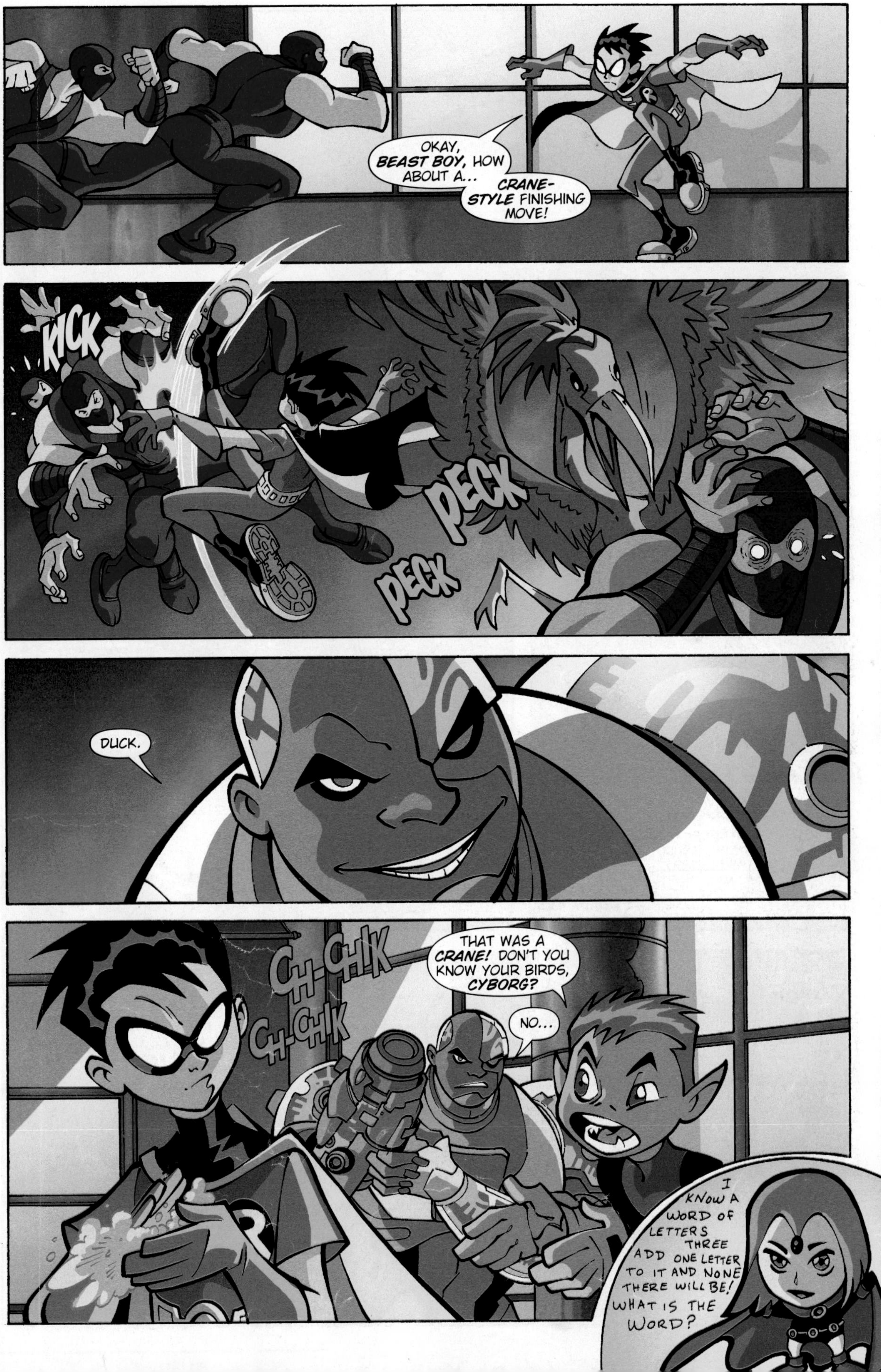
OKAY, BEAST BOY, HOW ABOUT A...
CRANE-STYLE FINISHING MOVE!
KICK
PECK
PECK
DUCK.
CH-CHIK
CH-CHIK
THAT WAS A CRANE! DON'T YOU KNOW YOUR BIRDS, CYBORG?
NO...
I KNOW A WORD OF LETTERS THREE ADD ONE LETTER TO IT AND NONE THERE WILL BE! WHAT IS THE WORD?

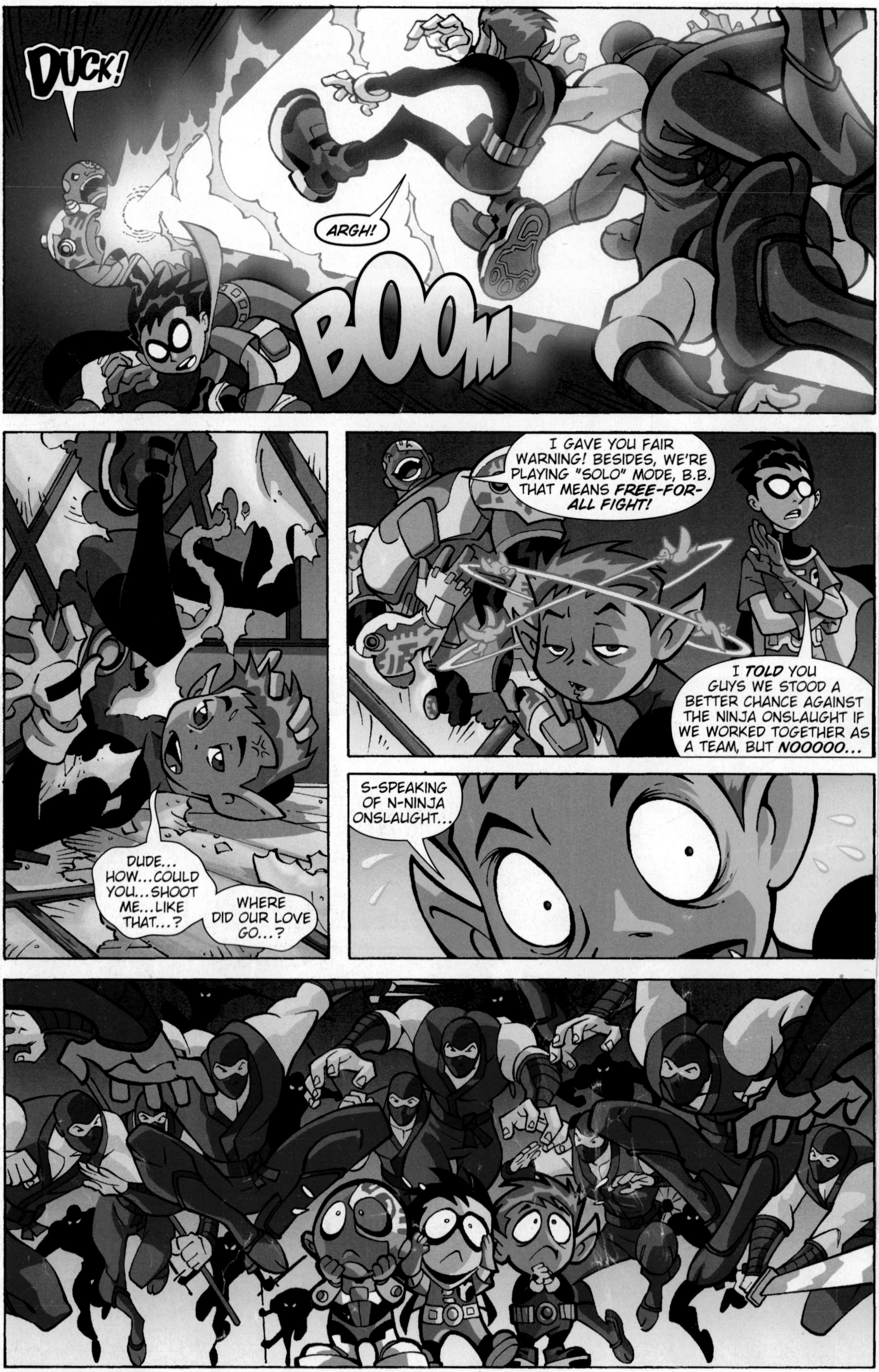
DUCK!
ARGH!
BOOM
DUDE... HOW...COULD YOU...SHOOT ME...LIKE THAT...?
WHERE DID OUR LOVE GO...?
I GAVE YOU FAIR WARNING! BESIDES, WE'RE PLAYING "SOLO" MODE, B.B. THAT MEANS FREE-FOR-ALL FIGHT!
I TOLD YOU GUYS WE STOOD A BETTER CHANCE AGAINST THE NINJA ONSLAUGHT IF WE WORKED TOGETHER AS A TEAM, BUT NOOOOO...
S-SPEAKING OF N-NINJA ONSLAUGHT...

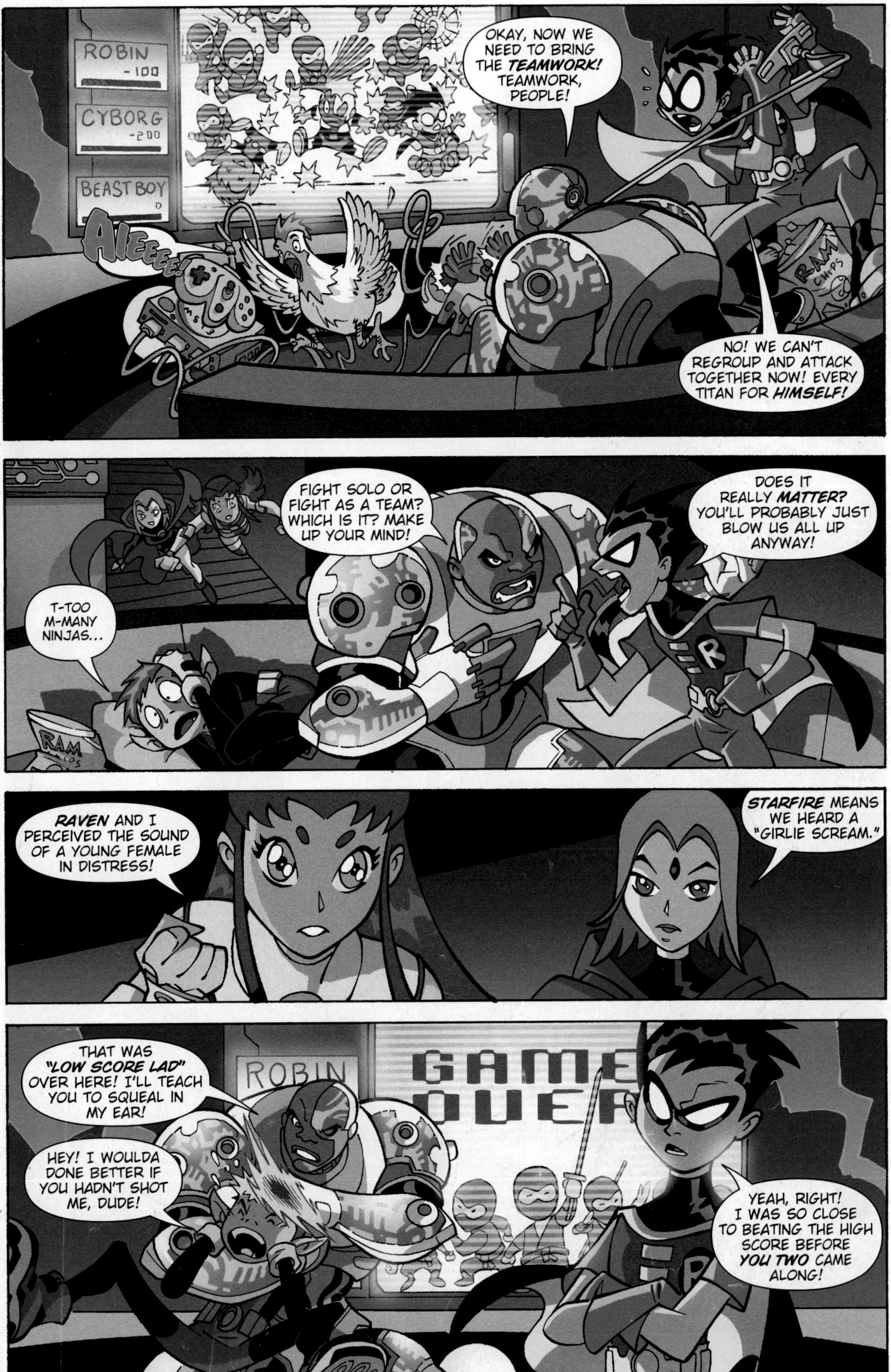

ROBIN -100
CYBORG -200
BEAST BOY 0
OKAY, NOW WE NEED TO BRING THE **TEAMWORK!** TEAMWORK, PEOPLE!
AIEEEE!
RAM CHIPS
NO! WE CAN'T REGROUP AND ATTACK TOGETHER NOW! EVERY TITAN FOR **HIMSELF!**
FIGHT SOLO OR FIGHT AS A TEAM? WHICH IS IT? MAKE UP YOUR MIND!
DOES IT REALLY **MATTER?** YOU'LL PROBABLY JUST BLOW US ALL UP ANYWAY!
T-TOO M-MANY NINJAS...
RAM
RAVEN AND I PERCEIVED THE SOUND OF A YOUNG FEMALE IN DISTRESS!
STARFIRE MEANS WE HEARD A "GIRLIE SCREAM."
ROBIN
GAME OVER
THAT WAS **"LOW SCORE LAD"** OVER HERE! I'LL TEACH YOU TO SQUEAL IN MY EAR!
HEY! I WOULDA DONE BETTER IF YOU HADN'T SHOT ME, DUDE!
YEAH, RIGHT! I WAS SO CLOSE TO BEATING THE HIGH SCORE BEFORE **YOU TWO** CAME ALONG!

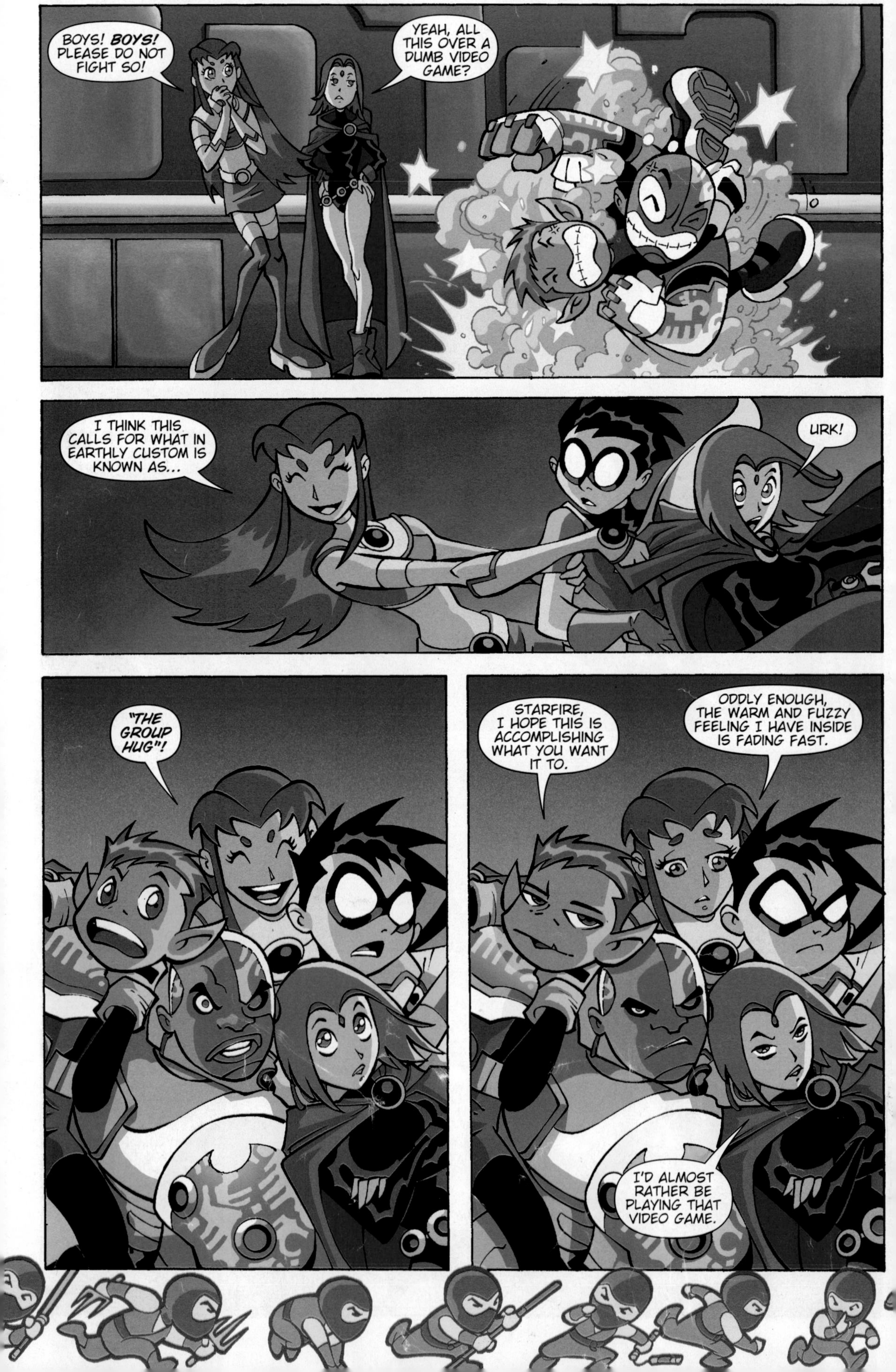
BOYS! BOYS! PLEASE DO NOT FIGHT SO!
YEAH, ALL THIS OVER A DUMB VIDEO GAME?
I THINK THIS CALLS FOR WHAT IN EARTHLY CUSTOM IS KNOWN AS...
URK!
"THE GROUP HUG"!
STARFIRE, I HOPE THIS IS ACCOMPLISHING WHAT YOU WANT IT TO.
ODDLY ENOUGH, THE WARM AND FUZZY FEELING I HAVE INSIDE IS FADING FAST.
I'D ALMOST RATHER BE PLAYING THAT VIDEO GAME.

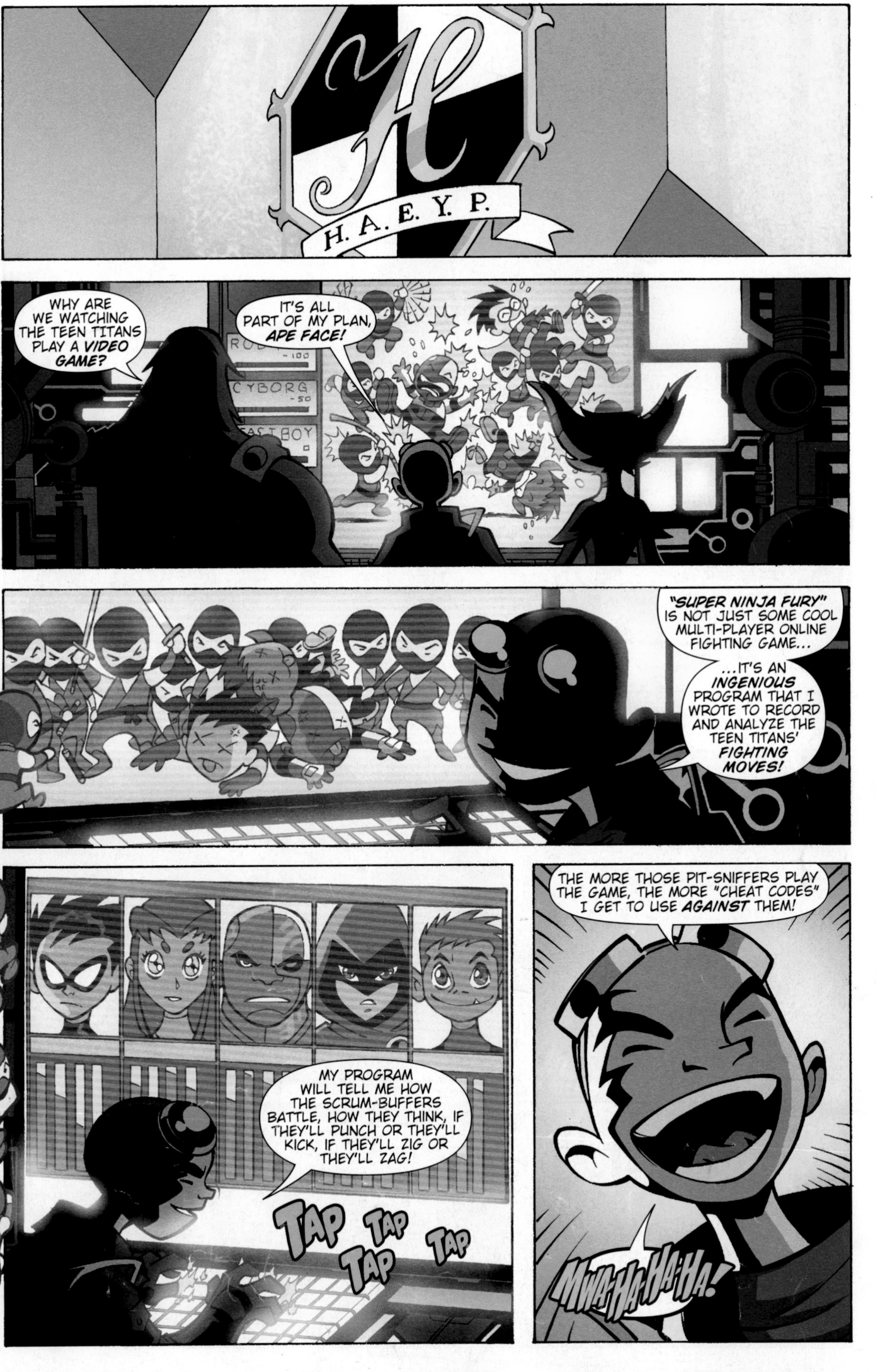
H
H. A. E. Y. P.
WHY ARE WE WATCHING THE TEEN TITANS PLAY A *VIDEO GAME?*
IT'S ALL PART OF MY PLAN, *APE FACE!*
CYBORG
"SUPER NINJA FURY" IS NOT JUST SOME COOL MULTI-PLAYER ONLINE FIGHTING GAME...
...IT'S AN *INGENIOUS* PROGRAM THAT I WROTE TO RECORD AND ANALYZE THE TEEN TITANS' *FIGHTING MOVES!*
MY PROGRAM WILL TELL ME HOW THE SCRUM-BUFFERS BATTLE, HOW THEY THINK, IF THEY'LL PUNCH OR THEY'LL KICK, IF THEY'LL ZIG OR THEY'LL ZAG!
TAP TAP TAP TAP
THE MORE THOSE PIT-SNIFFERS PLAY THE GAME, THE MORE "CHEAT CODES" I GET TO USE *AGAINST* THEM!
MWA-HA-HA-HA!

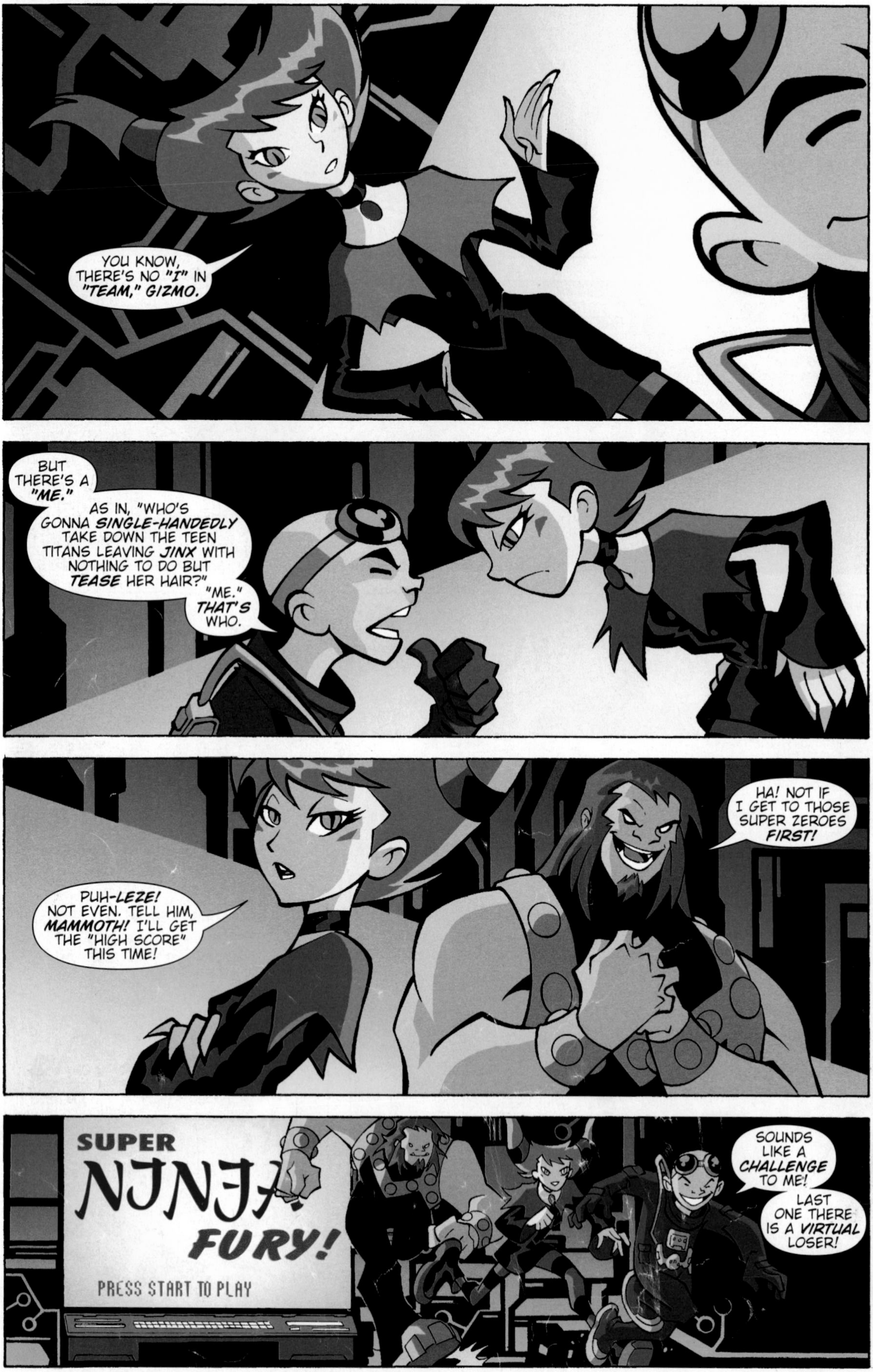
YOU KNOW, THERE'S NO "I" IN "TEAM," GIZMO.
BUT THERE'S A "ME."
AS IN, "WHO'S GONNA SINGLE-HANDEDLY TAKE DOWN THE TEEN TITANS LEAVING JINX WITH NOTHING TO DO BUT TEASE HER HAIR?"
"ME." THAT'S WHO.
HA! NOT IF I GET TO THOSE SUPER ZEROES FIRST!
PUH-LEZE! NOT EVEN. TELL HIM, MAMMOTH! I'LL GET THE "HIGH SCORE" THIS TIME!
SUPER
NINJA
FURY!
PRESS START TO PLAY
SOUNDS LIKE A CHALLENGE TO ME!
LAST ONE THERE IS A VIRTUAL LOSER!

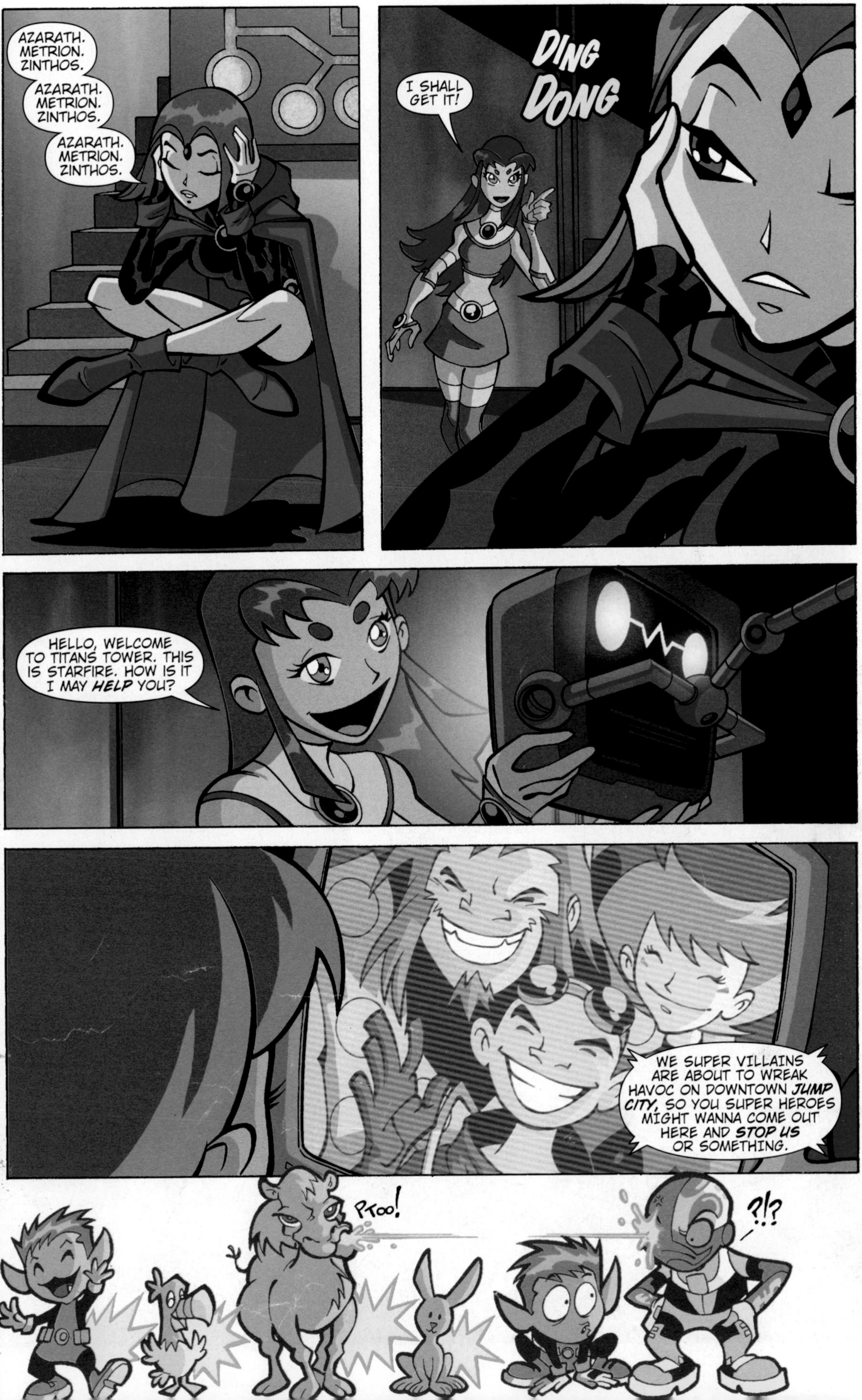
AZARATH. METRION. ZINTHOS.
AZARATH. METRION. ZINTHOS.
AZARATH. METRION. ZINTHOS.
I SHALL GET IT!
DING DONG
HELLO, WELCOME TO TITANS TOWER. THIS IS STARFIRE. HOW IS IT I MAY HELP YOU?
WE SUPER VILLAINS ARE ABOUT TO WREAK HAVOC ON DOWNTOWN JUMP CITY, SO YOU SUPER HEROES MIGHT WANNA COME OUT HERE AND STOP US OR SOMETHING.
PTOO!
?!?

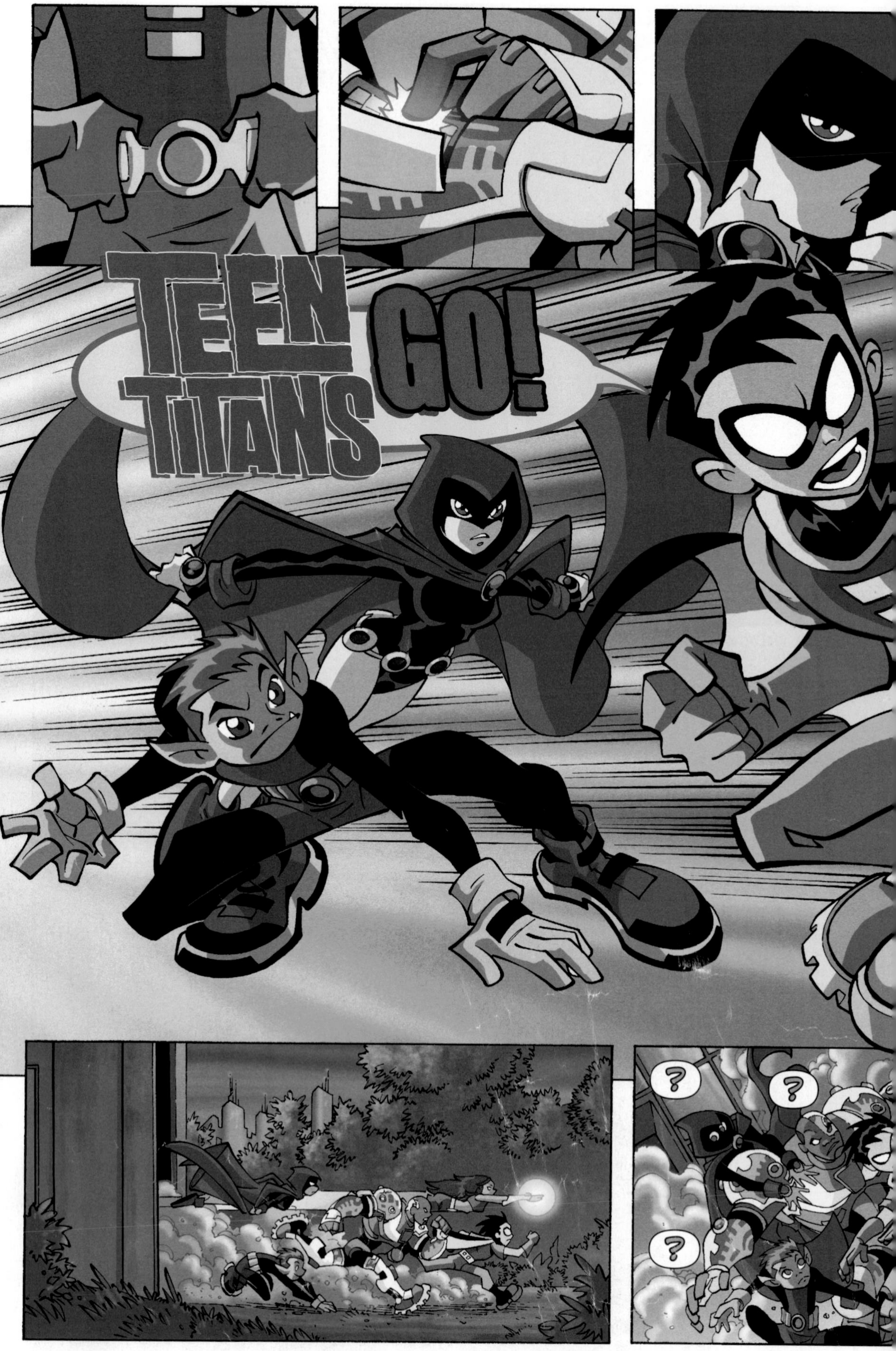
TEEN TITANS GO!
?
?
?

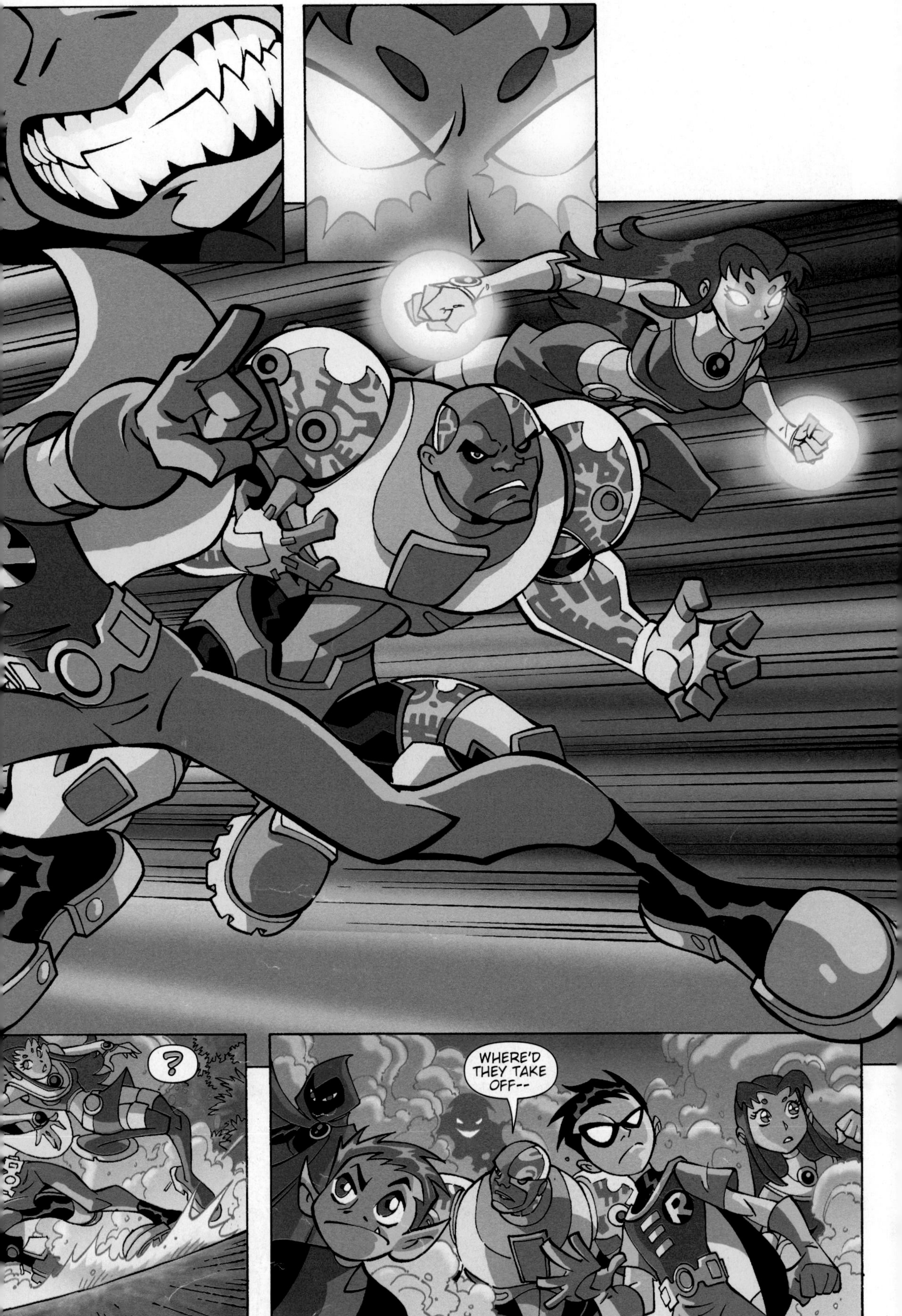
?
WHERE'D THEY TAKE OFF--

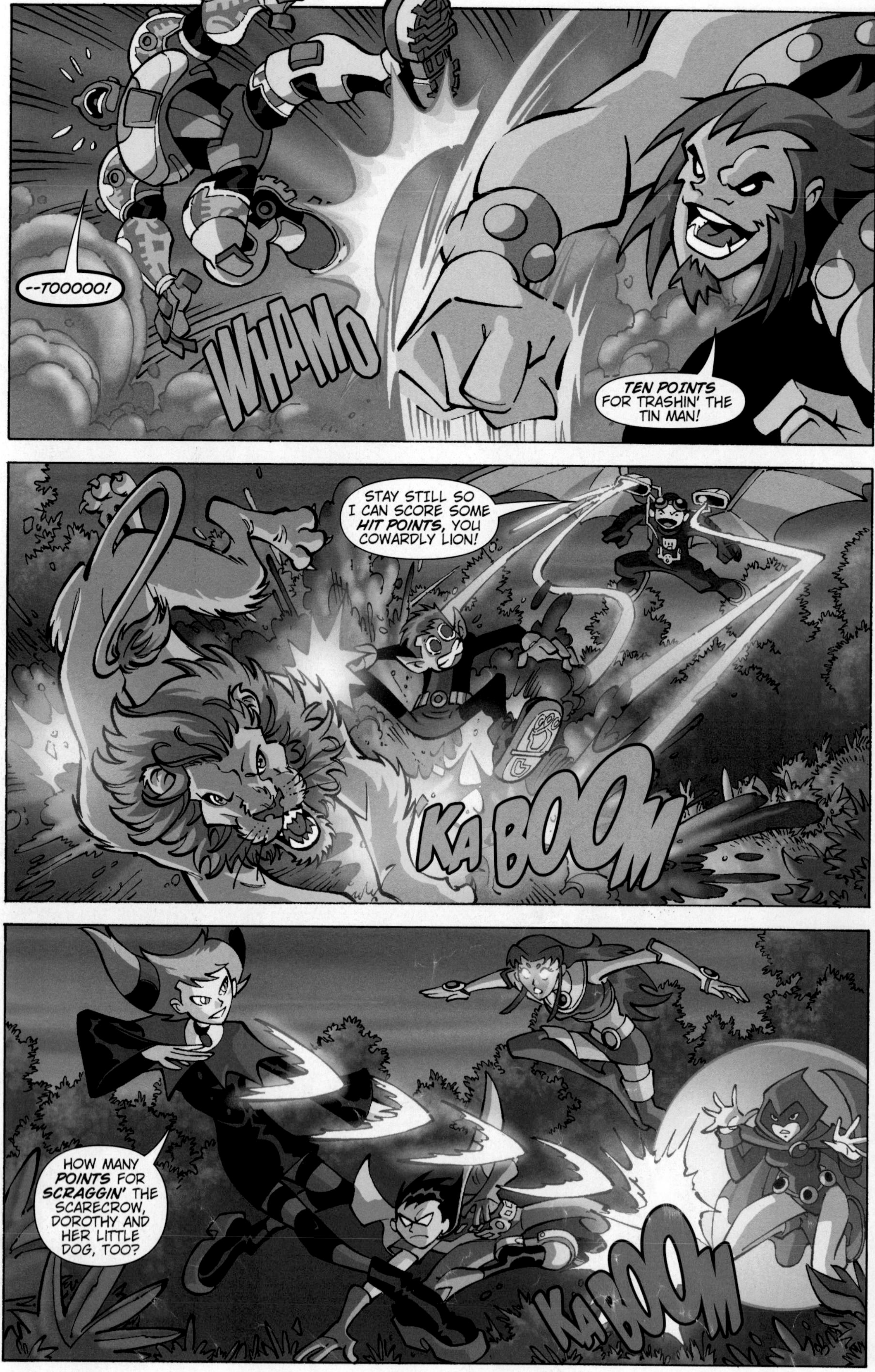
--TOOOOO!
WHAMO
TEN POINTS FOR TRASHIN' THE TIN MAN!
STAY STILL SO I CAN SCORE SOME HIT POINTS, YOU COWARDLY LION!
KA BOOM
HOW MANY POINTS FOR SCRAGGIN' THE SCARECROW, DOROTHY AND HER LITTLE DOG, TOO?
KA BOOM

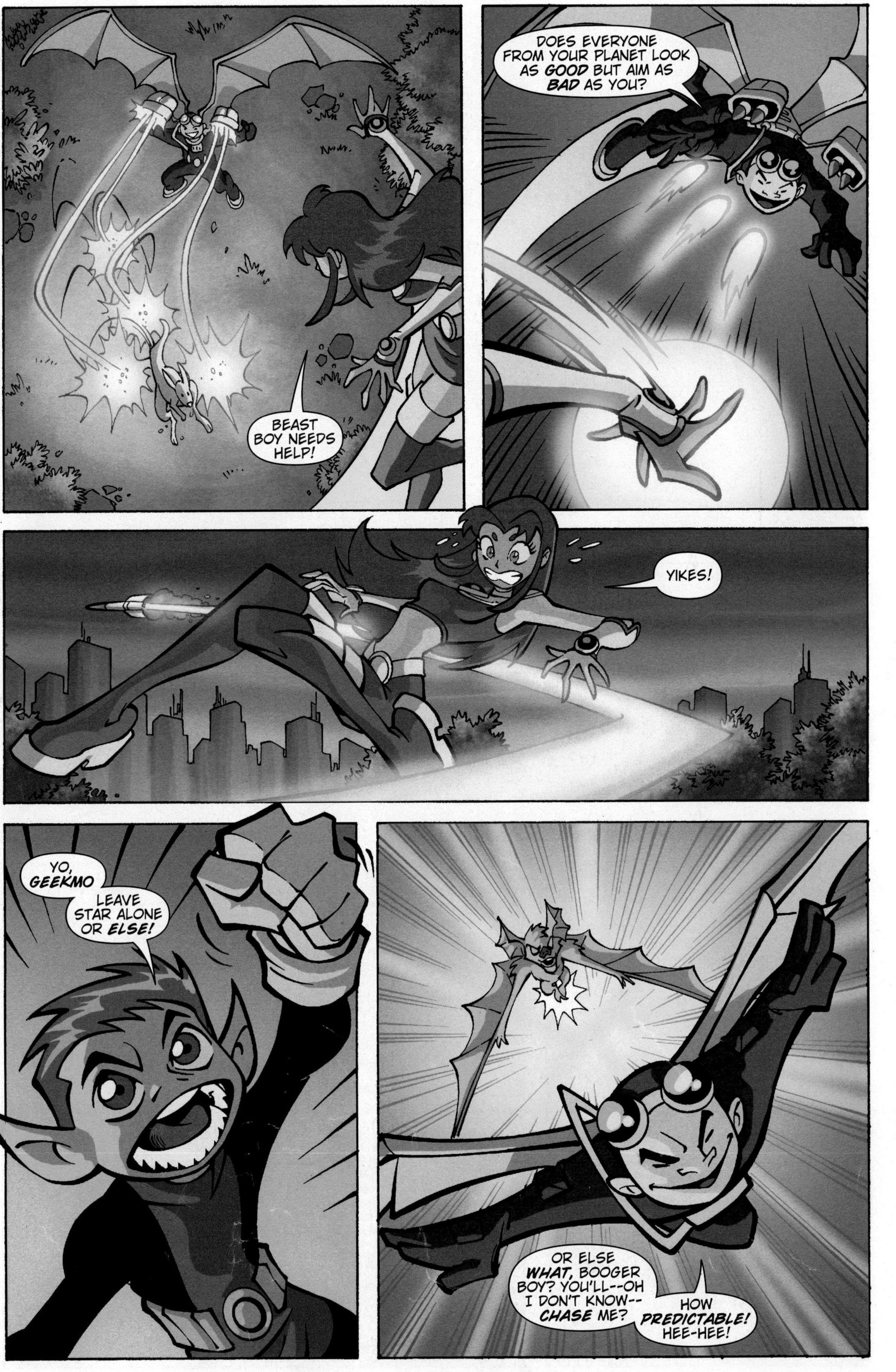
BEAST BOY NEEDS HELP!
DOES EVERYONE FROM YOUR PLANET LOOK AS GOOD BUT AIM AS BAD AS YOU?
YIKES!
YO, GEEKMO
LEAVE STAR ALONE OR ELSE!
OR ELSE WHAT, BOOGER BOY? YOU'LL--OH I DON'T KNOW-- CHASE ME?
HOW PREDICTABLE! HEE-HEE!

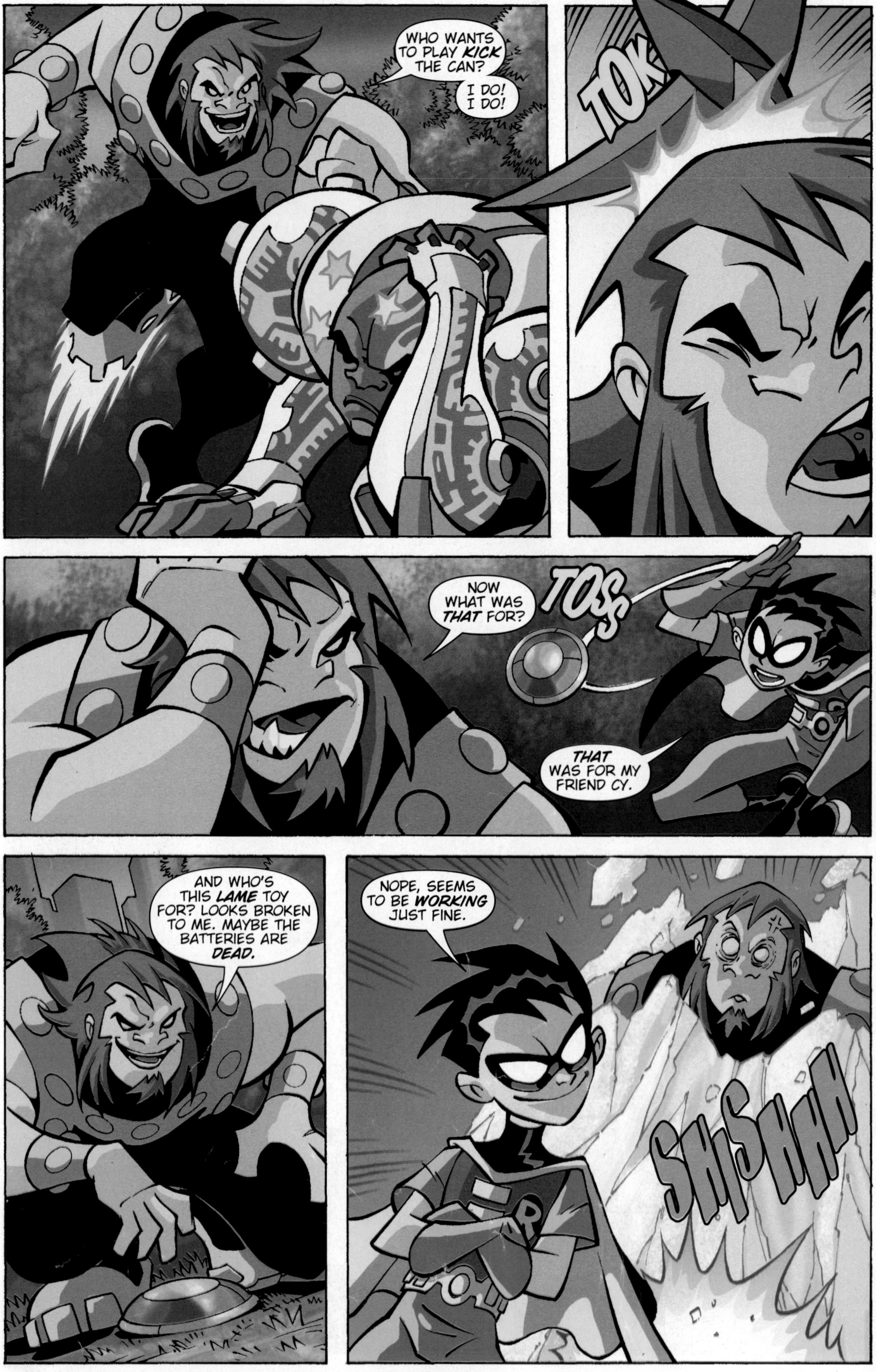
WHO WANTS TO PLAY KICK THE CAN?
I DO! I DO!
TOK
NOW WHAT WAS THAT FOR?
TOSS
THAT WAS FOR MY FRIEND CY.
AND WHO'S THIS LAME TOY FOR? LOOKS BROKEN TO ME. MAYBE THE BATTERIES ARE DEAD.
NOPE, SEEMS TO BE WORKING JUST FINE.
SHHSHHH

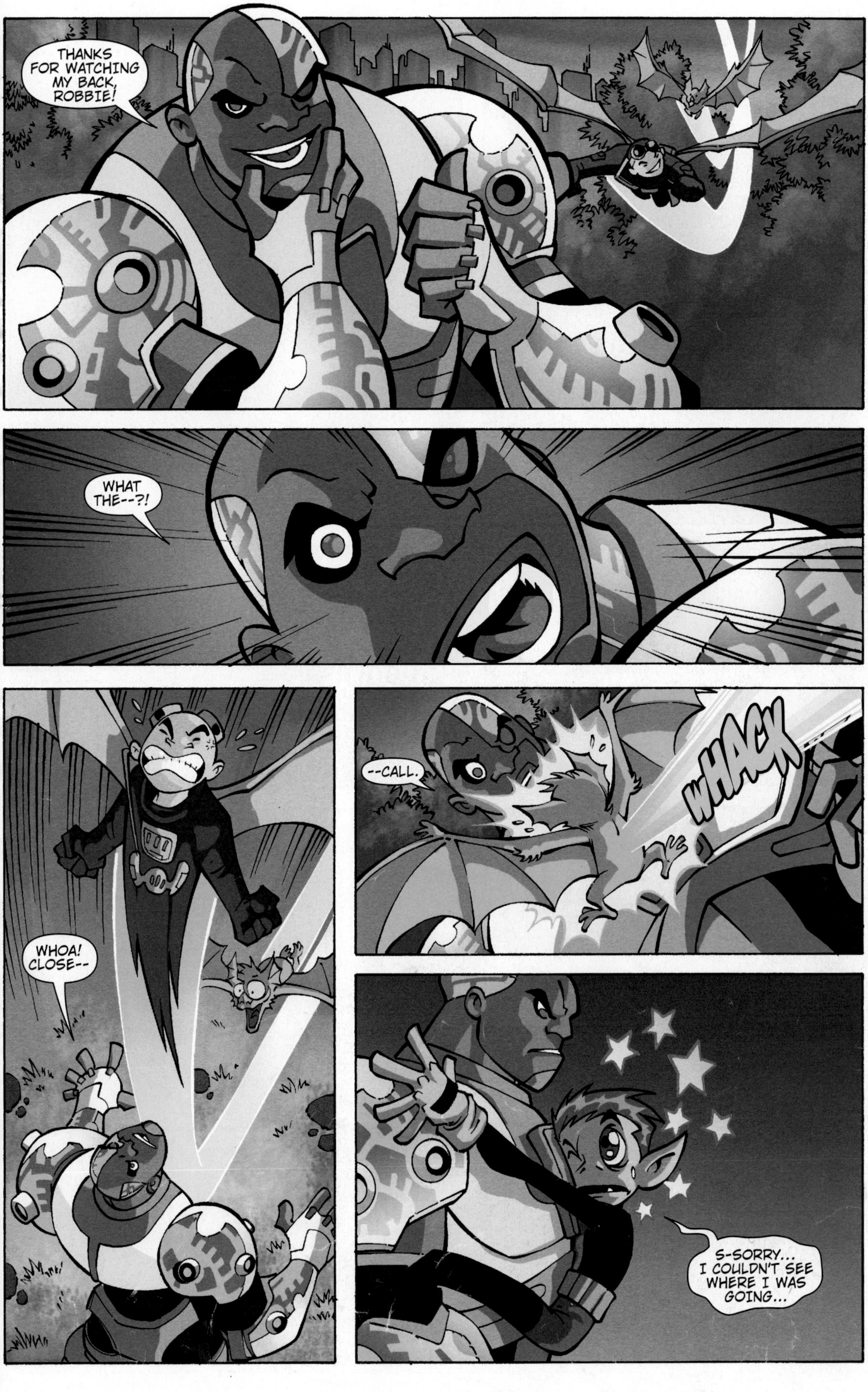
THANKS FOR WATCHING MY BACK, ROBBIE!
WHAT THE--?!
WHOA! CLOSE--
--CALL.
wHACK
S-SORRY... I COULDN'T SEE WHERE I WAS GOING...

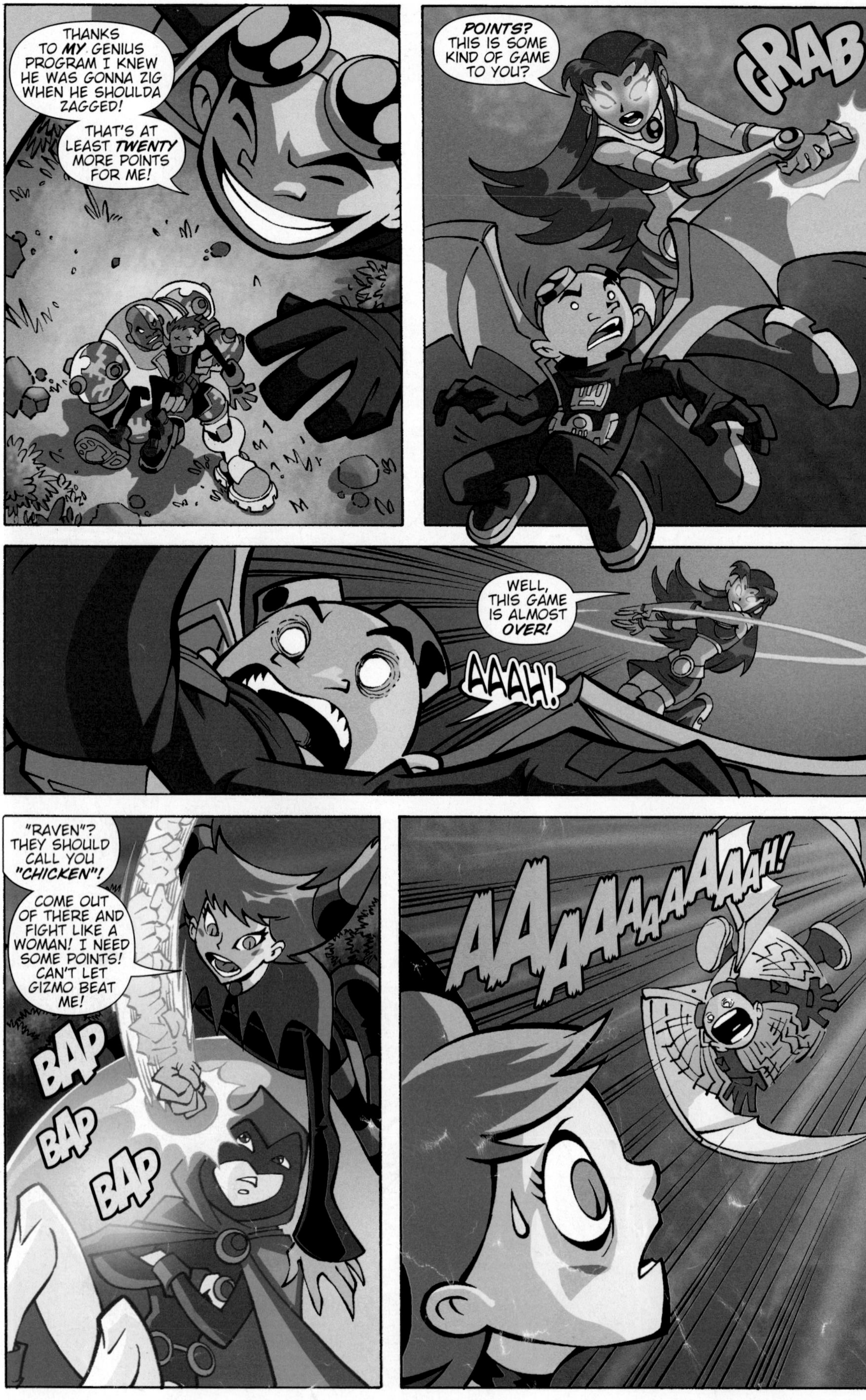
THANKS TO *MY* GENIUS PROGRAM I KNEW HE WAS GONNA ZIG WHEN HE SHOULDA ZAGGED!
THAT'S AT LEAST *TWENTY* MORE POINTS FOR ME!
POINTS? THIS IS SOME KIND OF GAME TO YOU?
GRAB
WELL, THIS GAME IS ALMOST *OVER!*
AAAH!
"RAVEN"? THEY SHOULD CALL YOU *"CHICKEN"*!
COME OUT OF THERE AND FIGHT LIKE A WOMAN! I NEED SOME POINTS! CAN'T LET GIZMO BEAT ME!
BAP
BAP
BAP
AAAAAAAAAAAH!

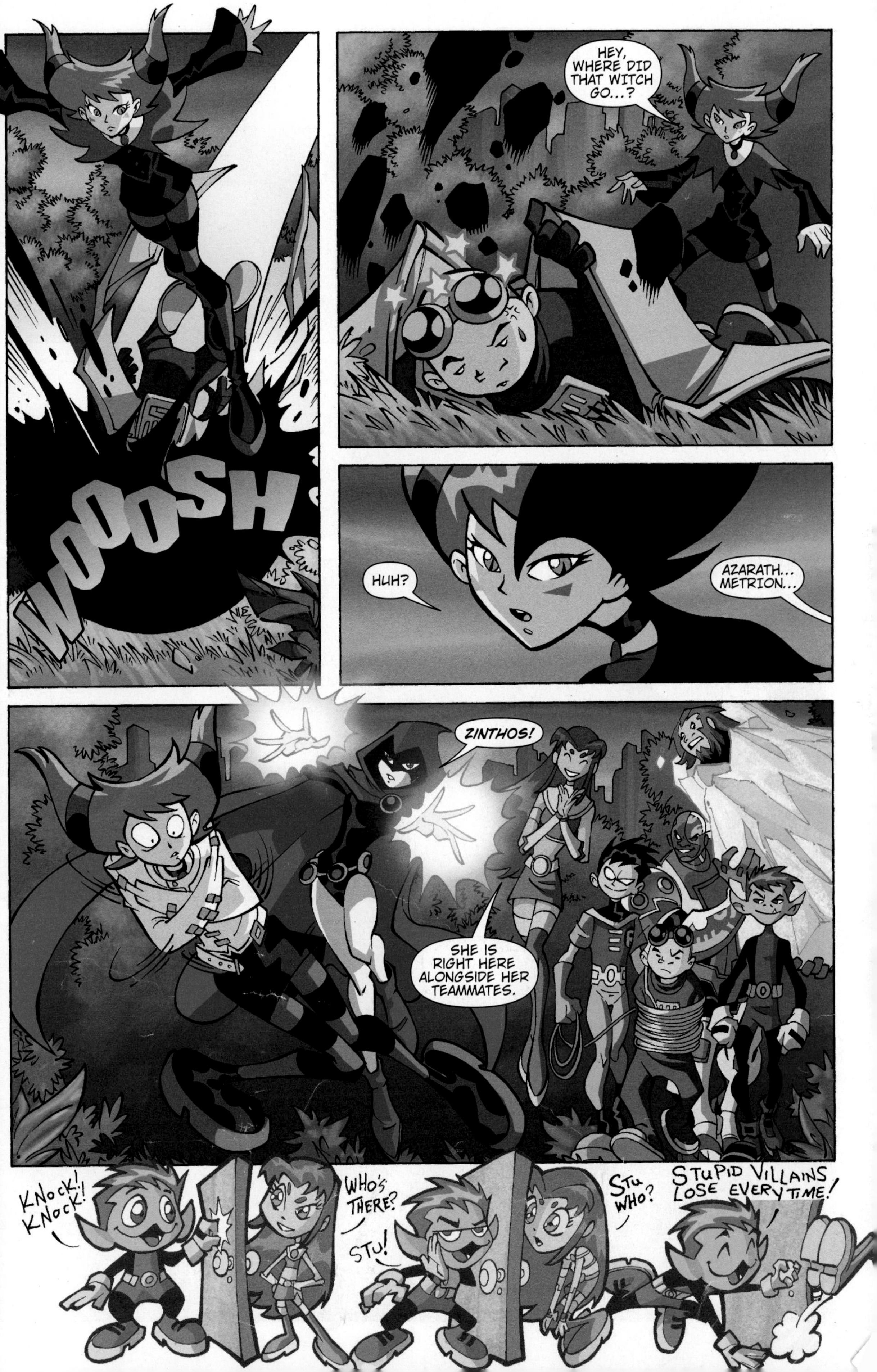
WOOOSH
HEY, WHERE DID THAT WITCH GO...?
HUH?
AZARATH... METRION...
ZINTHOS!
SHE IS RIGHT HERE ALONGSIDE HER TEAMMATES.
KNOCK! KNOCK!
WHO'S THERE?
STU!
STU WHO?
STUPID VILLAINS LOSE EVERY TIME!

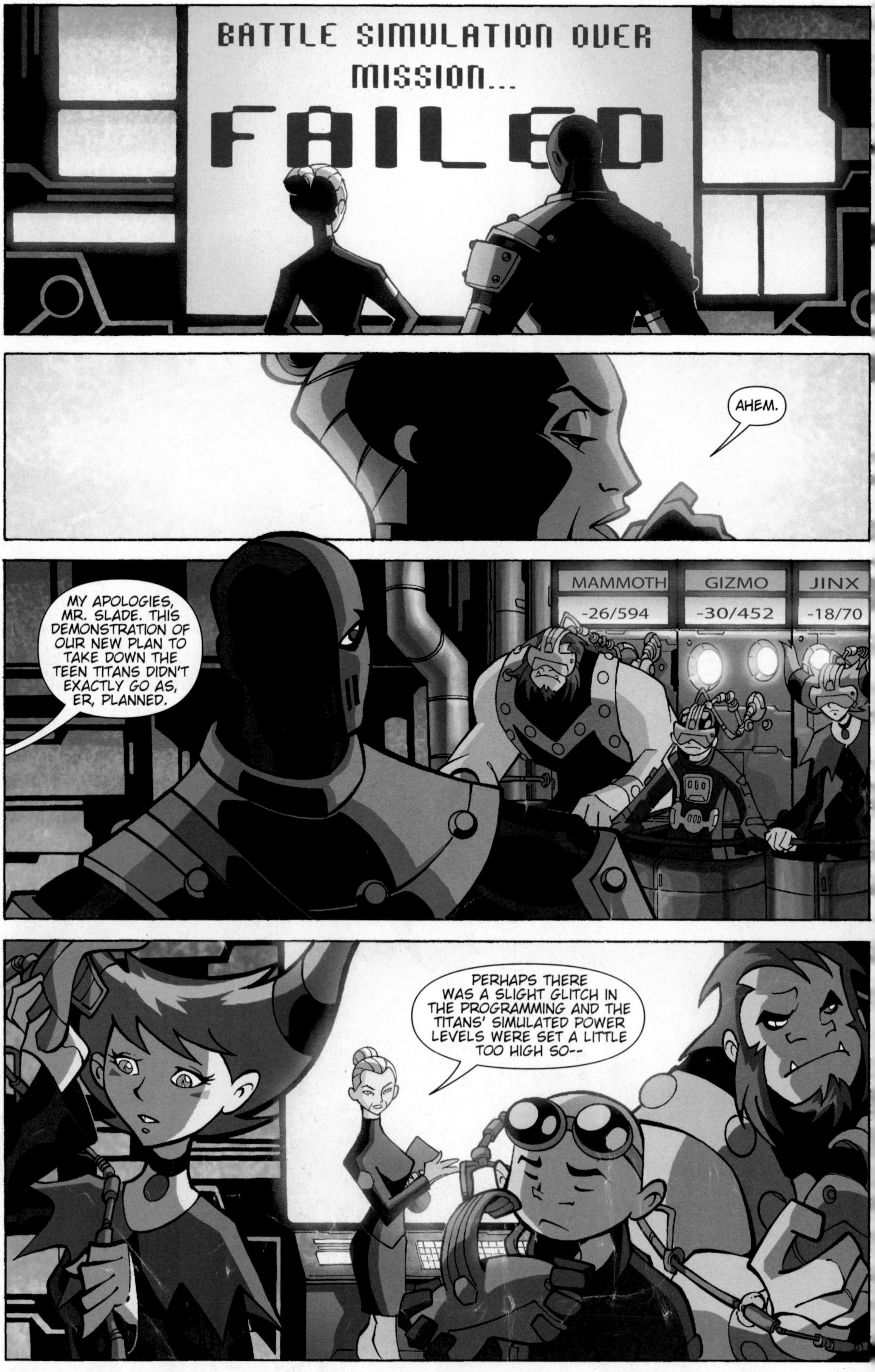
BATTLE SIMULATION OVER
MISSION...
FAILED
AHEM.
MAMMOTH
-26/594
GIZMO
-30/452
JINX
-18/70
MY APOLOGIES, MR. SLADE. THIS DEMONSTRATION OF OUR NEW PLAN TO TAKE DOWN THE TEEN TITANS DIDN'T EXACTLY GO AS, ER, PLANNED.
PERHAPS THERE WAS A SLIGHT GLITCH IN THE PROGRAMMING AND THE TITANS' SIMULATED POWER LEVELS WERE SET A LITTLE TOO HIGH SO--

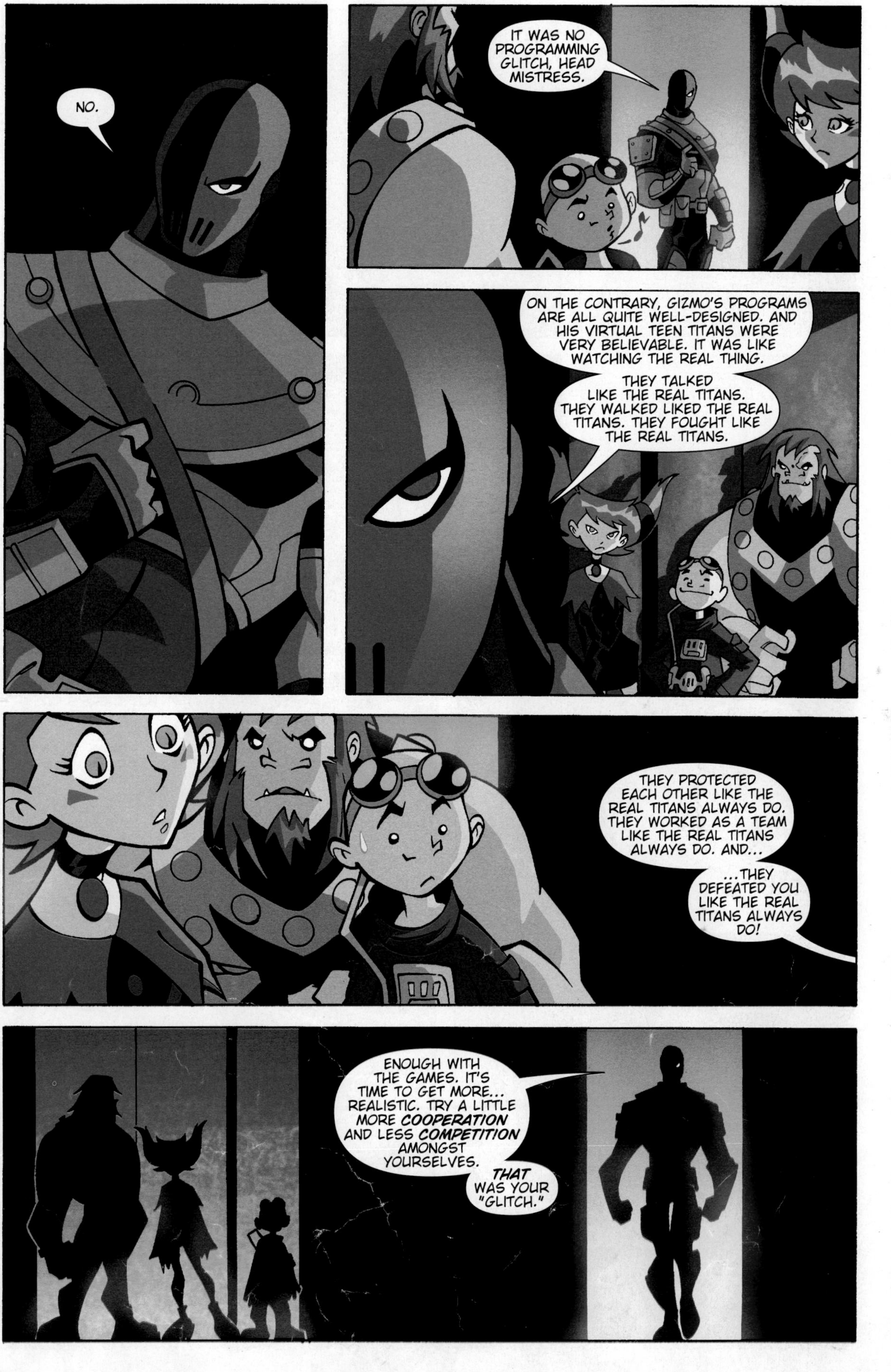
NO.
IT WAS NO PROGRAMMING GLITCH, HEAD MISTRESS.
ON THE CONTRARY, GIZMO'S PROGRAMS ARE ALL QUITE WELL-DESIGNED. AND HIS VIRTUAL TEEN TITANS WERE VERY BELIEVABLE. IT WAS LIKE WATCHING THE REAL THING.
THEY TALKED LIKE THE REAL TITANS. THEY WALKED LIKED THE REAL TITANS. THEY FOUGHT LIKE THE REAL TITANS.
THEY PROTECTED EACH OTHER LIKE THE REAL TITANS ALWAYS DO. THEY WORKED AS A TEAM LIKE THE REAL TITANS ALWAYS DO. AND...
...THEY DEFEATED YOU LIKE THE REAL TITANS ALWAYS DO!
ENOUGH WITH THE GAMES. IT'S TIME TO GET MORE... REALISTIC. TRY A LITTLE MORE COOPERATION AND LESS COMPETITION AMONGST YOURSELVES.
THAT WAS YOUR "GLITCH."

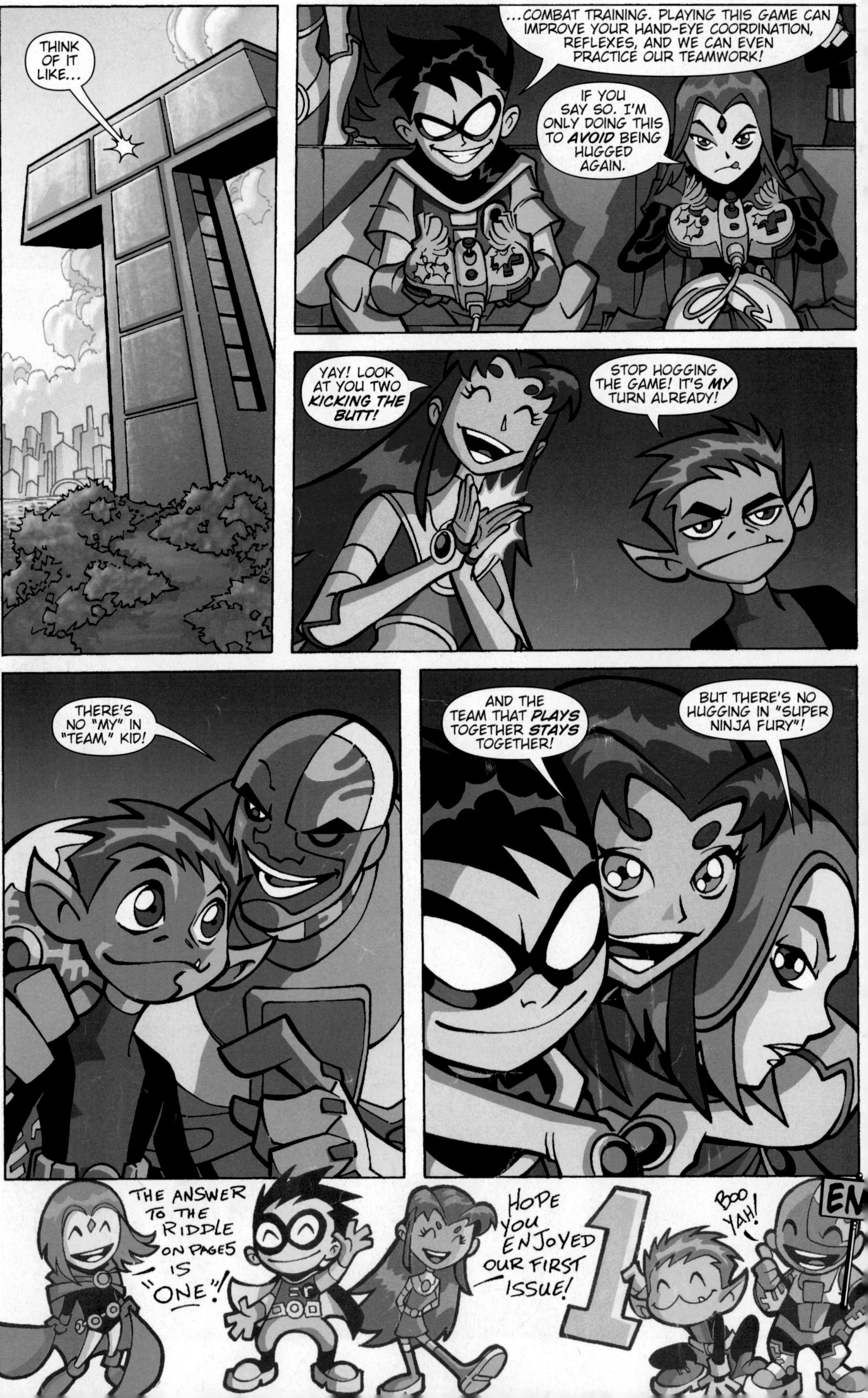
THINK OF IT LIKE...
...COMBAT TRAINING. PLAYING THIS GAME CAN IMPROVE YOUR HAND-EYE COORDINATION, REFLEXES, AND WE CAN EVEN PRACTICE OUR TEAMWORK!
IF YOU SAY SO. I'M ONLY DOING THIS TO AVOID BEING HUGGED AGAIN.
YAY! LOOK AT YOU TWO KICKING THE BUTT!
STOP HOGGING THE GAME! IT'S MY TURN ALREADY!
THERE'S NO "MY" IN "TEAM," KID!
AND THE TEAM THAT PLAYS TOGETHER STAYS TOGETHER!
BUT THERE'S NO HUGGING IN "SUPER NINJA FURY"!
THE ANSWER TO THE RIDDLE ON PAGE 5 IS "ONE"!
HOPE YOU ENJOYED OUR FIRST ISSUE!
1
BOO YAH!

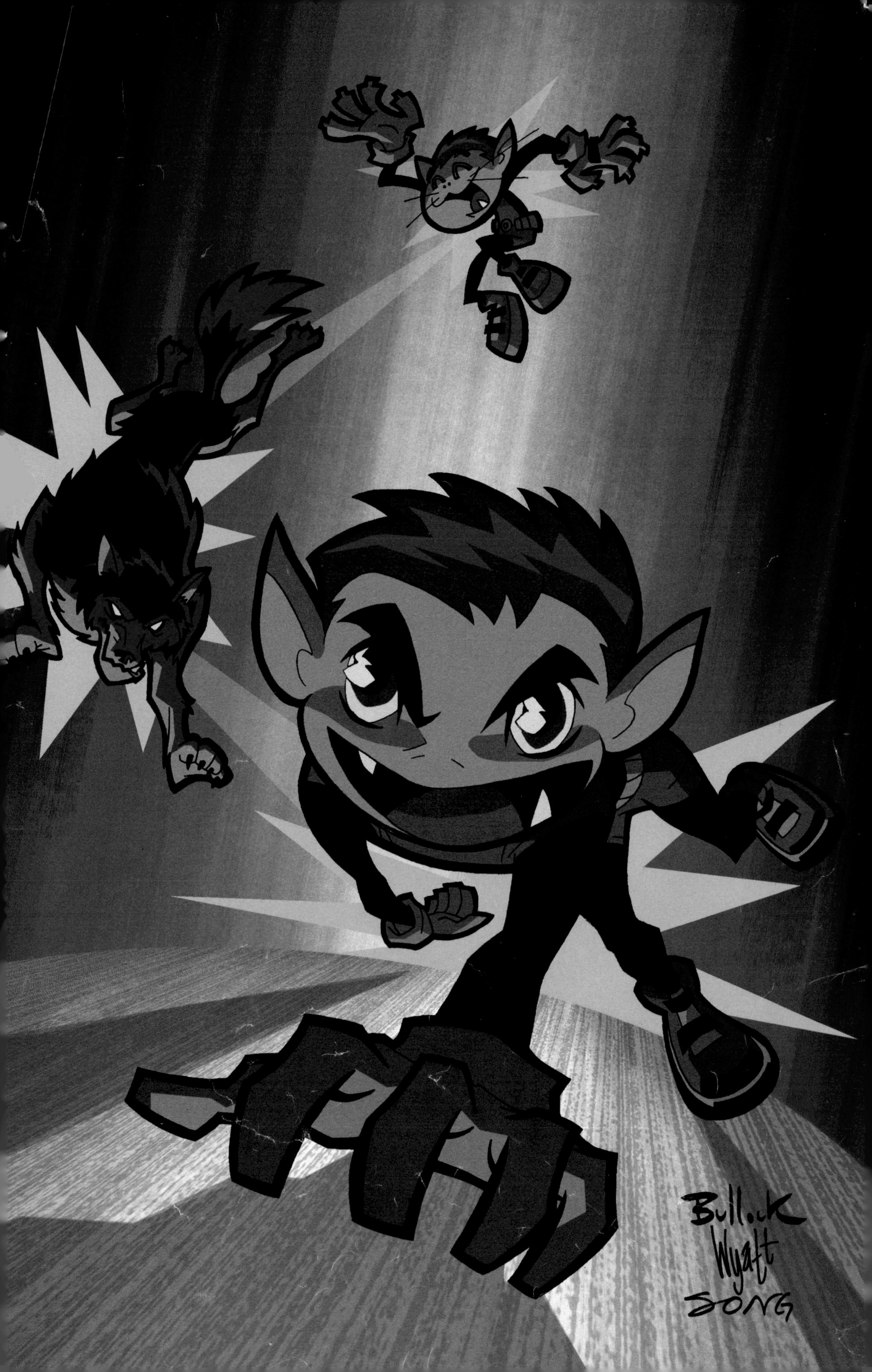
Bullock
Wyatt
Song

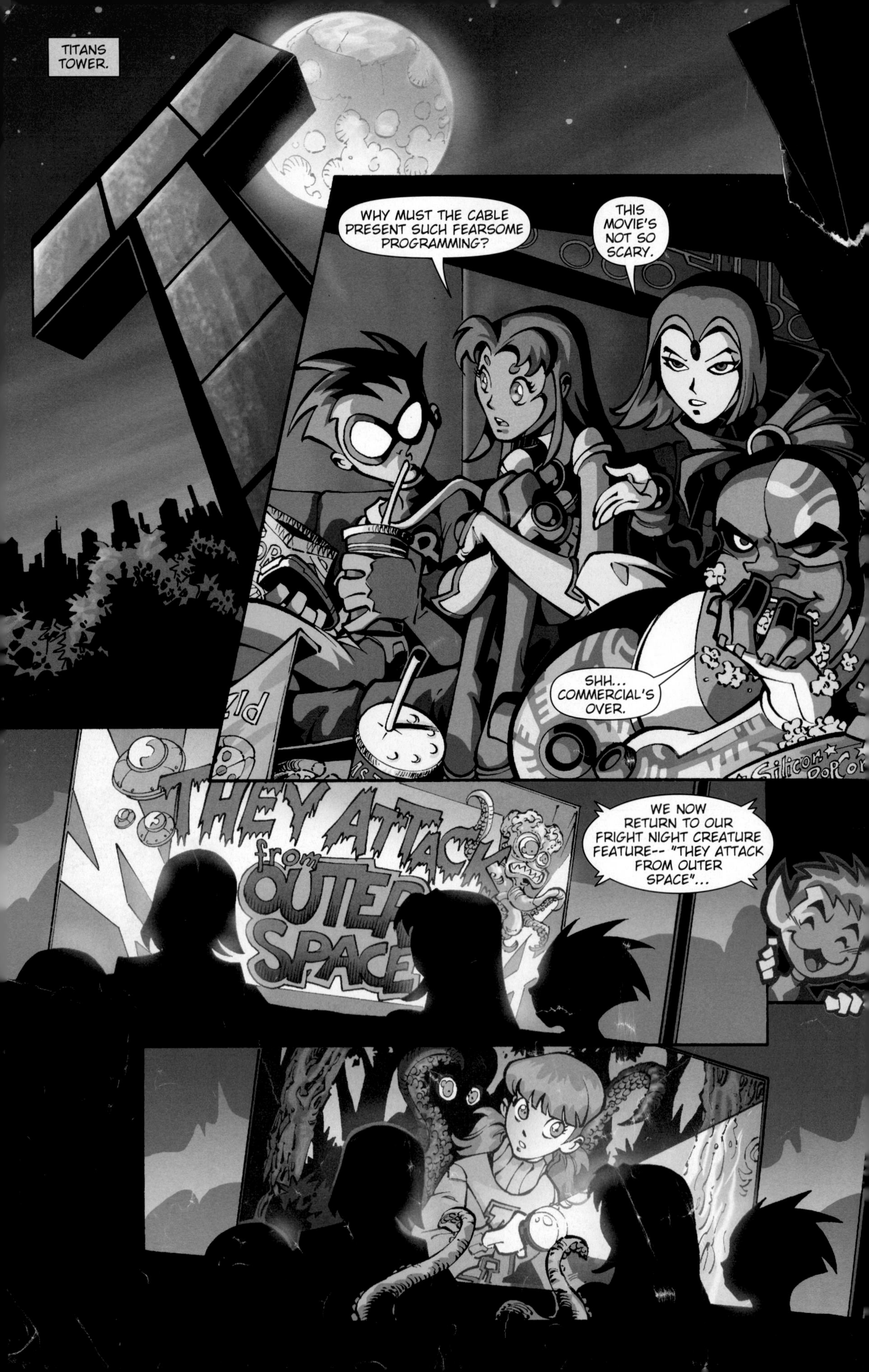
TITANS TOWER.
WHY MUST THE CABLE PRESENT SUCH FEARSOME PROGRAMMING?
THIS MOVIE'S NOT SO SCARY.
SHH... COMMERCIAL'S OVER.
Silicon PopCor
THEY ATTACK from OUTER SPACE
WE NOW RETURN TO OUR FRIGHT NIGHT CREATURE FEATURE-- "THEY ATTACK FROM OUTER SPACE"...

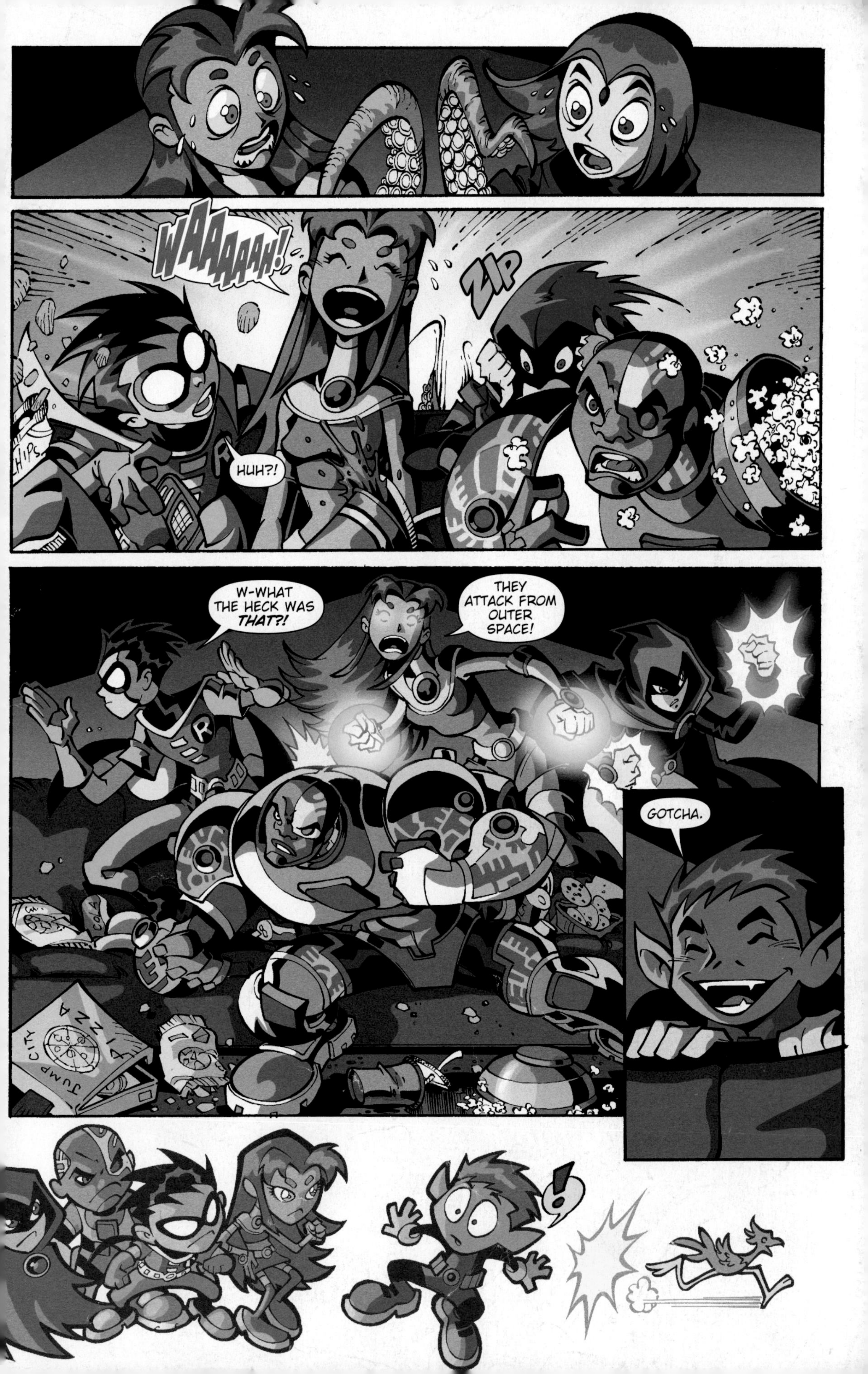
WAAAAAAH!
ZIP
HUH?!
CHIPS
W-WHAT THE HECK WAS THAT?!
THEY ATTACK FROM OUTER SPACE!
GOTCHA.
JUMP CITY
PIZZA

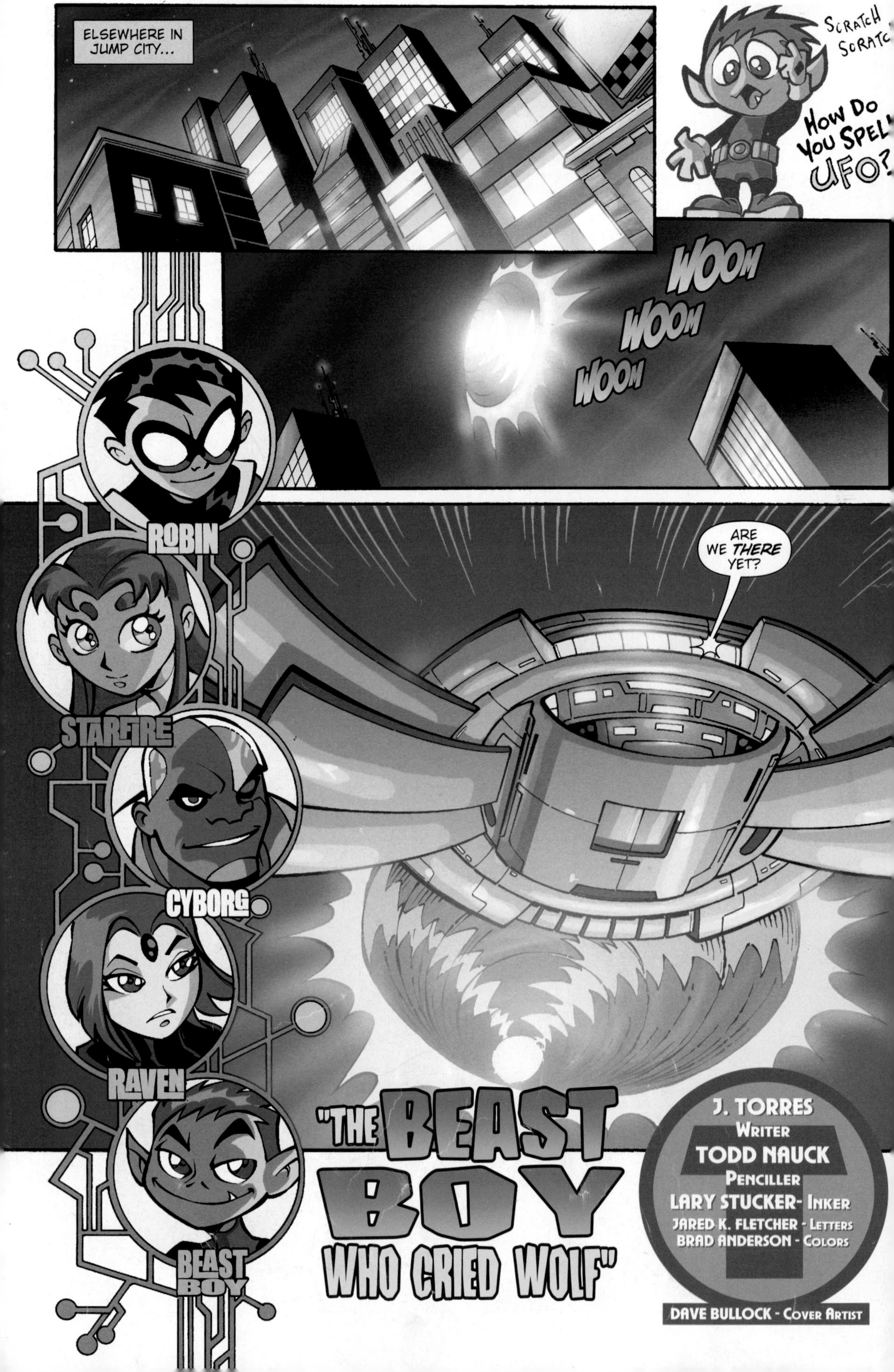

ELSEWHERE IN JUMP CITY...
SCRATCH SCRATC
HOW DO YOU SPEL UFO?
WOOM WOOM WOOM
ARE WE THERE YET?
ROBIN
STARFIRE
CYBORG
RAVEN
BEAST BOY
"THE BEAST BOY WHO CRIED WOLF"
J. TORRES Writer
TODD NAUCK Penciller
LARY STUCKER- Inker
JARED K. FLETCHER - Letters
BRAD ANDERSON - Colors
DAVE BULLOCK - Cover Artist

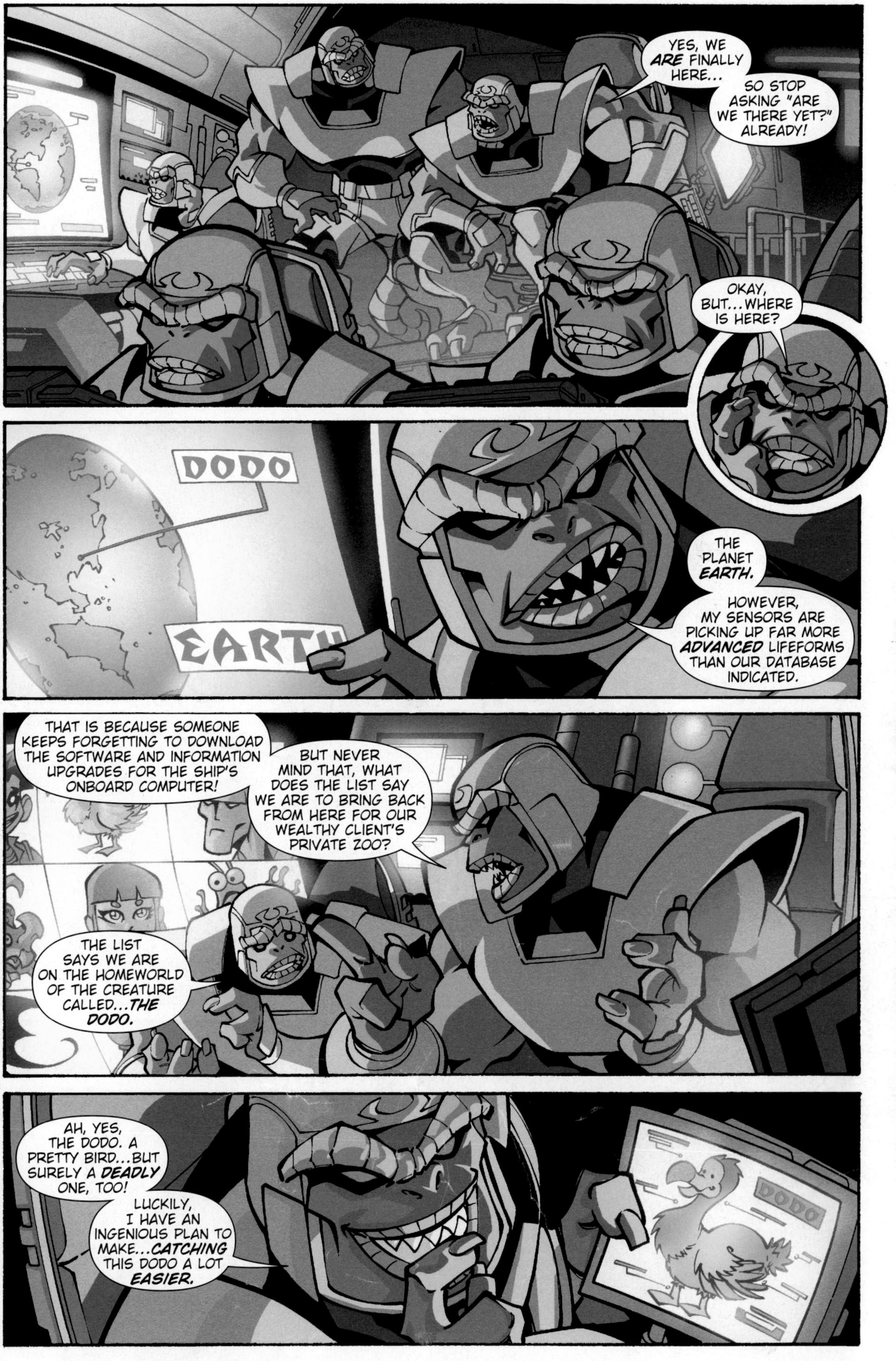
YES, WE ARE FINALLY HERE...
SO STOP ASKING "ARE WE THERE YET?" ALREADY!
OKAY, BUT...WHERE IS HERE?
DODO
EARTH
THE PLANET EARTH.
HOWEVER, MY SENSORS ARE PICKING UP FAR MORE ADVANCED LIFEFORMS THAN OUR DATABASE INDICATED.
THAT IS BECAUSE SOMEONE KEEPS FORGETTING TO DOWNLOAD THE SOFTWARE AND INFORMATION UPGRADES FOR THE SHIP'S ONBOARD COMPUTER!
BUT NEVER MIND THAT, WHAT DOES THE LIST SAY WE ARE TO BRING BACK FROM HERE FOR OUR WEALTHY CLIENT'S PRIVATE ZOO?
THE LIST SAYS WE ARE ON THE HOMEWORLD OF THE CREATURE CALLED...THE DODO.
AH, YES, THE DODO. A PRETTY BIRD...BUT SURELY A DEADLY ONE, TOO!
LUCKILY, I HAVE AN INGENIOUS PLAN TO MAKE...CATCHING THIS DODO A LOT EASIER.
DODO

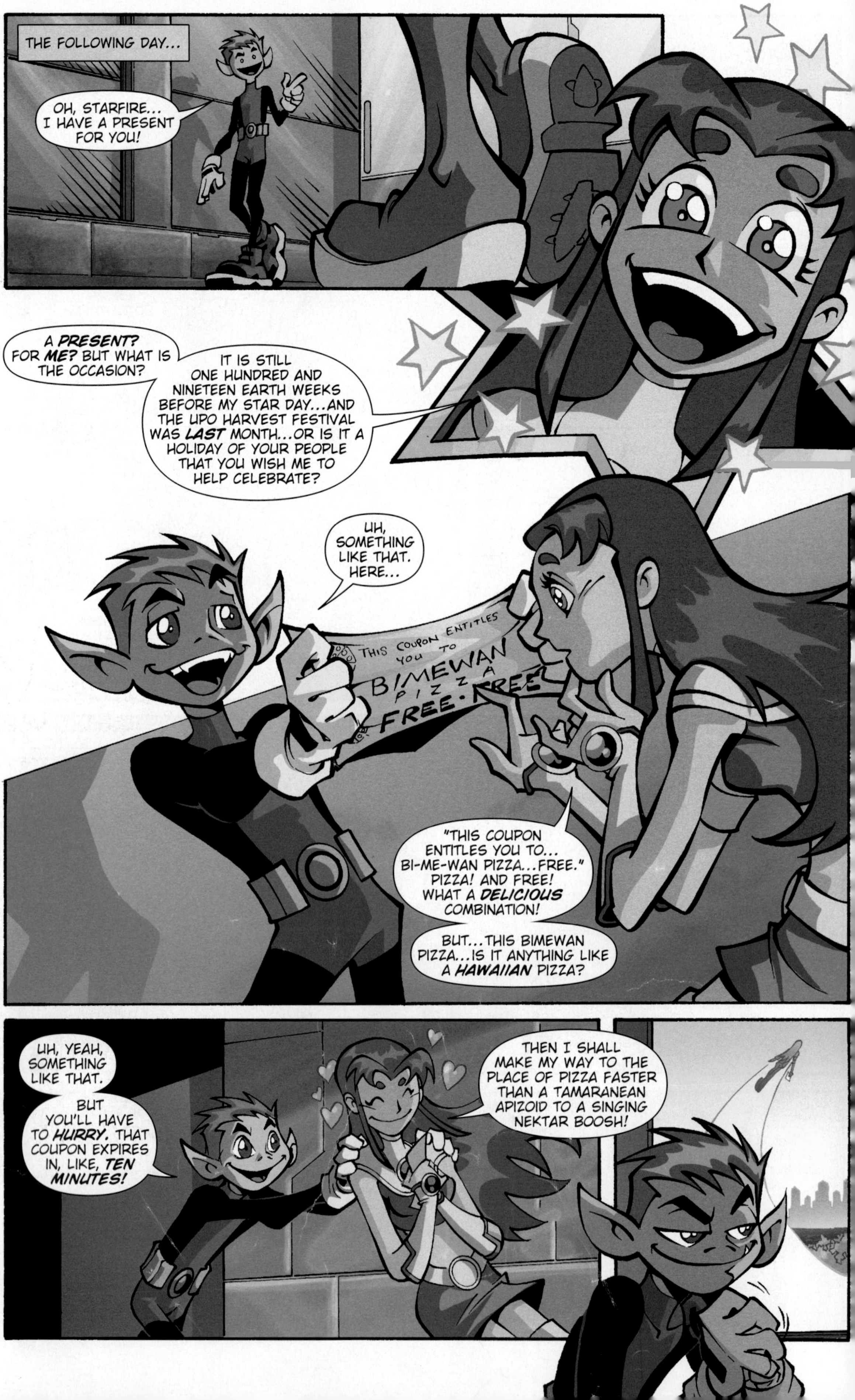
THE FOLLOWING DAY...
OH, STARFIRE... I HAVE A PRESENT FOR YOU!
A PRESENT? FOR ME? BUT WHAT IS THE OCCASION?
IT IS STILL ONE HUNDRED AND NINETEEN EARTH WEEKS BEFORE MY STAR DAY...AND THE UPO HARVEST FESTIVAL WAS LAST MONTH...OR IS IT A HOLIDAY OF YOUR PEOPLE THAT YOU WISH ME TO HELP CELEBRATE?
UH, SOMETHING LIKE THAT. HERE...
THIS COUPON ENTITLES YOU TO BIMEWAN PIZZA FREE. FREE
"THIS COUPON ENTITLES YOU TO... BI-ME-WAN PIZZA...FREE." PIZZA! AND FREE! WHAT A DELICIOUS COMBINATION!
BUT...THIS BIMEWAN PIZZA...IS IT ANYTHING LIKE A HAWAIIAN PIZZA?
UH, YEAH, SOMETHING LIKE THAT.
BUT YOU'LL HAVE TO HURRY. THAT COUPON EXPIRES IN, LIKE, TEN MINUTES!
THEN I SHALL MAKE MY WAY TO THE PLACE OF PIZZA FASTER THAN A TAMARANEAN APIZOID TO A SINGING NEKTAR BOOSH!

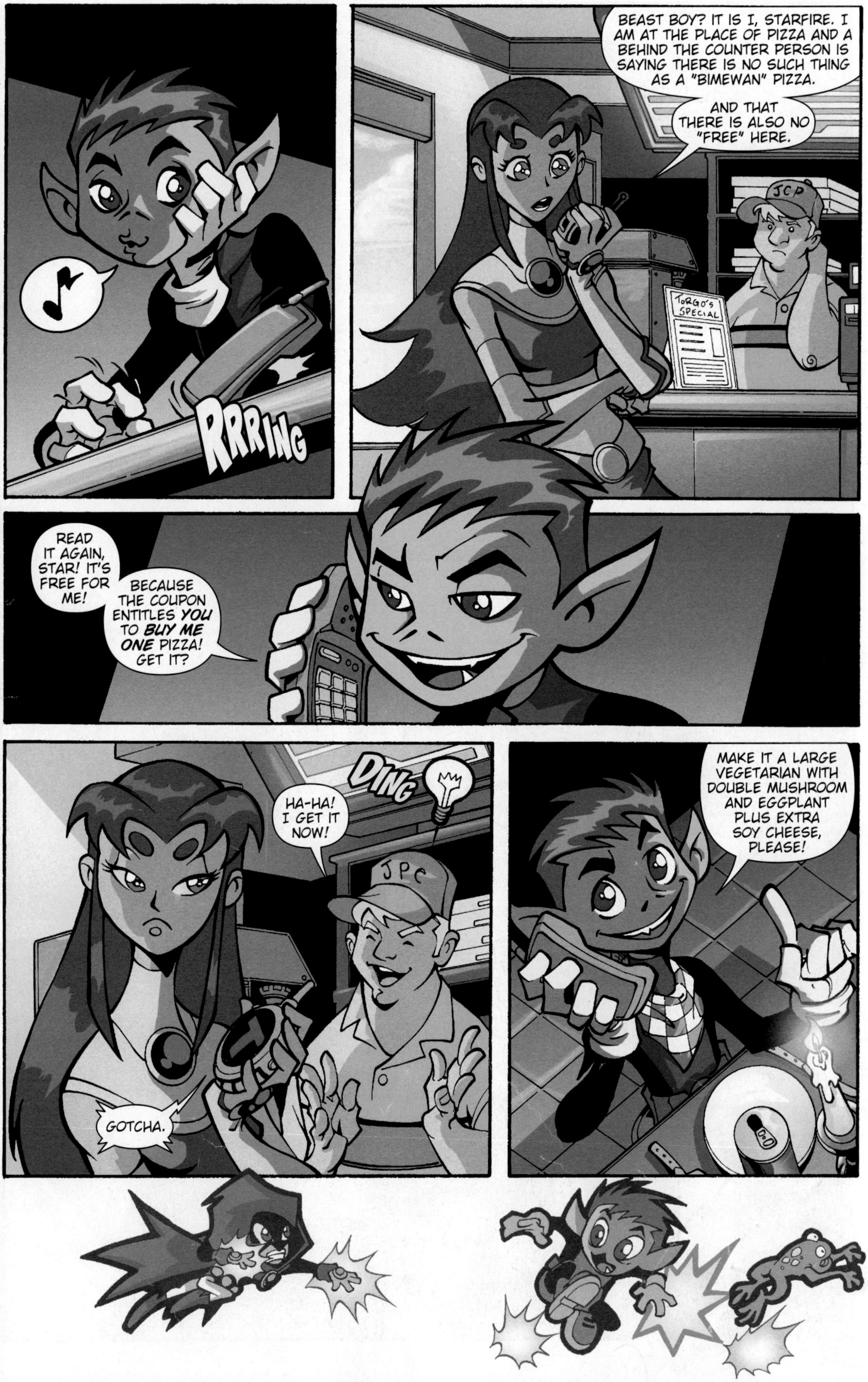
RRRING
BEAST BOY? IT IS I, STARFIRE. I AM AT THE PLACE OF PIZZA AND A BEHIND THE COUNTER PERSON IS SAYING THERE IS NO SUCH THING AS A "BIMEWAN" PIZZA.
AND THAT THERE IS ALSO NO "FREE" HERE.
JCP
TORGO'S SPECIAL
READ IT AGAIN, STAR! IT'S FREE FOR ME!
BECAUSE THE COUPON ENTITLES YOU TO BUY ME ONE PIZZA! GET IT?
DING
HA-HA! I GET IT NOW!
JPC
GOTCHA.
MAKE IT A LARGE VEGETARIAN WITH DOUBLE MUSHROOM AND EGGPLANT PLUS EXTRA SOY CHEESE, PLEASE!

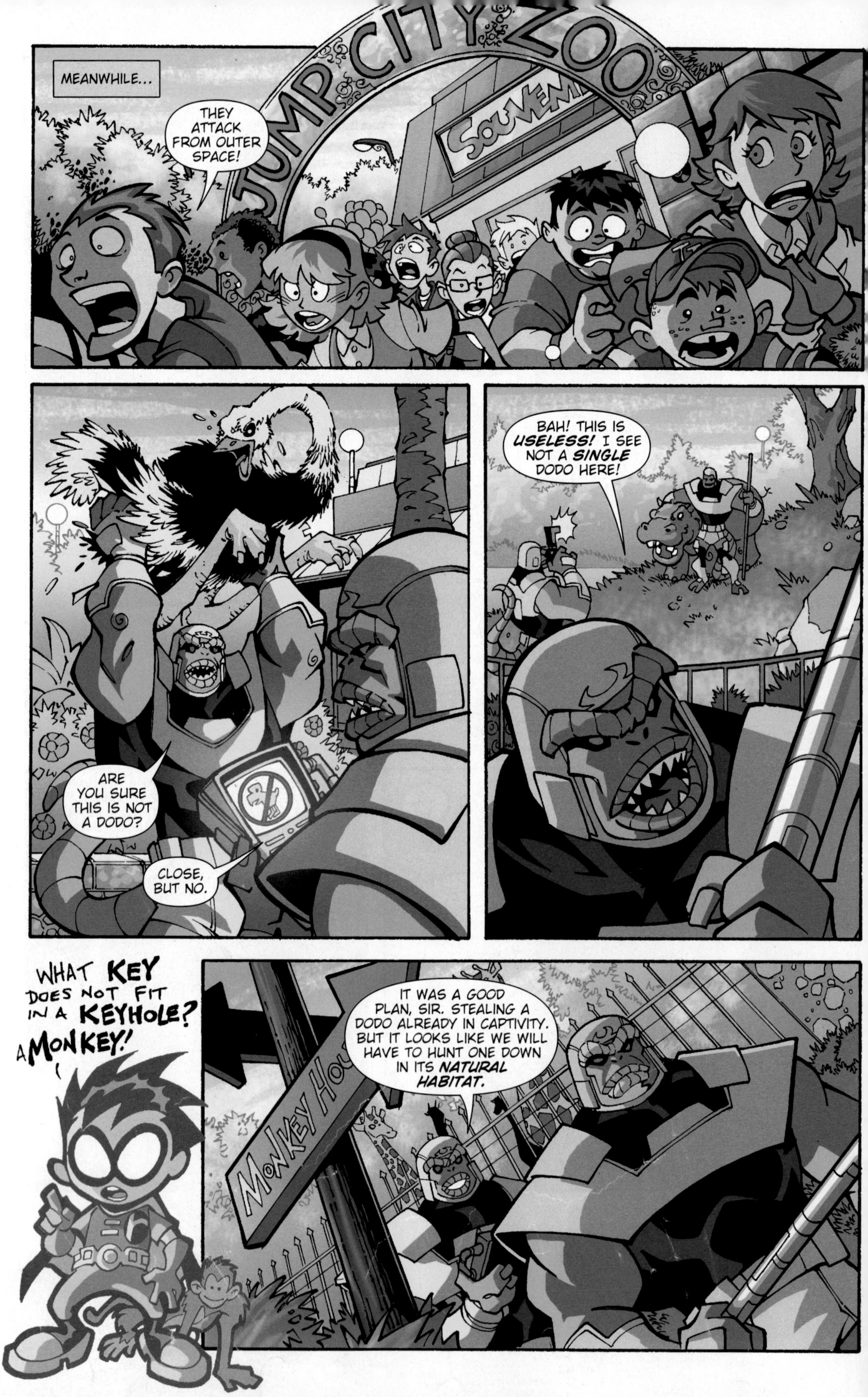
JUMP CITY ZOO
MEANWHILE...
THEY ATTACK FROM OUTER SPACE!
ARE YOU SURE THIS IS NOT A DODO?
CLOSE, BUT NO.
BAH! THIS IS USELESS! I SEE NOT A SINGLE DODO HERE!
IT WAS A GOOD PLAN, SIR. STEALING A DODO ALREADY IN CAPTIVITY. BUT IT LOOKS LIKE WE WILL HAVE TO HUNT ONE DOWN IN ITS NATURAL HABITAT.
WHAT KEY DOES NOT FIT IN A KEYHOLE? A MONKEY!

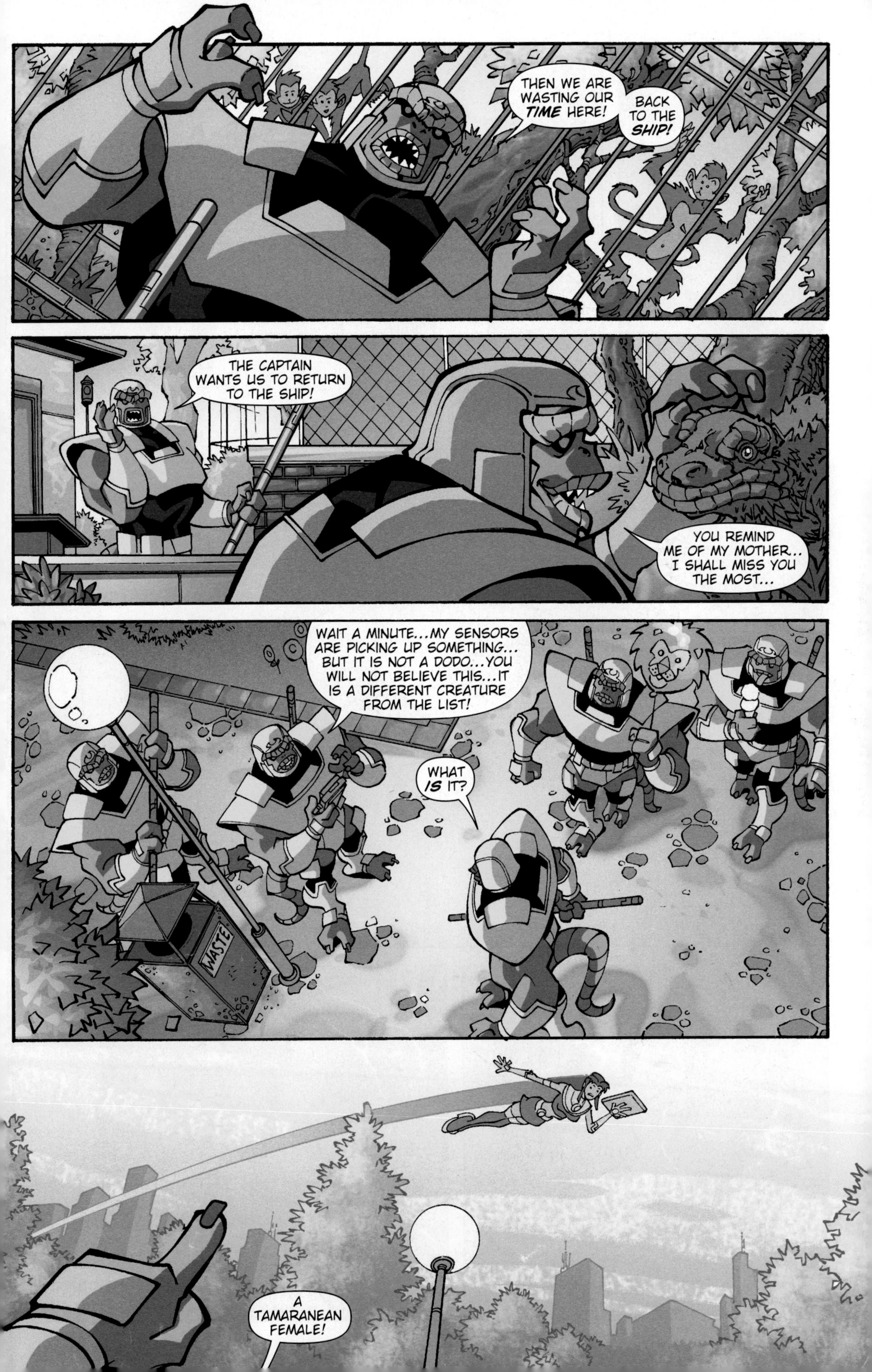
THEN WE ARE WASTING OUR *TIME* HERE!
BACK TO THE *SHIP!*
THE CAPTAIN WANTS US TO RETURN TO THE SHIP!
YOU REMIND ME OF MY MOTHER... I SHALL MISS YOU THE MOST...
WAIT A MINUTE...MY SENSORS ARE PICKING UP SOMETHING... BUT IT IS NOT A DODO...YOU WILL NOT BELIEVE THIS...IT IS A DIFFERENT CREATURE FROM THE LIST!
WHAT *IS* IT?
WASTE
A TAMARANEAN FEMALE!

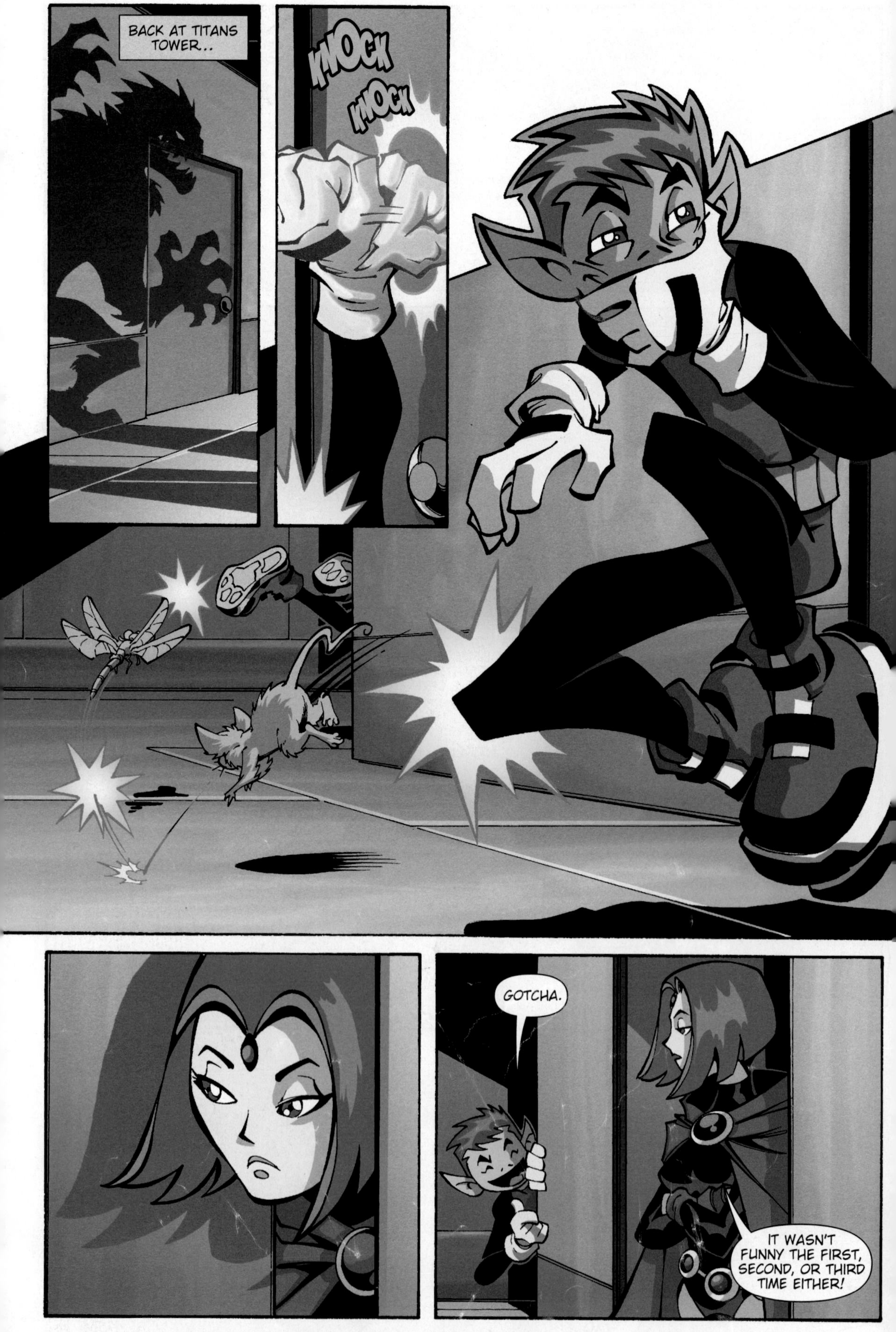
BACK AT TITANS TOWER...
KNOCK
KNOCK
GOTCHA.
IT WASN'T FUNNY THE FIRST, SECOND, OR THIRD TIME EITHER!

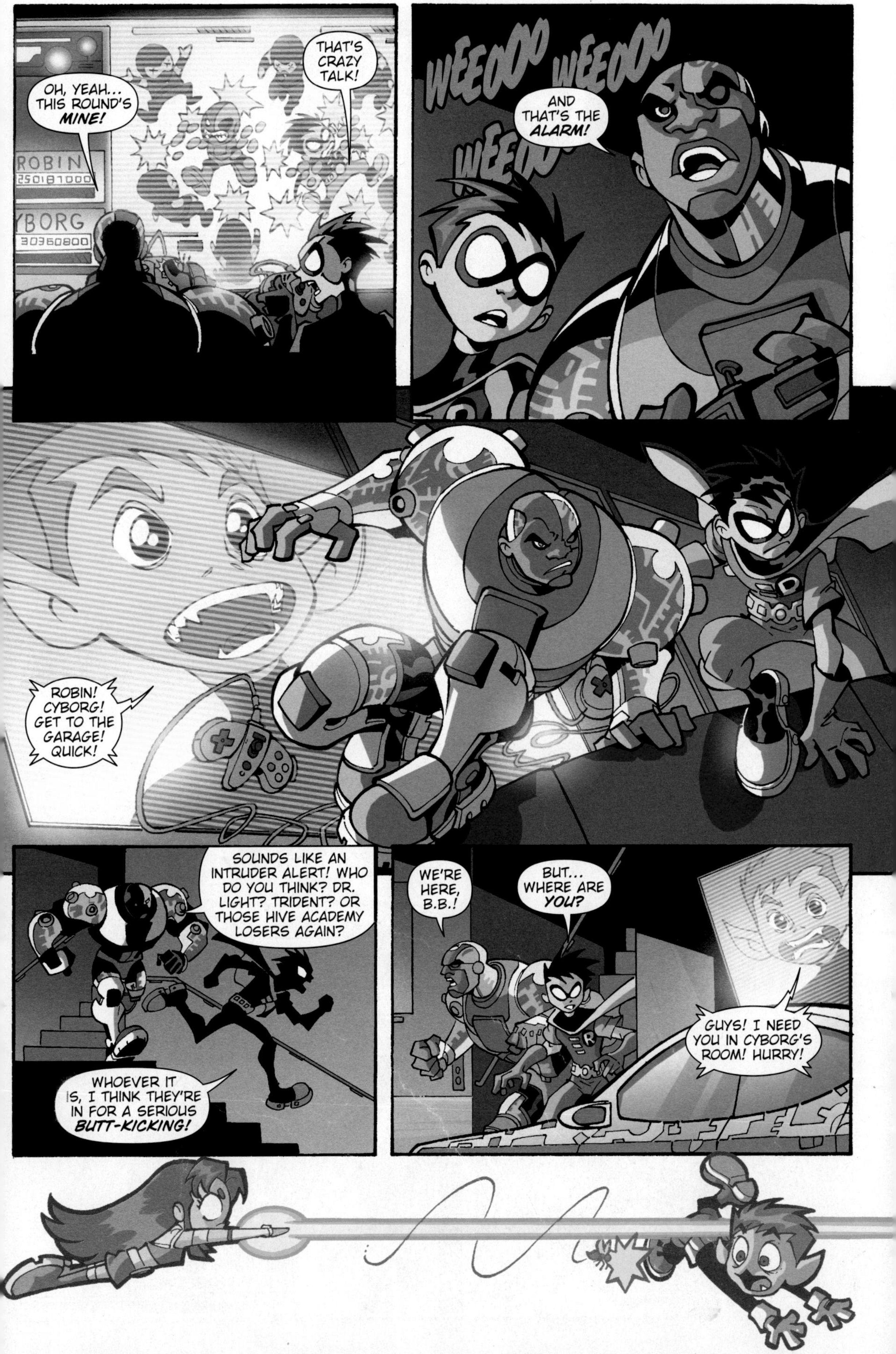
OH, YEAH... THIS ROUND'S MINE!
THAT'S CRAZY TALK!
ROBIN 250187000
YBORG 30360800
WEEOOO WEEOOO WEEOO
AND THAT'S THE ALARM!
ROBIN! CYBORG! GET TO THE GARAGE! QUICK!
SOUNDS LIKE AN INTRUDER ALERT! WHO DO YOU THINK? DR. LIGHT? TRIDENT? OR THOSE HIVE ACADEMY LOSERS AGAIN?
WHOEVER IT IS, I THINK THEY'RE IN FOR A SERIOUS BUTT-KICKING!
WE'RE HERE, B.B.!
BUT... WHERE ARE YOU?
GUYS! I NEED YOU IN CYBORG'S ROOM! HURRY!

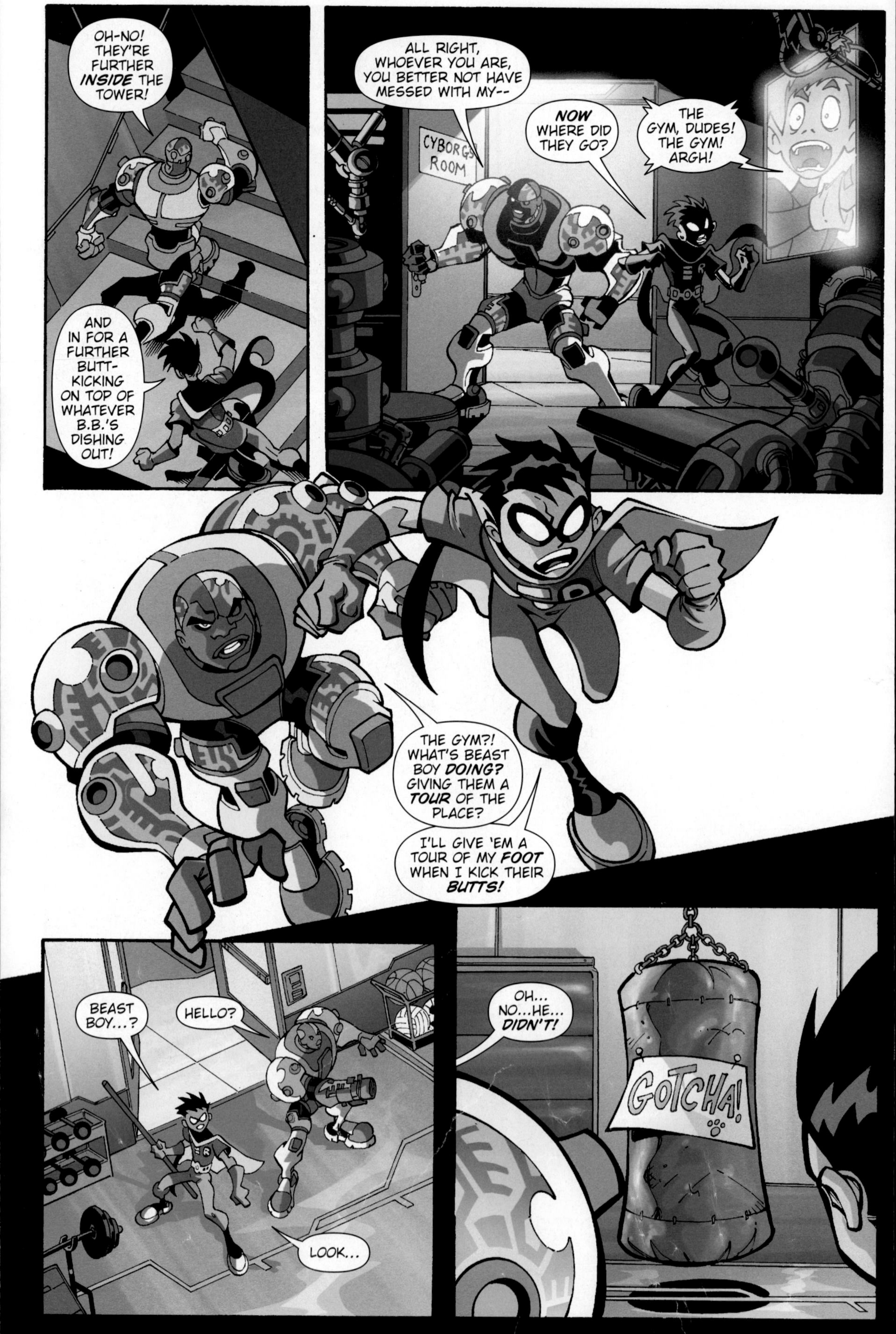
OH-NO! THEY'RE FURTHER ***INSIDE*** THE TOWER!
AND IN FOR A FURTHER BUTT-KICKING ON TOP OF WHATEVER B.B.'S DISHING OUT!
ALL RIGHT, WHOEVER YOU ARE, YOU BETTER NOT HAVE MESSED WITH MY--
CYBORG'S ROOM
NOW WHERE DID THEY GO?
THE GYM, DUDES! THE GYM! ARGH!
THE GYM?! WHAT'S BEAST BOY ***DOING?*** GIVING THEM A ***TOUR*** OF THE PLACE?
I'LL GIVE 'EM A TOUR OF MY ***FOOT*** WHEN I KICK THEIR ***BUTTS!***
BEAST BOY...?
HELLO?
LOOK...
OH... NO...HE... ***DIDN'T!***
GOTCHA!

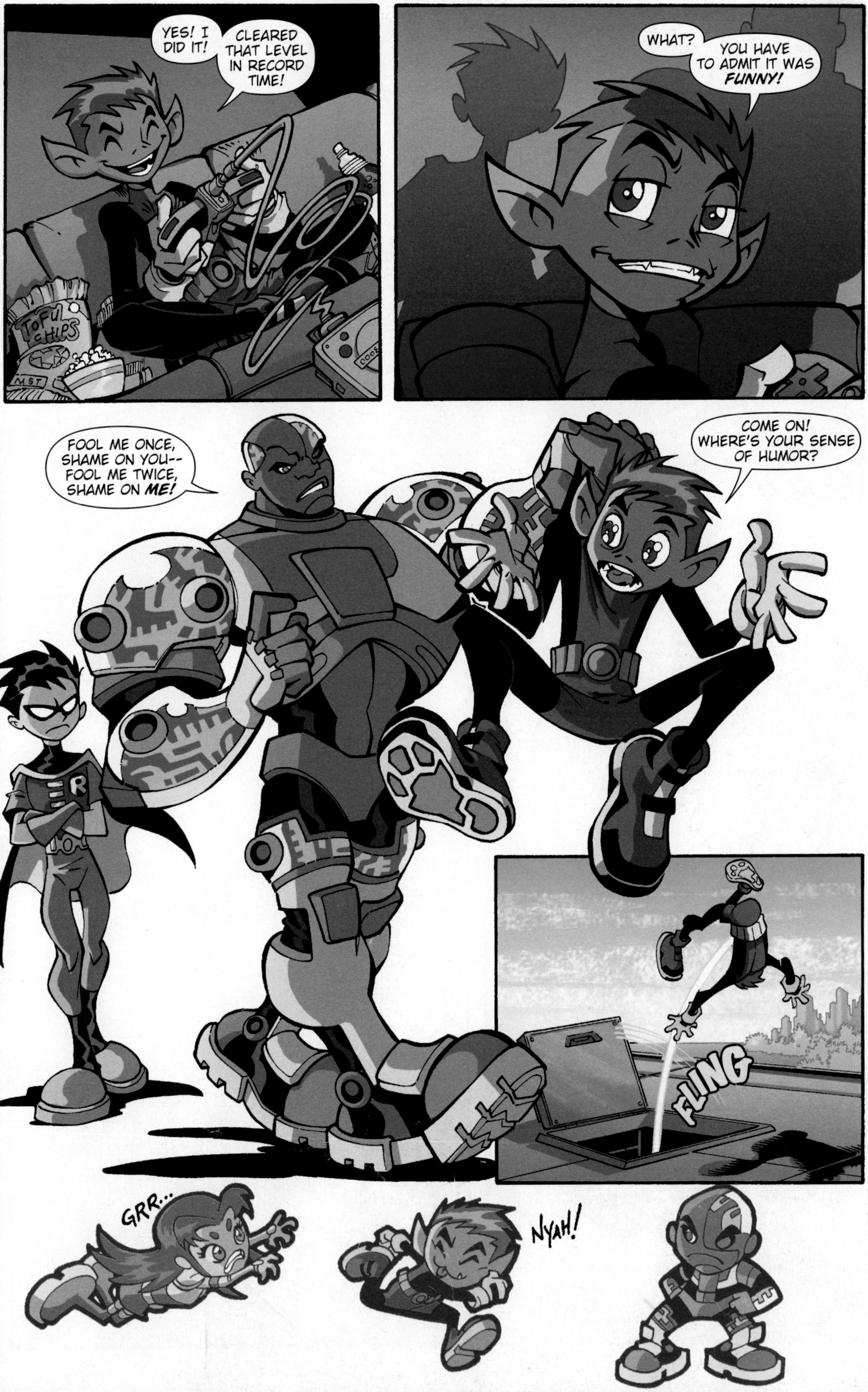
YES! I DID IT!
CLEARED THAT LEVEL IN RECORD TIME!
TOFU CHIPS
WHAT?
YOU HAVE TO ADMIT IT WAS FUNNY!
FOOL ME ONCE, SHAME ON YOU-- FOOL ME TWICE, SHAME ON ME!
COME ON! WHERE'S YOUR SENSE OF HUMOR?
FLING
GRR...
NYAH!

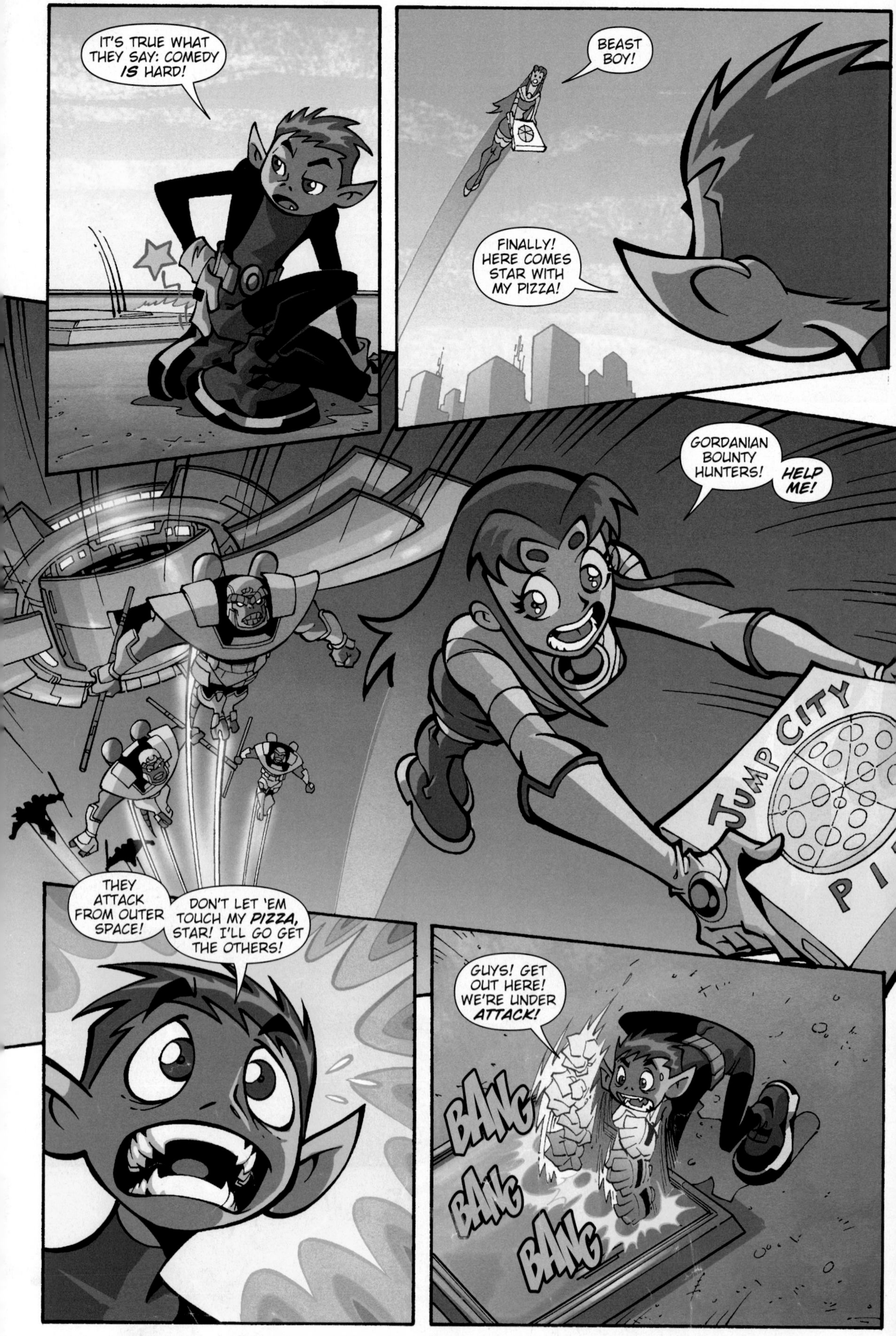
IT'S TRUE WHAT THEY SAY: COMEDY IS HARD!
BEAST BOY!
FINALLY! HERE COMES STAR WITH MY PIZZA!
GORDANIAN BOUNTY HUNTERS!
HELP ME!
JUMP CITY
THEY ATTACK FROM OUTER SPACE!
DON'T LET 'EM TOUCH MY PIZZA, STAR! I'LL GO GET THE OTHERS!
GUYS! GET OUT HERE! WE'RE UNDER ATTACK!
BANG
BANG
BANG

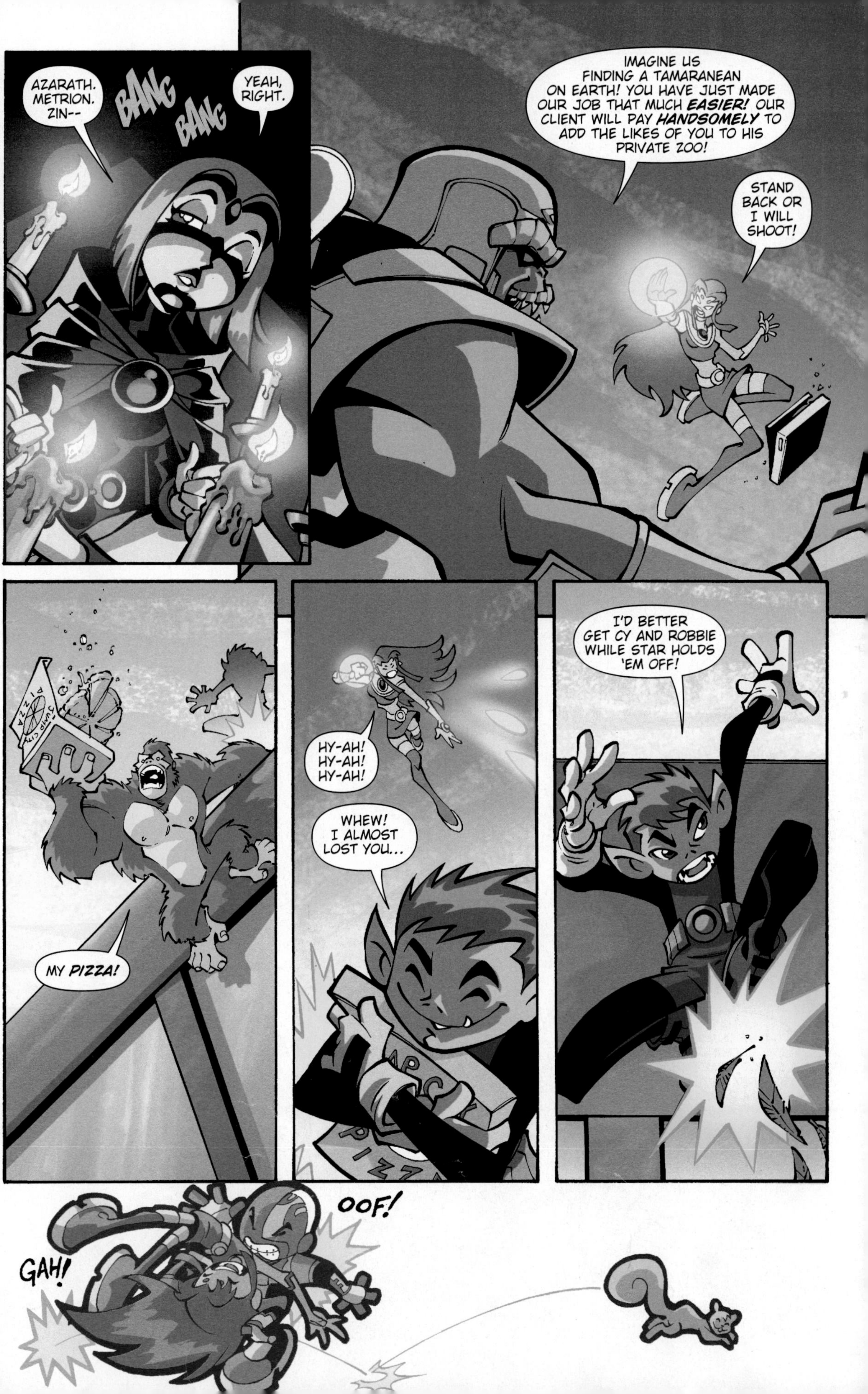
AZARATH. METRION. ZIN--
BANG
BANG
YEAH, RIGHT.
IMAGINE US FINDING A TAMARANEAN ON EARTH! YOU HAVE JUST MADE OUR JOB THAT MUCH EASIER! OUR CLIENT WILL PAY HANDSOMELY TO ADD THE LIKES OF YOU TO HIS PRIVATE ZOO!
STAND BACK OR I WILL SHOOT!
MY PIZZA!
HY-AH! HY-AH! HY-AH!
WHEW! I ALMOST LOST YOU...
I'D BETTER GET CY AND ROBBIE WHILE STAR HOLDS 'EM OFF!
OOF!
GAH!

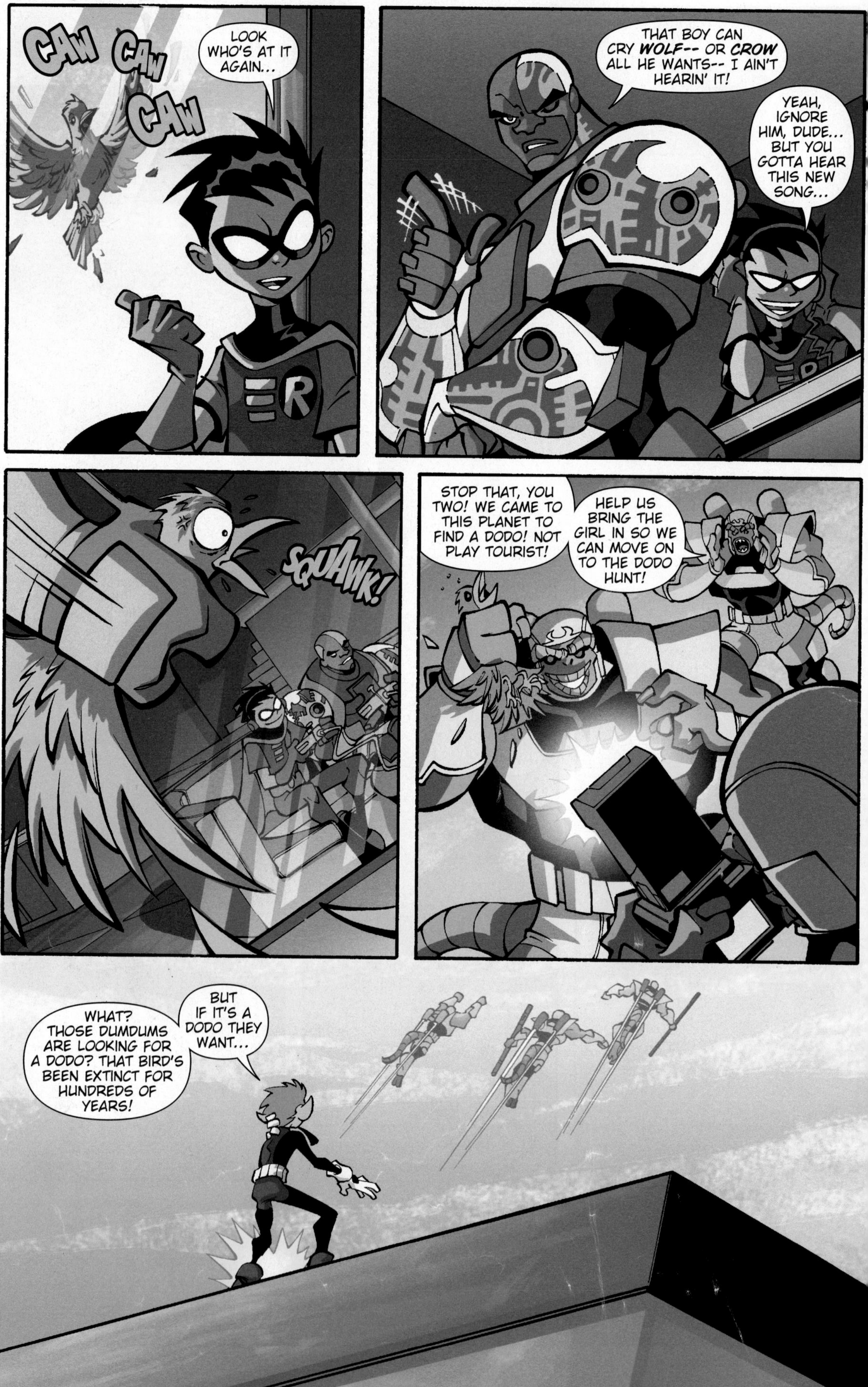
CAW CAW CAW
LOOK WHO'S AT IT AGAIN...
THAT BOY CAN CRY **WOLF**-- OR **CROW** ALL HE WANTS-- I AIN'T HEARIN' IT!
YEAH, IGNORE HIM, DUDE... BUT YOU GOTTA HEAR THIS NEW SONG...
SQUAWK!
STOP THAT, YOU TWO! WE CAME TO THIS PLANET TO FIND A DODO! NOT PLAY TOURIST!
HELP US BRING THE GIRL IN SO WE CAN MOVE ON TO THE DODO HUNT!
WHAT? THOSE DUMDUMS ARE LOOKING FOR A DODO? THAT BIRD'S BEEN EXTINCT FOR HUNDREDS OF YEARS!
BUT IF IT'S A DODO THEY WANT...

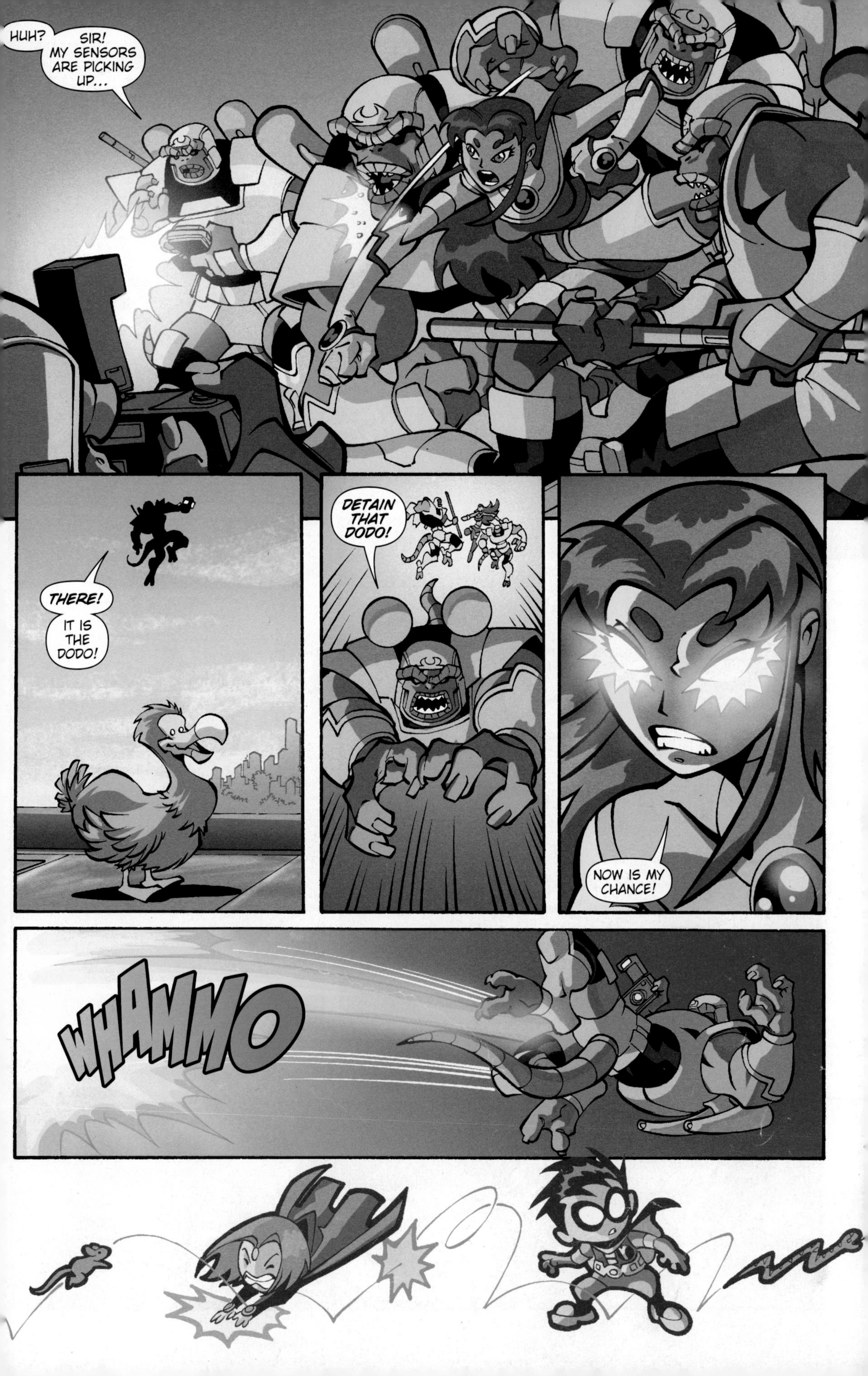
HUH?
SIR! MY SENSORS ARE PICKING UP...
THERE! IT IS THE DODO!
DETAIN THAT DODO!
NOW IS MY CHANCE!
WHAMMO

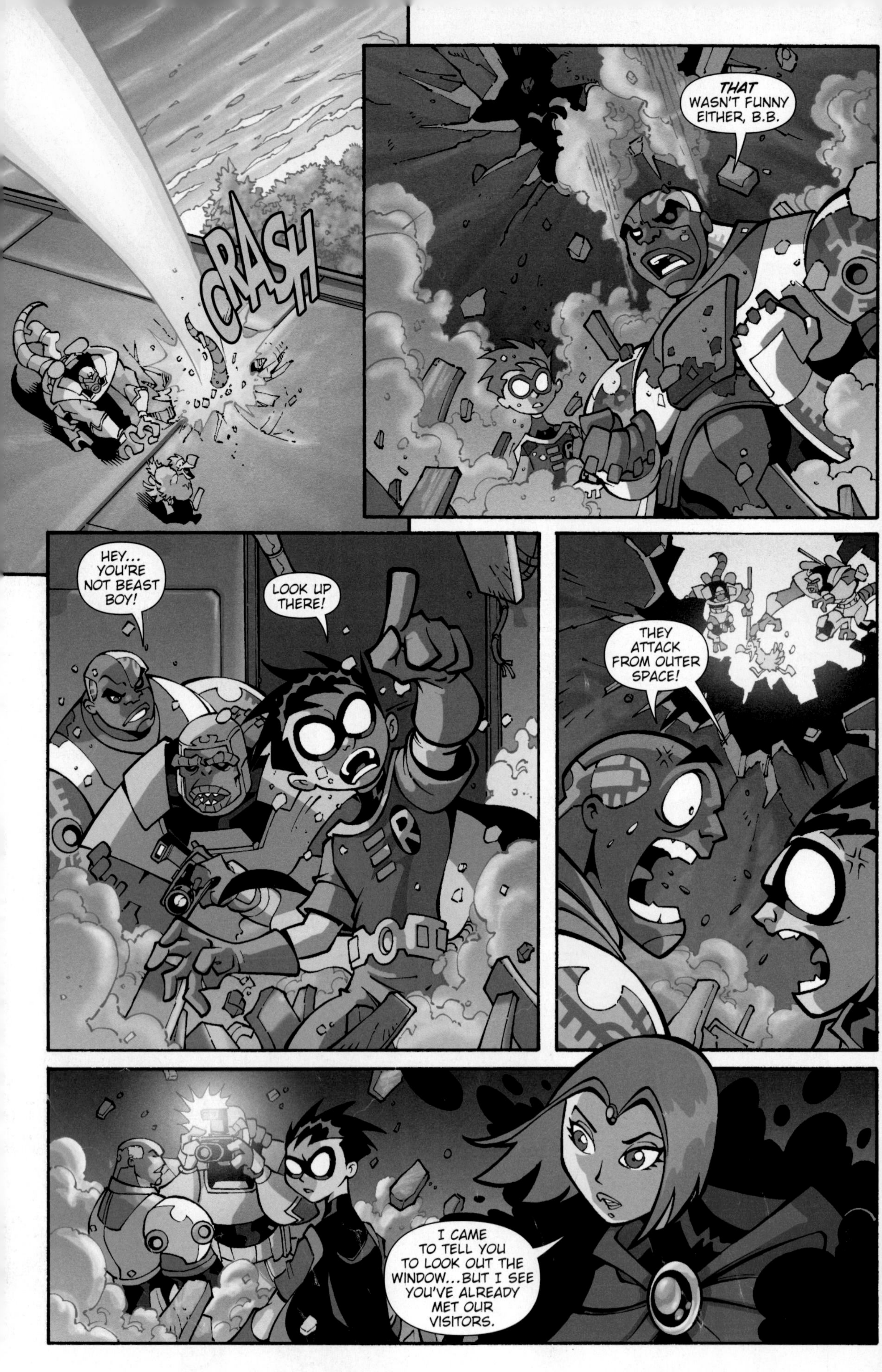
CRASH
THAT WASN'T FUNNY EITHER, B.B.
HEY... YOU'RE NOT BEAST BOY!
LOOK UP THERE!
THEY ATTACK FROM OUTER SPACE!
I CAME TO TELL YOU TO LOOK OUT THE WINDOW...BUT I SEE YOU'VE ALREADY MET OUR VISITORS.

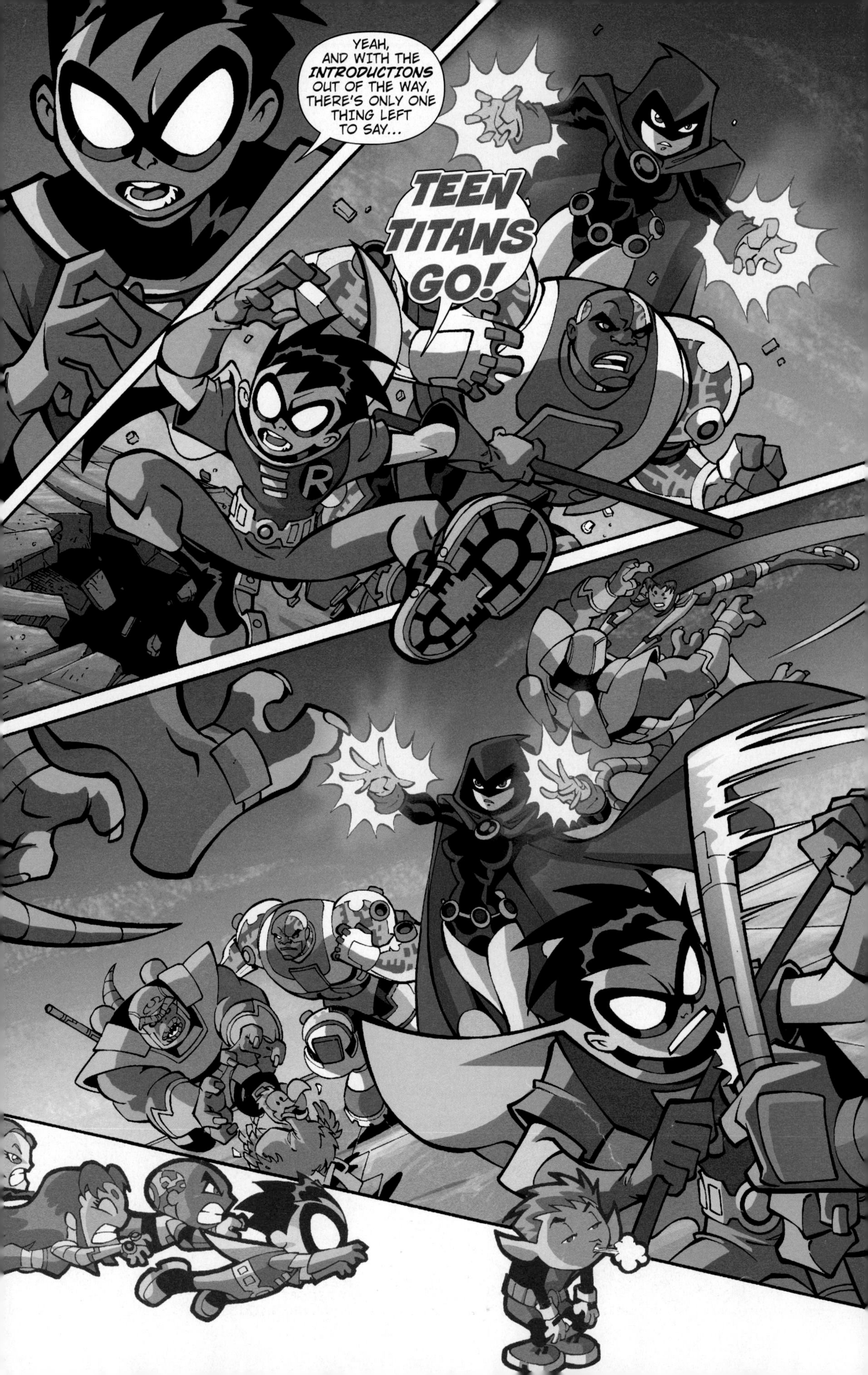
YEAH, AND WITH THE *INTRODUCTIONS* OUT OF THE WAY, THERE'S ONLY ONE THING LEFT TO SAY...
TEEN TITANS GO!

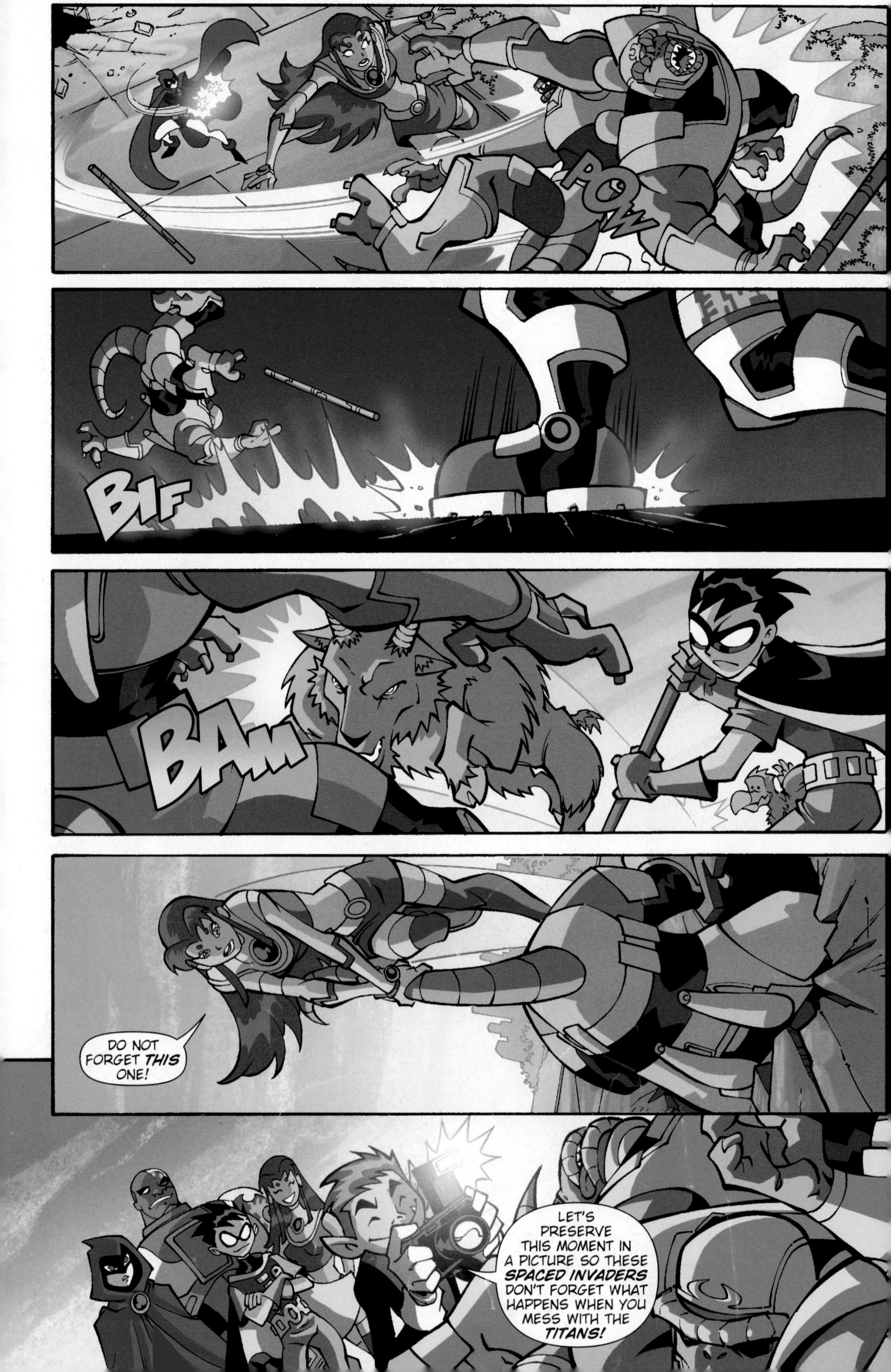
POW
BIF
BAM
DO NOT FORGET THIS ONE!
LET'S PRESERVE THIS MOMENT IN A PICTURE SO THESE SPACED INVADERS DON'T FORGET WHAT HAPPENS WHEN YOU MESS WITH THE TITANS!

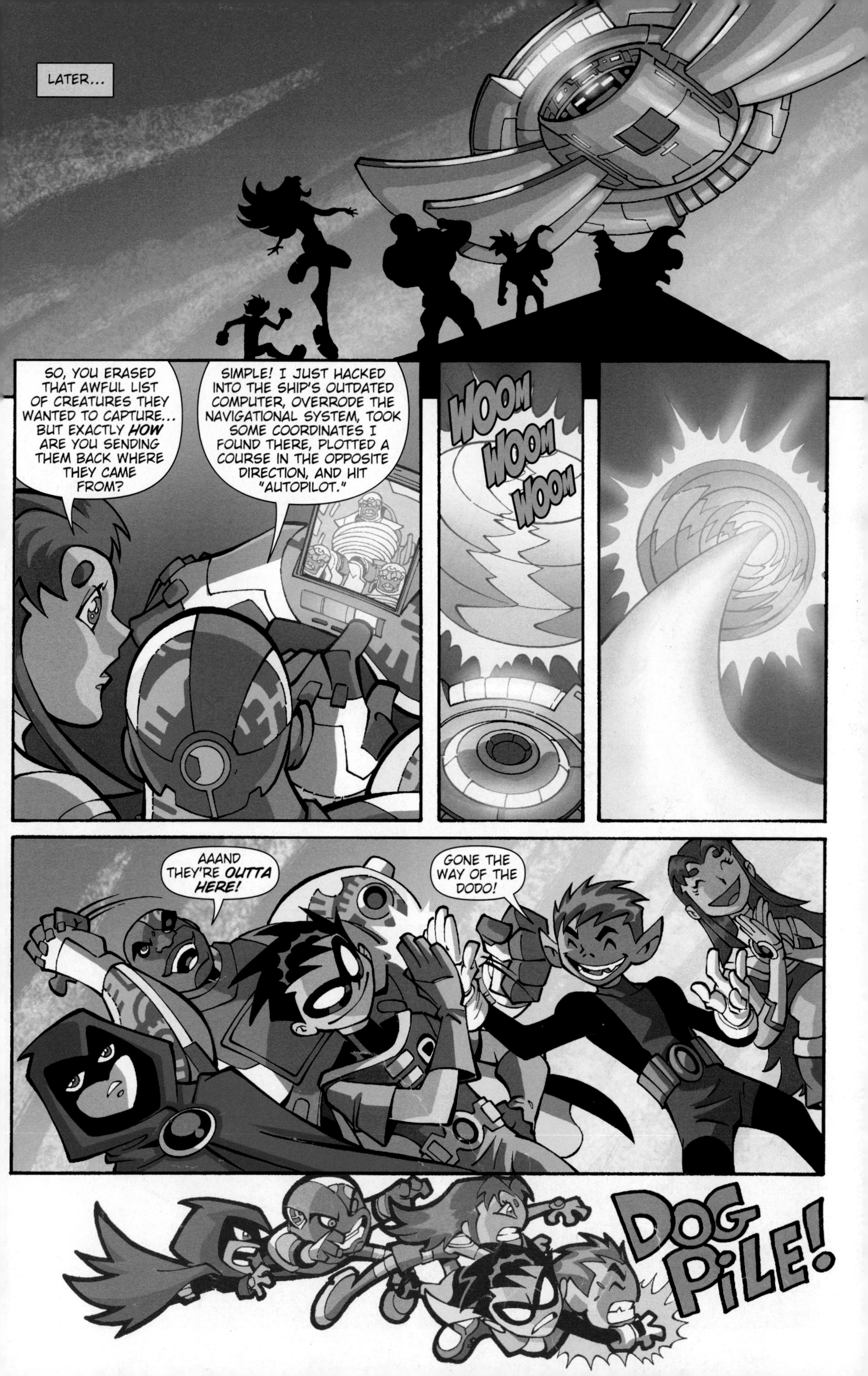
LATER...
SO, YOU ERASED THAT AWFUL LIST OF CREATURES THEY WANTED TO CAPTURE... BUT EXACTLY HOW ARE YOU SENDING THEM BACK WHERE THEY CAME FROM?
SIMPLE! I JUST HACKED INTO THE SHIP'S OUTDATED COMPUTER, OVERRODE THE NAVIGATIONAL SYSTEM, TOOK SOME COORDINATES I FOUND THERE, PLOTTED A COURSE IN THE OPPOSITE DIRECTION, AND HIT "AUTOPILOT."
WOOM
WOOM
WOOM
AAAND THEY'RE OUTTA HERE!
GONE THE WAY OF THE DODO!
DOG PILE!

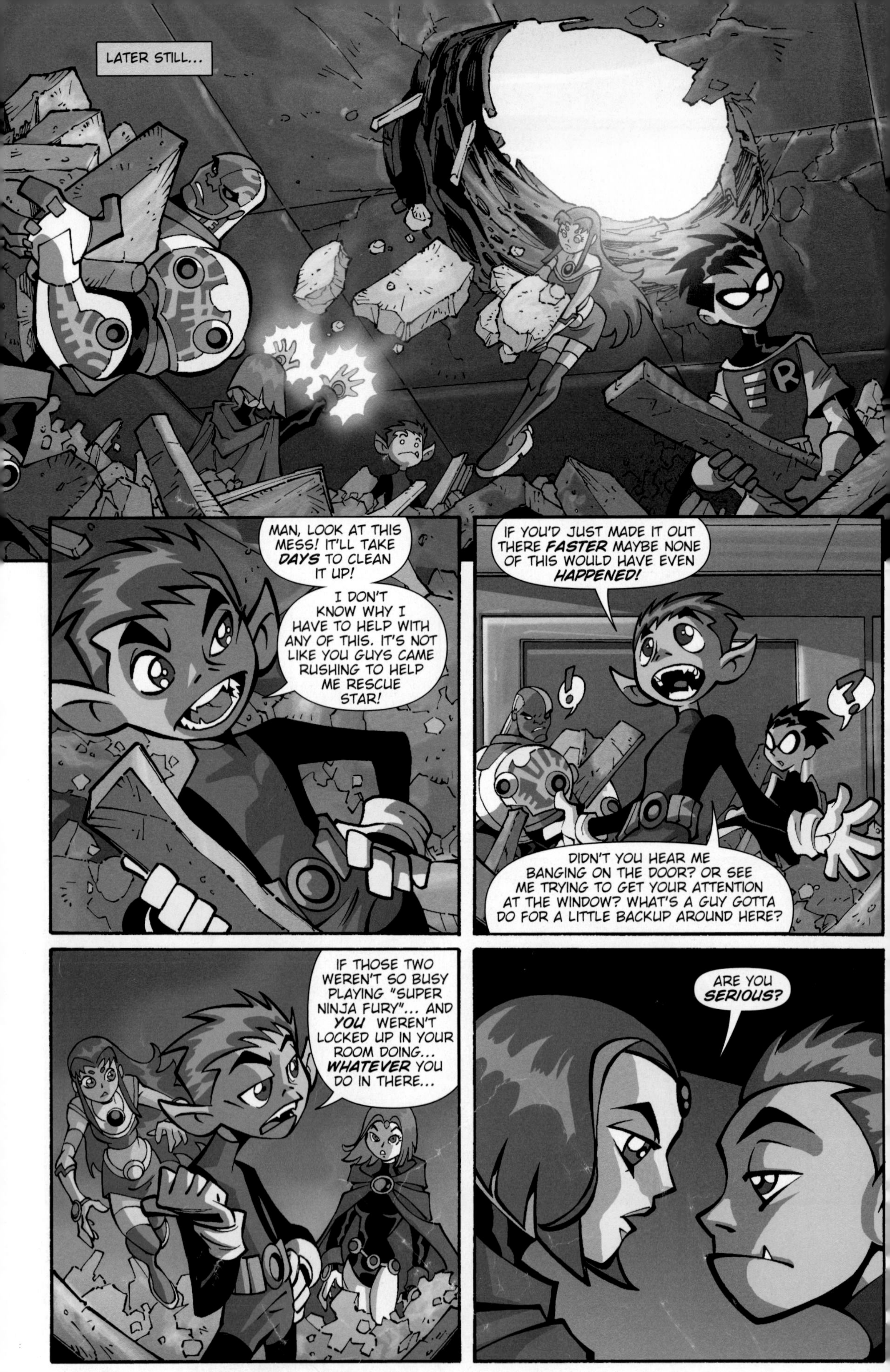
LATER STILL...
MAN, LOOK AT THIS MESS! IT'LL TAKE DAYS TO CLEAN IT UP!
I DON'T KNOW WHY I HAVE TO HELP WITH ANY OF THIS. IT'S NOT LIKE YOU GUYS CAME RUSHING TO HELP ME RESCUE STAR!
IF YOU'D JUST MADE IT OUT THERE FASTER MAYBE NONE OF THIS WOULD HAVE EVEN HAPPENED!
DIDN'T YOU HEAR ME BANGING ON THE DOOR? OR SEE ME TRYING TO GET YOUR ATTENTION AT THE WINDOW? WHAT'S A GUY GOTTA DO FOR A LITTLE BACKUP AROUND HERE?
IF THOSE TWO WEREN'T SO BUSY PLAYING "SUPER NINJA FURY"... AND YOU WEREN'T LOCKED UP IN YOUR ROOM DOING... WHATEVER YOU DO IN THERE...
ARE YOU SERIOUS?

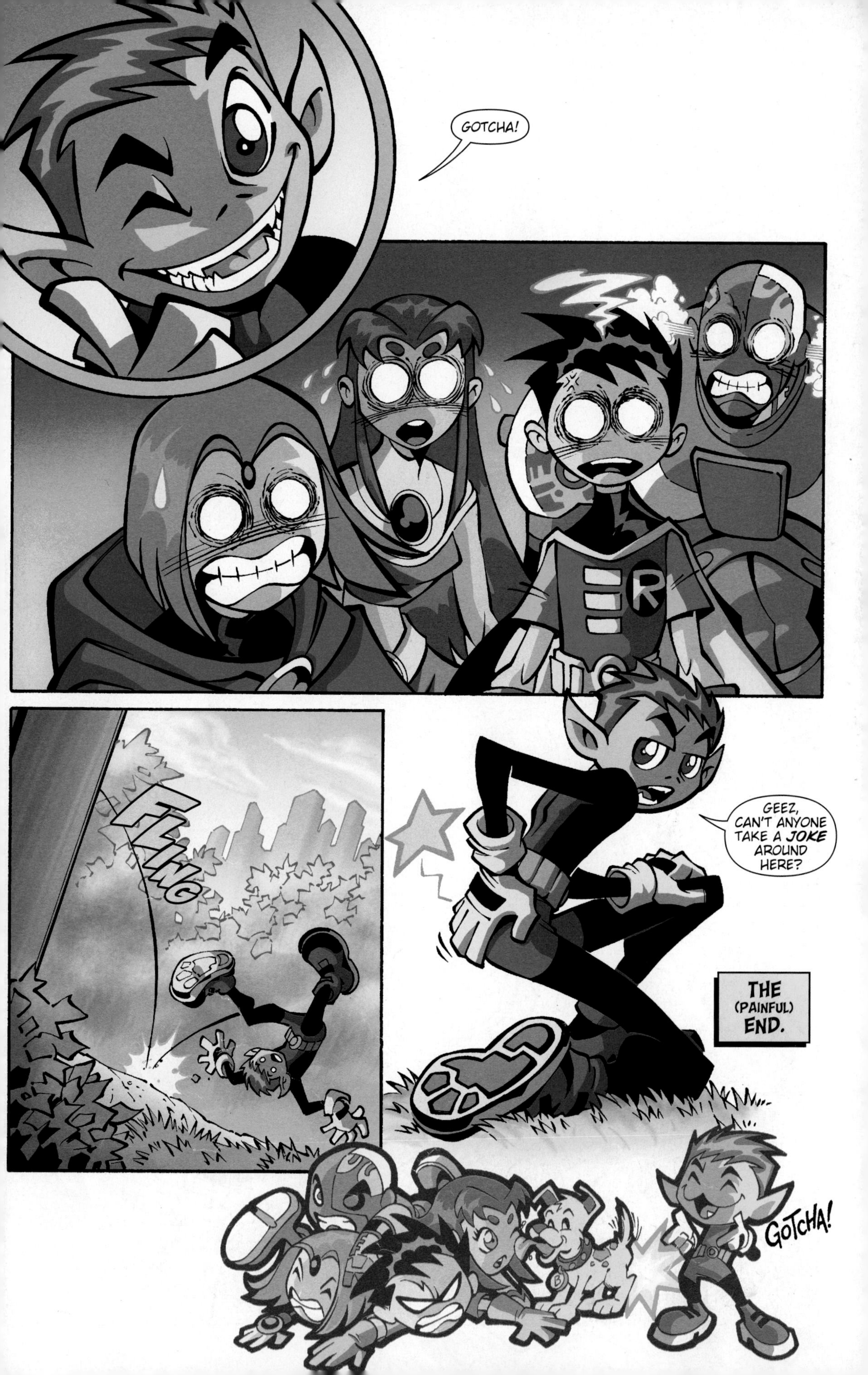
GOTCHA!
FLING
GEEZ, CAN'T ANYONE TAKE A JOKE AROUND HERE?
THE (PAINFUL) END.
GOTCHA!

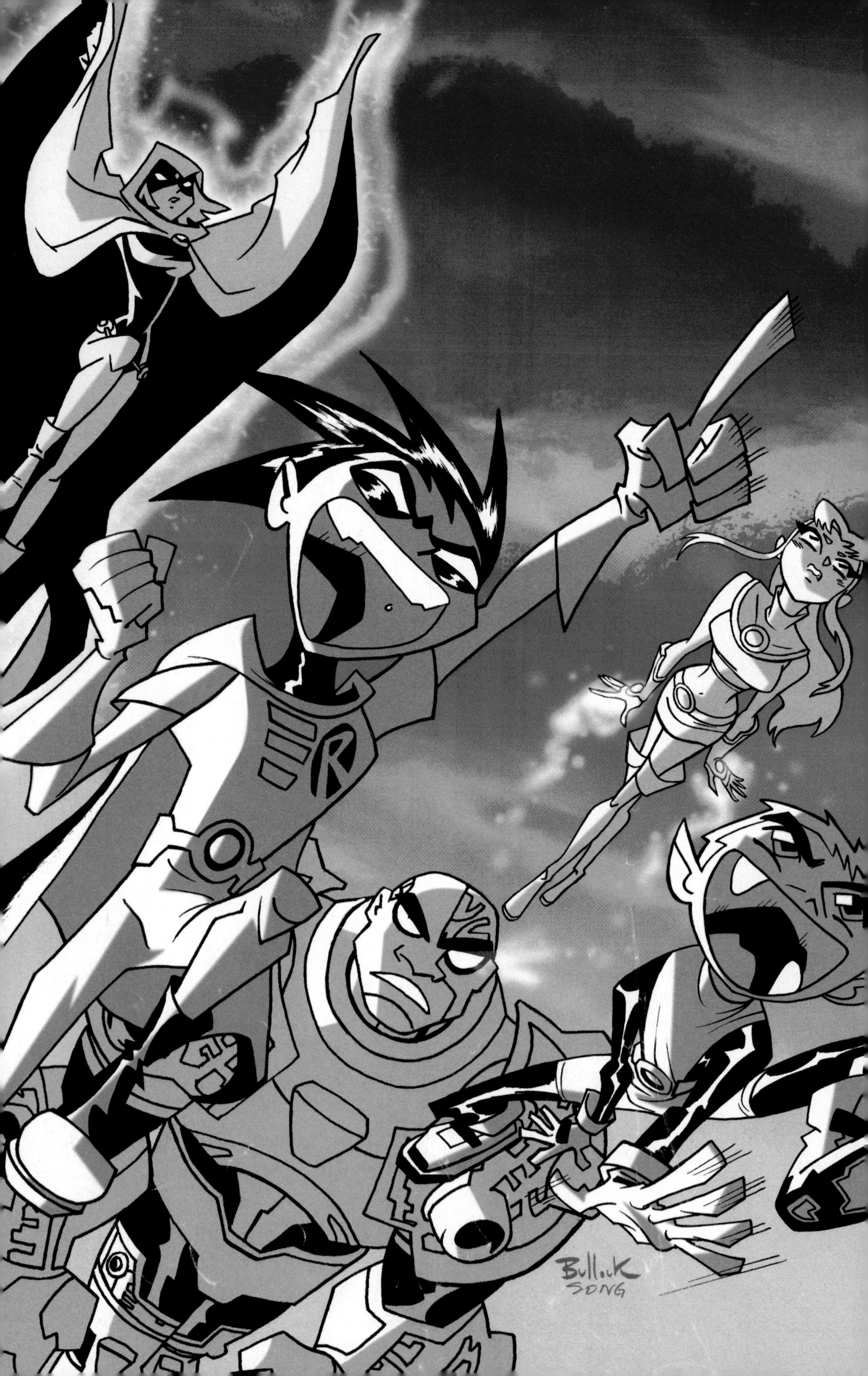
Bullock
Song

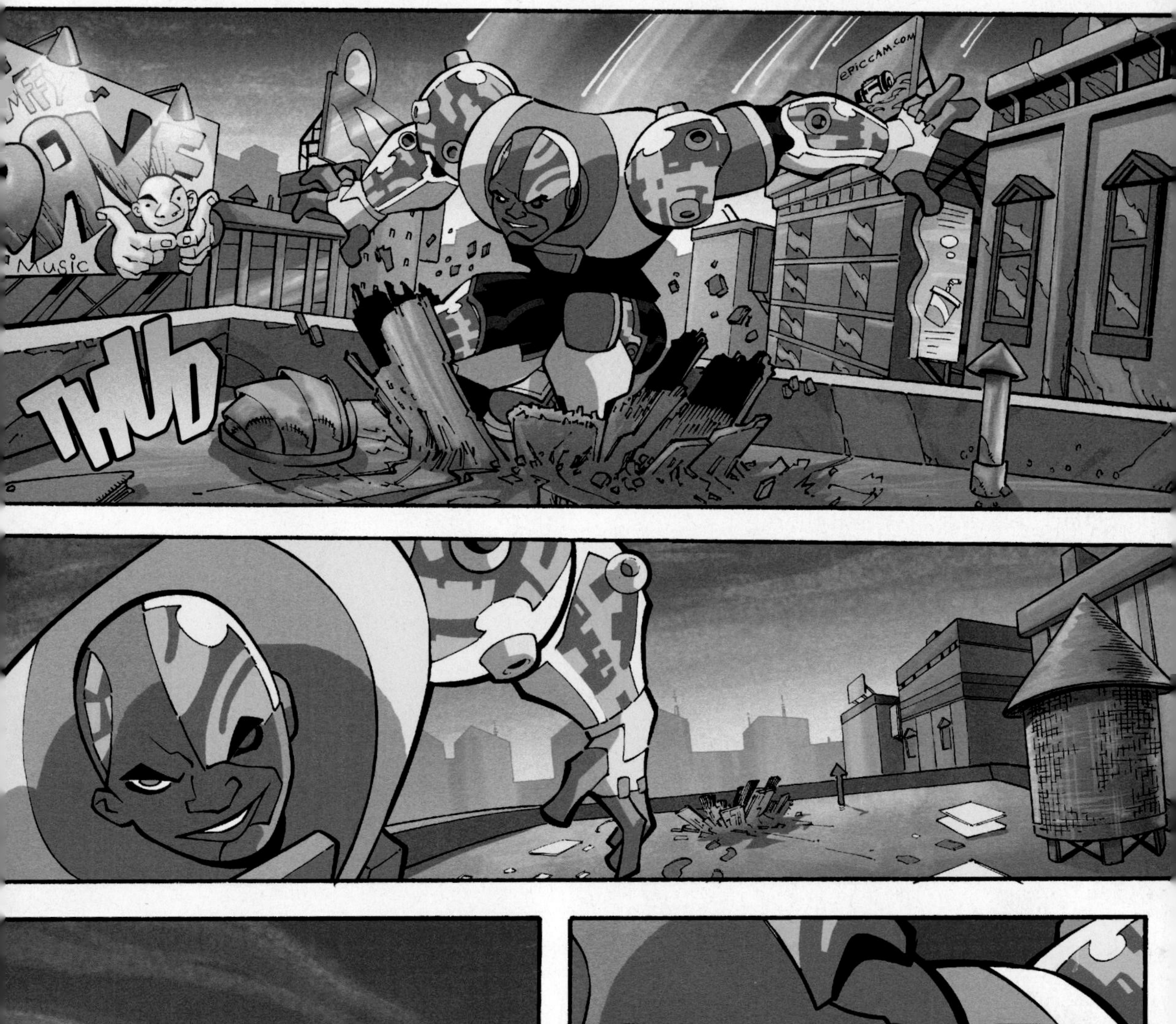
Music
EPICCAM.COM
THUD
OH, YEAH...

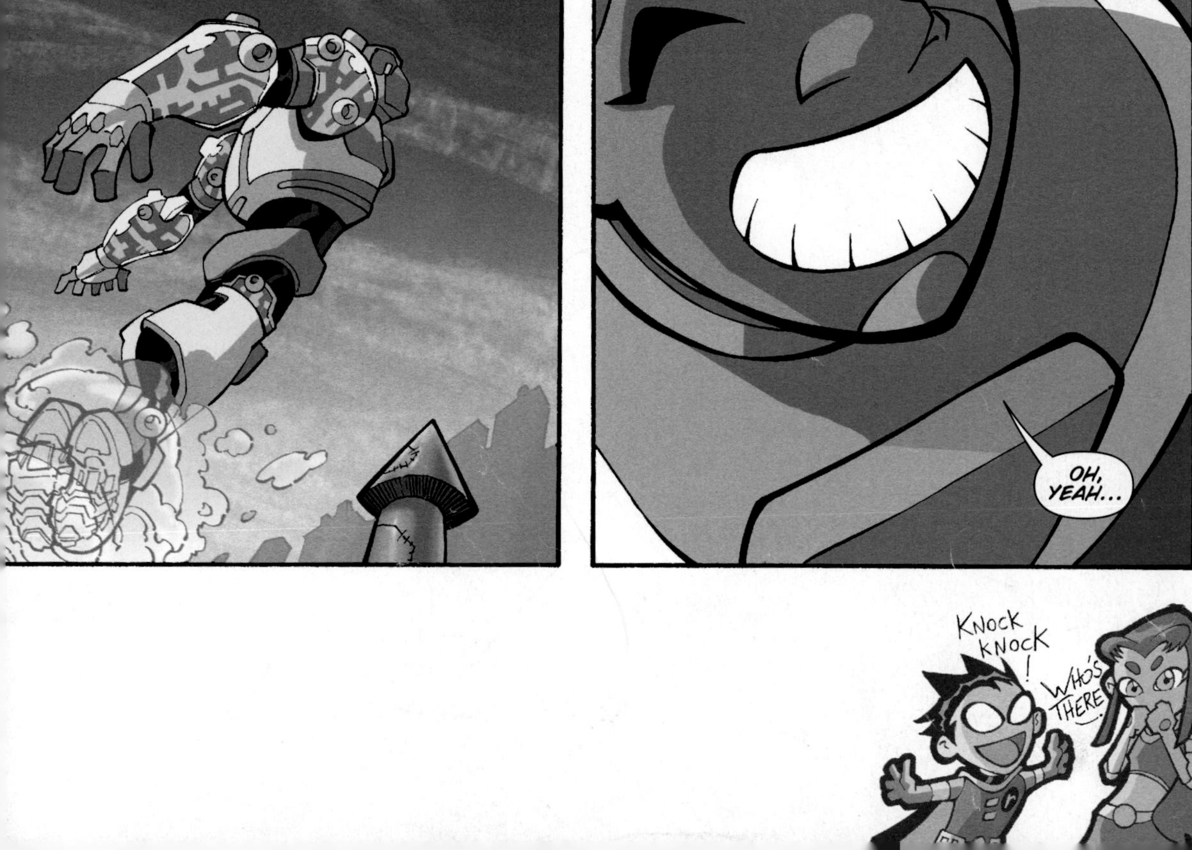
KNOCK KNOCK!
WHO'S THERE?

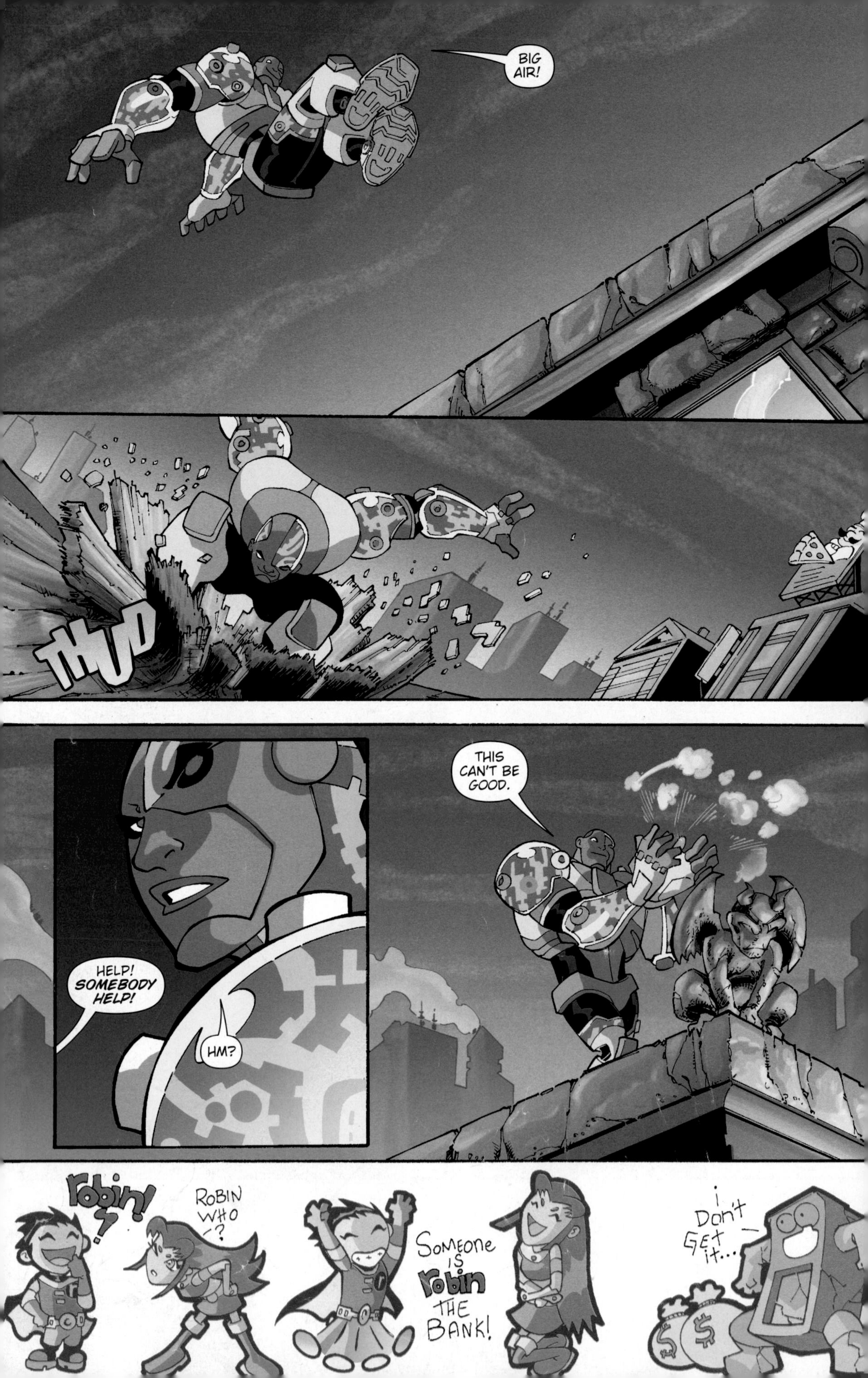

BIG AIR!
THUD
HELP! SOMEBODY HELP!
HM?
THIS CAN'T BE GOOD.
robin!?
ROBIN WHO-?
SOMEONE IS robin THE BANK!
I Don't GET it...

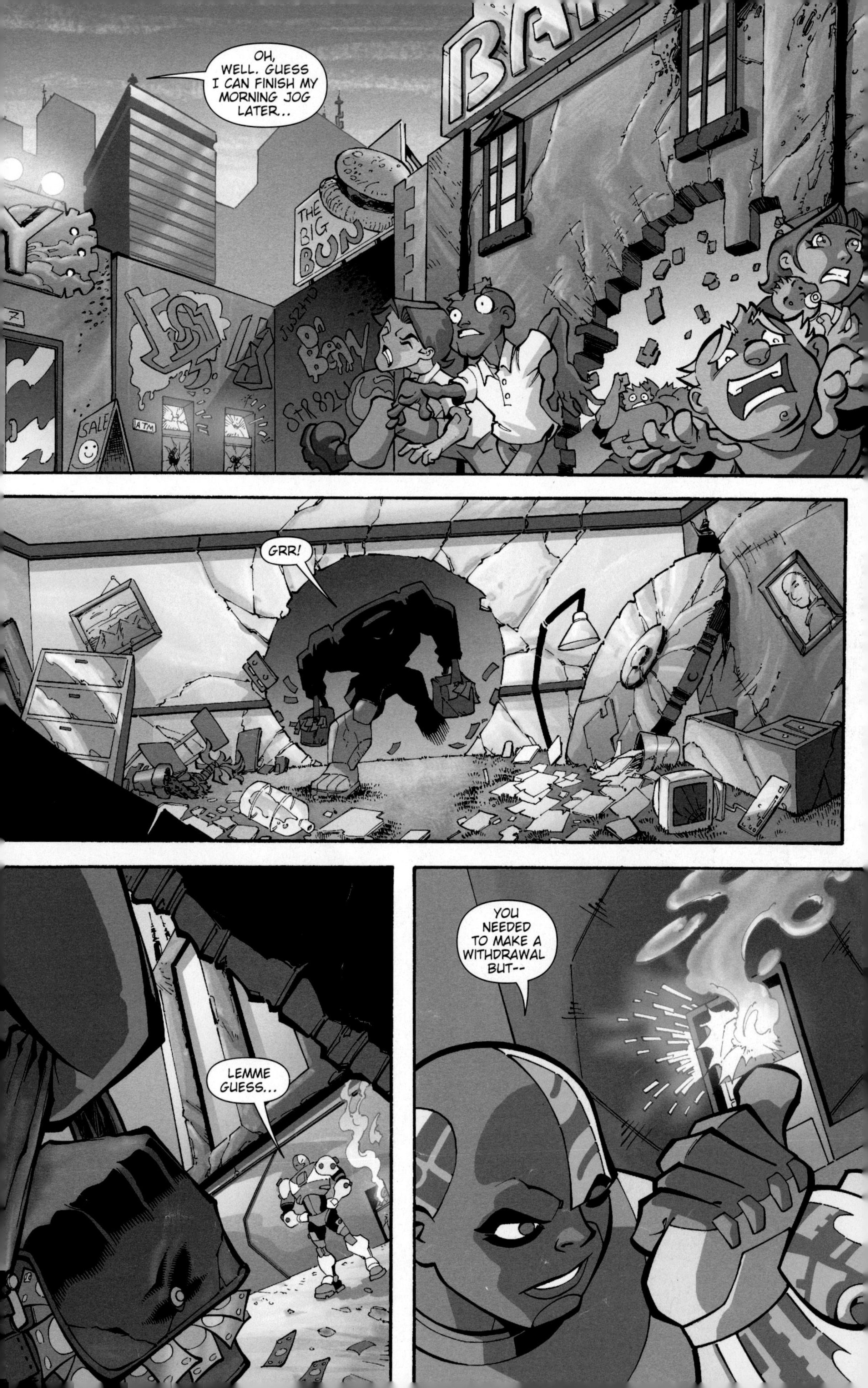
OH, WELL. GUESS I CAN FINISH MY MORNING JOG LATER...
THE BIG BUN
SALE
ATM
GRR!
LEMME GUESS...
YOU NEEDED TO MAKE A WITHDRAWAL BUT--

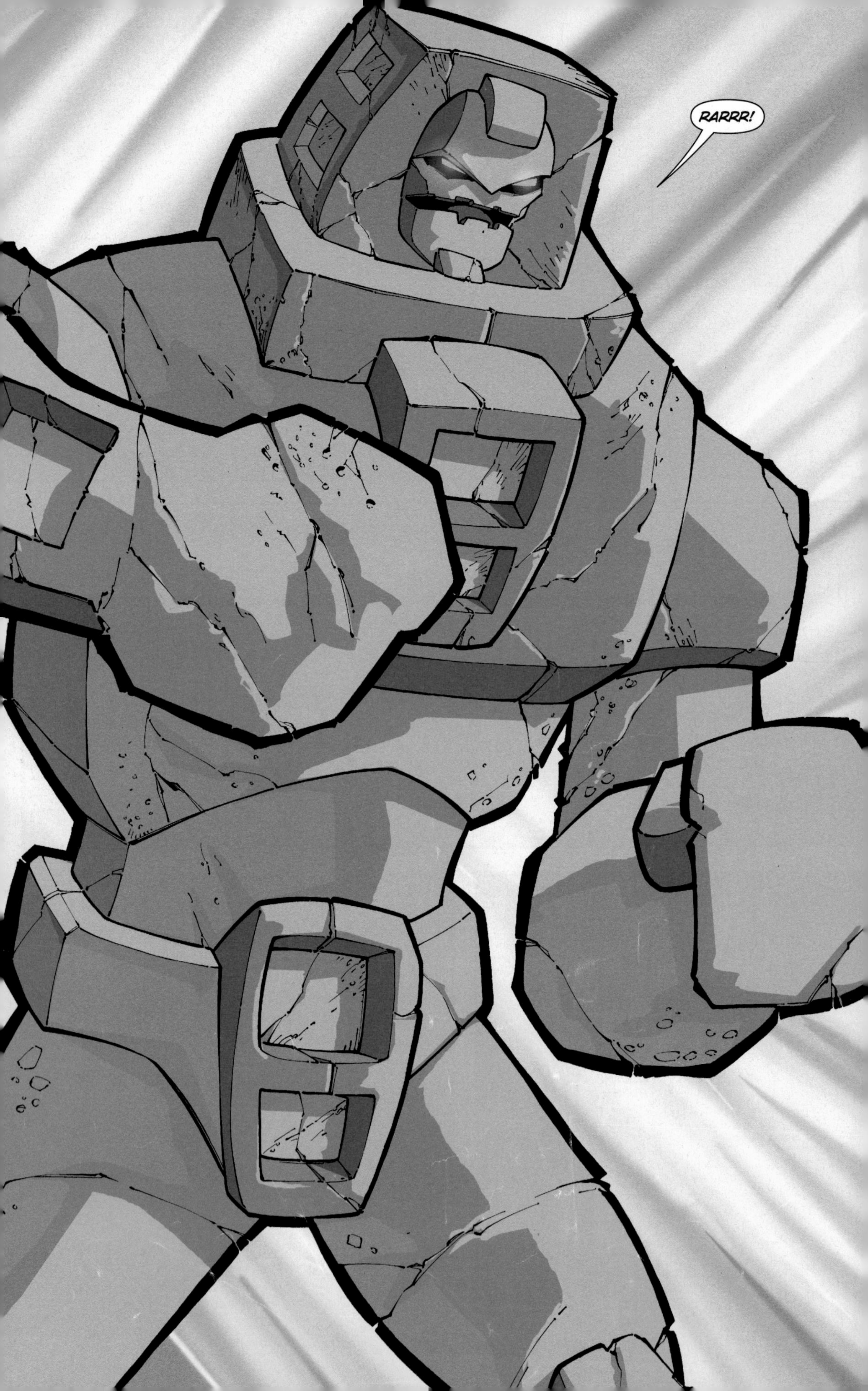
RARRR!

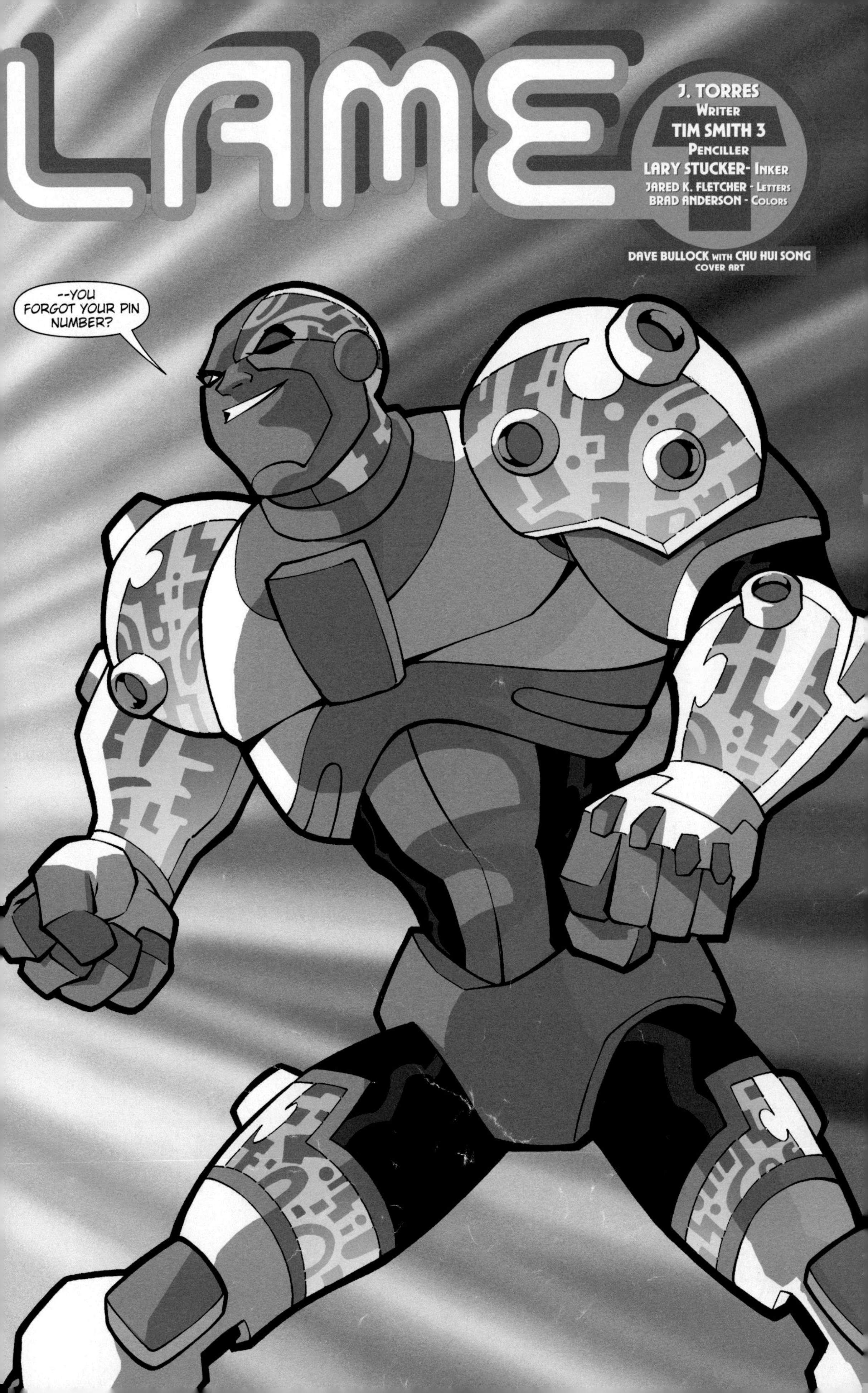
LAME
J. TORRES
WRITER
TIM SMITH 3
PENCILLER
LARY STUCKER- INKER
JARED K. FLETCHER - LETTERS
BRAD ANDERSON - COLORS
DAVE BULLOCK WITH CHU HUI SONG
COVER ART
--YOU FORGOT YOUR PIN NUMBER?

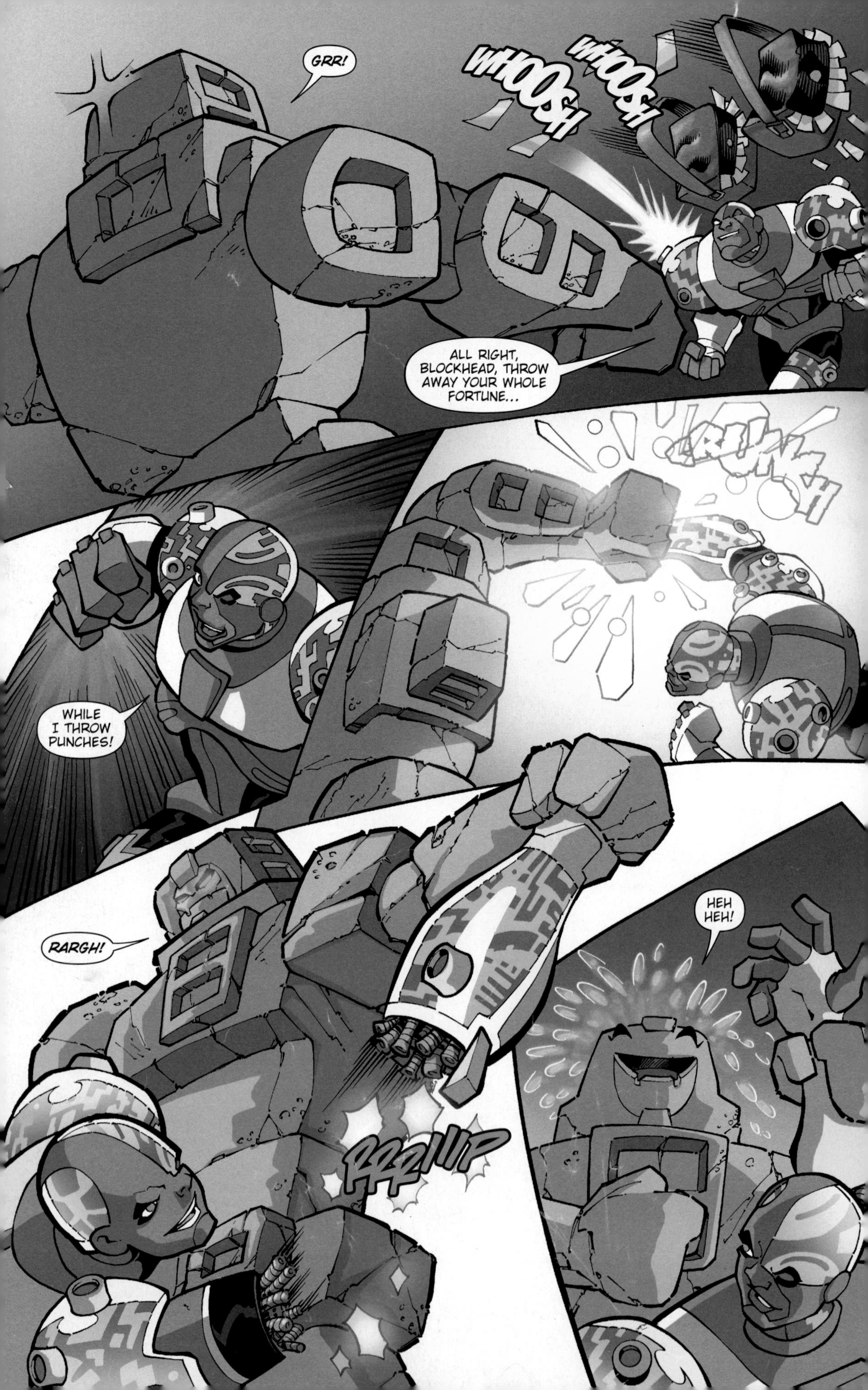
GRR!
WHOOSH
WHOOSH
ALL RIGHT, BLOCKHEAD, THROW AWAY YOUR WHOLE FORTUNE...
KRUNCH
WHILE I THROW PUNCHES!
RARGH!
RRRIIIP
HEH HEH!

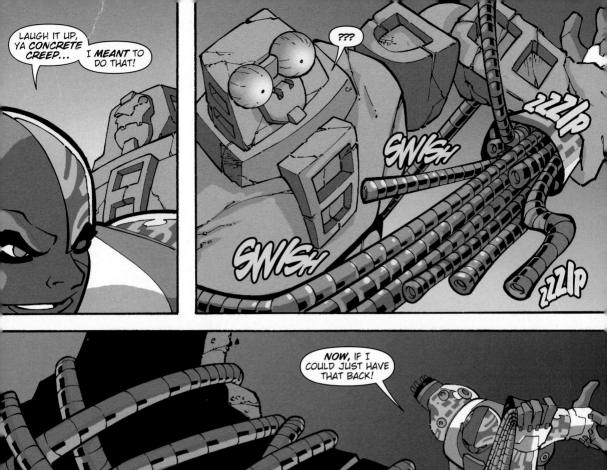

LAUGH IT UP, YA *CONCRETE CREEP*... I *MEANT* TO DO THAT!

???

SWISH

SWISH

ZZZIP

ZZZIP

NOW, IF I COULD JUST HAVE THAT BACK!

YANK

KER-RASH!

THANKS, *CYBORG!* WE'LL TAKE IT FROM HERE.

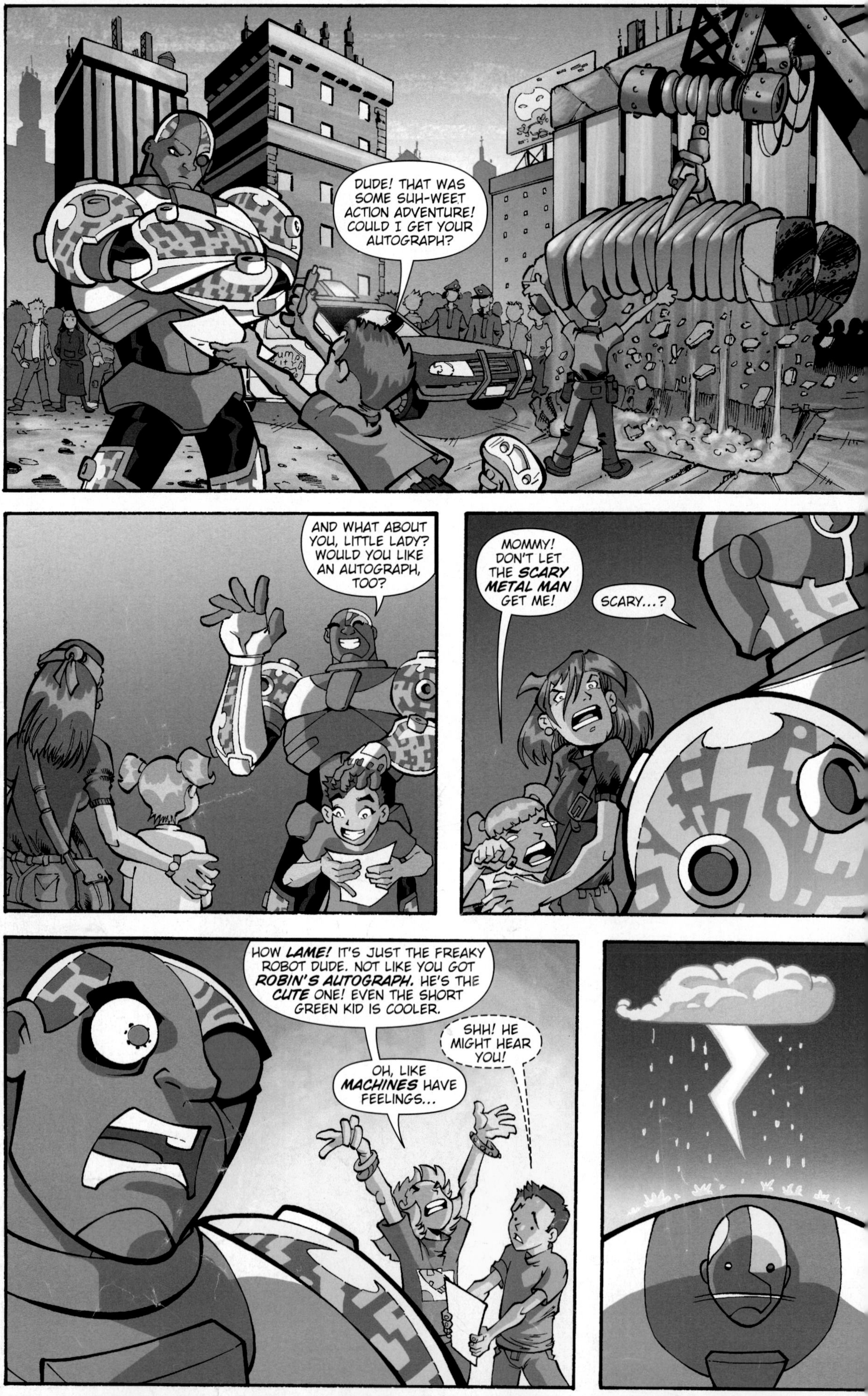
DUDE! THAT WAS SOME SUH-WEET ACTION ADVENTURE! COULD I GET YOUR AUTOGRAPH?
AND WHAT ABOUT YOU, LITTLE LADY? WOULD YOU LIKE AN AUTOGRAPH, TOO?
MOMMY! DON'T LET THE SCARY METAL MAN GET ME!
SCARY...?
HOW LAME! IT'S JUST THE FREAKY ROBOT DUDE. NOT LIKE YOU GOT ROBIN'S AUTOGRAPH. HE'S THE CUTE ONE! EVEN THE SHORT GREEN KID IS COOLER.
SHH! HE MIGHT HEAR YOU!
OH, LIKE MACHINES HAVE FEELINGS...

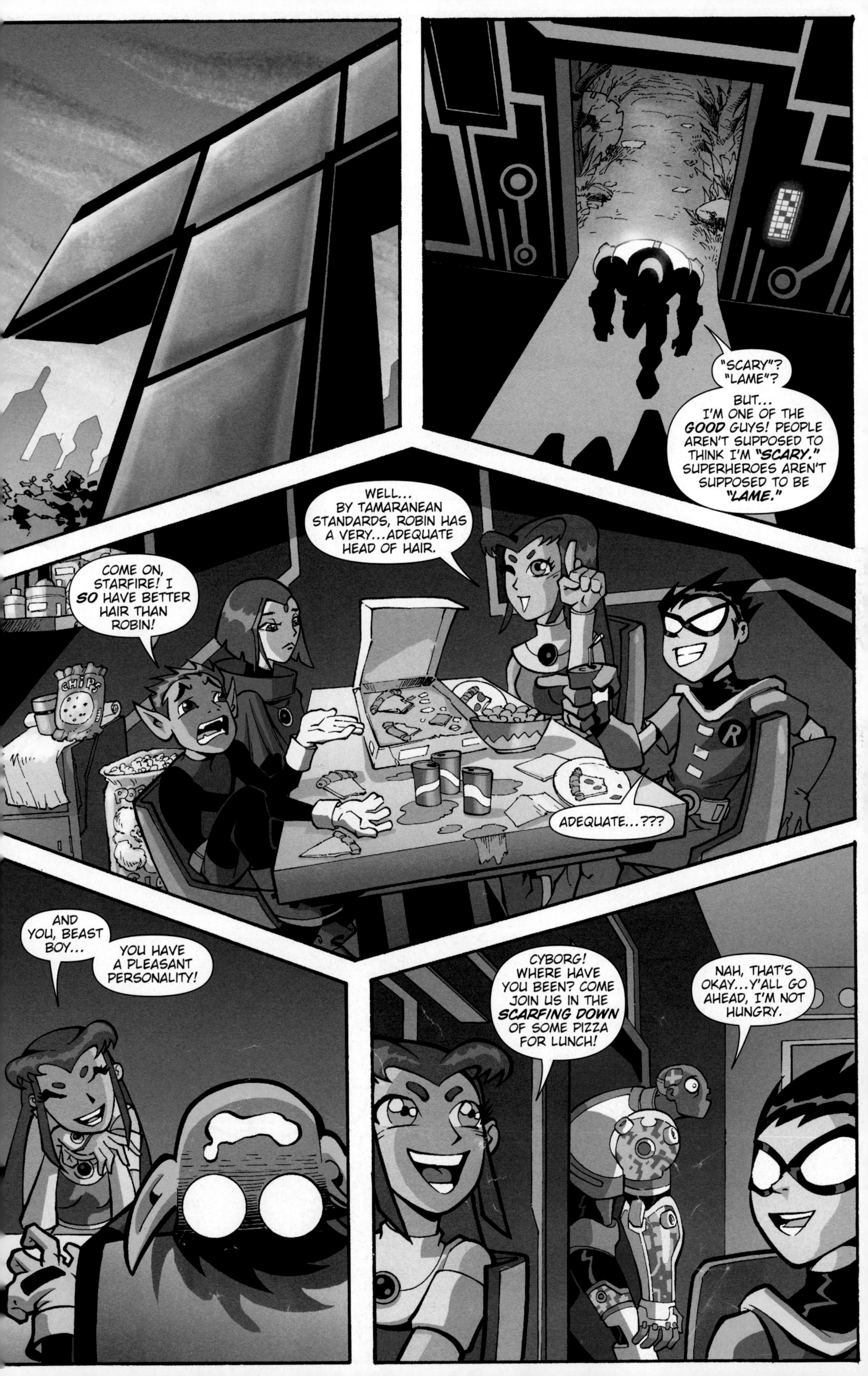
"SCARY"? "LAME"?
BUT... I'M ONE OF THE GOOD GUYS! PEOPLE AREN'T SUPPOSED TO THINK I'M "SCARY." SUPERHEROES AREN'T SUPPOSED TO BE "LAME."
COME ON, STARFIRE! I SO HAVE BETTER HAIR THAN ROBIN!
WELL... BY TAMARANEAN STANDARDS, ROBIN HAS A VERY...ADEQUATE HEAD OF HAIR.
ADEQUATE...???
AND YOU, BEAST BOY...
YOU HAVE A PLEASANT PERSONALITY!
CYBORG! WHERE HAVE YOU BEEN? COME JOIN US IN THE SCARFING DOWN OF SOME PIZZA FOR LUNCH!
NAH, THAT'S OKAY...Y'ALL GO AHEAD, I'M NOT HUNGRY.

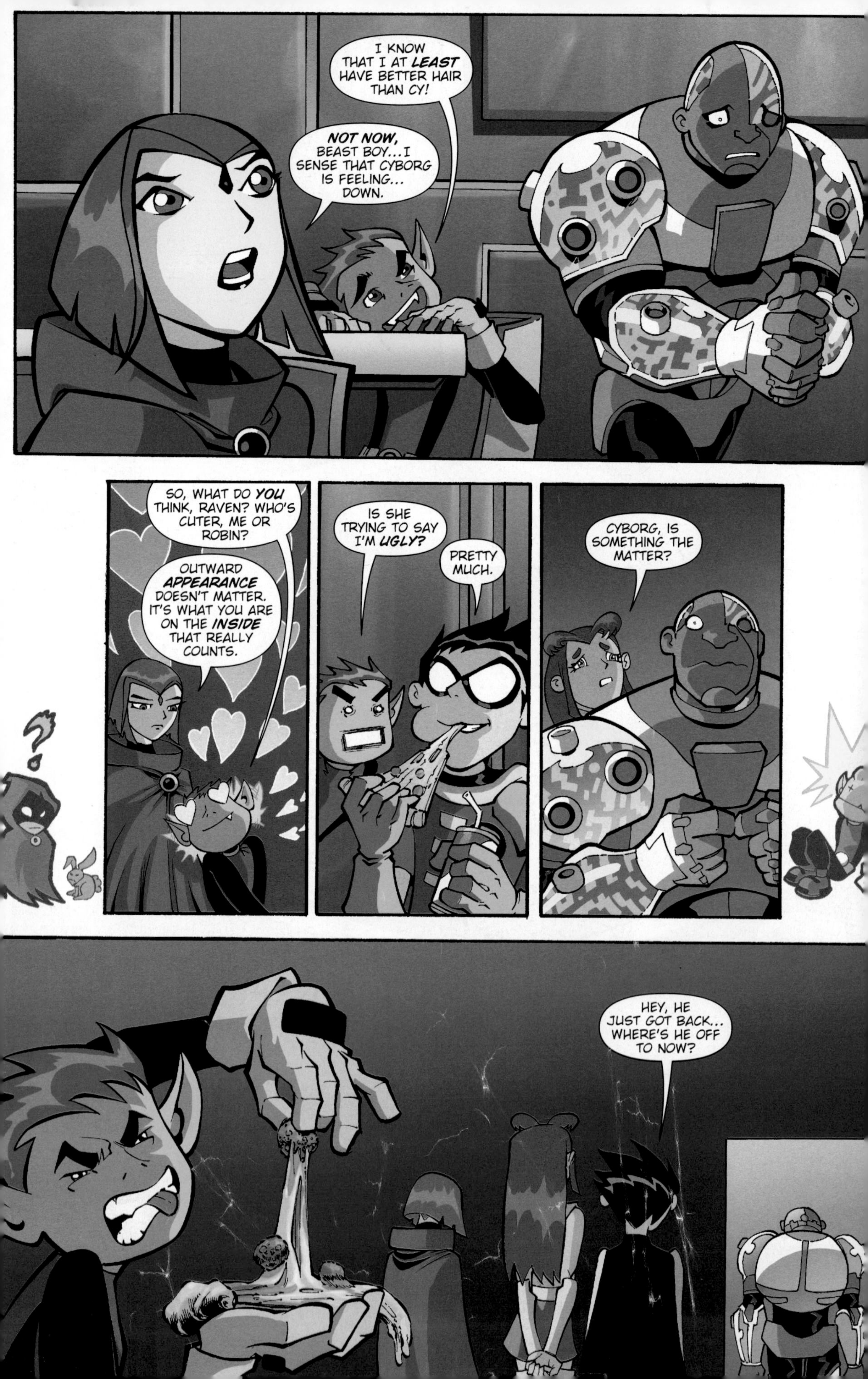

I KNOW THAT I AT LEAST HAVE BETTER HAIR THAN CY!
NOT NOW, BEAST BOY...I SENSE THAT CYBORG IS FEELING... DOWN.
SO, WHAT DO YOU THINK, RAVEN? WHO'S CUTER, ME OR ROBIN?
OUTWARD APPEARANCE DOESN'T MATTER. IT'S WHAT YOU ARE ON THE INSIDE THAT REALLY COUNTS.
IS SHE TRYING TO SAY I'M UGLY?
PRETTY MUCH.
CYBORG, IS SOMETHING THE MATTER?
HEY, HE JUST GOT BACK... WHERE'S HE OFF TO NOW?

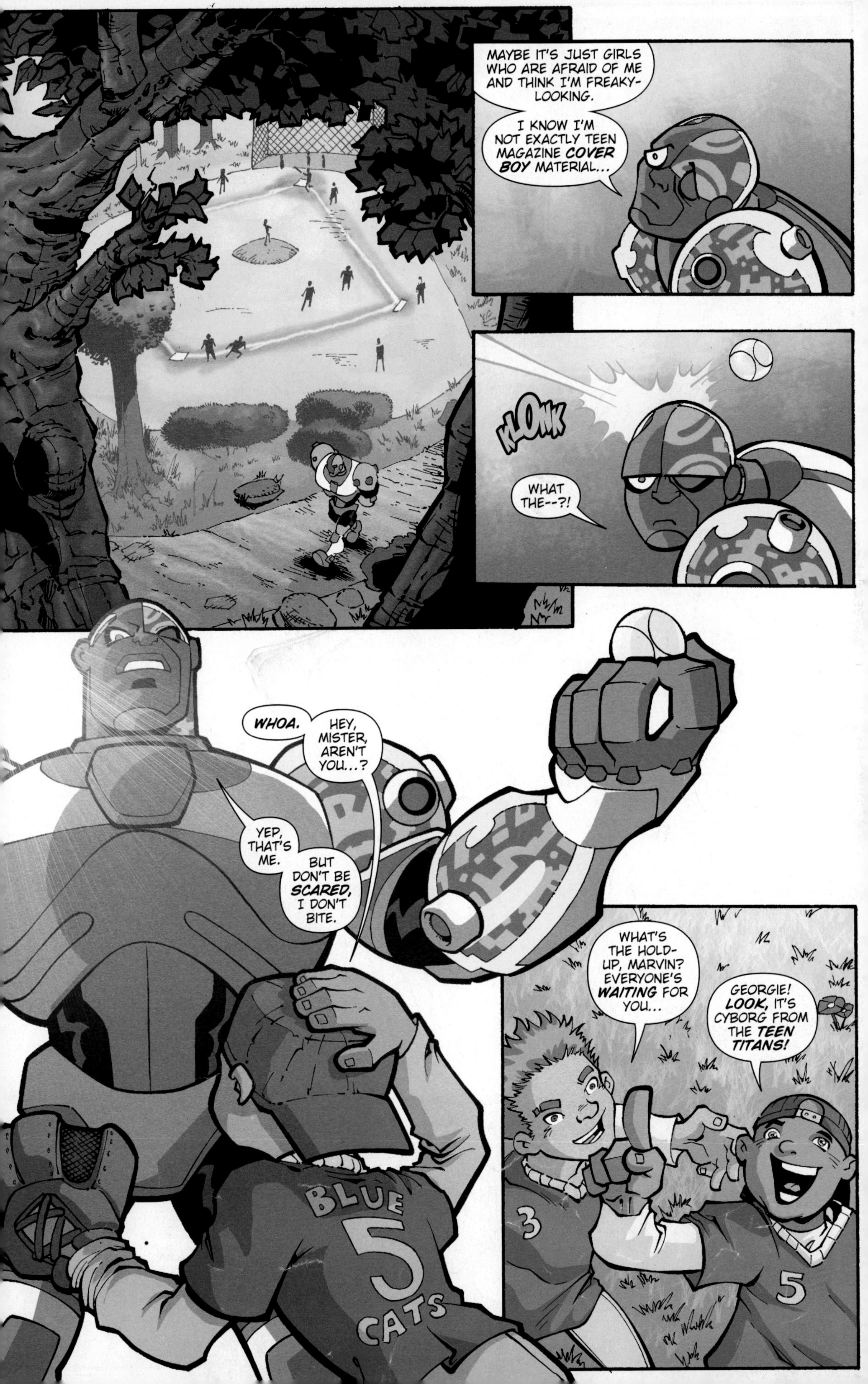
MAYBE IT'S JUST GIRLS WHO ARE AFRAID OF ME AND THINK I'M FREAKY-LOOKING.
I KNOW I'M NOT EXACTLY TEEN MAGAZINE COVER BOY MATERIAL...
KLONK
WHAT THE--?!
WHOA.
HEY, MISTER, AREN'T YOU...?
YEP, THAT'S ME.
BUT DON'T BE SCARED, I DON'T BITE.
BLUE
5
CATS
WHAT'S THE HOLD-UP, MARVIN? EVERYONE'S WAITING FOR YOU...
GEORGIE! LOOK, IT'S CYBORG FROM THE TEEN TITANS!
3
5

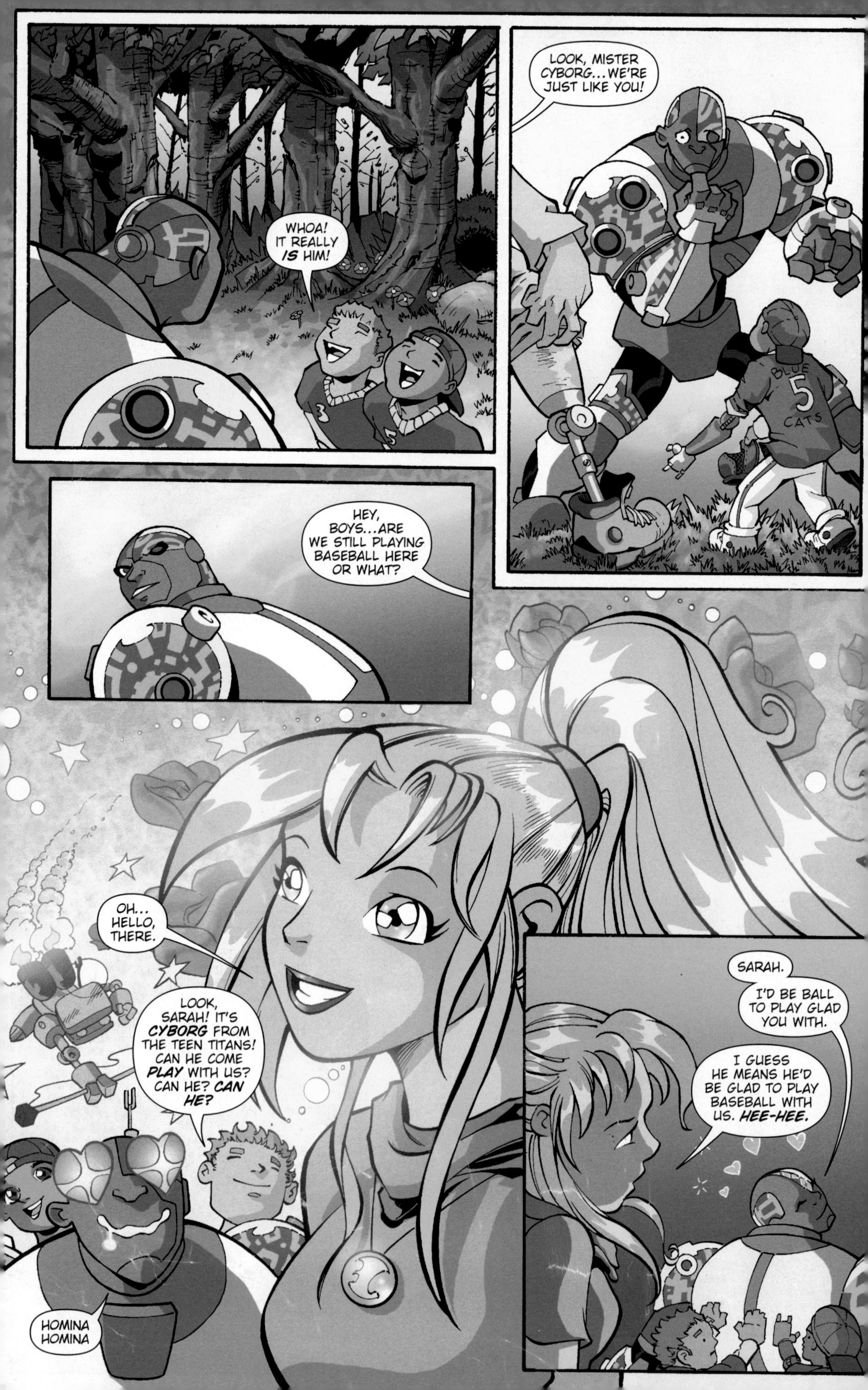

WHOA! IT REALLY IS HIM!
LOOK, MISTER CYBORG... WE'RE JUST LIKE YOU!
BLUE 5 CATS
HEY, BOYS... ARE WE STILL PLAYING BASEBALL HERE OR WHAT?
OH... HELLO, THERE.
LOOK, SARAH! IT'S CYBORG FROM THE TEEN TITANS! CAN HE COME PLAY WITH US? CAN HE? CAN HE?
HOMINA HOMINA
SARAH.
I'D BE BALL TO PLAY GLAD YOU WITH.
I GUESS HE MEANS HE'D BE GLAD TO PLAY BASEBALL WITH US. HEE-HEE.

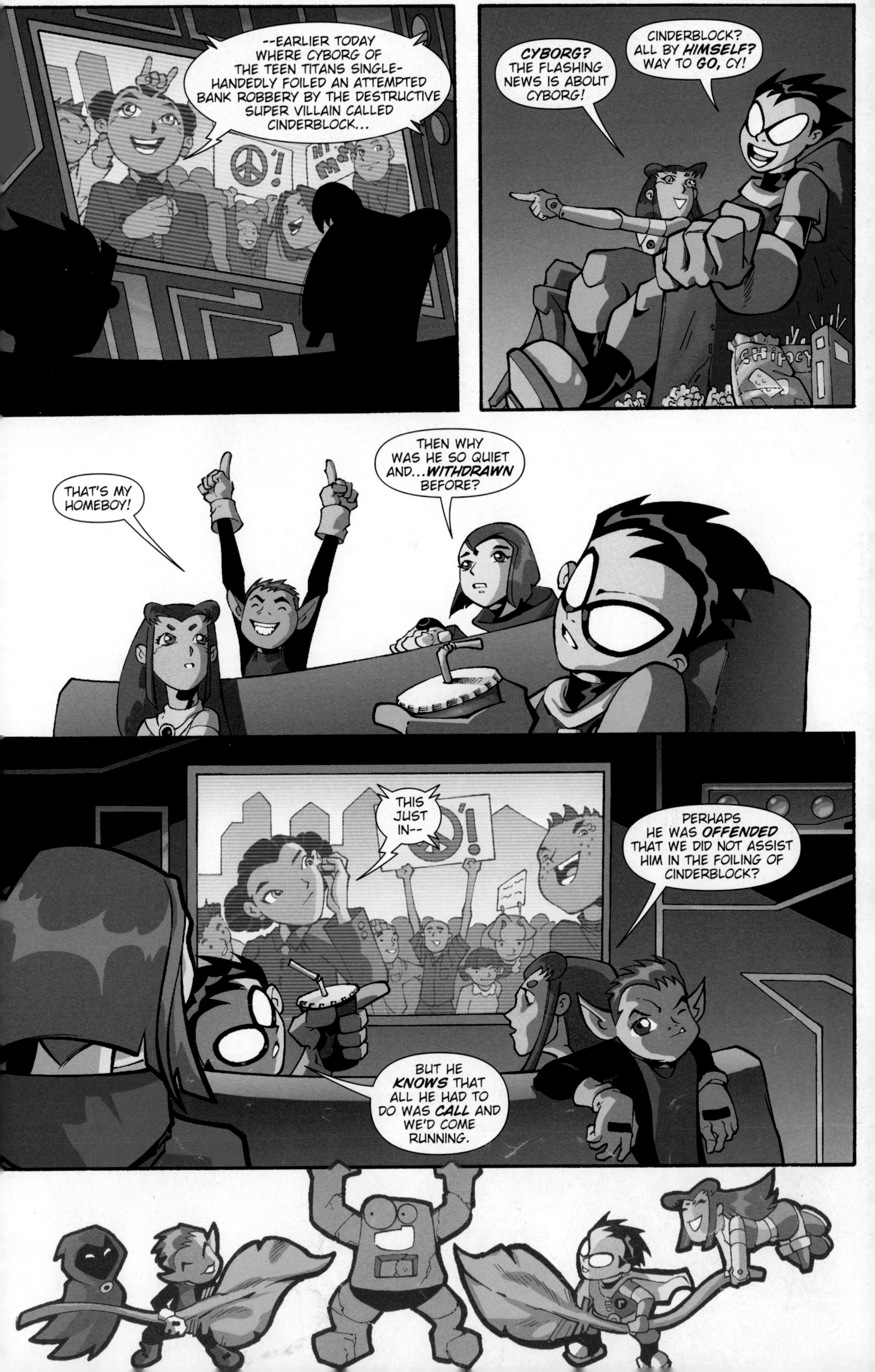
--EARLIER TODAY WHERE CYBORG OF THE TEEN TITANS SINGLE-HANDEDLY FOILED AN ATTEMPTED BANK ROBBERY BY THE DESTRUCTIVE SUPER VILLAIN CALLED CINDERBLOCK...
CYBORG? THE FLASHING NEWS IS ABOUT CYBORG!
CINDERBLOCK? ALL BY HIMSELF? WAY TO GO, CY!
THAT'S MY HOMEBOY!
THEN WHY WAS HE SO QUIET AND...WITHDRAWN BEFORE?
THIS JUST IN--
PERHAPS HE WAS OFFENDED THAT WE DID NOT ASSIST HIM IN THE FOILING OF CINDERBLOCK?
BUT HE KNOWS THAT ALL HE HAD TO DO WAS CALL AND WE'D COME RUNNING.

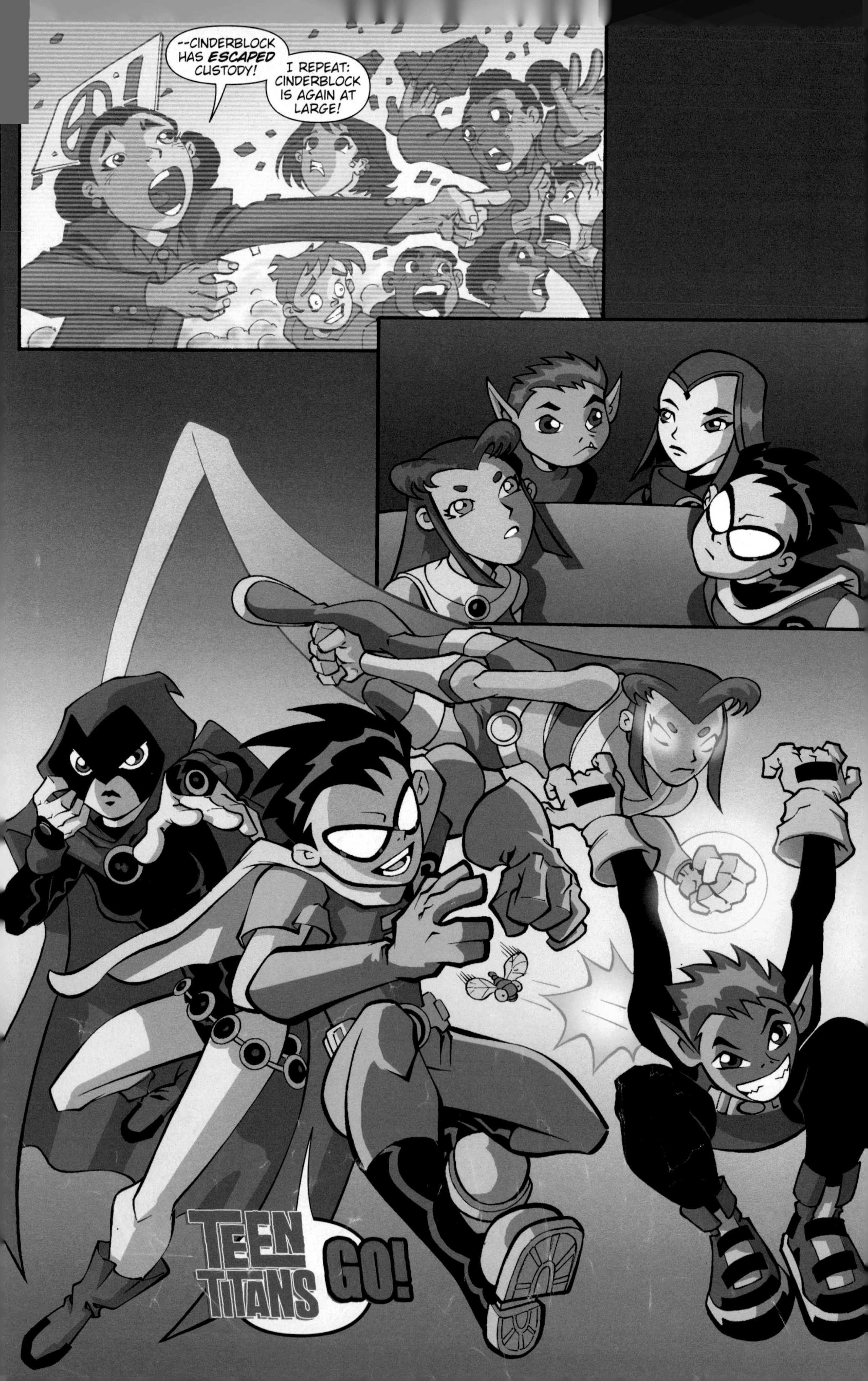
--CINDERBLOCK HAS ESCAPED CUSTODY!
I REPEAT: CINDERBLOCK IS AGAIN AT LARGE!
TEEN TITANS GO!

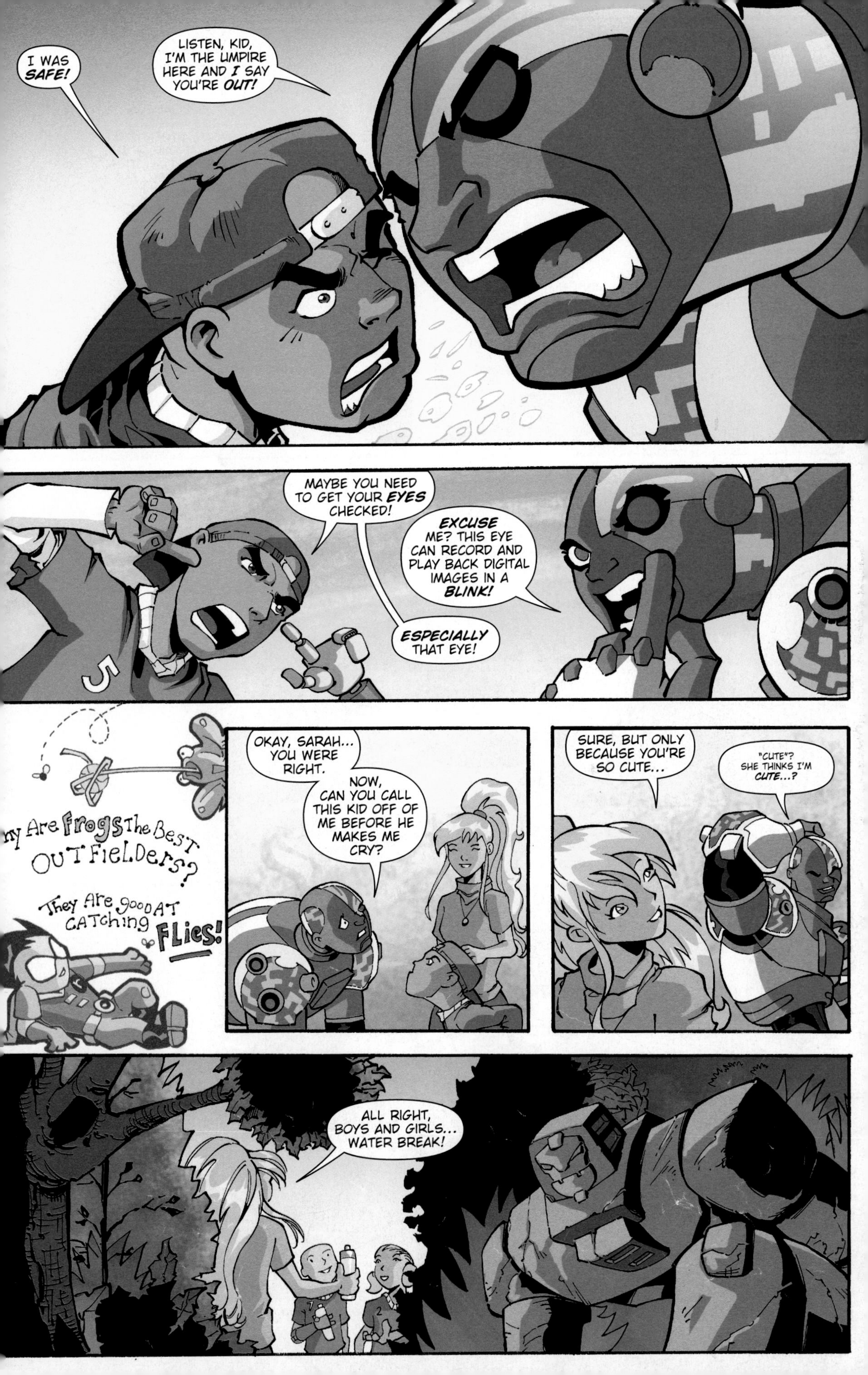
I WAS SAFE!
LISTEN, KID, I'M THE UMPIRE HERE AND I SAY YOU'RE OUT!
MAYBE YOU NEED TO GET YOUR EYES CHECKED!
EXCUSE ME? THIS EYE CAN RECORD AND PLAY BACK DIGITAL IMAGES IN A BLINK!
ESPECIALLY THAT EYE!
ny Are Frogs The Best OUTFIELDers?
They Are good AT CATching FLies!
OKAY, SARAH... YOU WERE RIGHT.
NOW, CAN YOU CALL THIS KID OFF OF ME BEFORE HE MAKES ME CRY?
SURE, BUT ONLY BECAUSE YOU'RE SO CUTE...
"CUTE"? SHE THINKS I'M CUTE...?
ALL RIGHT, BOYS AND GIRLS... WATER BREAK!

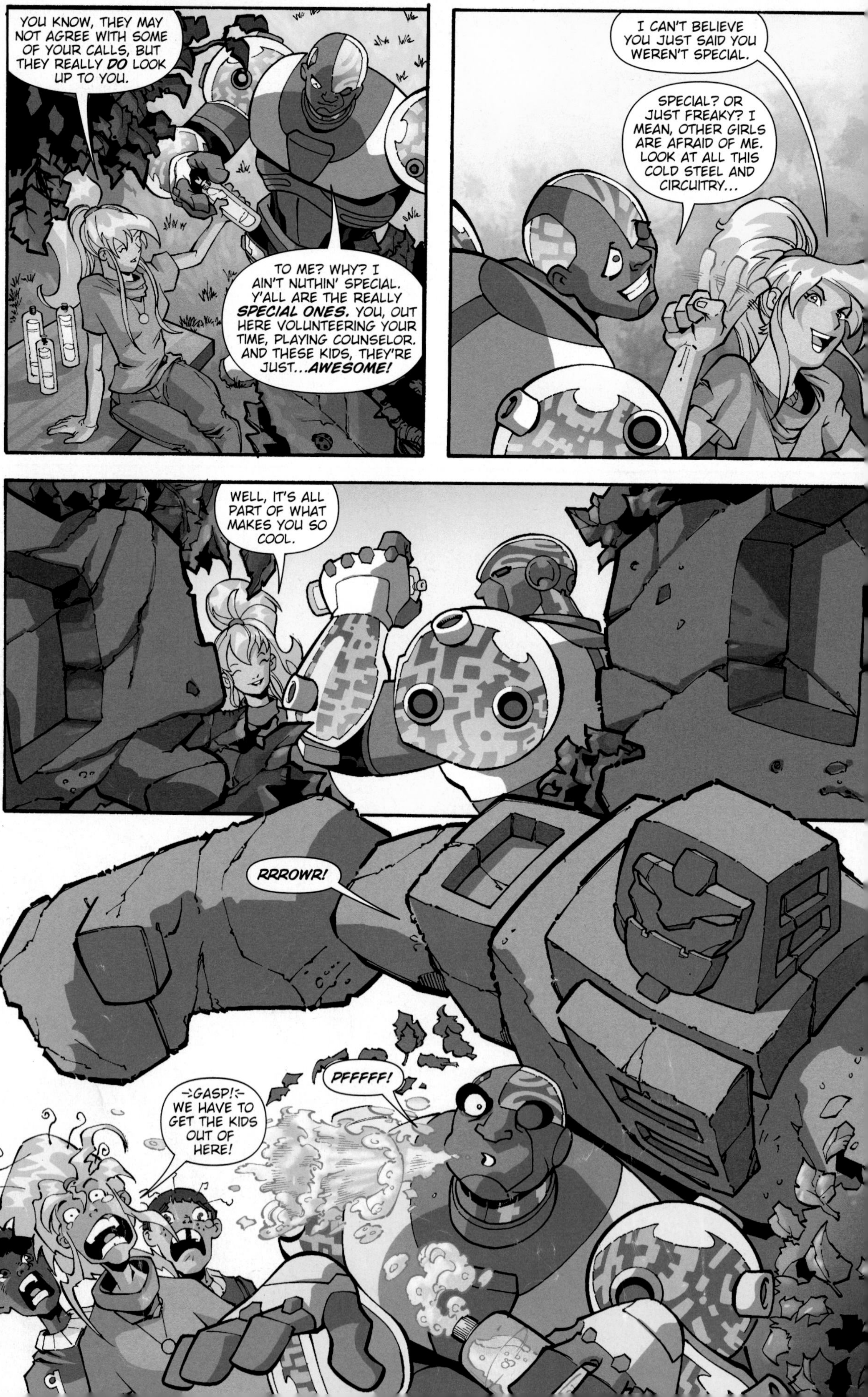
YOU KNOW, THEY MAY NOT AGREE WITH SOME OF YOUR CALLS, BUT THEY REALLY DO LOOK UP TO YOU.
TO ME? WHY? I AIN'T NUTHIN' SPECIAL. Y'ALL ARE THE REALLY SPECIAL ONES. YOU, OUT HERE VOLUNTEERING YOUR TIME, PLAYING COUNSELOR. AND THESE KIDS, THEY'RE JUST...AWESOME!
I CAN'T BELIEVE YOU JUST SAID YOU WEREN'T SPECIAL.
SPECIAL? OR JUST FREAKY? I MEAN, OTHER GIRLS ARE AFRAID OF ME. LOOK AT ALL THIS COLD STEEL AND CIRCUITRY...
WELL, IT'S ALL PART OF WHAT MAKES YOU SO COOL.
RRROWR!
PFFFFF!
-GASP!- WE HAVE TO GET THE KIDS OUT OF HERE!

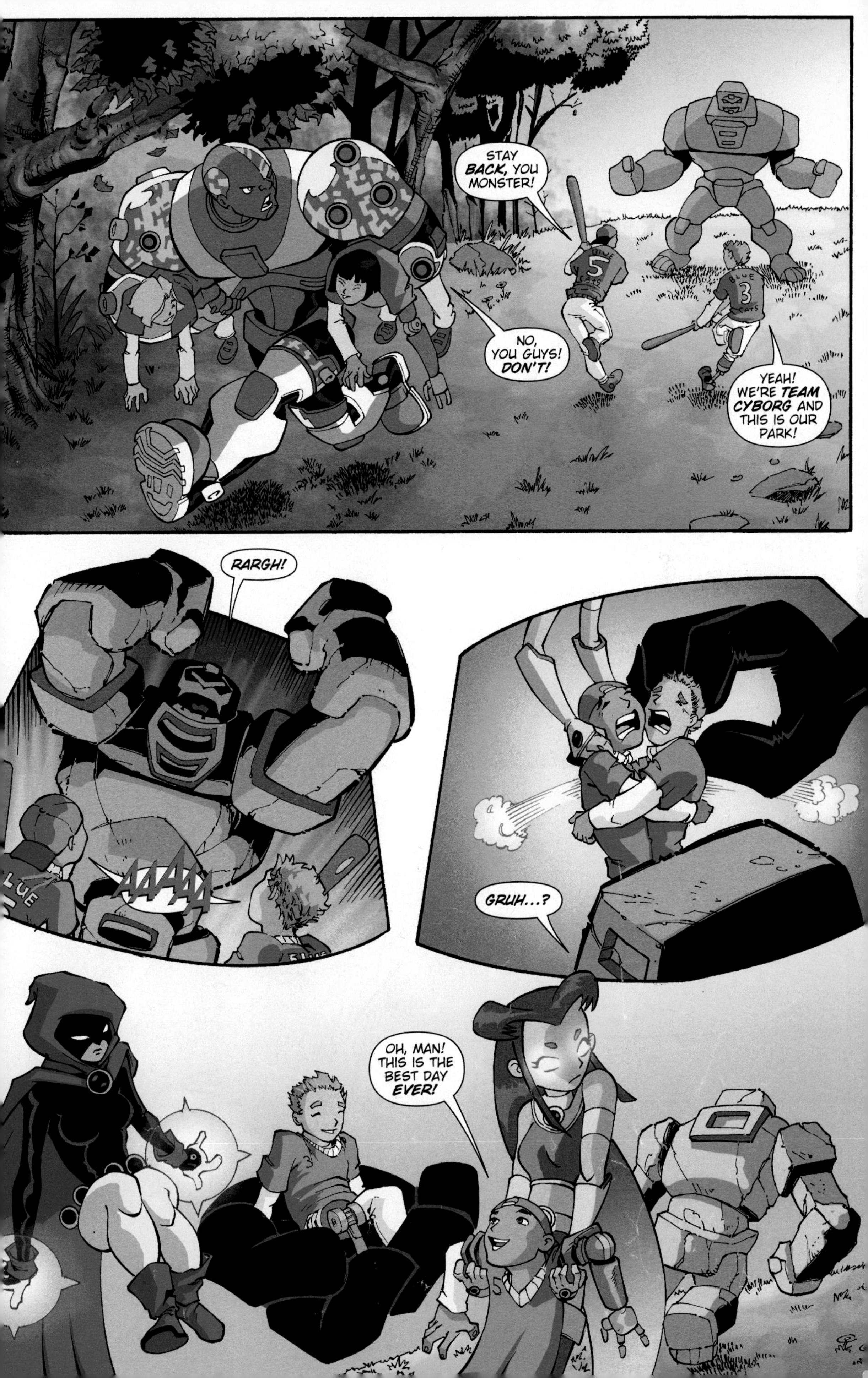
STAY BACK, YOU MONSTER!
NO, YOU GUYS! DON'T!
YEAH! WE'RE TEAM CYBORG AND THIS IS OUR PARK!
RARGH!
AAAAA
GRUH...?
OH, MAN! THIS IS THE BEST DAY EVER!

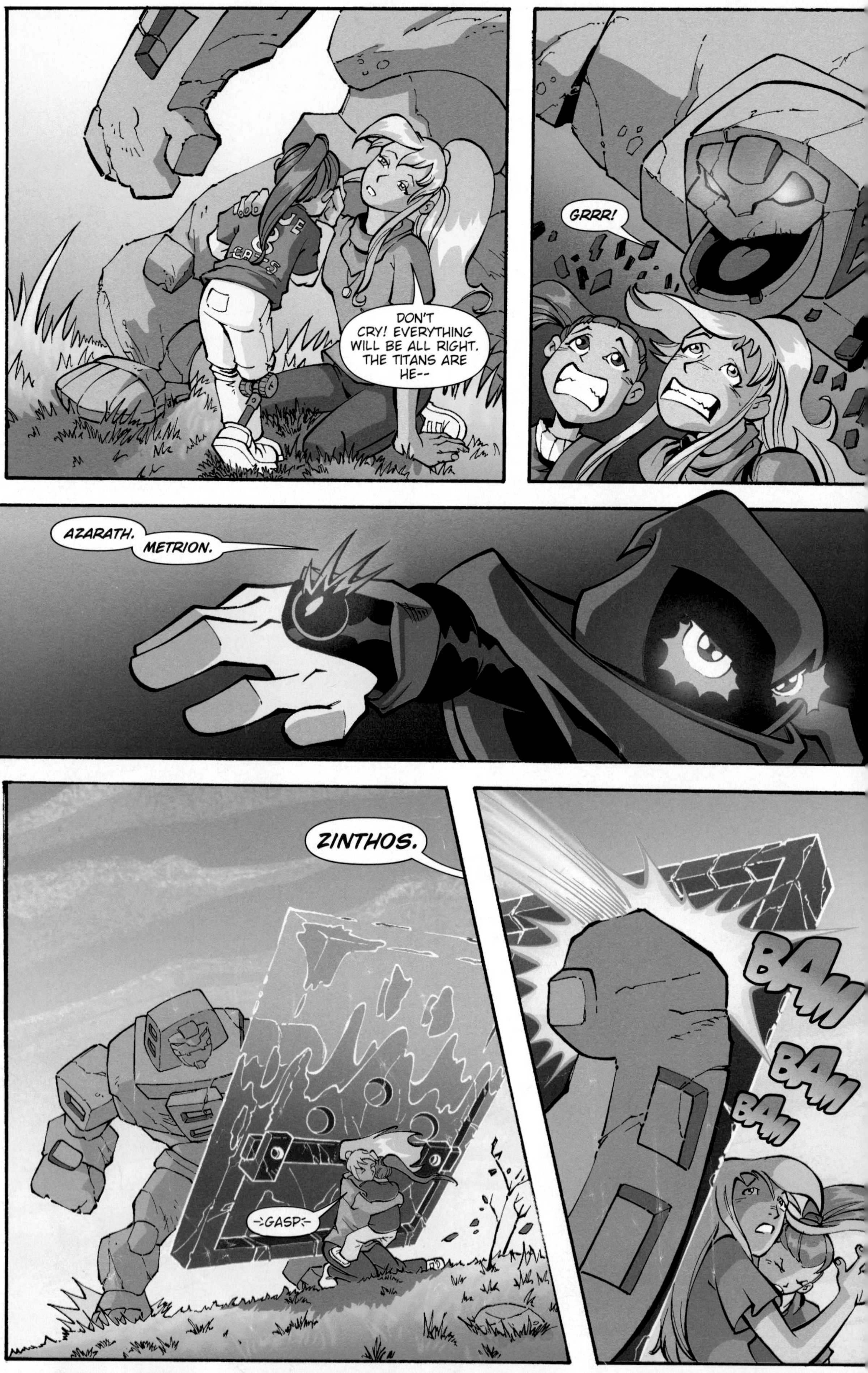
DON'T CRY! EVERYTHING WILL BE ALL RIGHT. THE TITANS ARE HE--
GRRR!
AZARATH.
METRION.
ZINTHOS.
-GASP-
BAM
BAM
BAM

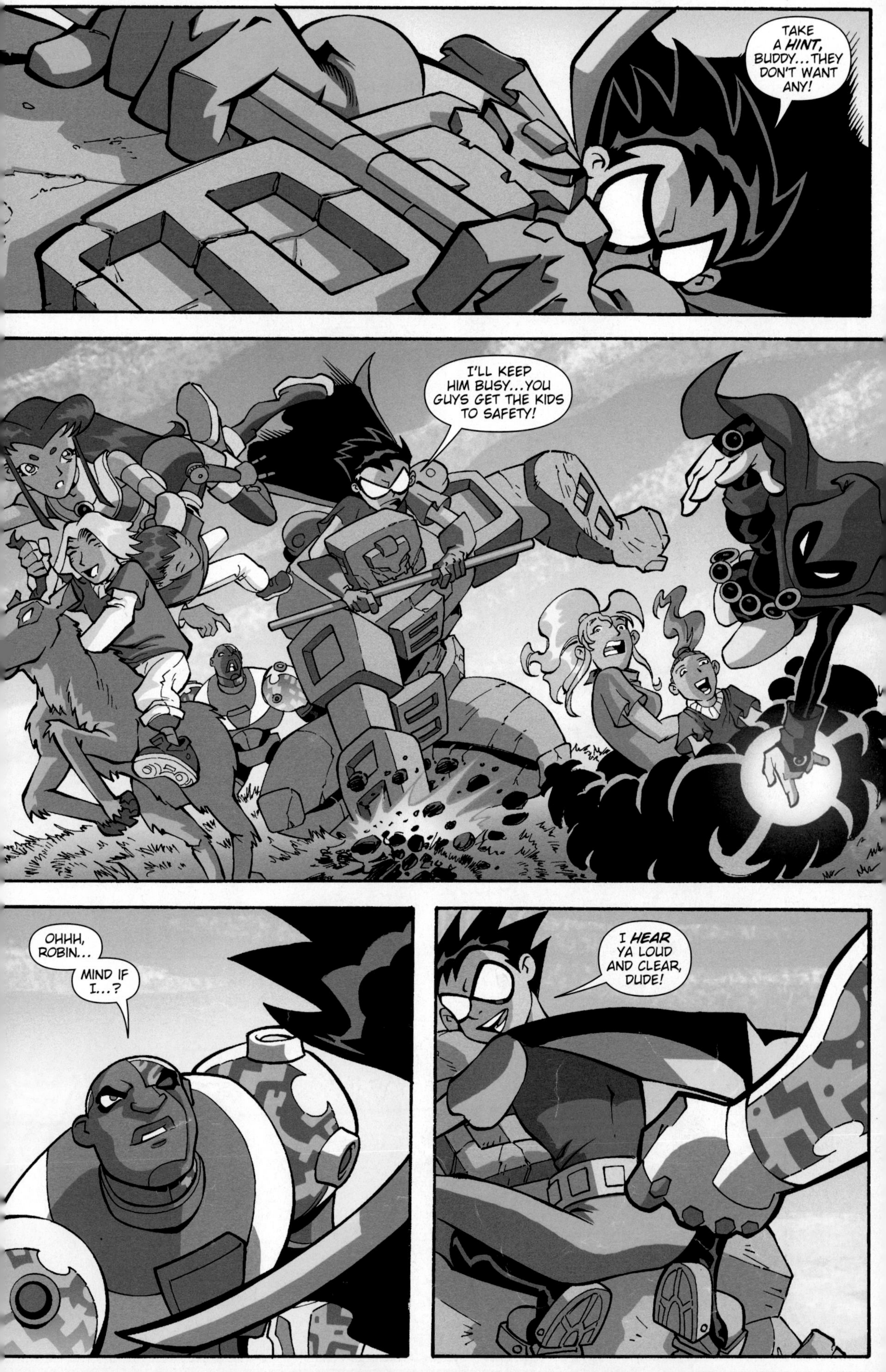
TAKE A HINT, BUDDY...THEY DON'T WANT ANY!
I'LL KEEP HIM BUSY...YOU GUYS GET THE KIDS TO SAFETY!
OHHH, ROBIN...
MIND IF I...?
I HEAR YA LOUD AND CLEAR, DUDE!

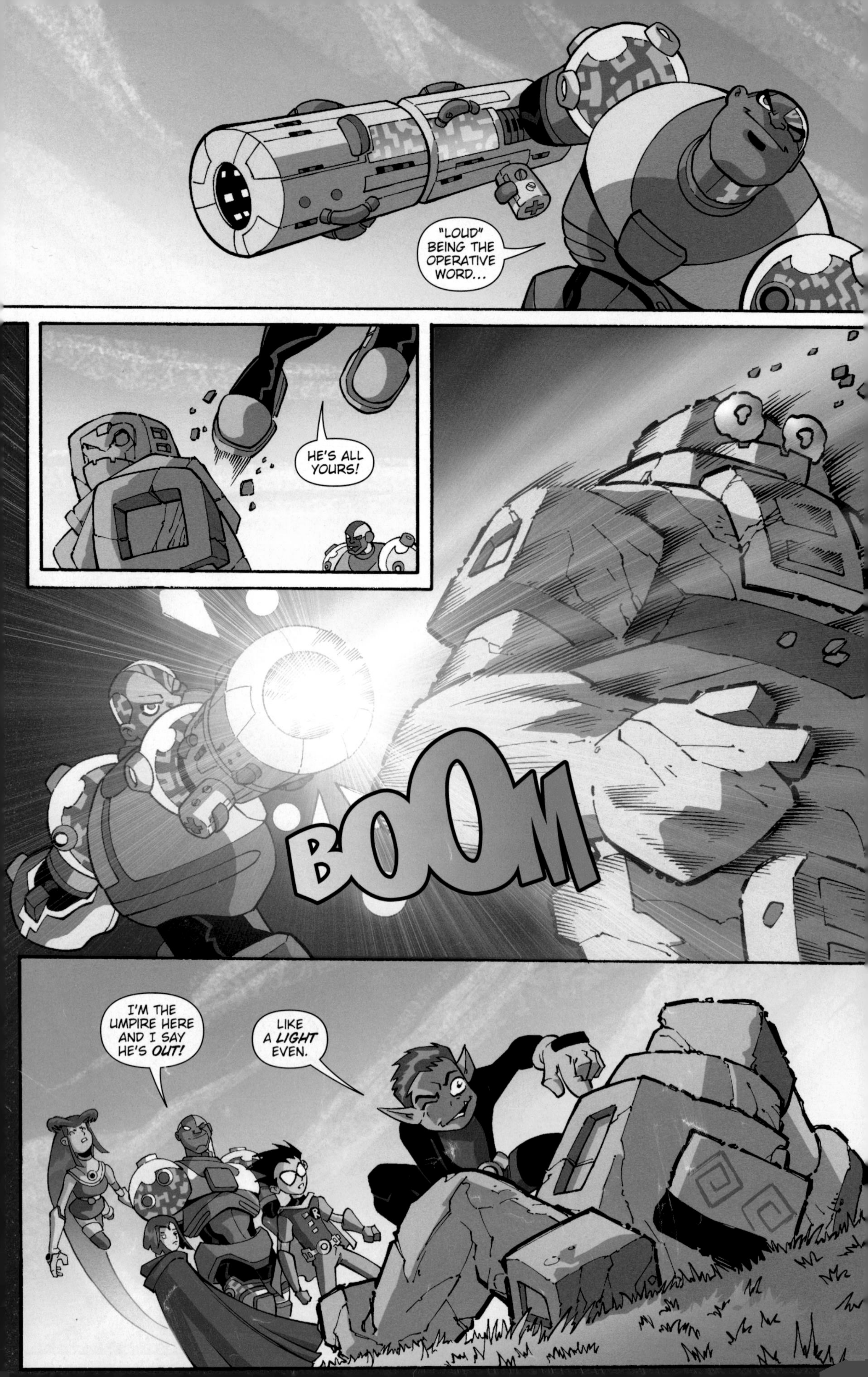
"LOUD" BEING THE OPERATIVE WORD...
HE'S ALL YOURS!
BOOM
I'M THE UMPIRE HERE AND I SAY HE'S *OUT!*
LIKE A *LIGHT* EVEN.

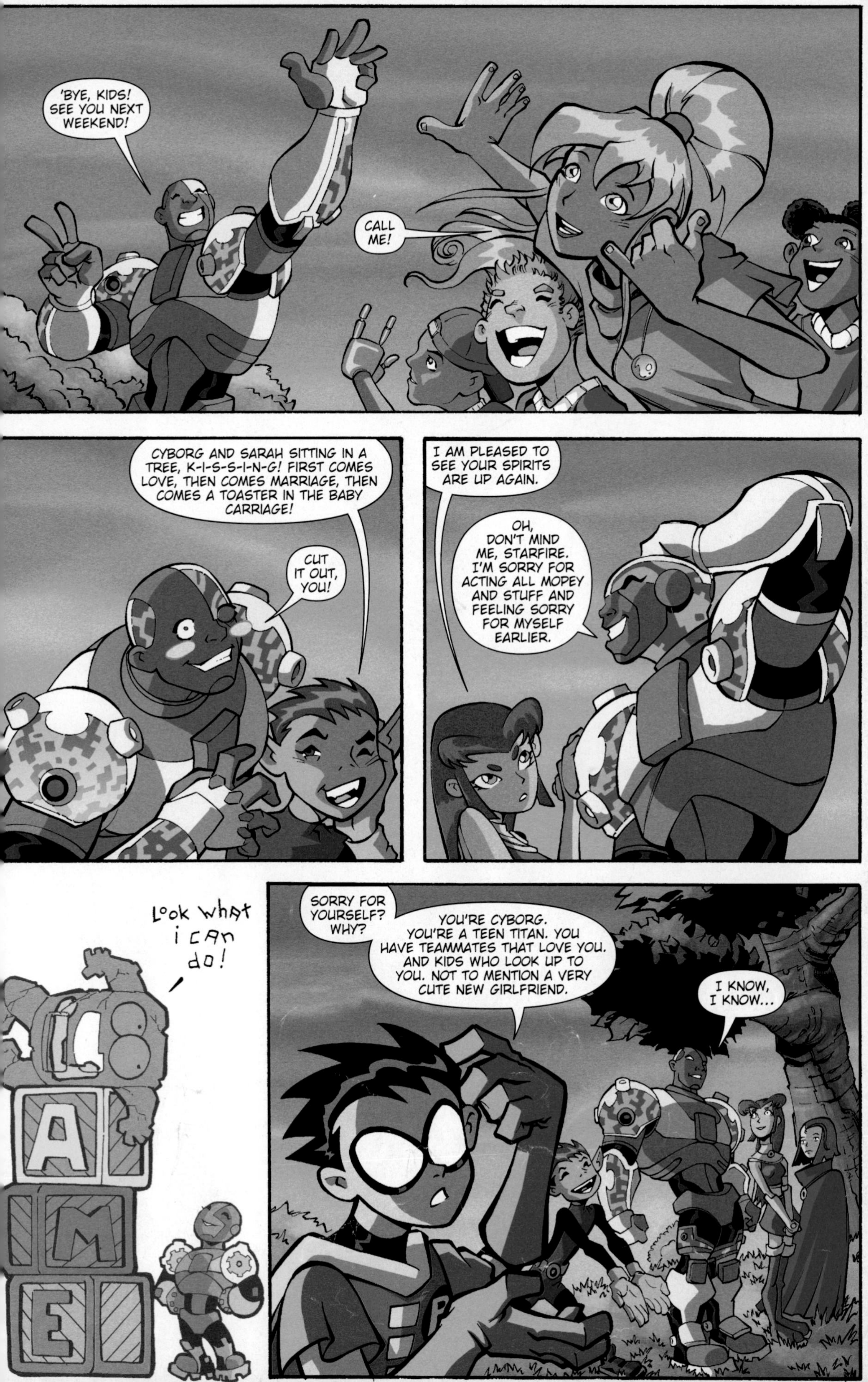

'BYE, KIDS! SEE YOU NEXT WEEKEND!
CALL ME!
CYBORG AND SARAH SITTING IN A TREE, K-I-S-S-I-N-G! FIRST COMES LOVE, THEN COMES MARRIAGE, THEN COMES A TOASTER IN THE BABY CARRIAGE!
CUT IT OUT, YOU!
I AM PLEASED TO SEE YOUR SPIRITS ARE UP AGAIN.
OH, DON'T MIND ME, STARFIRE. I'M SORRY FOR ACTING ALL MOPEY AND STUFF AND FEELING SORRY FOR MYSELF EARLIER.
Look what i can do!
C
A
M
E
SORRY FOR YOURSELF? WHY?
YOU'RE CYBORG. YOU'RE A TEEN TITAN. YOU HAVE TEAMMATES THAT LOVE YOU. AND KIDS WHO LOOK UP TO YOU. NOT TO MENTION A VERY CUTE NEW GIRLFRIEND.
I KNOW, I KNOW...

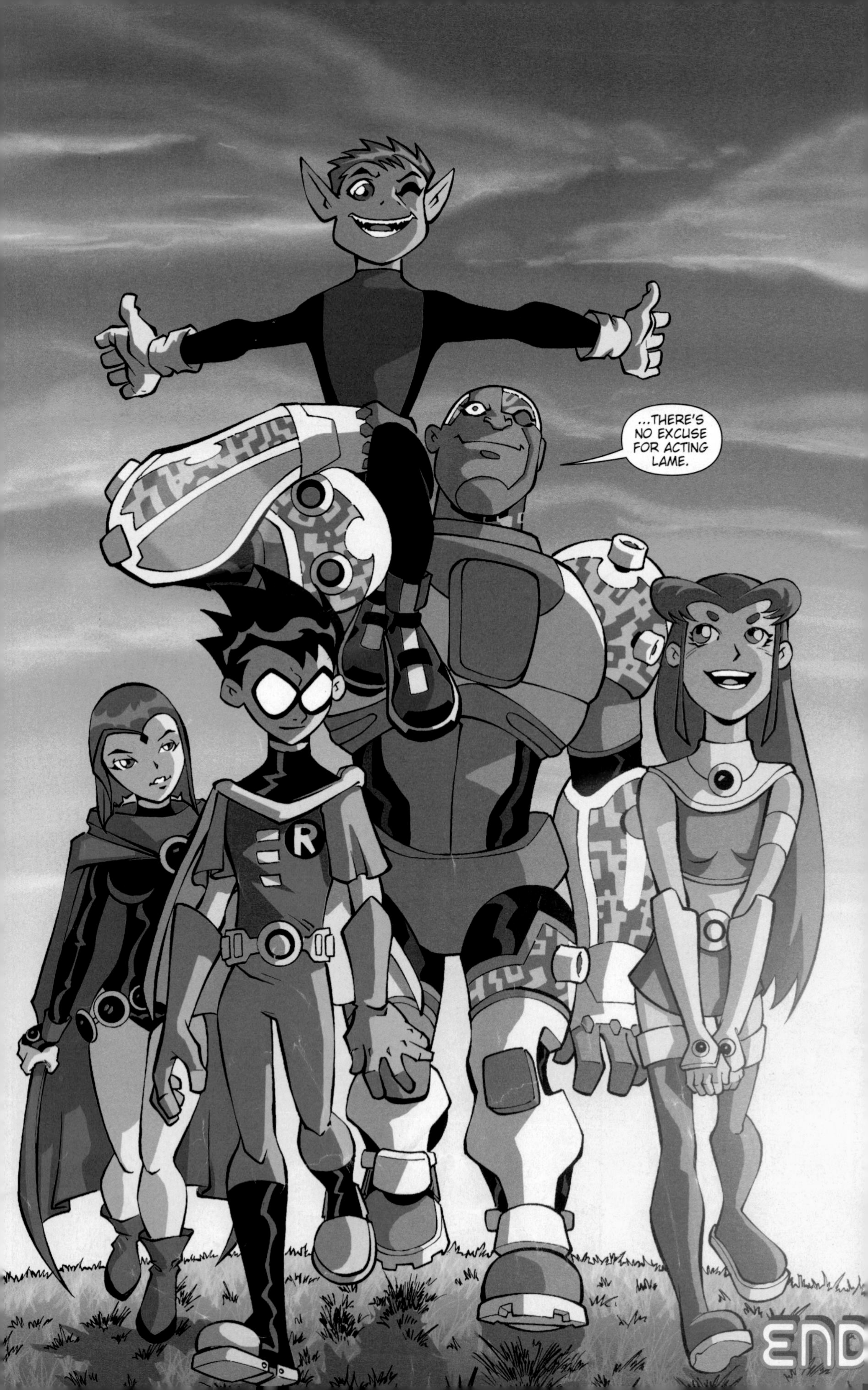
...THERE'S NO EXCUSE FOR ACTING LAME.
END

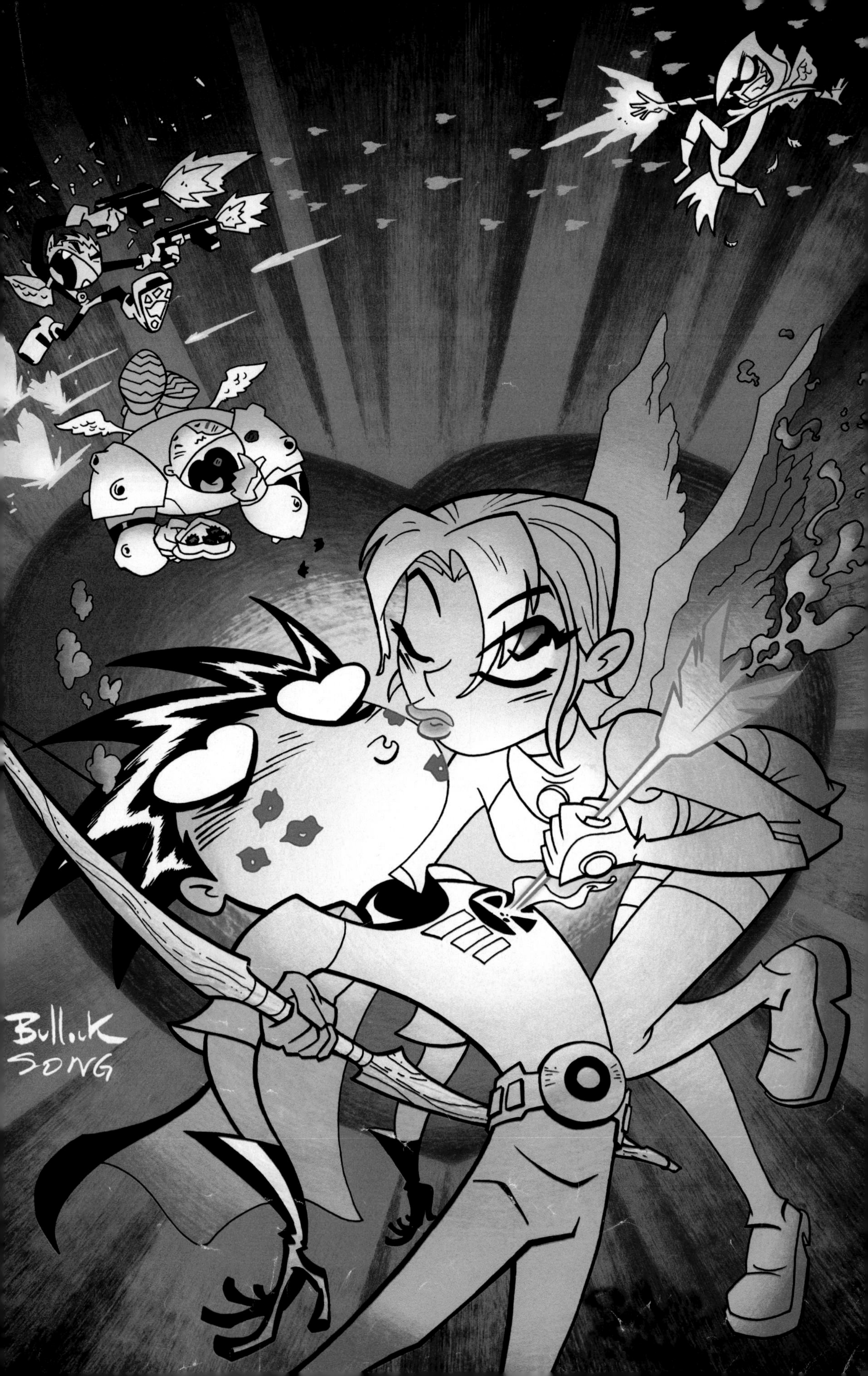
Bullock
SONG

EEN

TANS

GO

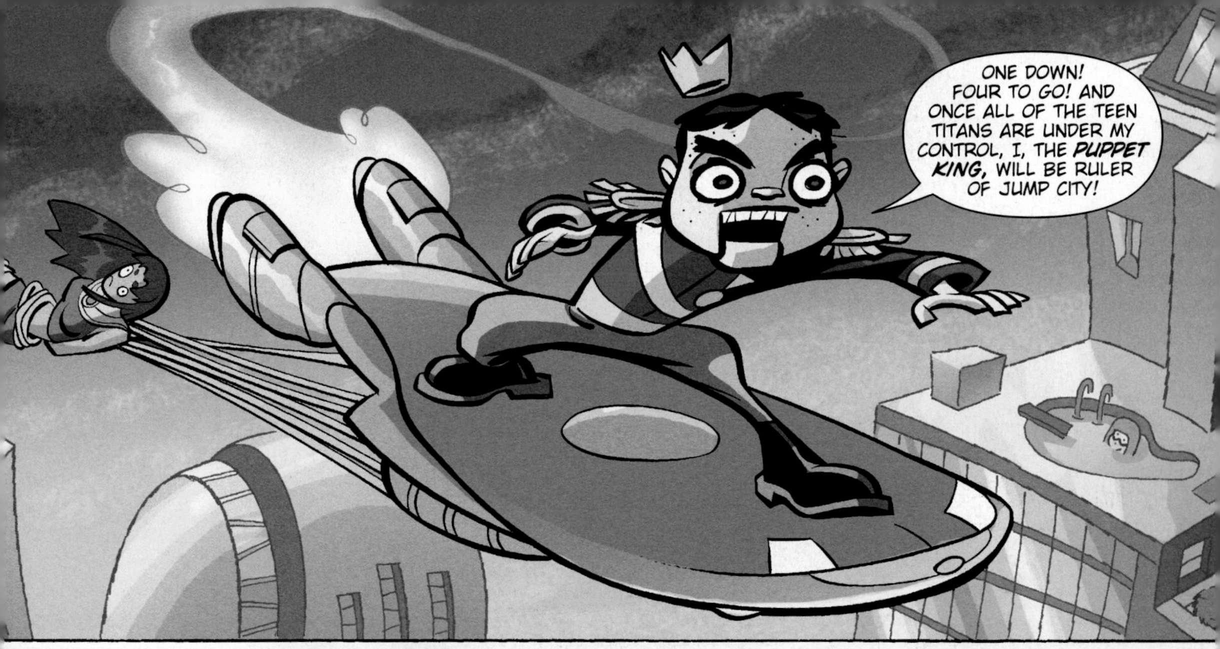
ONE DOWN! FOUR TO GO! AND ONCE ALL OF THE TEEN TITANS ARE UNDER MY CONTROL, I, THE PUPPET KING, WILL BE RULER OF JUMP CITY!

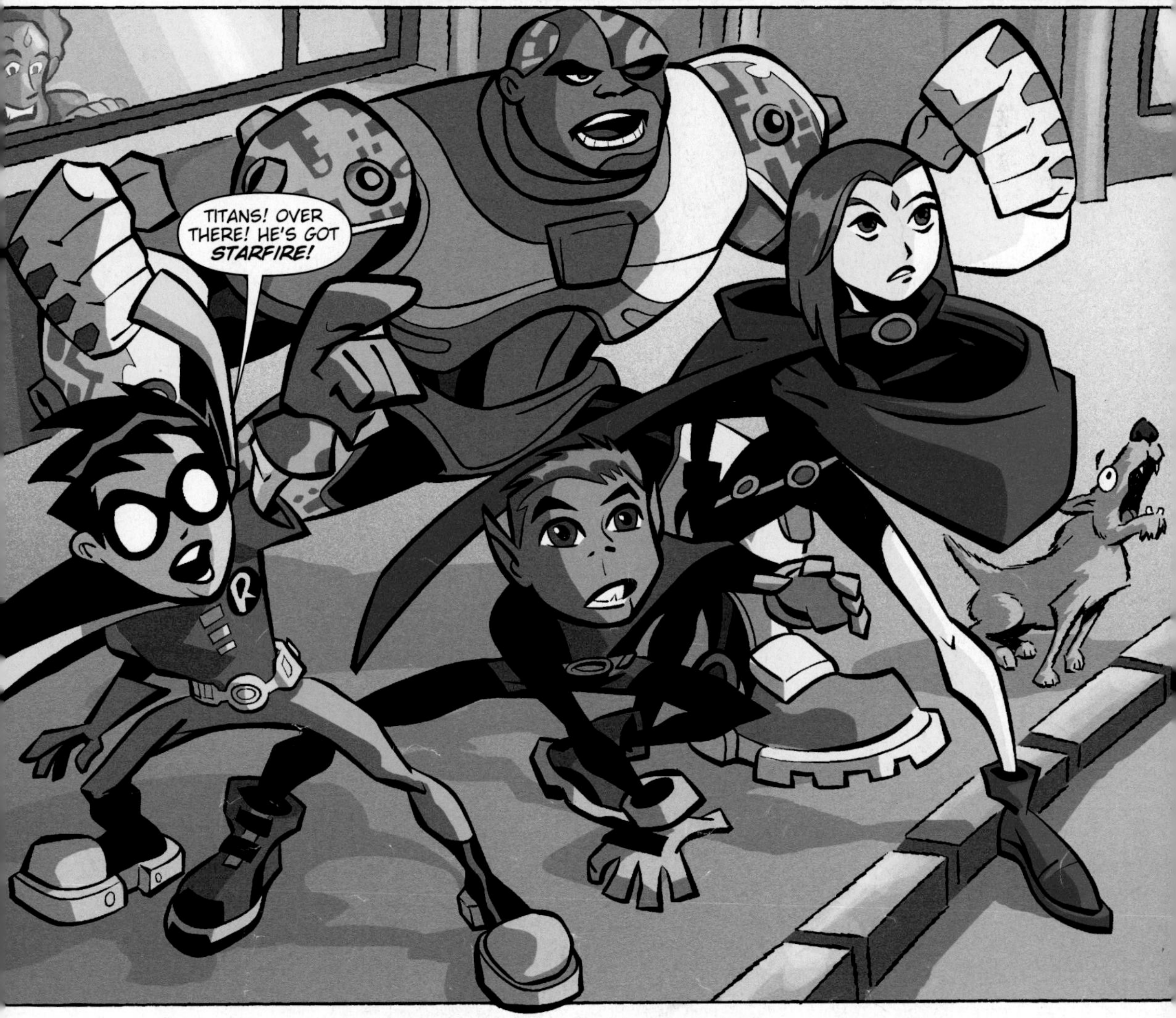
TITANS! OVER THERE! HE'S GOT STARFIRE!

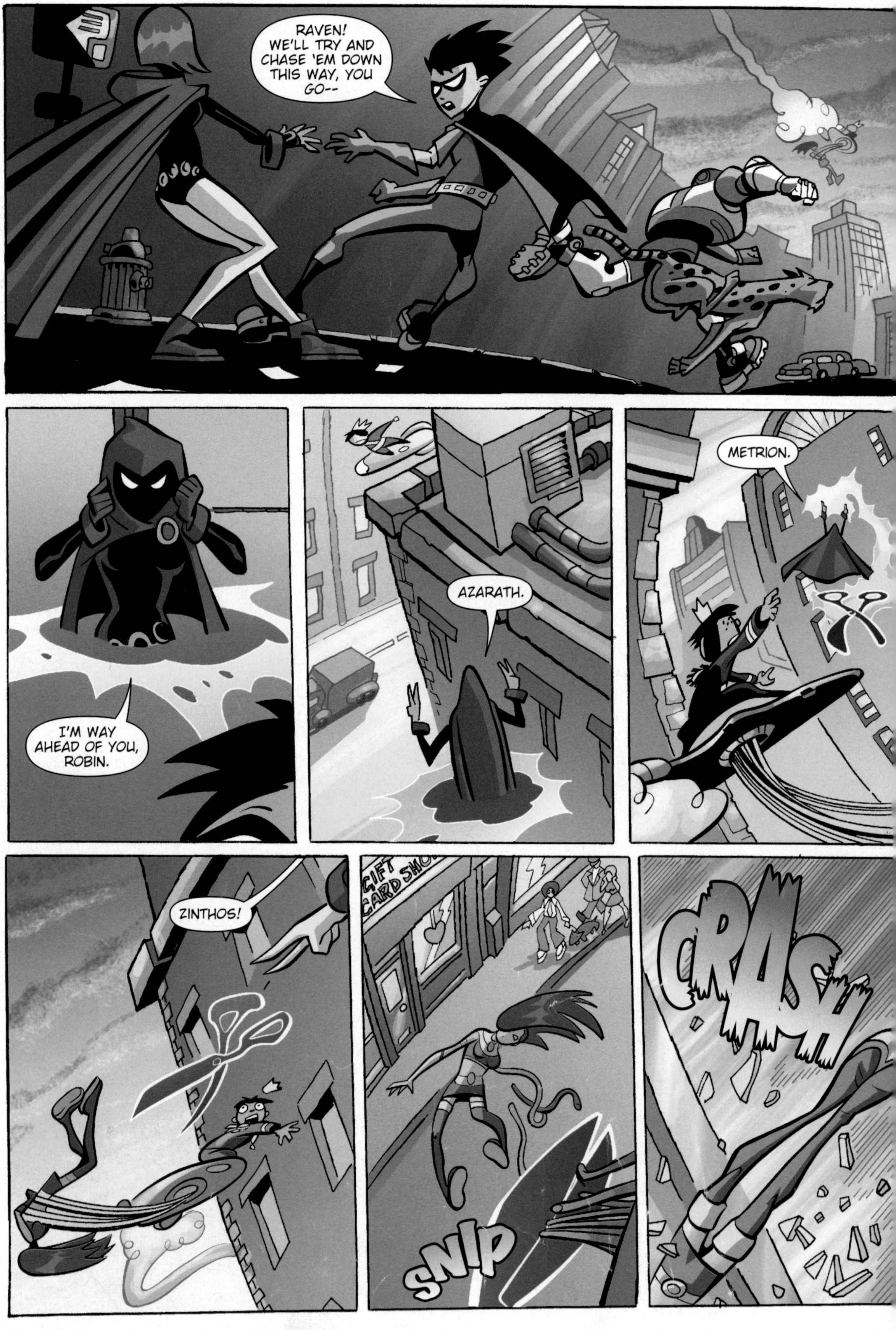
RAVEN! WE'LL TRY AND CHASE 'EM DOWN THIS WAY, YOU GO--
I'M WAY AHEAD OF YOU, ROBIN.
AZARATH.
METRION.
ZINTHOS!
GIFT CARD SHO
SNIP
CRASH

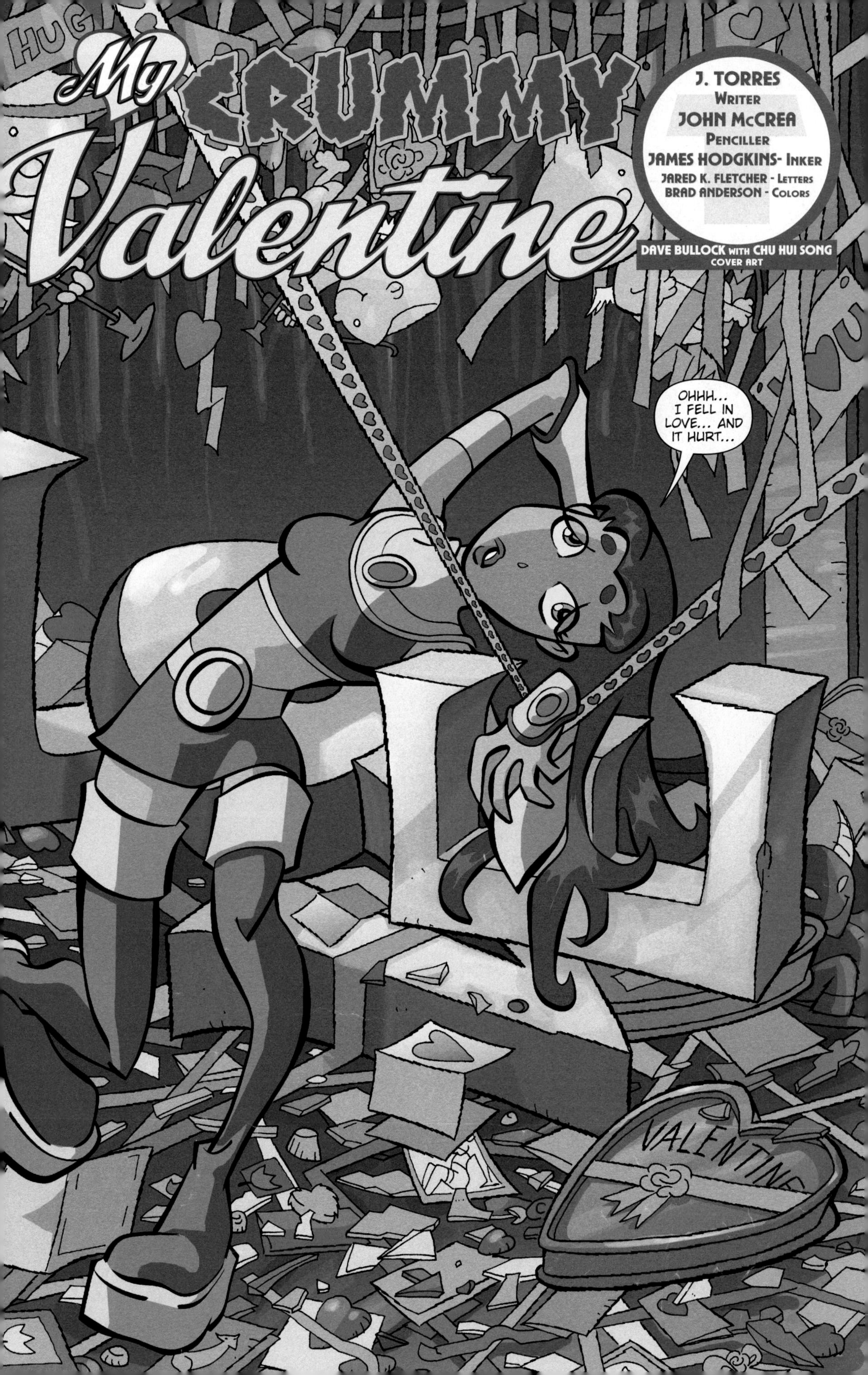
My CRUMMY Valentine
J. TORRES
WRITER
JOHN McCREA
PENCILLER
JAMES HODGKINS- INKER
JARED K. FLETCHER - LETTERS
BRAD ANDERSON - COLORS
DAVE BULLOCK WITH CHU HUI SONG
COVER ART
HUG
OHHH... I FELL IN LOVE... AND IT HURT...
VALENTINE

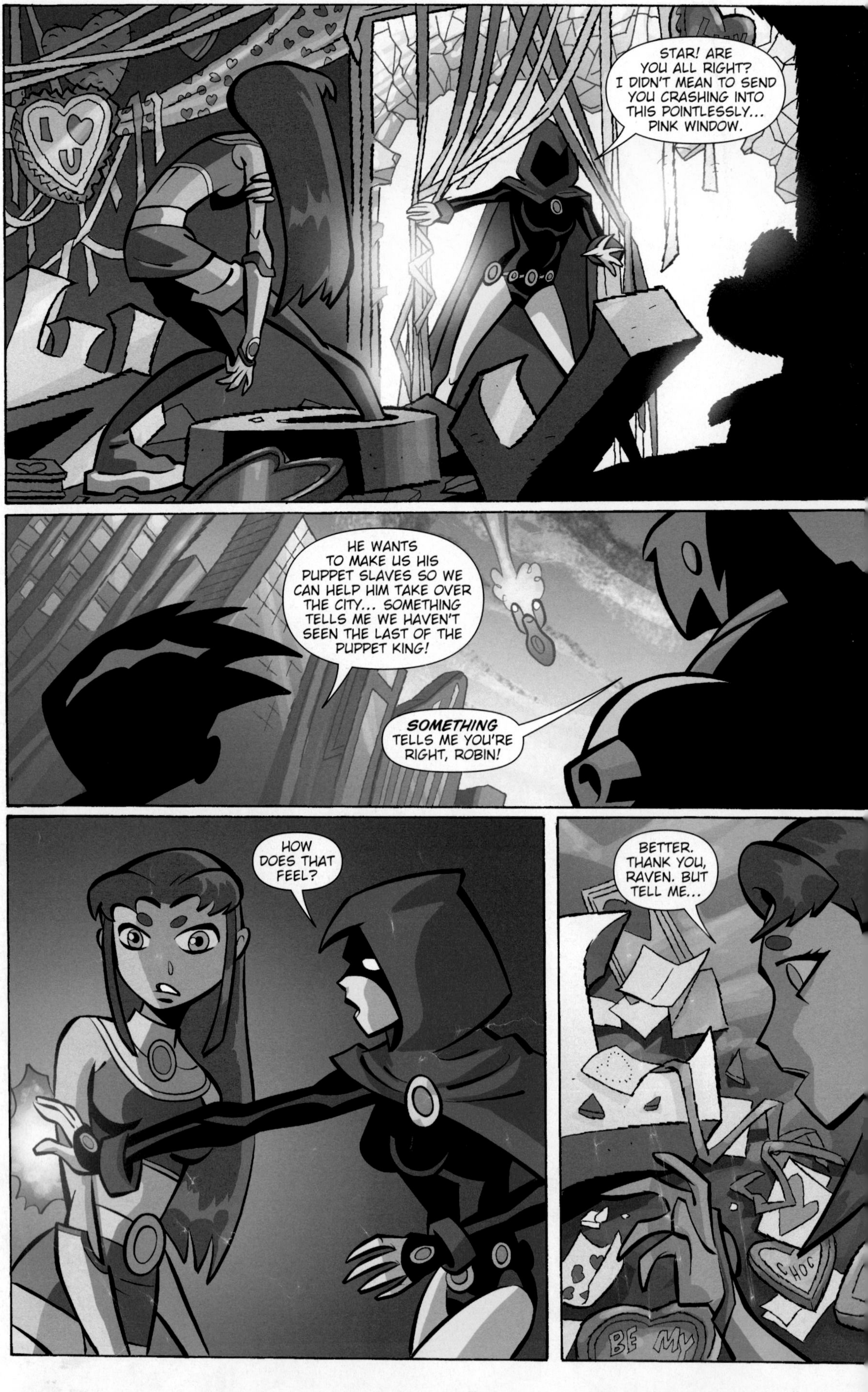
STAR! ARE YOU ALL RIGHT? I DIDN'T MEAN TO SEND YOU CRASHING INTO THIS POINTLESSLY... PINK WINDOW.
HE WANTS TO MAKE US HIS PUPPET SLAVES SO WE CAN HELP HIM TAKE OVER THE CITY... SOMETHING TELLS ME WE HAVEN'T SEEN THE LAST OF THE PUPPET KING!
SOMETHING TELLS ME YOU'RE RIGHT, ROBIN!
HOW DOES THAT FEEL?
BETTER. THANK YOU, RAVEN. BUT TELL ME...
I LOVE U
CHOC
BE MY

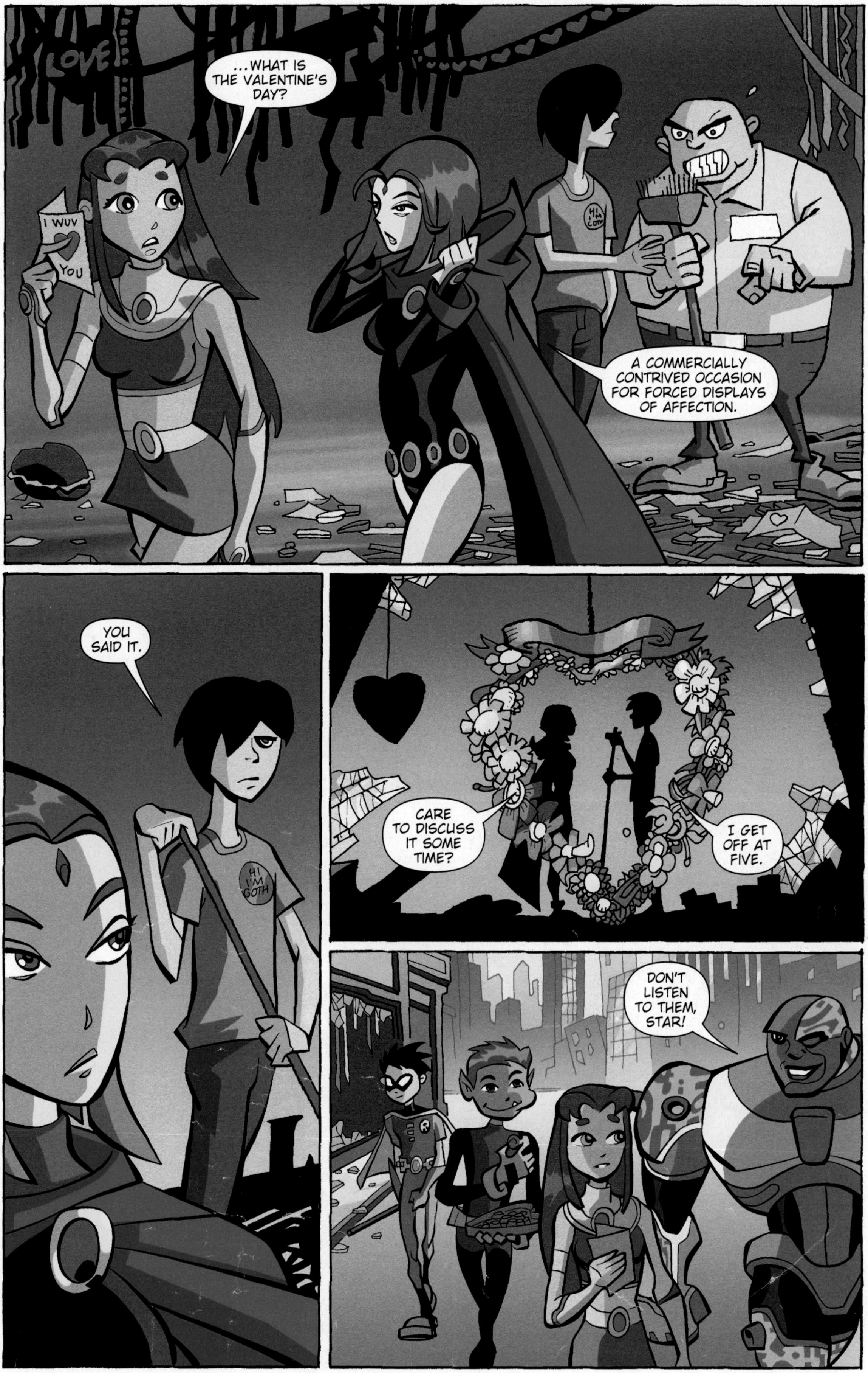
LOVE
...WHAT IS THE VALENTINE'S DAY?
I WUV YOU
HI I'M GOTH
A COMMERCIALLY CONTRIVED OCCASION FOR FORCED DISPLAYS OF AFFECTION.
YOU SAID IT.
HI I'M GOTH
CARE TO DISCUSS IT SOME TIME?
I GET OFF AT FIVE.
DON'T LISTEN TO THEM, STAR!

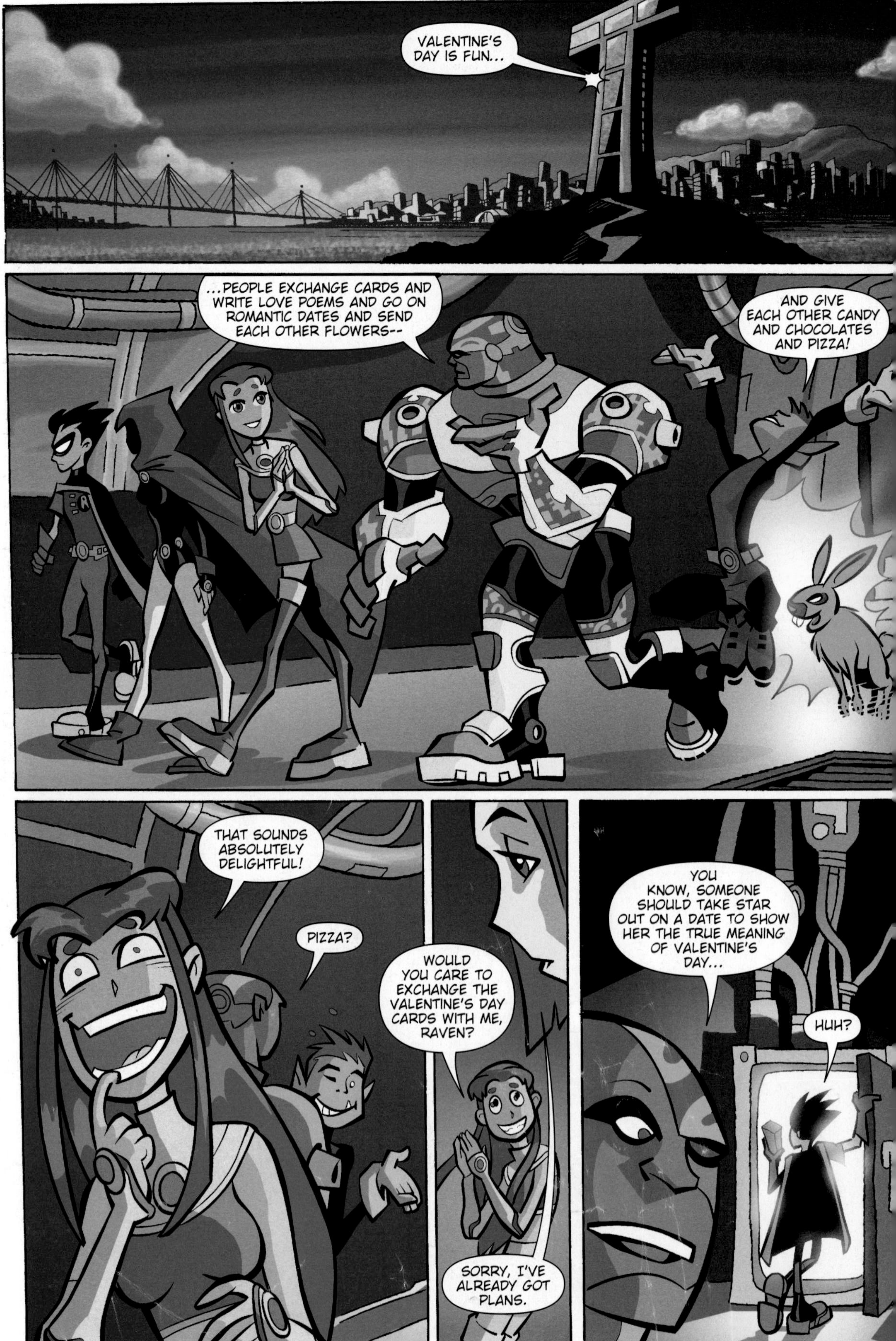
VALENTINE'S DAY IS FUN...
...PEOPLE EXCHANGE CARDS AND WRITE LOVE POEMS AND GO ON ROMANTIC DATES AND SEND EACH OTHER FLOWERS--
AND GIVE EACH OTHER CANDY AND CHOCOLATES AND PIZZA!
THAT SOUNDS ABSOLUTELY DELIGHTFUL!
PIZZA?
WOULD YOU CARE TO EXCHANGE THE VALENTINE'S DAY CARDS WITH ME, RAVEN?
SORRY, I'VE ALREADY GOT PLANS.
YOU KNOW, SOMEONE SHOULD TAKE STAR OUT ON A DATE TO SHOW HER THE TRUE MEANING OF VALENTINE'S DAY...
HUH?

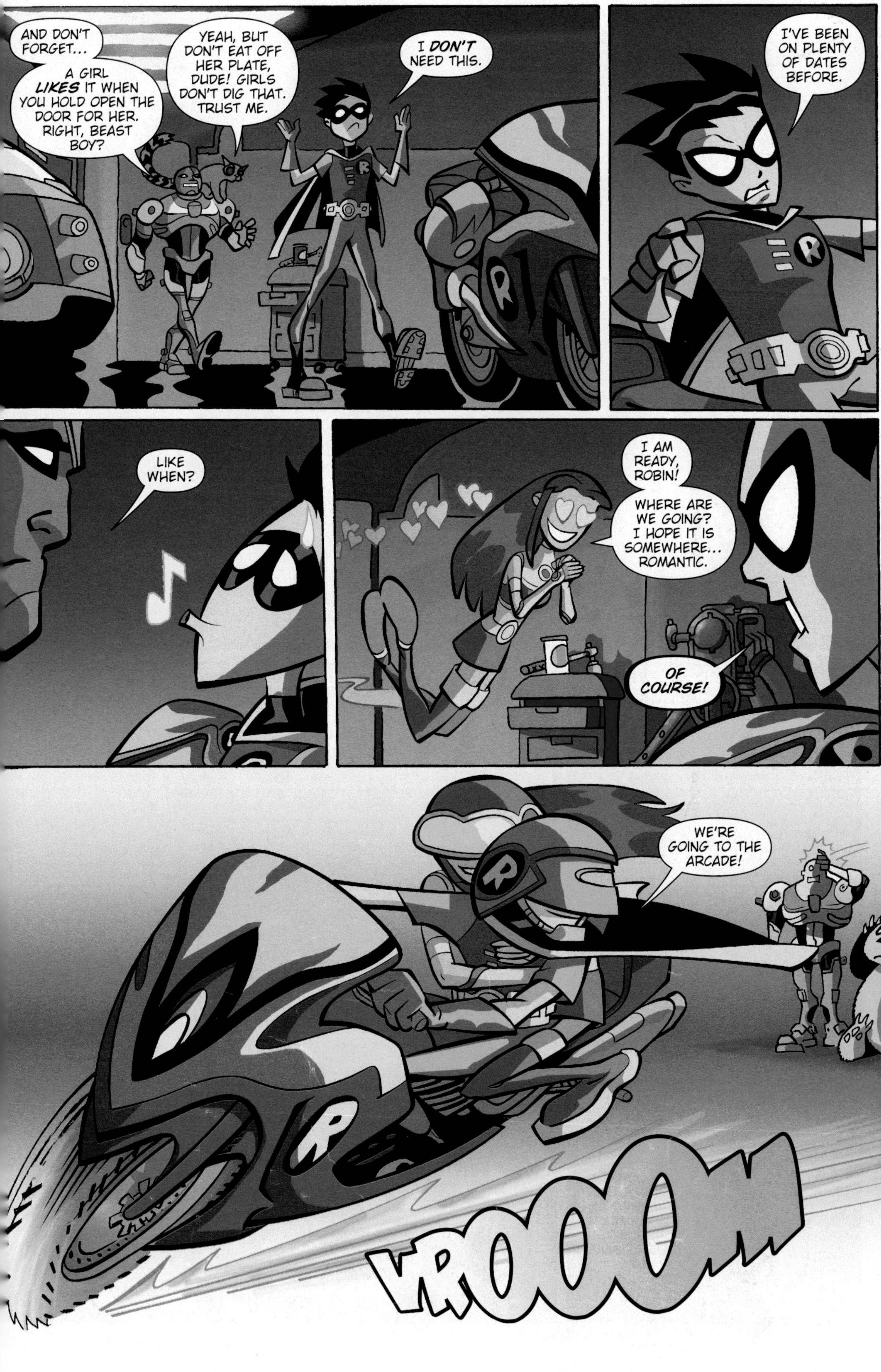
AND DON'T FORGET...
A GIRL LIKES IT WHEN YOU HOLD OPEN THE DOOR FOR HER. RIGHT, BEAST BOY?
YEAH, BUT DON'T EAT OFF HER PLATE, DUDE! GIRLS DON'T DIG THAT. TRUST ME.
I DON'T NEED THIS.
I'VE BEEN ON PLENTY OF DATES BEFORE.
LIKE WHEN?
I AM READY, ROBIN!
WHERE ARE WE GOING? I HOPE IT IS SOMEWHERE... ROMANTIC.
OF COURSE!
WE'RE GOING TO THE ARCADE!
VROOOOM

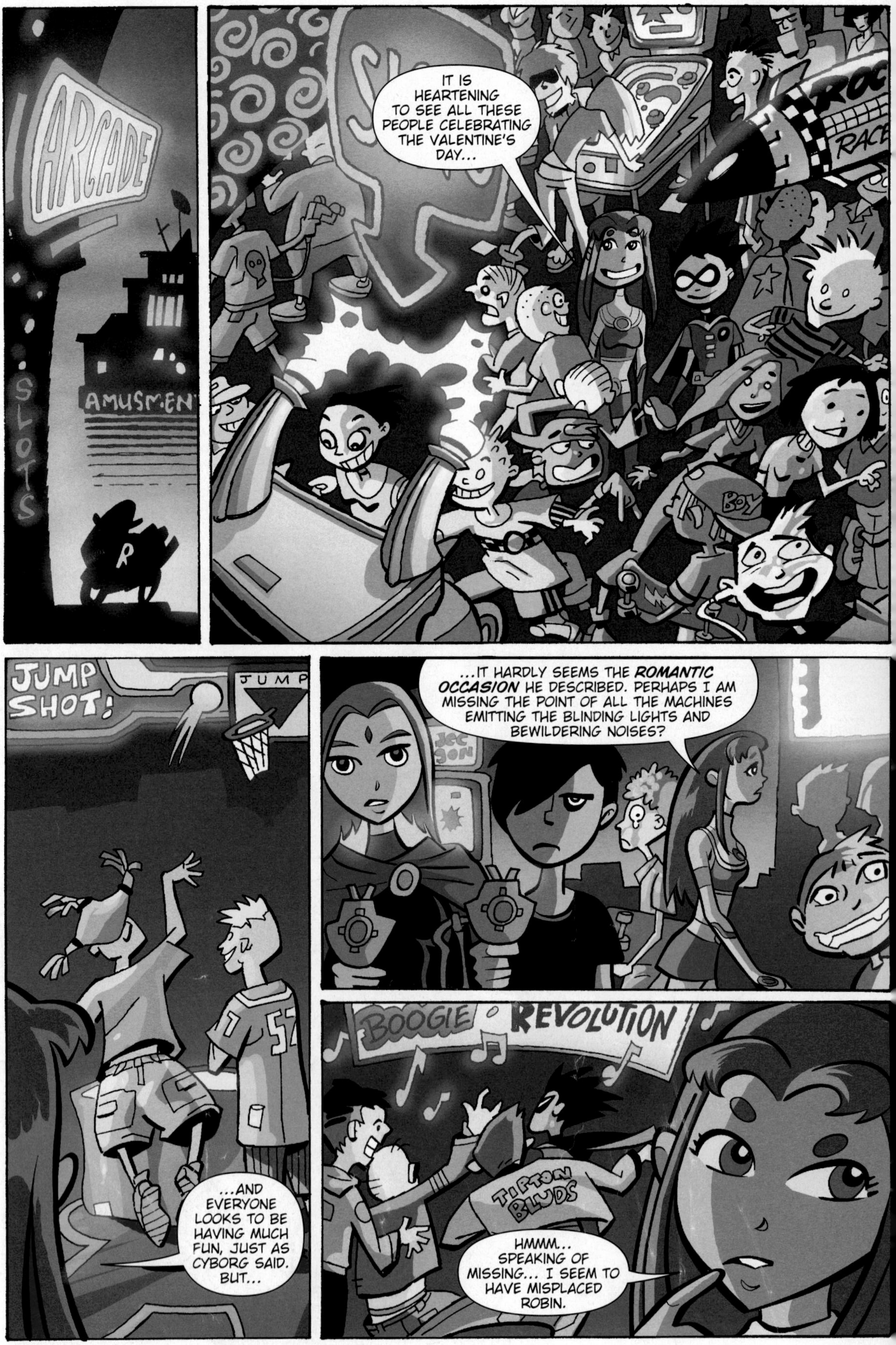
ARCADE
AMUSMENT
SLOTS
IT IS HEARTENING TO SEE ALL THESE PEOPLE CELEBRATING THE VALENTINE'S DAY...
JUMP SHOT!
JUMP
...IT HARDLY SEEMS THE ROMANTIC OCCASION HE DESCRIBED. PERHAPS I AM MISSING THE POINT OF ALL THE MACHINES EMITTING THE BLINDING LIGHTS AND BEWILDERING NOISES?
...AND EVERYONE LOOKS TO BE HAVING MUCH FUN, JUST AS CYBORG SAID. BUT...
BOOGIE REVOLUTION
TIPTON BLUDS
HMMM... SPEAKING OF MISSING... I SEEM TO HAVE MISPLACED ROBIN.

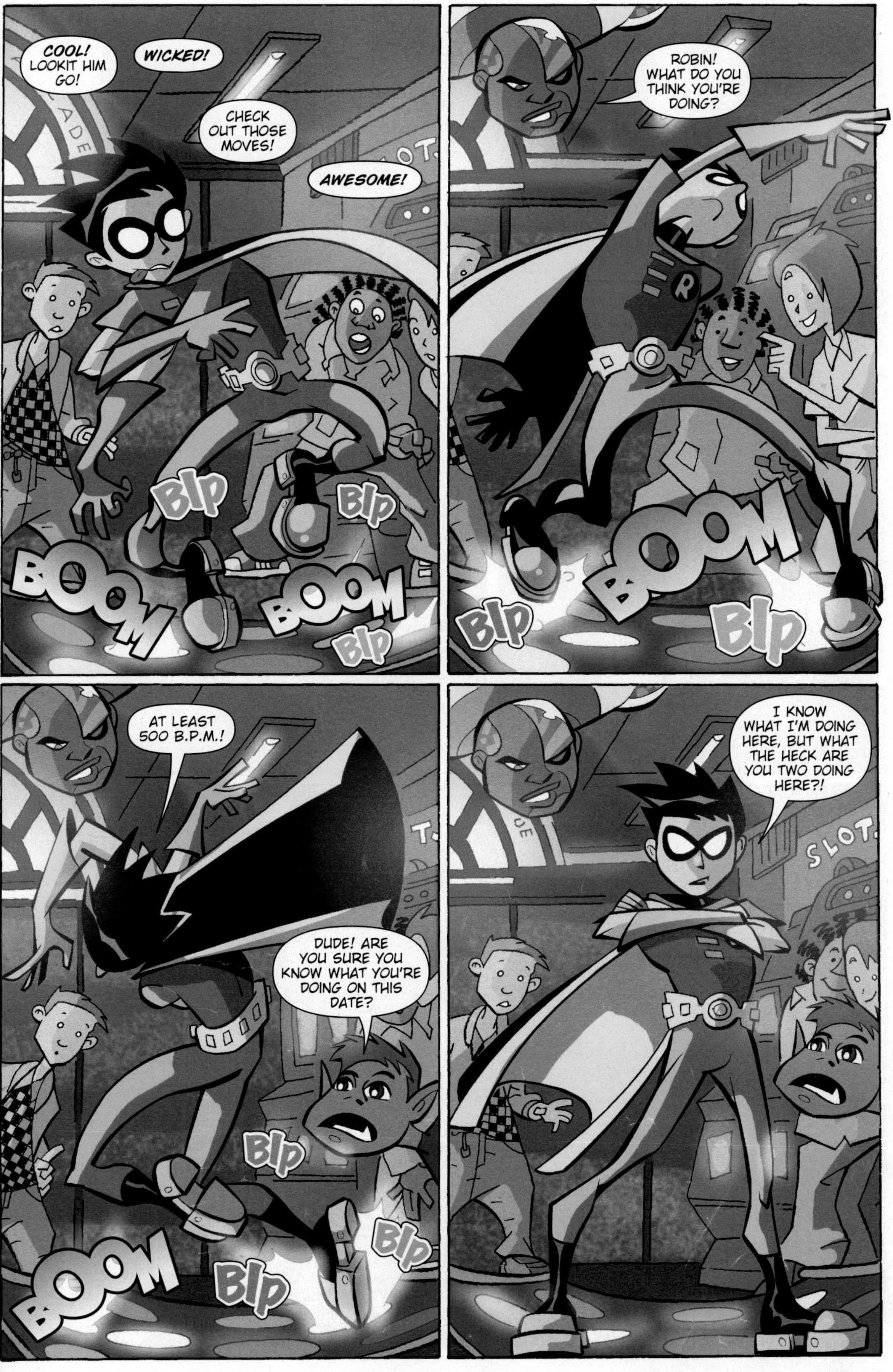
COOL! LOOKIT HIM GO!
WICKED!
CHECK OUT THOSE MOVES!
AWESOME!
BLIP
BLIP
BOOM
BOOM
BLIP
ROBIN! WHAT DO YOU THINK YOU'RE DOING?
BOOM
BLIP
BLIP
AT LEAST 500 B.P.M.!
DUDE! ARE YOU SURE YOU KNOW WHAT YOU'RE DOING ON THIS DATE?
BLIP
BLIP
BOOM
BLIP
I KNOW WHAT I'M DOING HERE, BUT WHAT THE HECK ARE YOU TWO DOING HERE?!

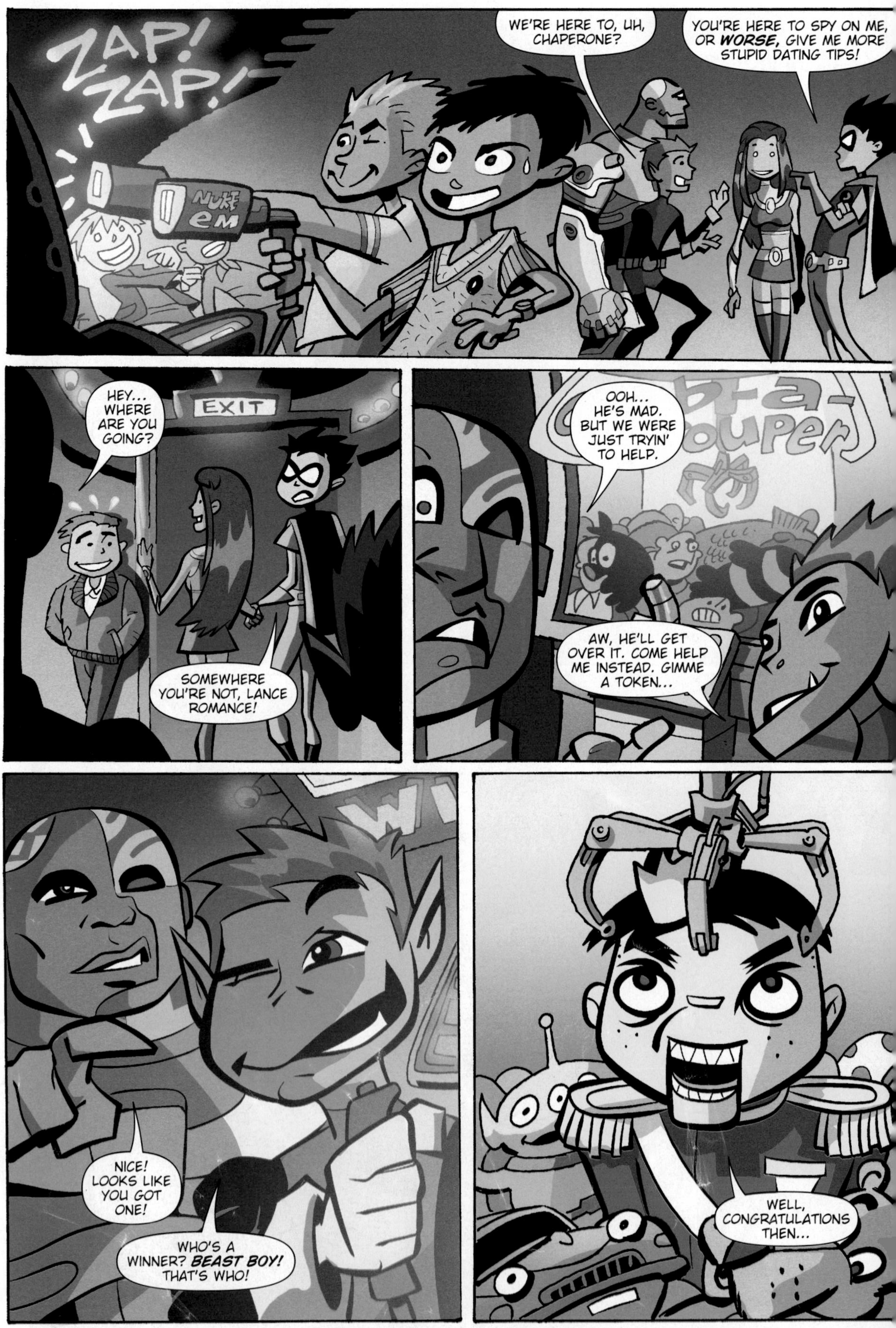
ZAP! ZAP!
NUKE EM
WE'RE HERE TO, UH, CHAPERONE?
YOU'RE HERE TO SPY ON ME, OR ***WORSE,*** GIVE ME MORE STUPID DATING TIPS!
EXIT
HEY... WHERE ARE YOU GOING?
SOMEWHERE YOU'RE NOT, LANCE ROMANCE!
OOH... HE'S MAD. BUT WE WERE JUST TRYIN' TO HELP.
AW, HE'LL GET OVER IT. COME HELP ME INSTEAD. GIMME A TOKEN...
NICE! LOOKS LIKE YOU GOT ONE!
WHO'S A WINNER? ***BEAST BOY!*** THAT'S WHO!
WELL, CONGRATULATIONS THEN...

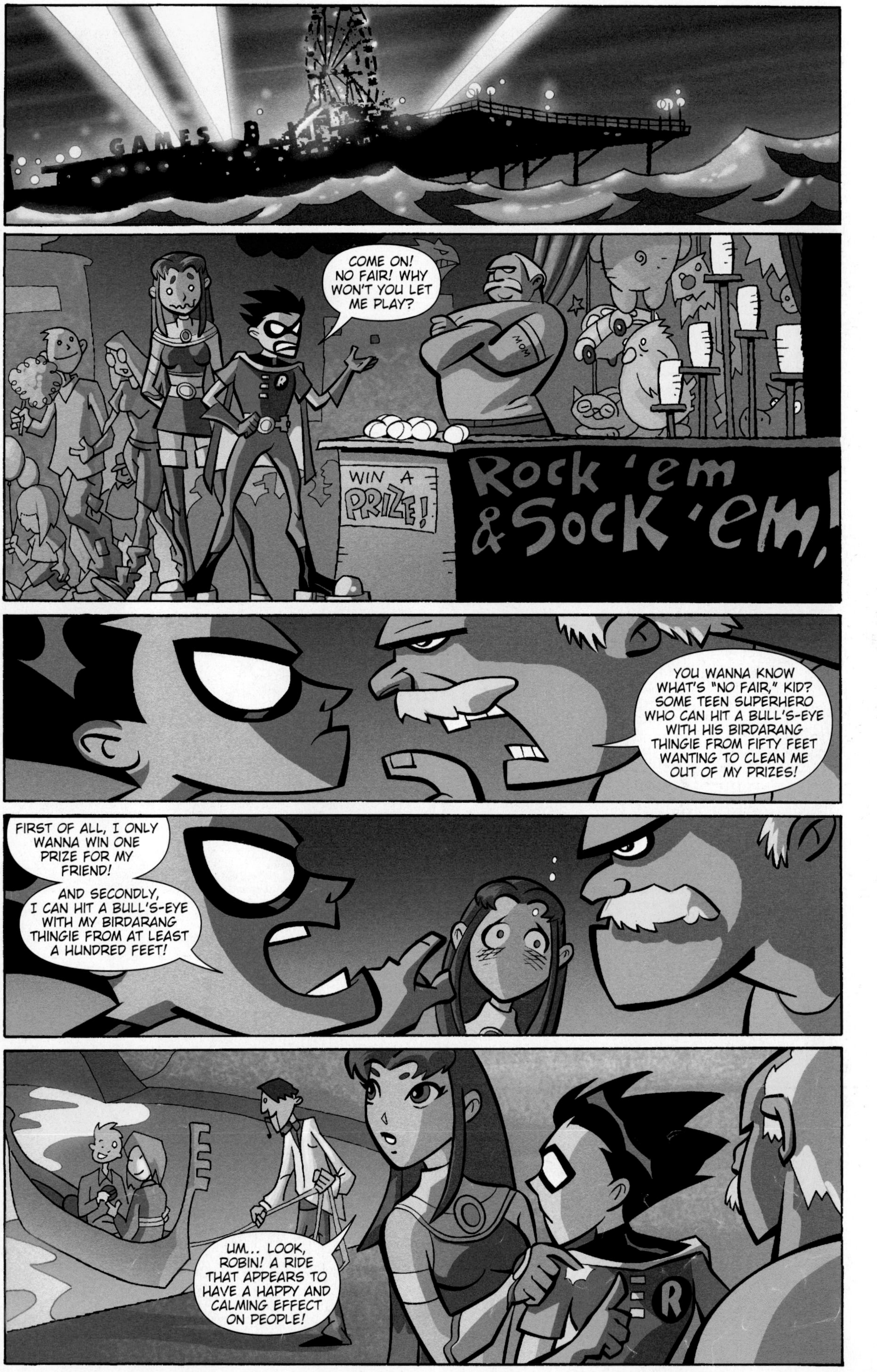
GAMES
COME ON! NO FAIR! WHY WON'T YOU LET ME PLAY?
MOM
WIN A PRIZE!
Rock 'em & Sock 'em!
YOU WANNA KNOW WHAT'S "NO FAIR," KID? SOME TEEN SUPERHERO WHO CAN HIT A BULL'S-EYE WITH HIS BIRDARANG THINGIE FROM FIFTY FEET WANTING TO CLEAN ME OUT OF MY PRIZES!
FIRST OF ALL, I ONLY WANNA WIN ONE PRIZE FOR MY FRIEND!
AND SECONDLY, I CAN HIT A BULL'S-EYE WITH MY BIRDARANG THINGIE FROM AT LEAST A HUNDRED FEET!
UM... LOOK, ROBIN! A RIDE THAT APPEARS TO HAVE A HAPPY AND CALMING EFFECT ON PEOPLE!

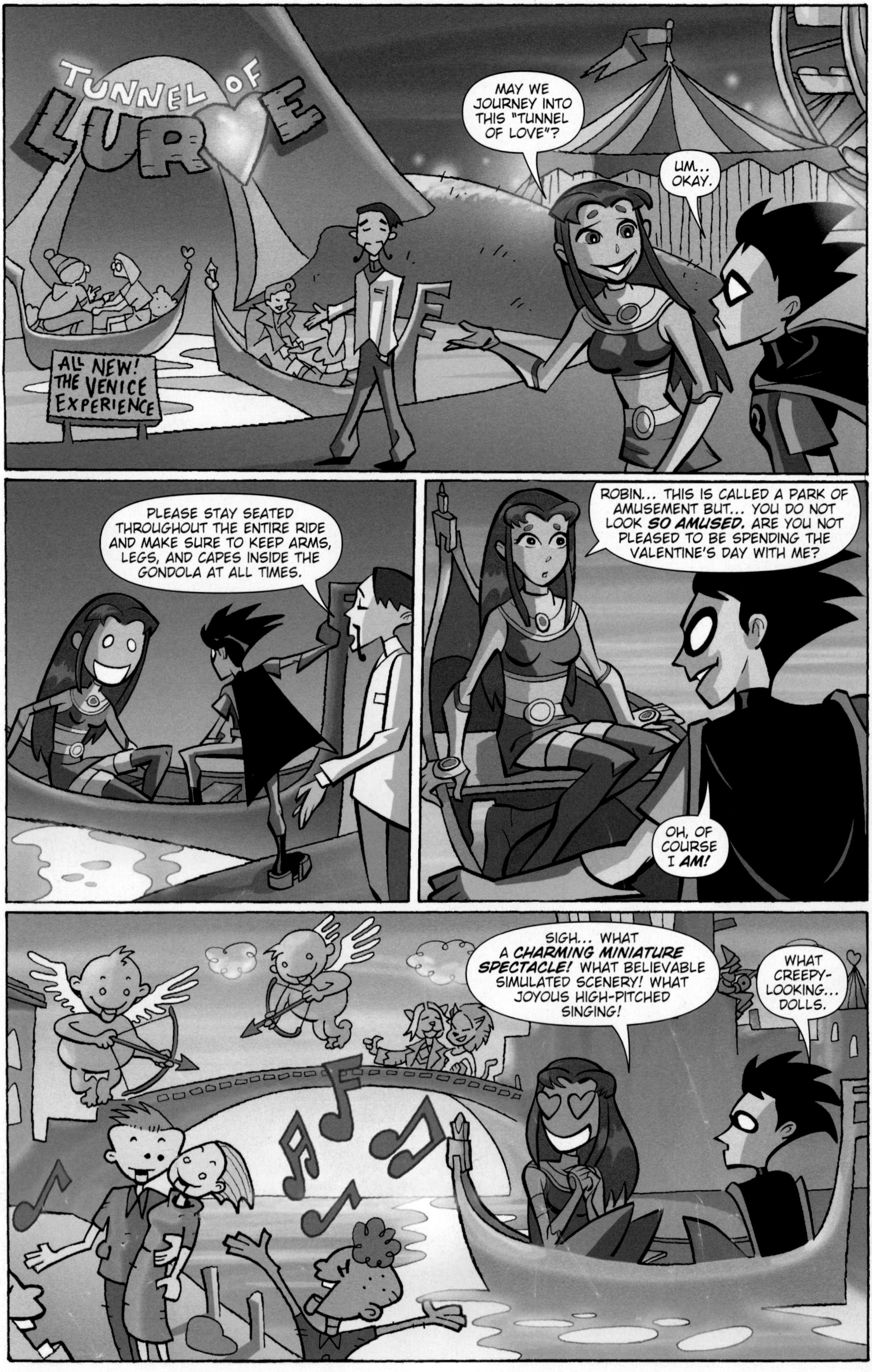
TUNNEL OF LURVE
ALL NEW! THE VENICE EXPERIENCE
MAY WE JOURNEY INTO THIS "TUNNEL OF LOVE"?
UM... OKAY.
PLEASE STAY SEATED THROUGHOUT THE ENTIRE RIDE AND MAKE SURE TO KEEP ARMS, LEGS, AND CAPES INSIDE THE GONDOLA AT ALL TIMES.
ROBIN... THIS IS CALLED A PARK OF AMUSEMENT BUT... YOU DO NOT LOOK SO AMUSED. ARE YOU NOT PLEASED TO BE SPENDING THE VALENTINE'S DAY WITH ME?
OH, OF COURSE I AM!
SIGH... WHAT A CHARMING MINIATURE SPECTACLE! WHAT BELIEVABLE SIMULATED SCENERY! WHAT JOYOUS HIGH-PITCHED SINGING!
WHAT CREEPY-LOOKING... DOLLS.

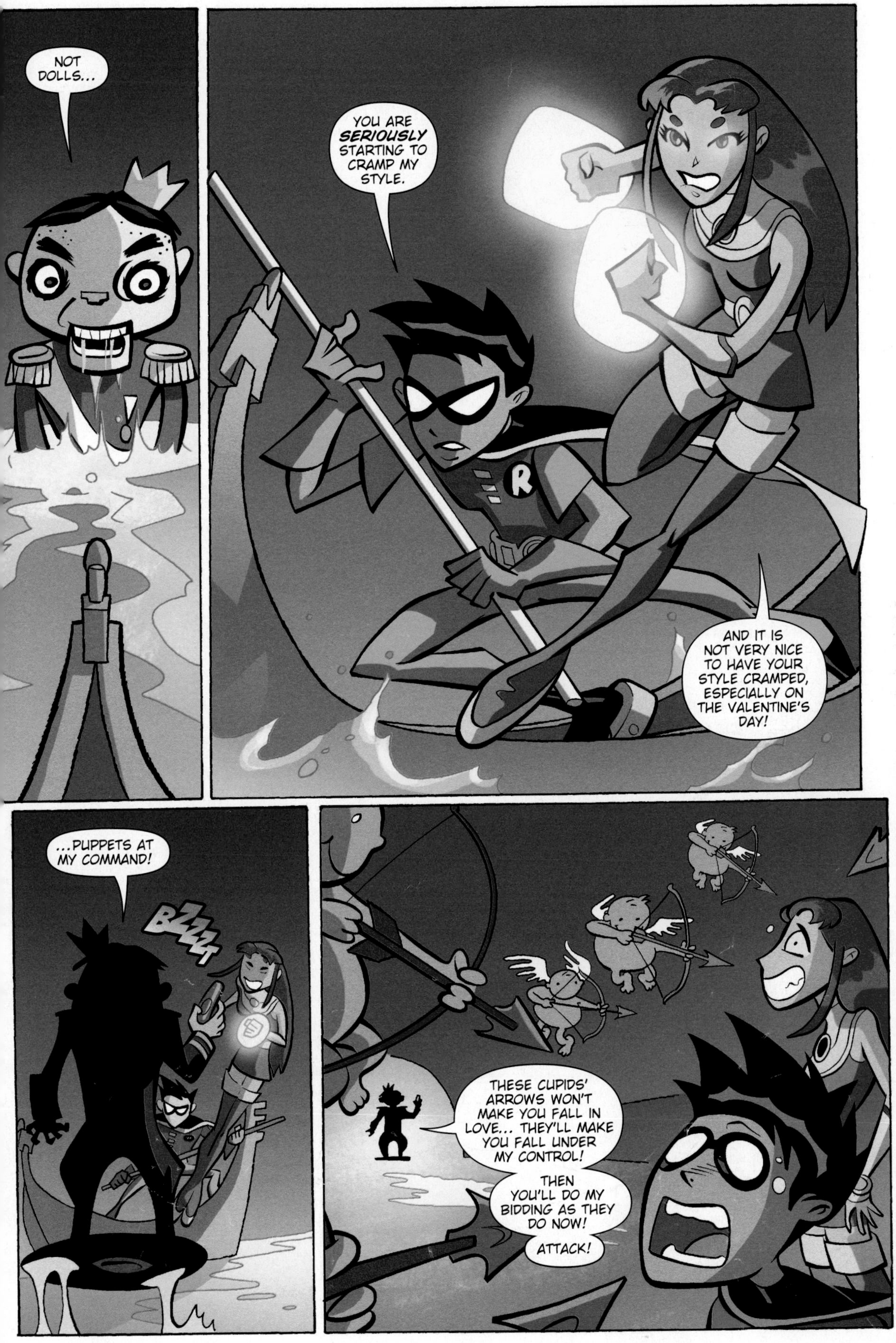
NOT DOLLS...
YOU ARE SERIOUSLY STARTING TO CRAMP MY STYLE.
AND IT IS NOT VERY NICE TO HAVE YOUR STYLE CRAMPED, ESPECIALLY ON THE VALENTINE'S DAY!
...PUPPETS AT MY COMMAND!
BZZZT
THESE CUPIDS' ARROWS WON'T MAKE YOU FALL IN LOVE... THEY'LL MAKE YOU FALL UNDER MY CONTROL!
THEN YOU'LL DO MY BIDDING AS THEY DO NOW!
ATTACK!

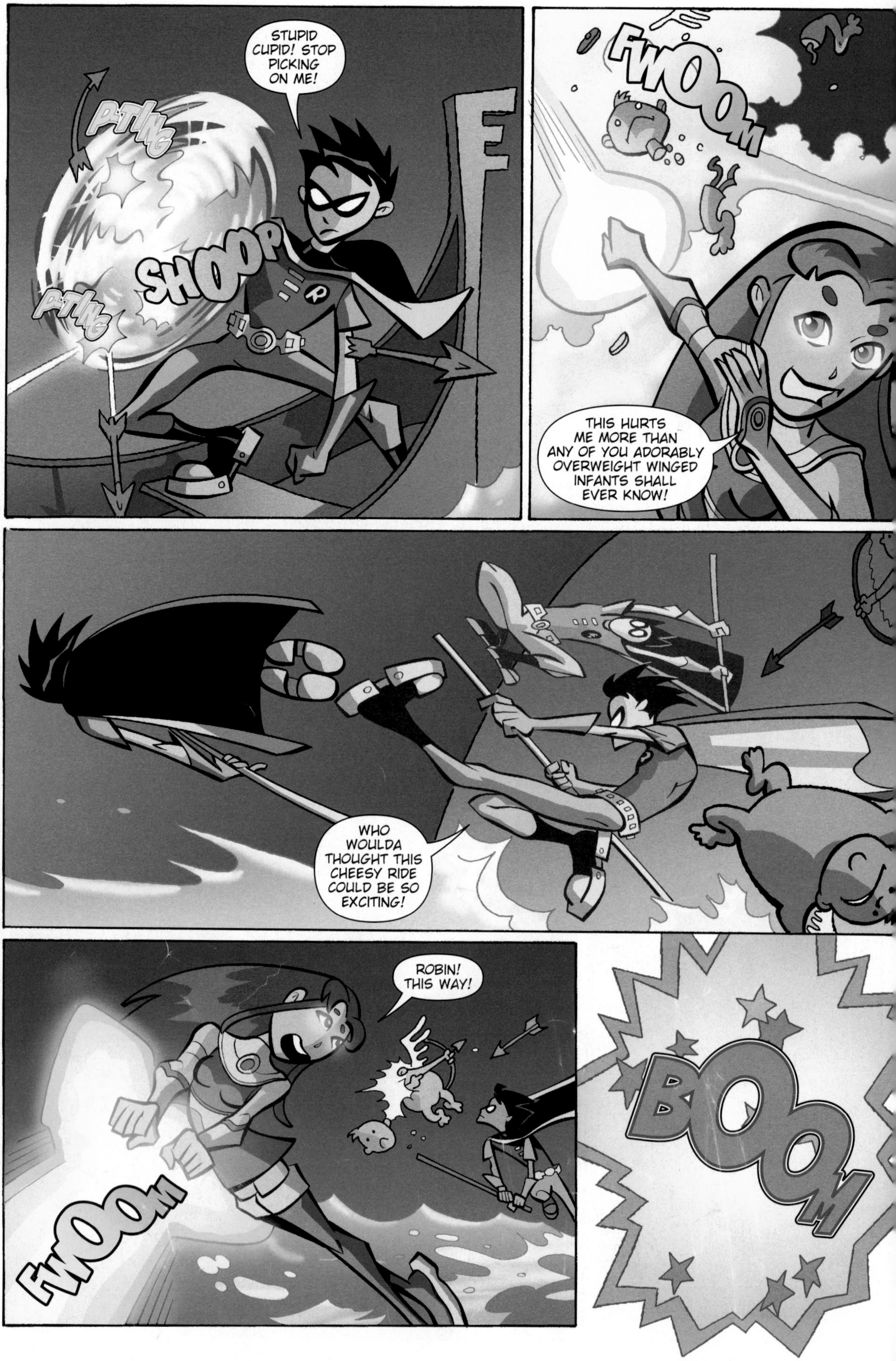
STUPID CUPID! STOP PICKING ON ME!
P-TING
SHOOP
P-TING
FWOOOM
THIS HURTS ME MORE THAN ANY OF YOU ADORABLY OVERWEIGHT WINGED INFANTS SHALL EVER KNOW!
WHO WOULDA THOUGHT THIS CHEESY RIDE COULD BE SO EXCITING!
ROBIN! THIS WAY!
FWOOOM
BOOOM

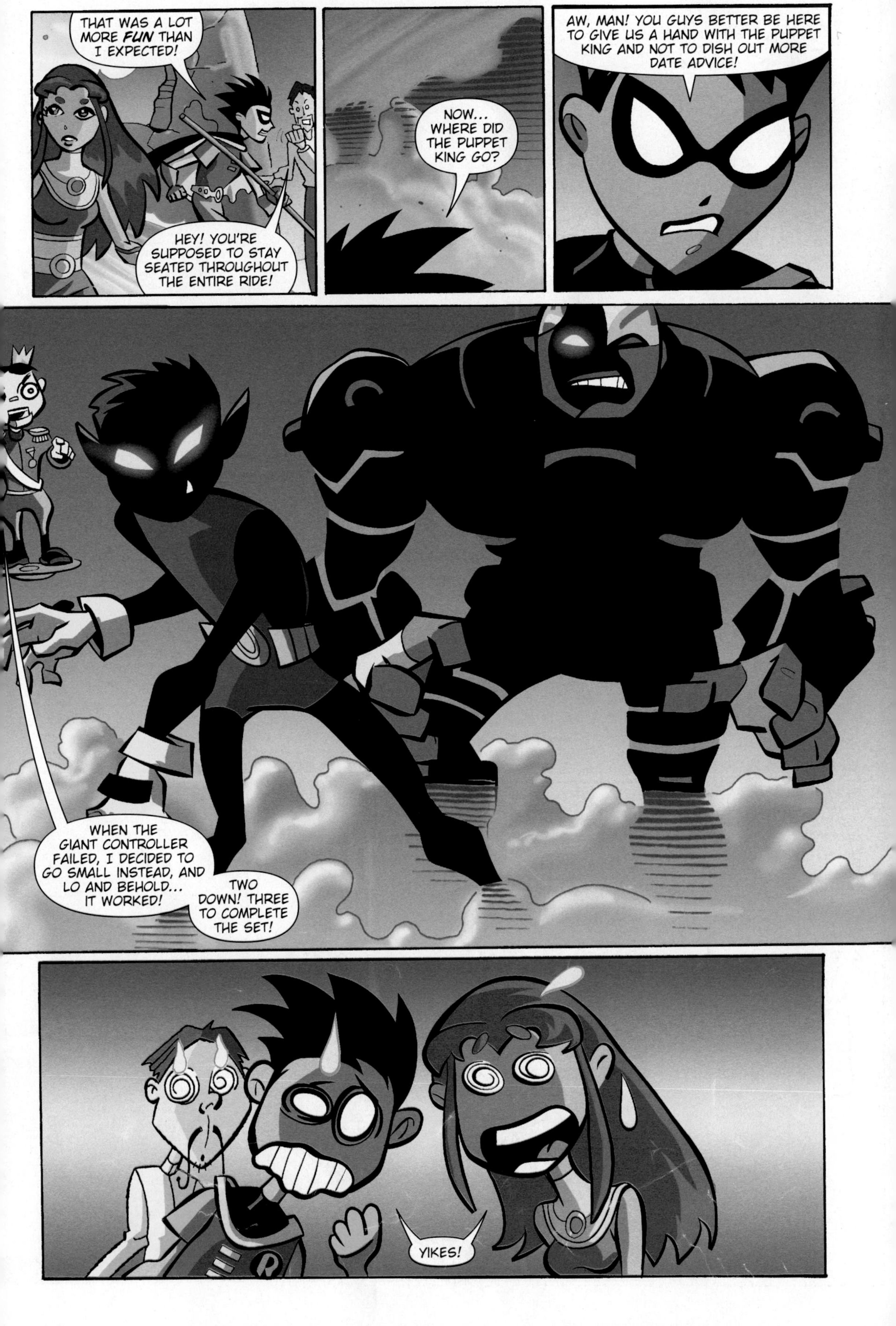
THAT WAS A LOT MORE FUN THAN I EXPECTED!
HEY! YOU'RE SUPPOSED TO STAY SEATED THROUGHOUT THE ENTIRE RIDE!
NOW... WHERE DID THE PUPPET KING GO?
AW, MAN! YOU GUYS BETTER BE HERE TO GIVE US A HAND WITH THE PUPPET KING AND NOT TO DISH OUT MORE DATE ADVICE!
WHEN THE GIANT CONTROLLER FAILED, I DECIDED TO GO SMALL INSTEAD, AND LO AND BEHOLD... IT WORKED!
TWO DOWN! THREE TO COMPLETE THE SET!
YIKES!

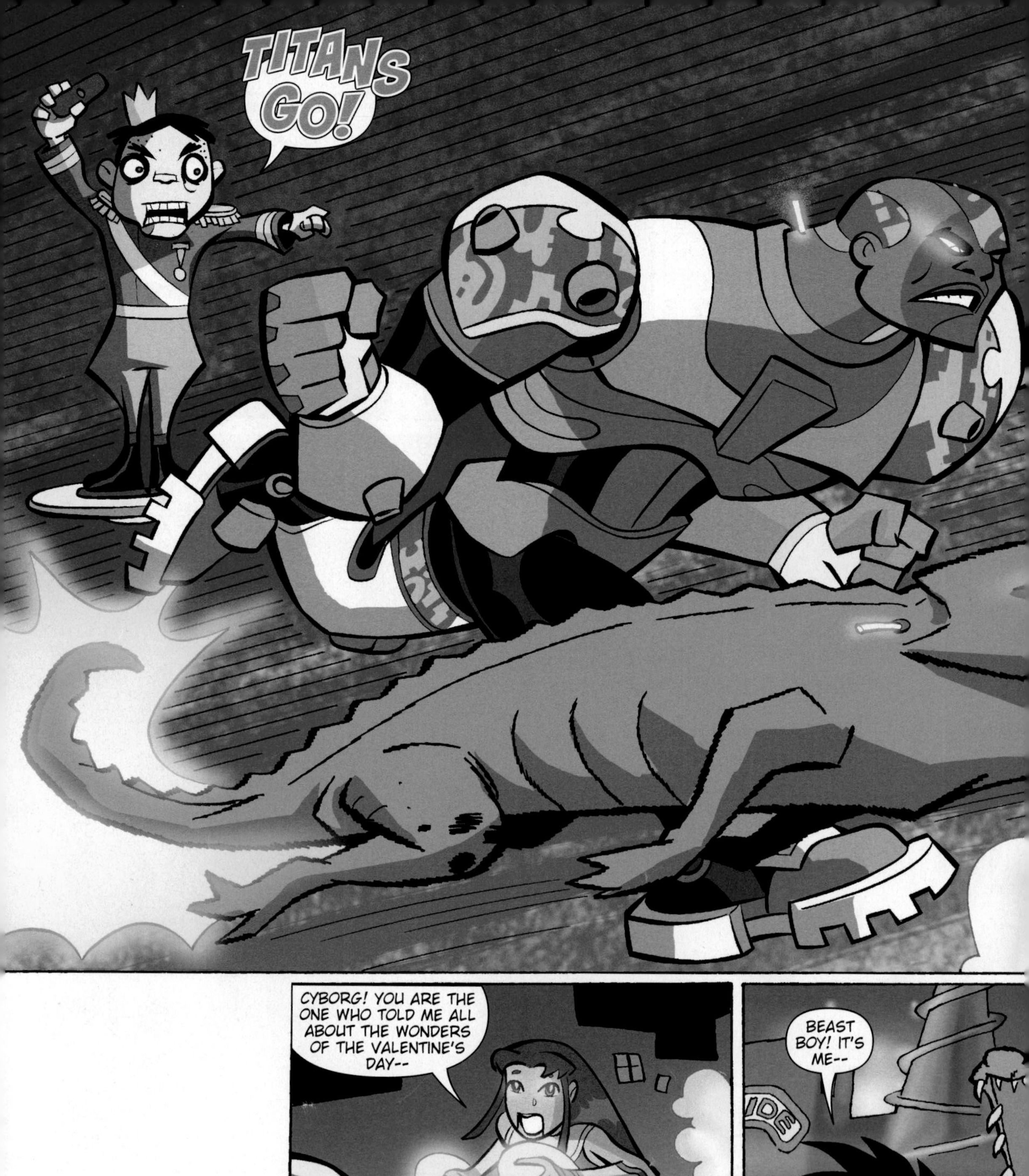
TITANS GO!

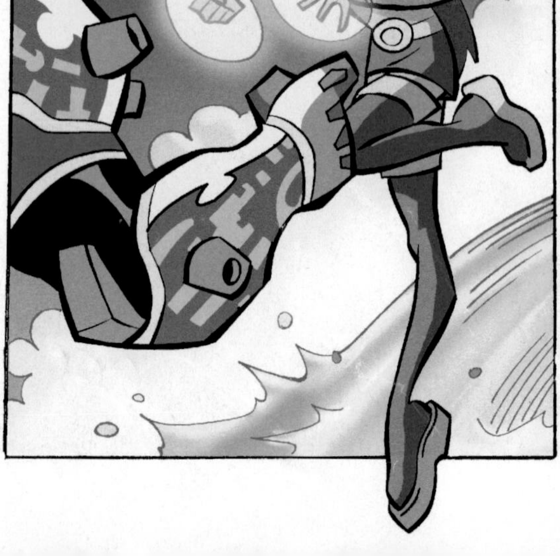
CYBORG! YOU ARE THE ONE WHO TOLD ME ALL ABOUT THE WONDERS OF THE VALENTINE'S DAY--

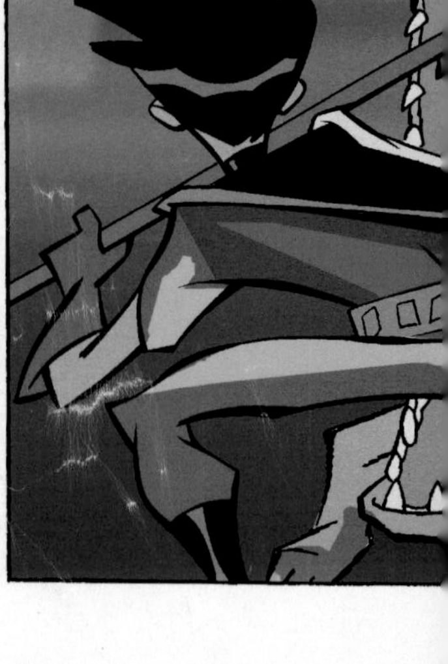
BEAST BOY! IT'S ME--

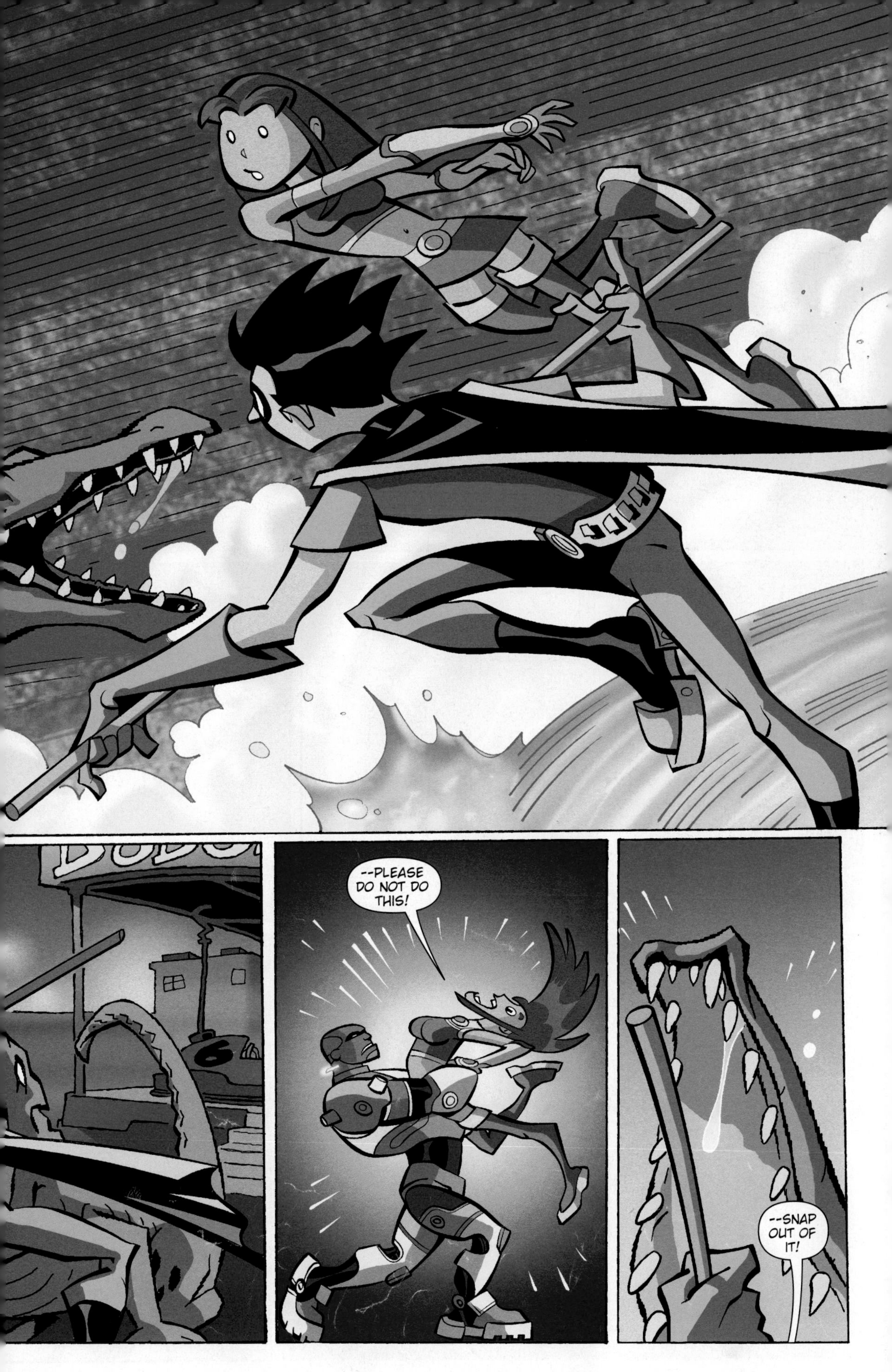
--PLEASE DO NOT DO THIS!
--SNAP OUT OF IT!

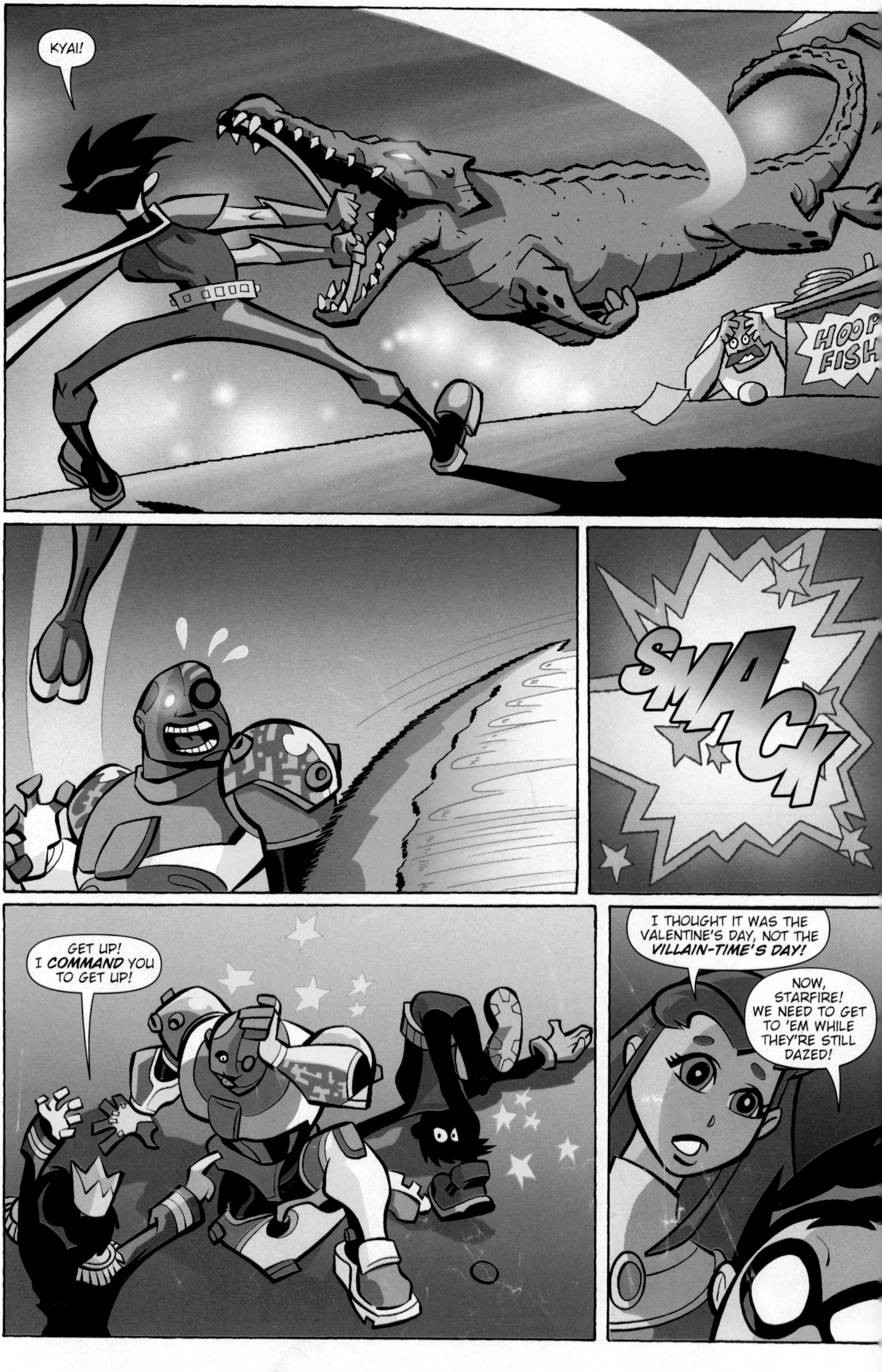
KYAI!
HOOP FISH
SMACK
GET UP! I COMMAND YOU TO GET UP!
I THOUGHT IT WAS THE VALENTINE'S DAY, NOT THE VILLAIN-TIME'S DAY!
NOW, STARFIRE! WE NEED TO GET TO 'EM WHILE THEY'RE STILL DAZED!

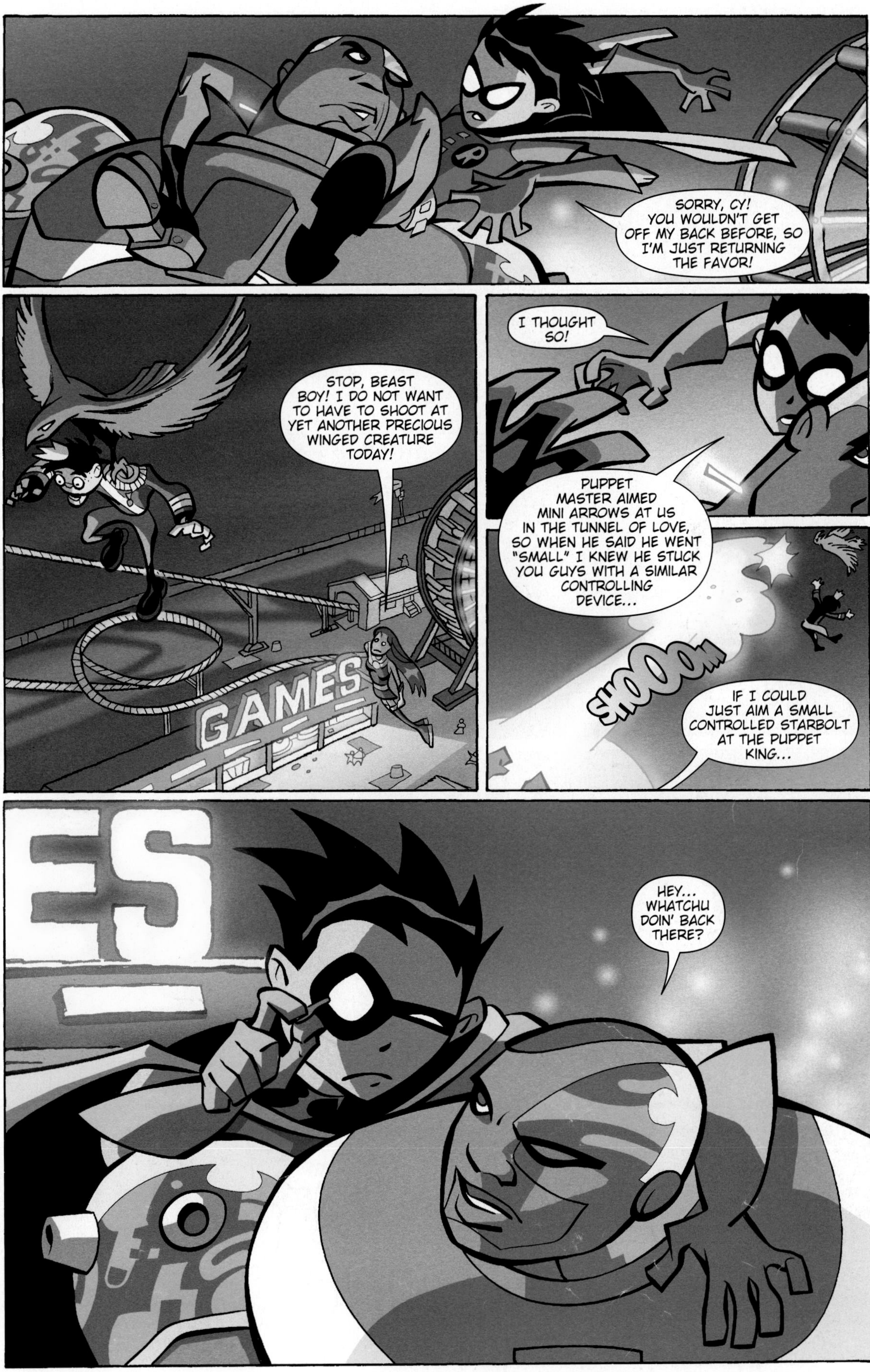
SORRY, CY! YOU WOULDN'T GET OFF MY BACK BEFORE, SO I'M JUST RETURNING THE FAVOR!
STOP, BEAST BOY! I DO NOT WANT TO HAVE TO SHOOT AT YET ANOTHER PRECIOUS WINGED CREATURE TODAY!
GAMES
I THOUGHT SO!
PUPPET MASTER AIMED MINI ARROWS AT US IN THE TUNNEL OF LOVE, SO WHEN HE SAID HE WENT "SMALL" I KNEW HE STUCK YOU GUYS WITH A SIMILAR CONTROLLING DEVICE...
SHOOOOM
IF I COULD JUST AIM A SMALL CONTROLLED STARBOLT AT THE PUPPET KING...
HEY... WHATCHU DOIN' BACK THERE?

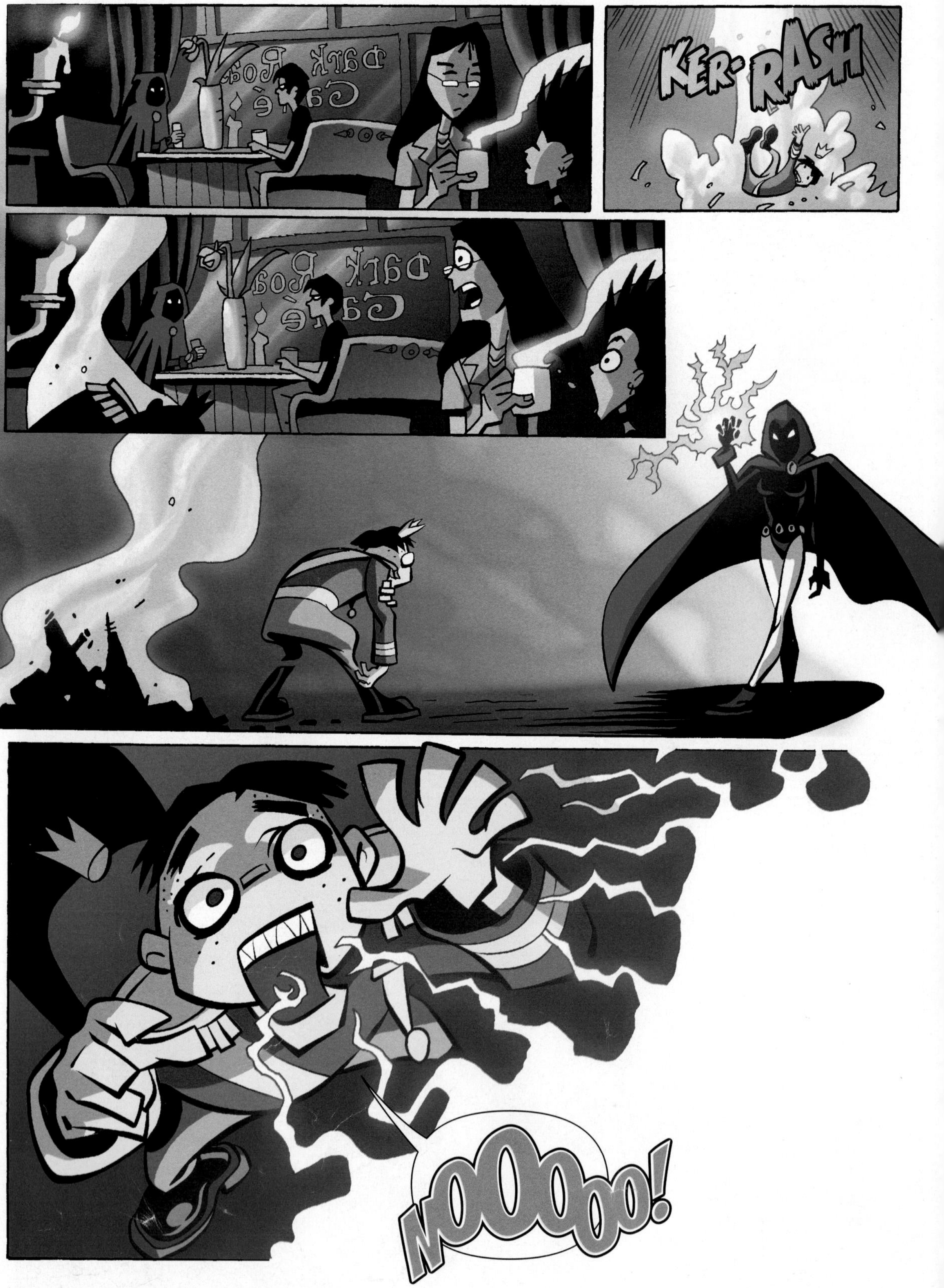
KER-RASH
NOOOOOO!

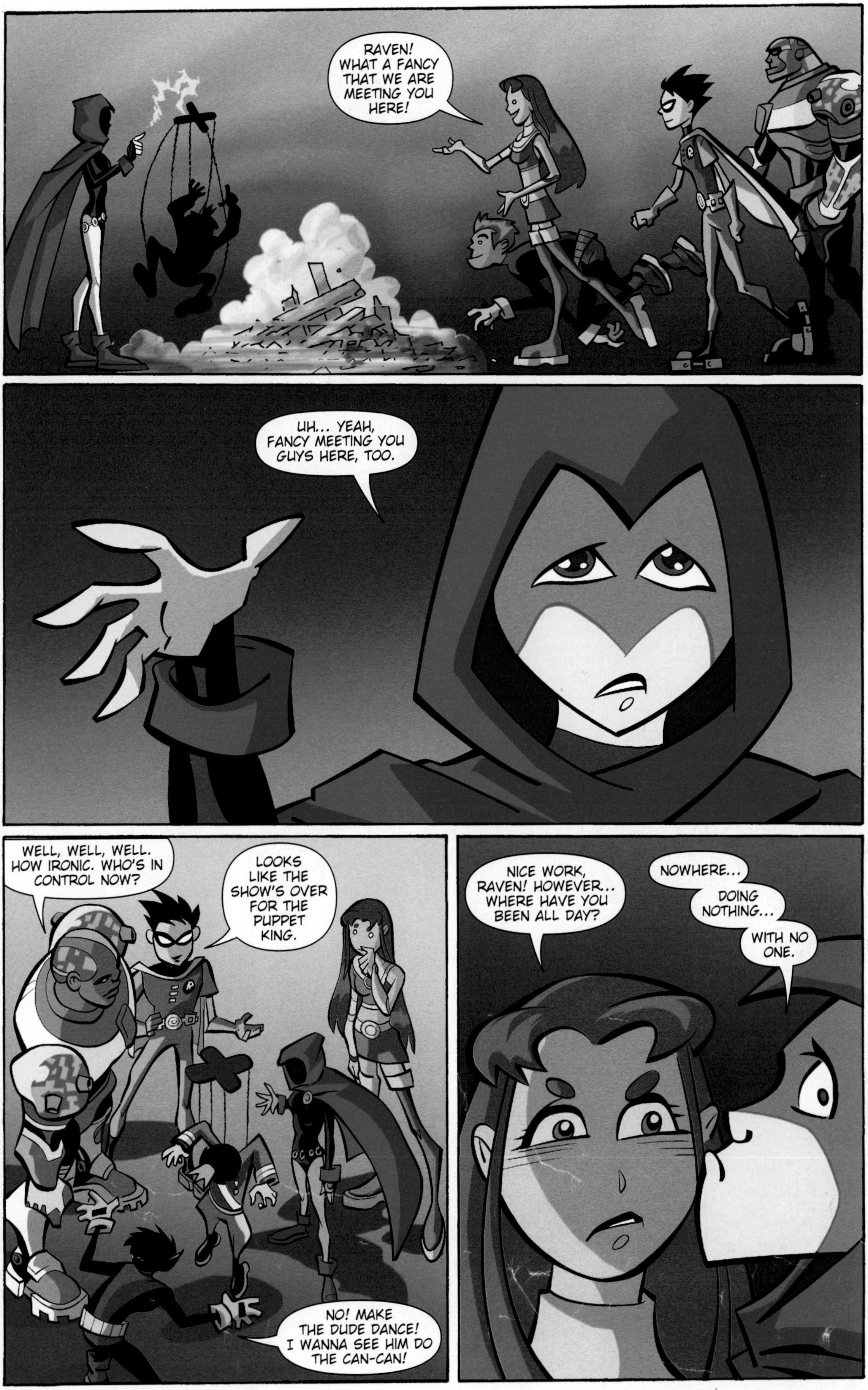
RAVEN! WHAT A FANCY THAT WE ARE MEETING YOU HERE!
UH... YEAH, FANCY MEETING YOU GUYS HERE, TOO.
WELL, WELL, WELL. HOW IRONIC. WHO'S IN CONTROL NOW?
LOOKS LIKE THE SHOW'S OVER FOR THE PUPPET KING.
NO! MAKE THE DUDE DANCE! I WANNA SEE HIM DO THE CAN-CAN!
NICE WORK, RAVEN! HOWEVER... WHERE HAVE YOU BEEN ALL DAY?
NOWHERE...
DOING NOTHING...
WITH NO ONE.

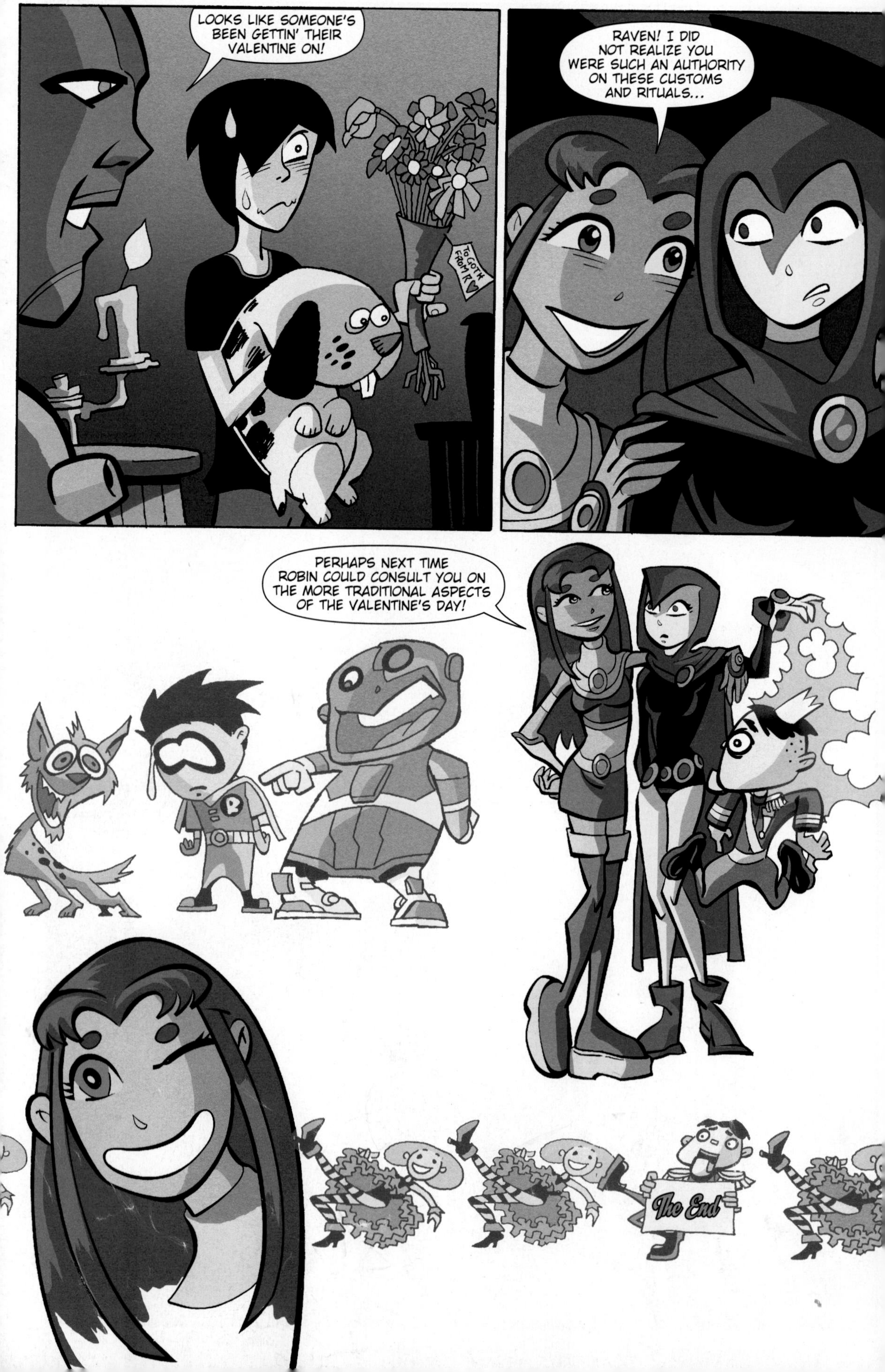
LOOKS LIKE SOMEONE'S BEEN GETTIN' THEIR VALENTINE ON!
TO GOTH FROM R
RAVEN! I DID NOT REALIZE YOU WERE SUCH AN AUTHORITY ON THESE CUSTOMS AND RITUALS...
PERHAPS NEXT TIME ROBIN COULD CONSULT YOU ON THE MORE TRADITIONAL ASPECTS OF THE VALENTINE'S DAY!
The End

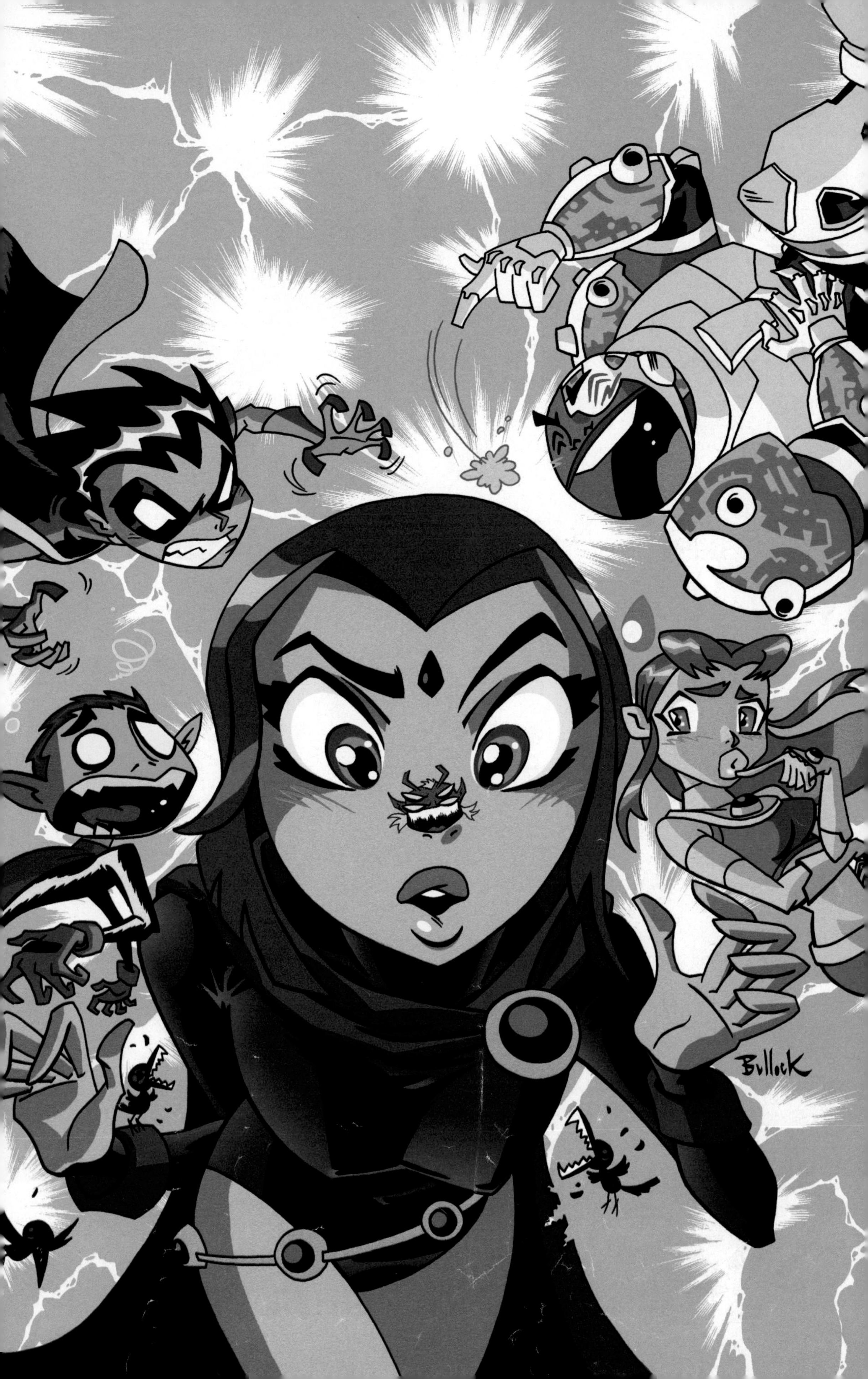
Bullock

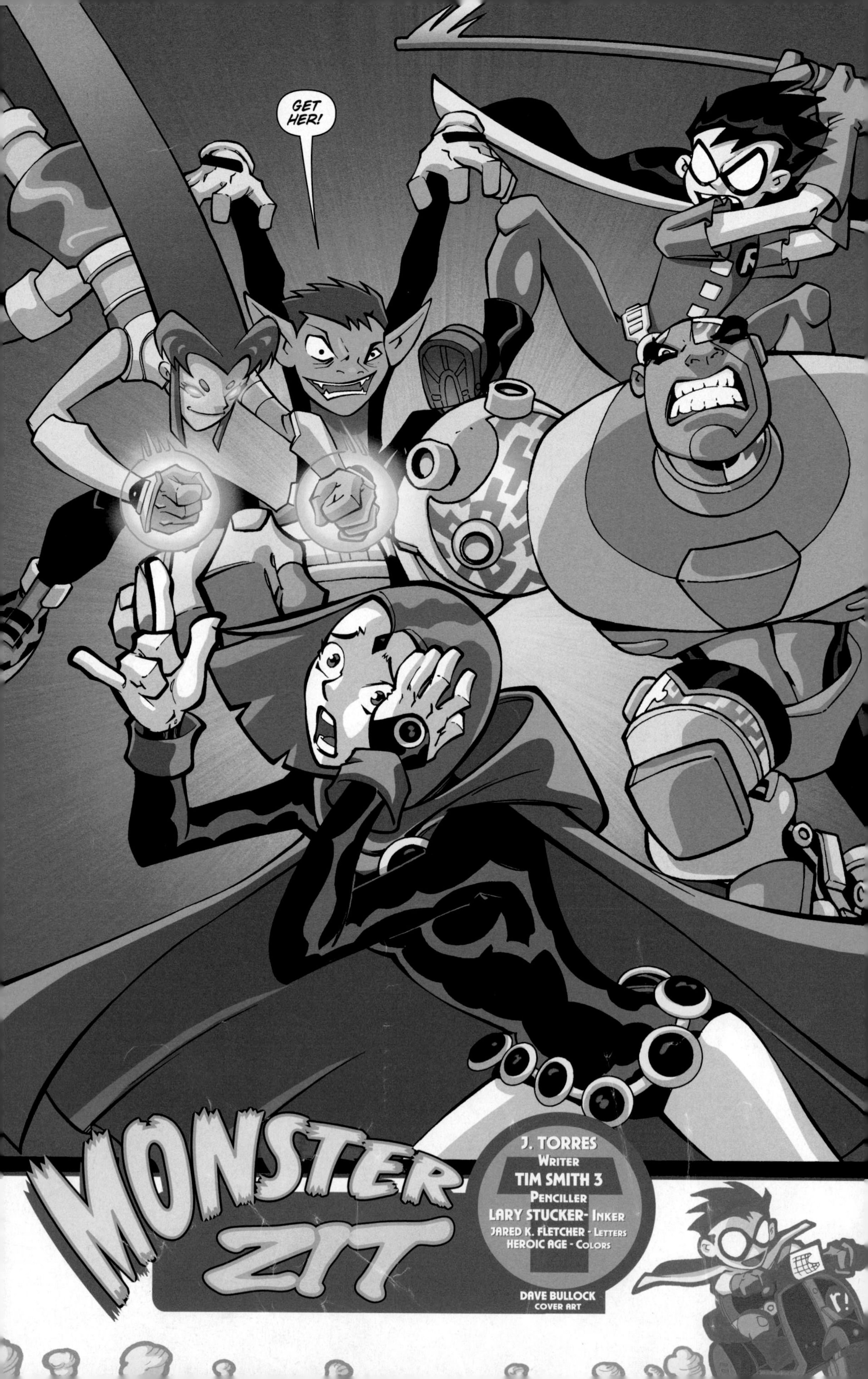
GET HER!
MONSTER ZIT
J. TORRES
Writer
TIM SMITH 3
Penciller
LARY STUCKER- Inker
JARED K. FLETCHER - Letters
HEROIC AGE - Colors
DAVE BULLOCK
COVER ART

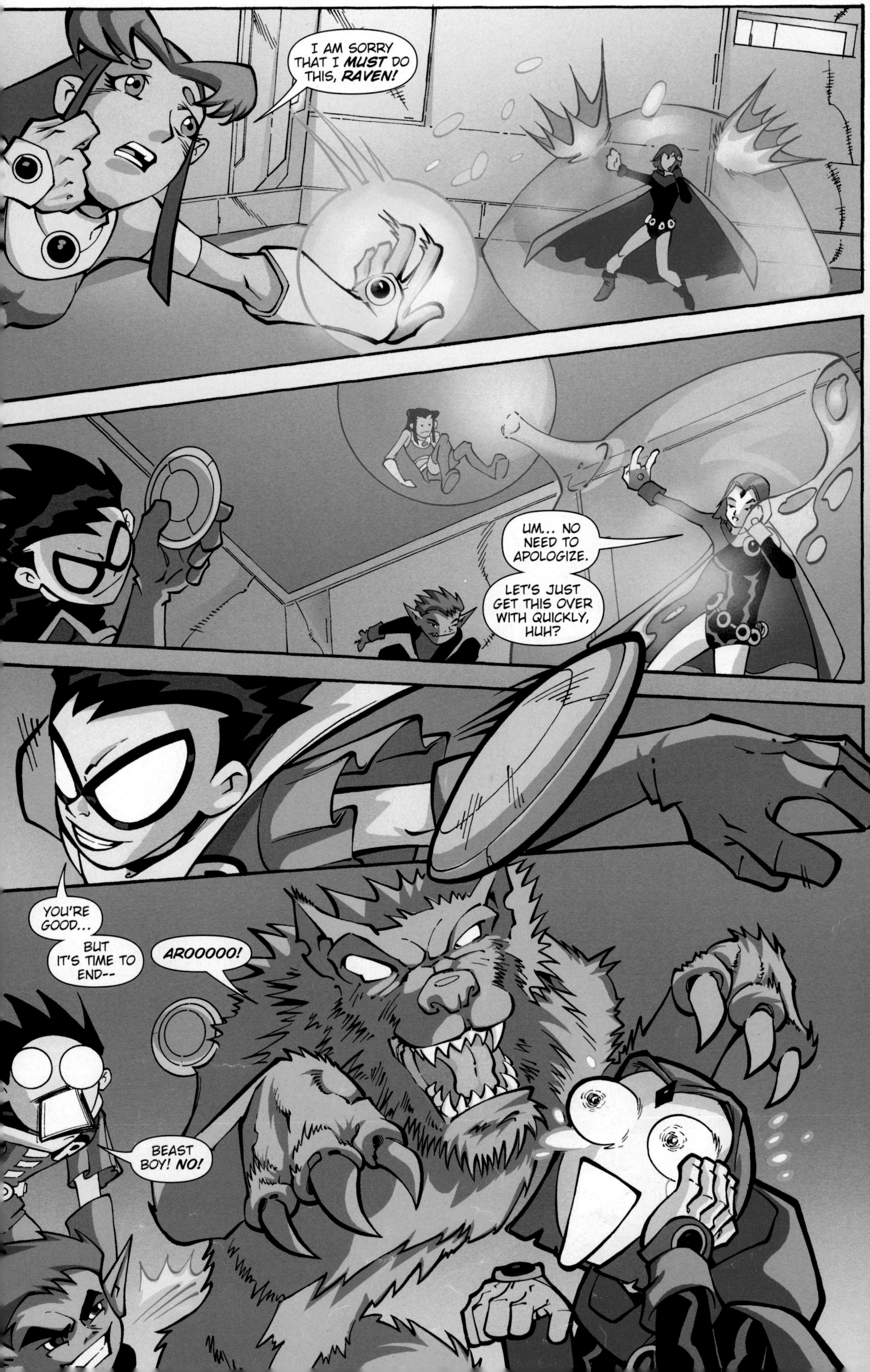
I AM SORRY THAT I **MUST** DO THIS, **RAVEN!**
UM... NO NEED TO APOLOGIZE.
LET'S JUST GET THIS OVER WITH QUICKLY, HUH?
YOU'RE GOOD...
BUT IT'S TIME TO END--
AROOOOO!
BEAST BOY! **NO!**

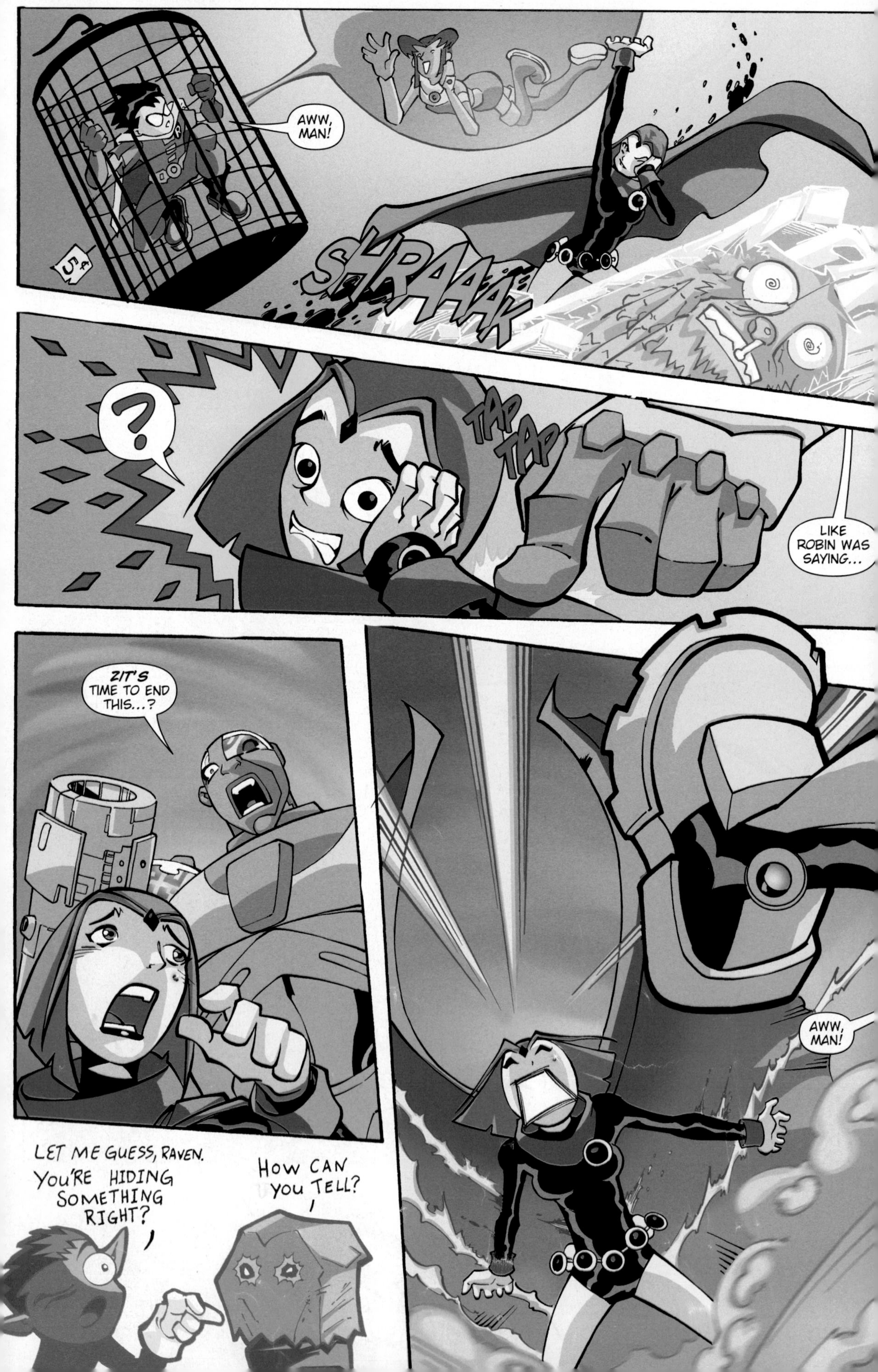
AWW, MAN!
SHRAAAK
?
TAP TAP
LIKE ROBIN WAS SAYING...
ZIT'S TIME TO END THIS...?
AWW, MAN!
LET ME GUESS, RAVEN. YOU'RE HIDING SOMETHING RIGHT?
HOW CAN YOU TELL?

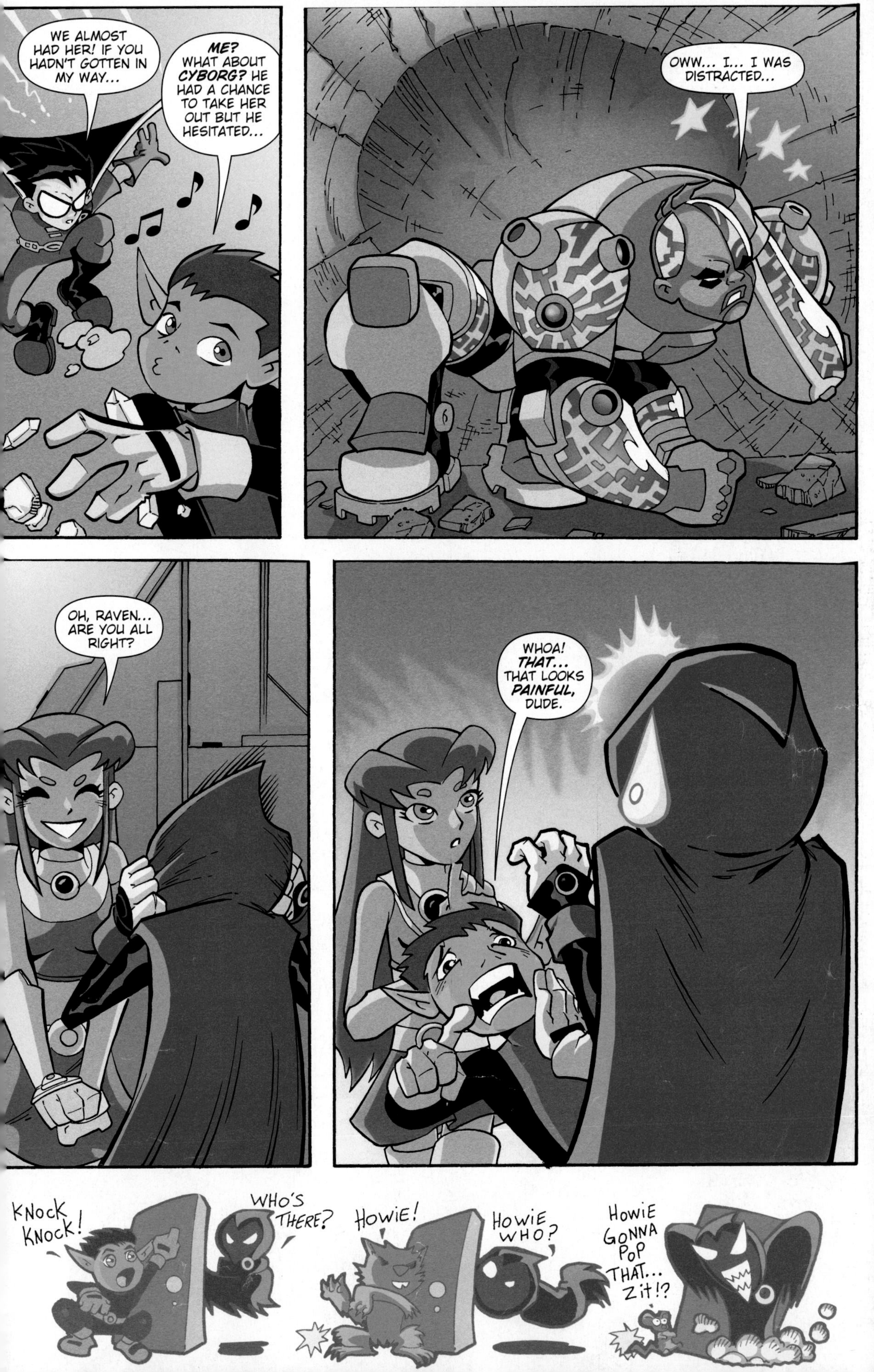
WE ALMOST HAD HER! IF YOU HADN'T GOTTEN IN MY WAY...
ME? WHAT ABOUT CYBORG? HE HAD A CHANCE TO TAKE HER OUT BUT HE HESITATED...
OWW... I... I WAS DISTRACTED...
OH, RAVEN... ARE YOU ALL RIGHT?
WHOA! THAT... THAT LOOKS PAINFUL, DUDE.
KNOCK KNOCK!
WHO'S THERE?
HOWIE!
HOWIE WHO?
HOWIE GONNA POP THAT... ZIT!?

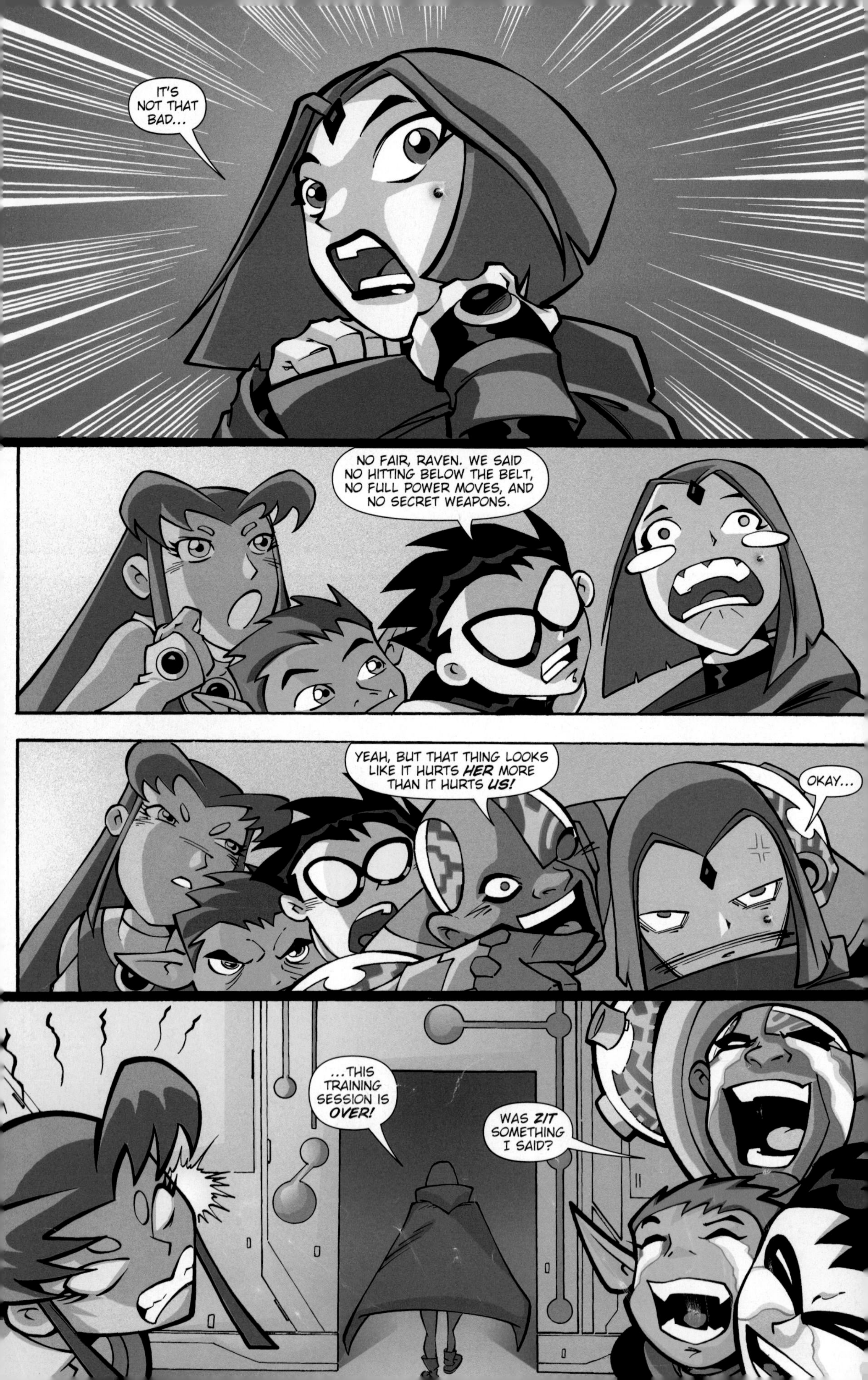
IT'S NOT THAT BAD...
NO FAIR, RAVEN. WE SAID NO HITTING BELOW THE BELT, NO FULL POWER MOVES, AND NO SECRET WEAPONS.
YEAH, BUT THAT THING LOOKS LIKE IT HURTS HER MORE THAN IT HURTS US!
OKAY...
...THIS TRAINING SESSION IS OVER!
WAS ZIT SOMETHING I SAID?

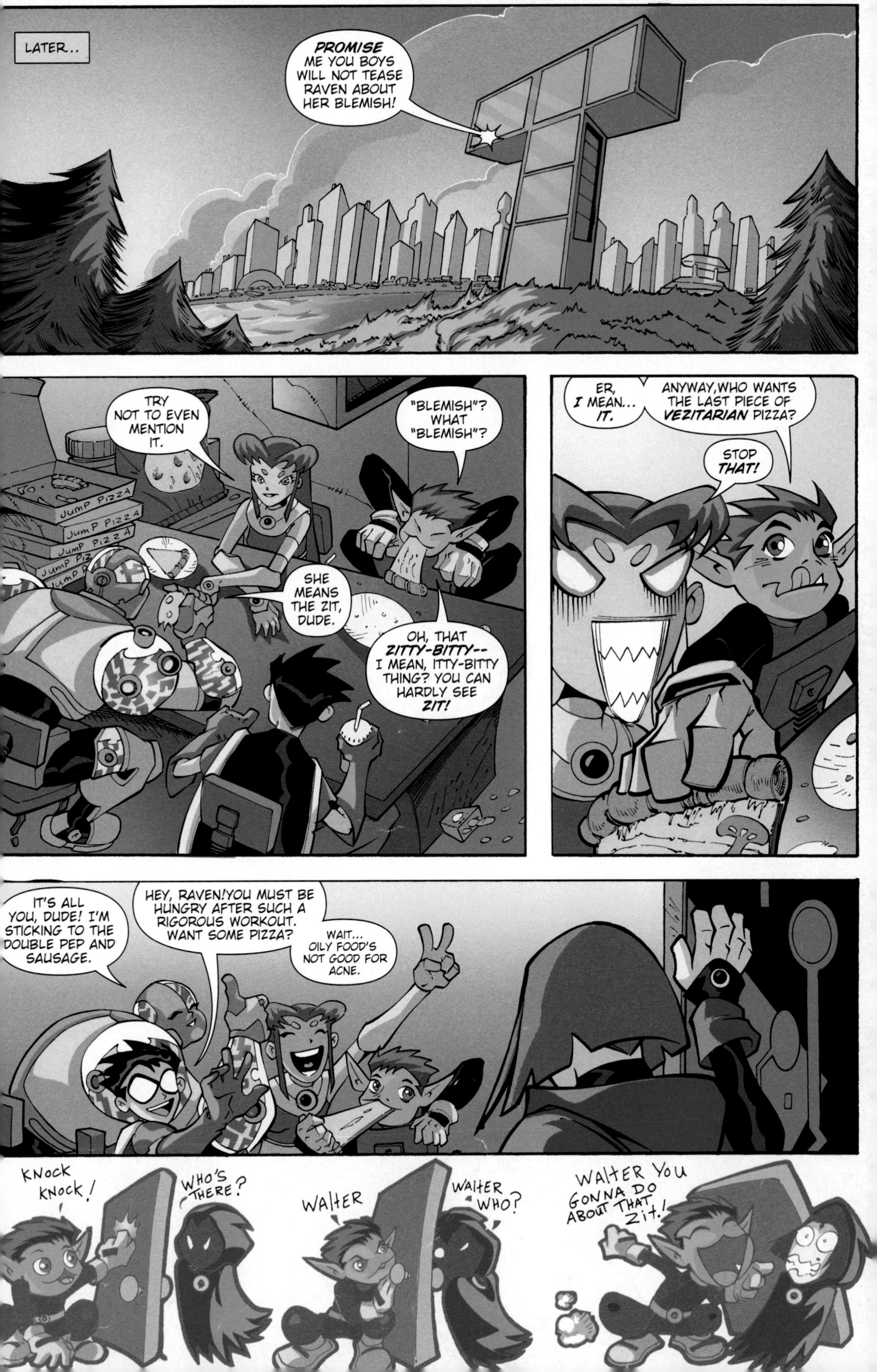
LATER...
PROMISE ME YOU BOYS WILL NOT TEASE RAVEN ABOUT HER BLEMISH!
TRY NOT TO EVEN MENTION IT.
"BLEMISH"? WHAT "BLEMISH"?
JUMP PIZZA
SHE MEANS THE ZIT, DUDE.
OH, THAT ZITTY-BITTY-- I MEAN, ITTY-BITTY THING? YOU CAN HARDLY SEE ZIT!
ER, I MEAN... IT.
ANYWAY, WHO WANTS THE LAST PIECE OF VEZITARIAN PIZZA?
STOP THAT!
IT'S ALL YOU, DUDE! I'M STICKING TO THE DOUBLE PEP AND SAUSAGE.
HEY, RAVEN! YOU MUST BE HUNGRY AFTER SUCH A RIGOROUS WORKOUT. WANT SOME PIZZA?
WAIT... OILY FOOD'S NOT GOOD FOR ACNE.
KNOCK KNOCK!
WHO'S THERE?
WALTER
WALTER WHO?
WALTER YOU GONNA DO ABOUT THAT ZIT!

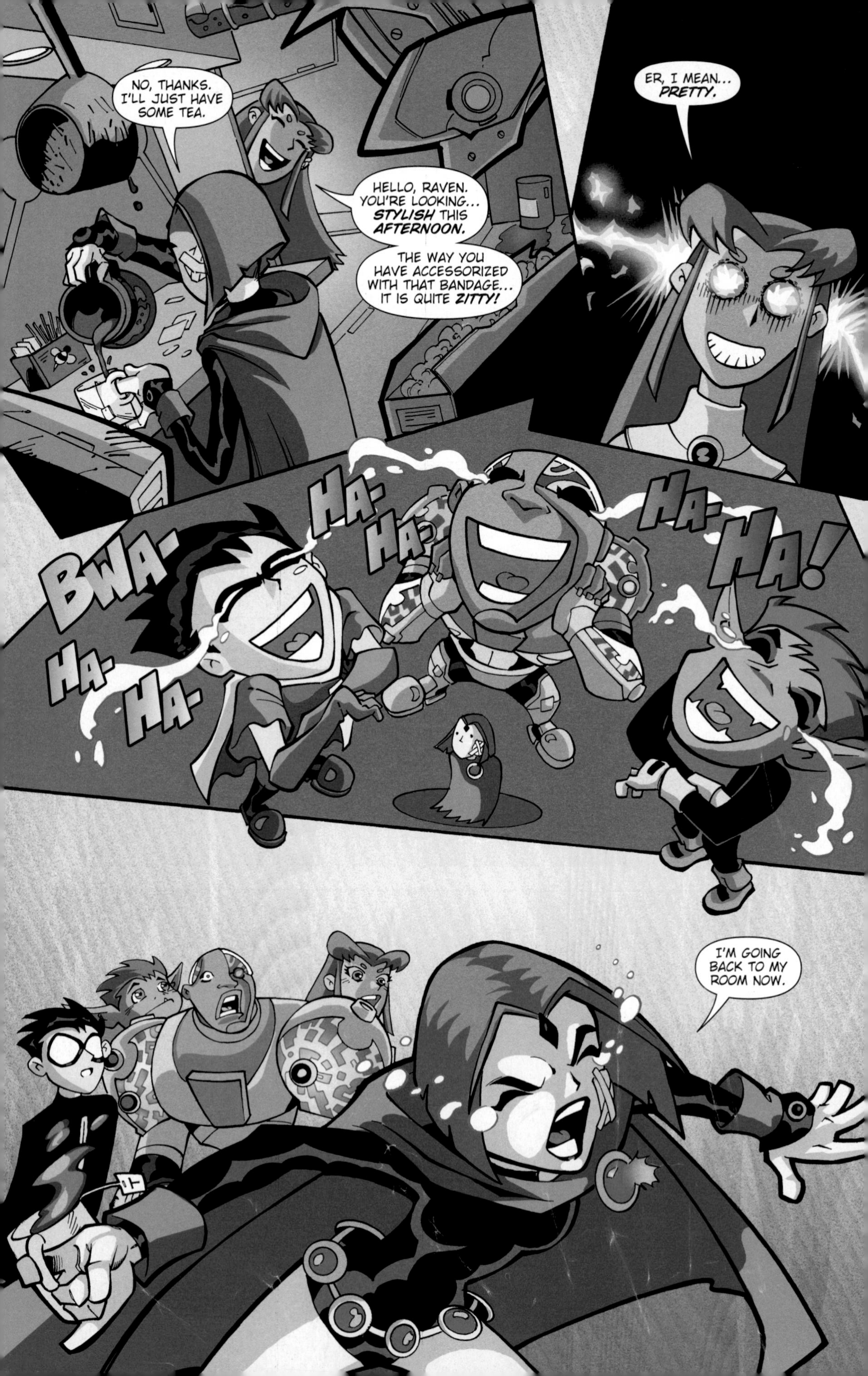
NO, THANKS. I'LL JUST HAVE SOME TEA.
HELLO, RAVEN. YOU'RE LOOKING... STYLISH THIS AFTERNOON.
THE WAY YOU HAVE ACCESSORIZED WITH THAT BANDAGE... IT IS QUITE ZITTY!
ER, I MEAN... PRETTY.
BWA-HA-HA-
HA-HA-
HA-HA!
I'M GOING BACK TO MY ROOM NOW.

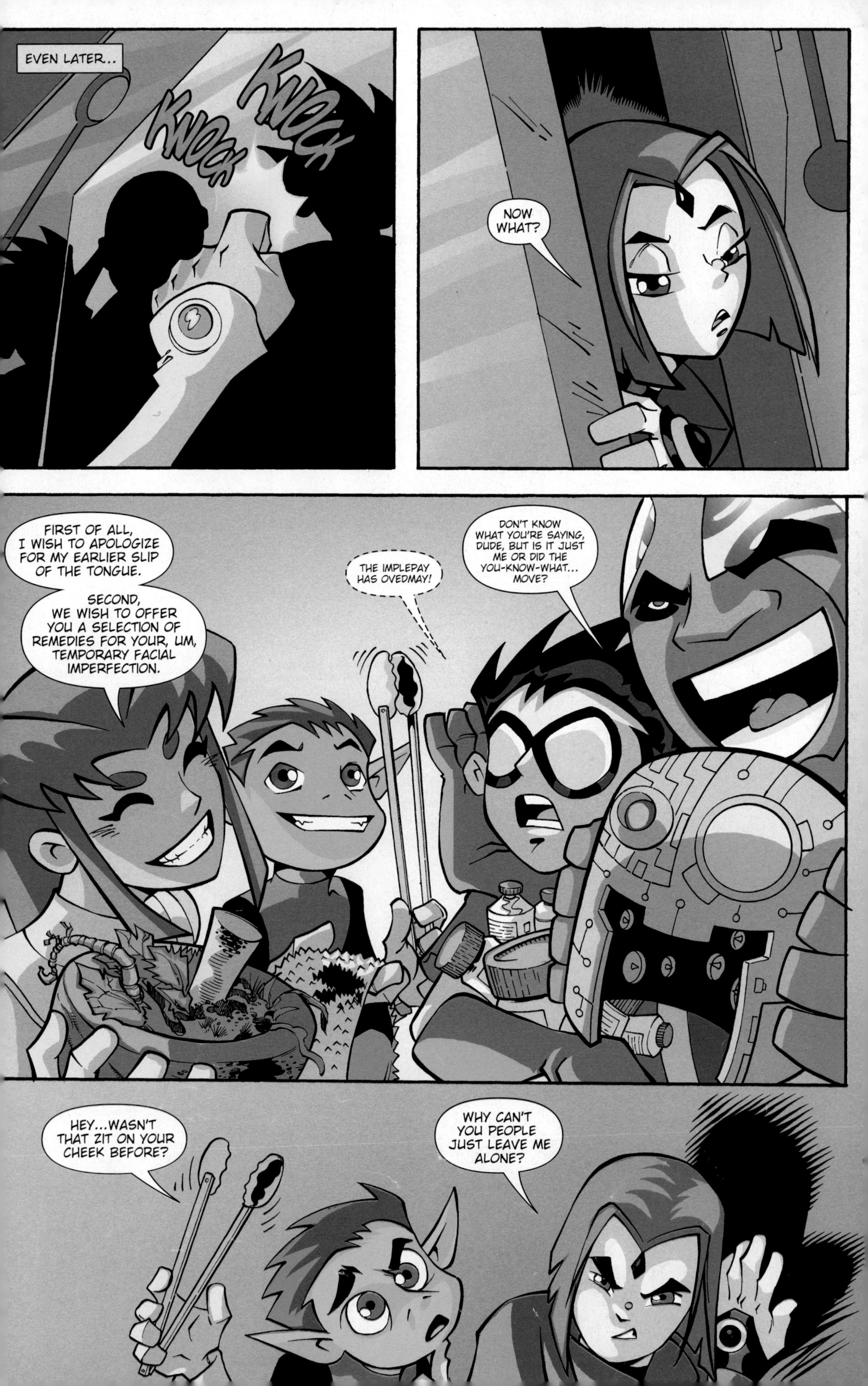
EVEN LATER...
KNOCK KNOCK
NOW WHAT?
FIRST OF ALL, I WISH TO APOLOGIZE FOR MY EARLIER SLIP OF THE TONGUE.
SECOND, WE WISH TO OFFER YOU A SELECTION OF REMEDIES FOR YOUR, UM, TEMPORARY FACIAL IMPERFECTION.
THE IMPLEPAY HAS OVEDMAY!
DON'T KNOW WHAT YOU'RE SAYING, DUDE, BUT IS IT JUST ME OR DID THE YOU-KNOW-WHAT... MOVE?
HEY...WASN'T THAT ZIT ON YOUR CHEEK BEFORE?
WHY CAN'T YOU PEOPLE JUST LEAVE ME ALONE?

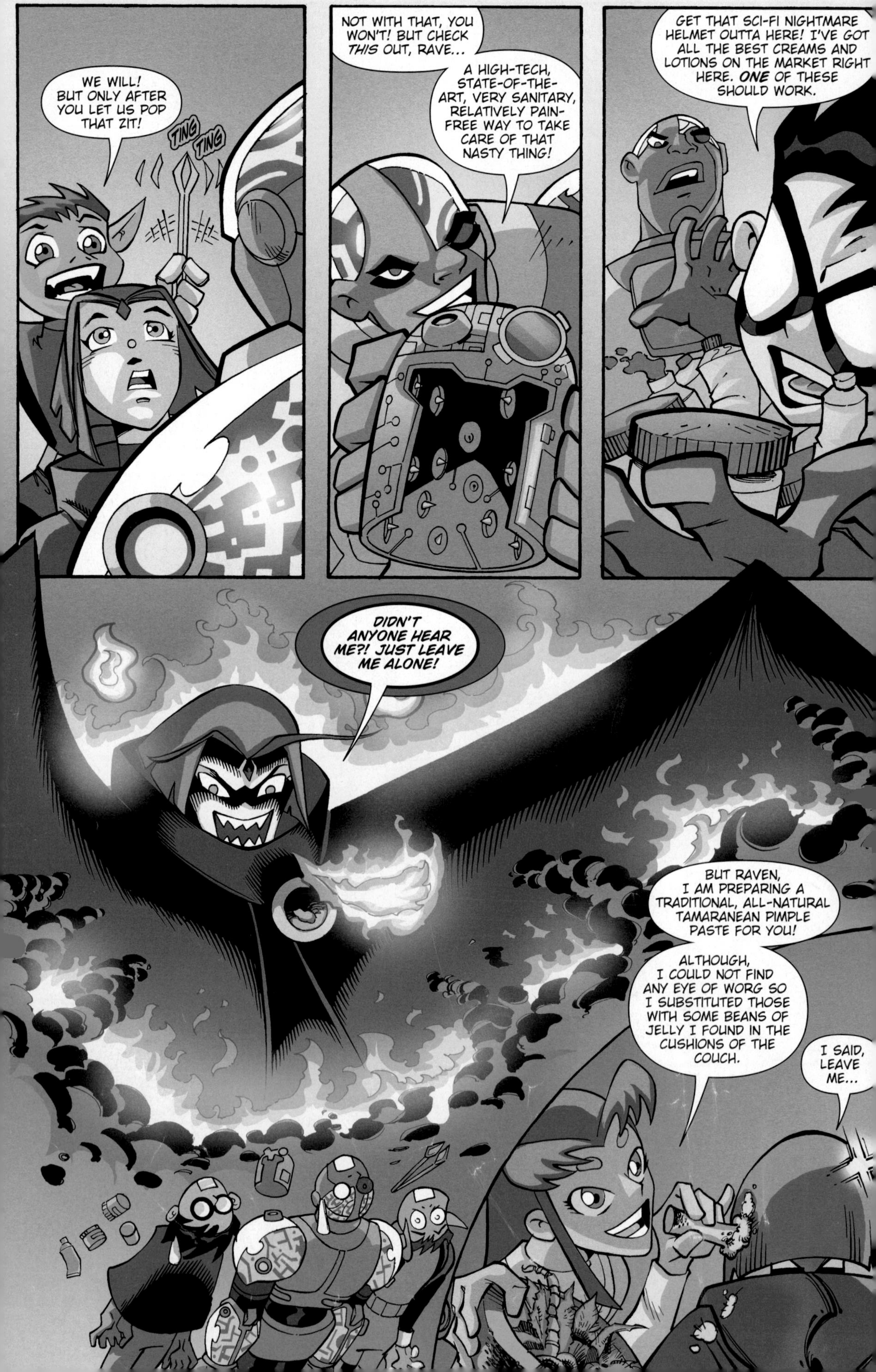
WE WILL! BUT ONLY AFTER YOU LET US POP THAT ZIT!
TING TING
NOT WITH THAT, YOU WON'T! BUT CHECK THIS OUT, RAVE...
A HIGH-TECH, STATE-OF-THE-ART, VERY SANITARY, RELATIVELY PAIN-FREE WAY TO TAKE CARE OF THAT NASTY THING!
GET THAT SCI-FI NIGHTMARE HELMET OUTTA HERE! I'VE GOT ALL THE BEST CREAMS AND LOTIONS ON THE MARKET RIGHT HERE. ONE OF THESE SHOULD WORK.
DIDN'T ANYONE HEAR ME?! JUST LEAVE ME ALONE!
BUT RAVEN, I AM PREPARING A TRADITIONAL, ALL-NATURAL TAMARANEAN PIMPLE PASTE FOR YOU!
ALTHOUGH, I COULD NOT FIND ANY EYE OF WORG SO I SUBSTITUTED THOSE WITH SOME BEANS OF JELLY I FOUND IN THE CUSHIONS OF THE COUCH.
I SAID, LEAVE ME...

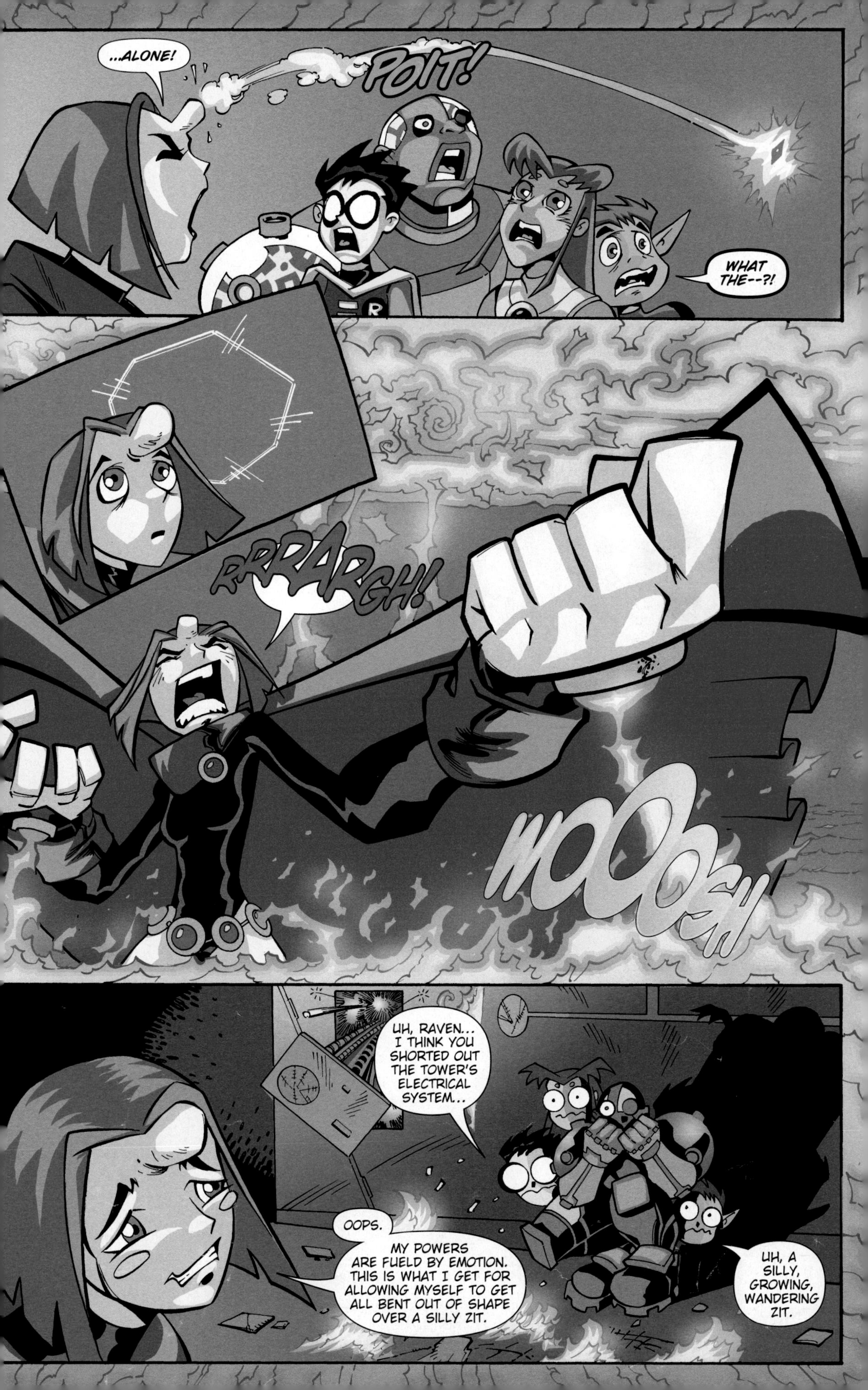
...ALONE!
POIT!
WHAT THE--?!
RRRARGH!
WOOOSH
UH, RAVEN... I THINK YOU SHORTED OUT THE TOWER'S ELECTRICAL SYSTEM...
OOPS.
MY POWERS ARE FUELD BY EMOTION. THIS IS WHAT I GET FOR ALLOWING MYSELF TO GET ALL BENT OUT OF SHAPE OVER A SILLY ZIT.
UH, A SILLY, GROWING, WANDERING ZIT.

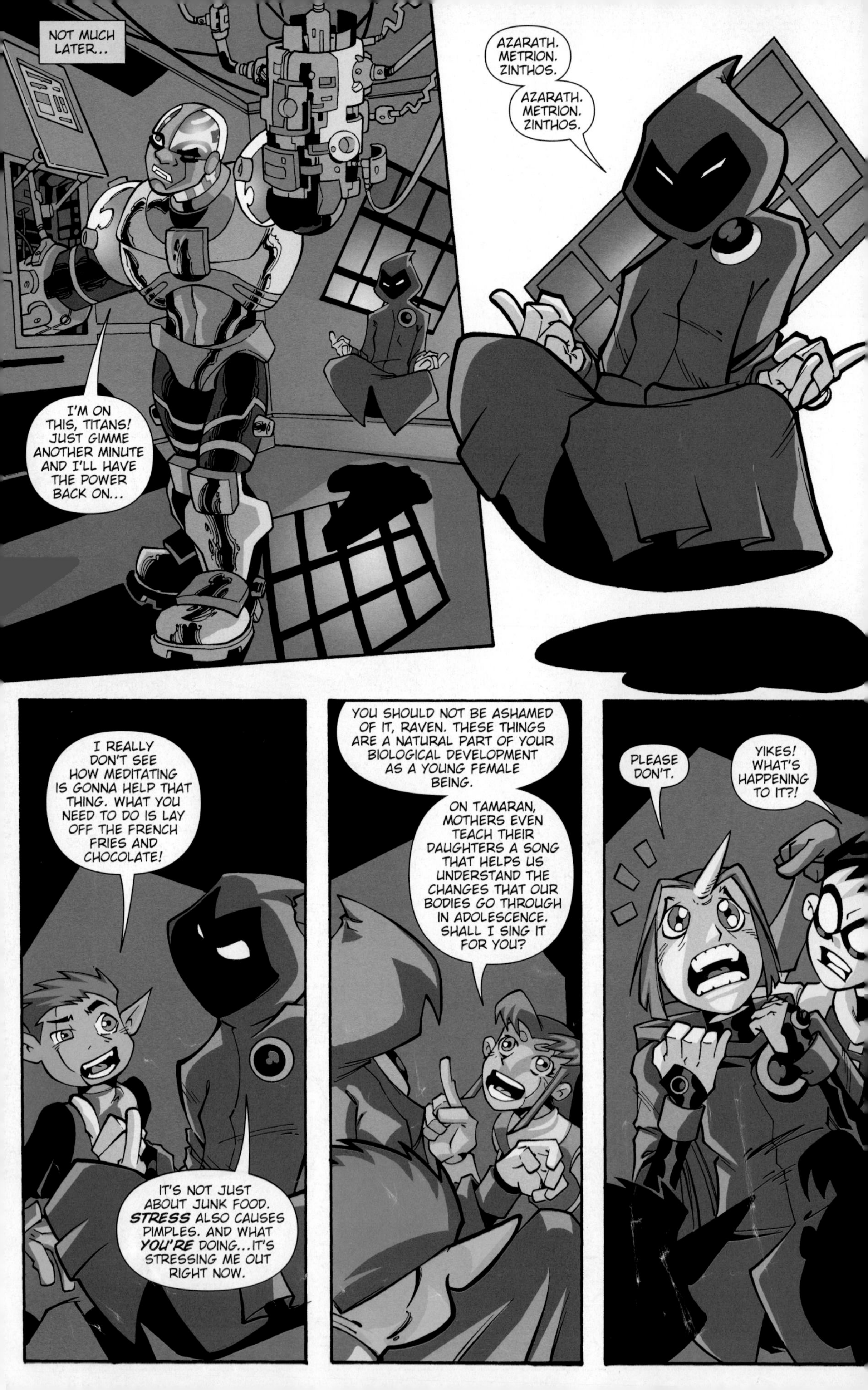
NOT MUCH LATER...
I'M ON THIS, TITANS! JUST GIMME ANOTHER MINUTE AND I'LL HAVE THE POWER BACK ON...
AZARATH. METRION. ZINTHOS.
AZARATH. METRION. ZINTHOS.
I REALLY DON'T SEE HOW MEDITATING IS GONNA HELP THAT THING. WHAT YOU NEED TO DO IS LAY OFF THE FRENCH FRIES AND CHOCOLATE!
IT'S NOT JUST ABOUT JUNK FOOD. STRESS ALSO CAUSES PIMPLES. AND WHAT YOU'RE DOING...IT'S STRESSING ME OUT RIGHT NOW.
YOU SHOULD NOT BE ASHAMED OF IT, RAVEN. THESE THINGS ARE A NATURAL PART OF YOUR BIOLOGICAL DEVELOPMENT AS A YOUNG FEMALE BEING.
ON TAMARAN, MOTHERS EVEN TEACH THEIR DAUGHTERS A SONG THAT HELPS US UNDERSTAND THE CHANGES THAT OUR BODIES GO THROUGH IN ADOLESCENCE. SHALL I SING IT FOR YOU?
PLEASE DON'T.
YIKES! WHAT'S HAPPENING TO IT?!

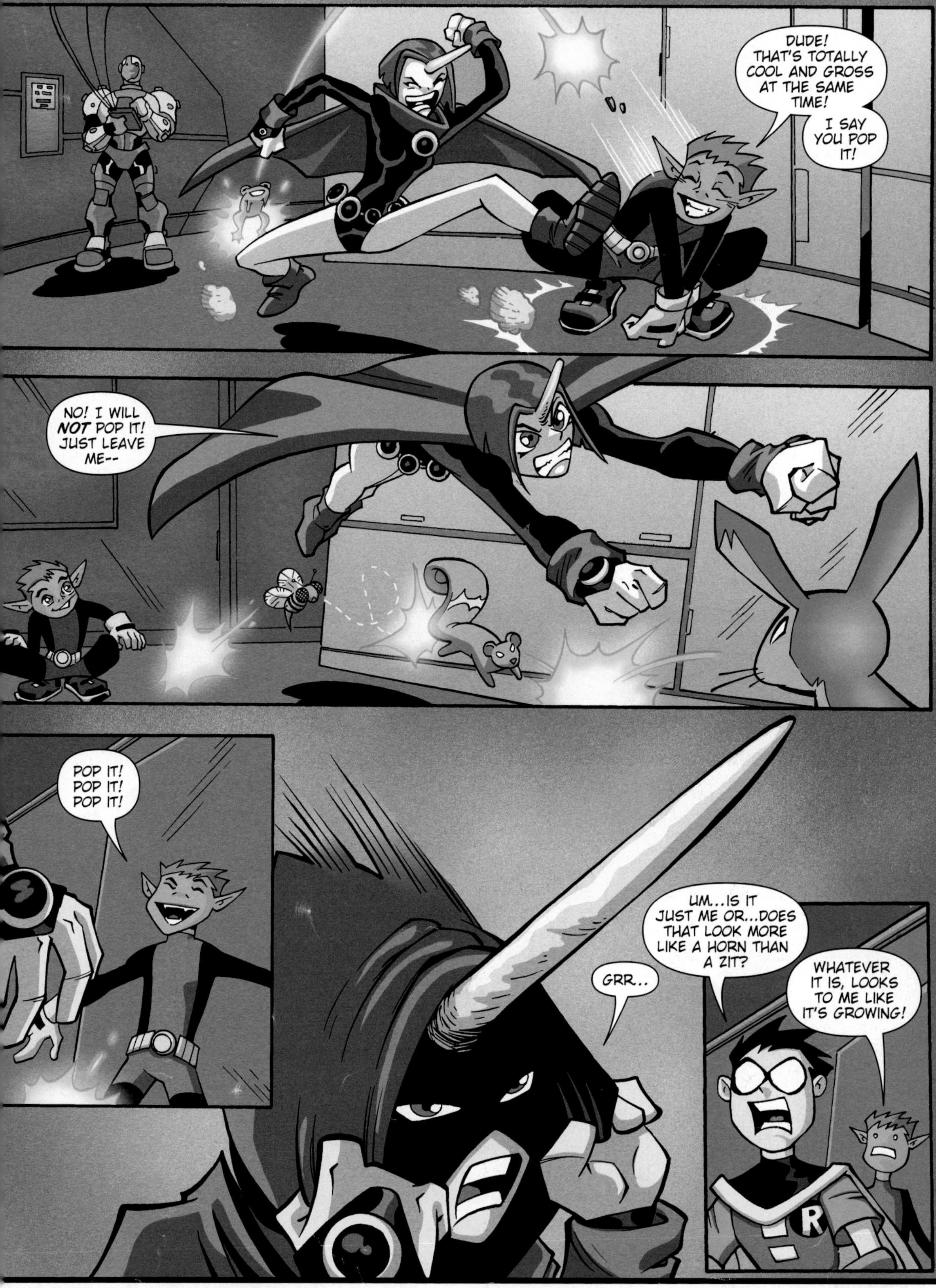
DUDE! THAT'S TOTALLY COOL AND GROSS AT THE SAME TIME!
I SAY YOU POP IT!
NO! I WILL NOT POP IT! JUST LEAVE ME--
POP IT! POP IT! POP IT!
GRR..
UM...IS IT JUST ME OR...DOES THAT LOOK MORE LIKE A HORN THAN A ZIT?
WHATEVER IT IS, LOOKS TO ME LIKE IT'S GROWING!

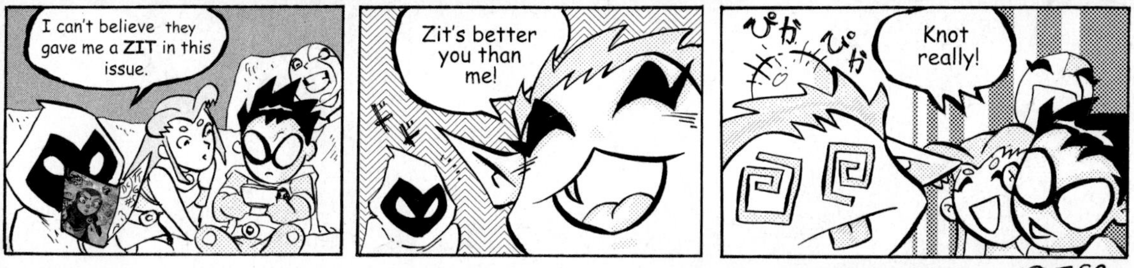
I can't believe they gave me a ZIT in this issue.
Zit's better you than me!
ぴか ぴか
Knot really!

©TS3

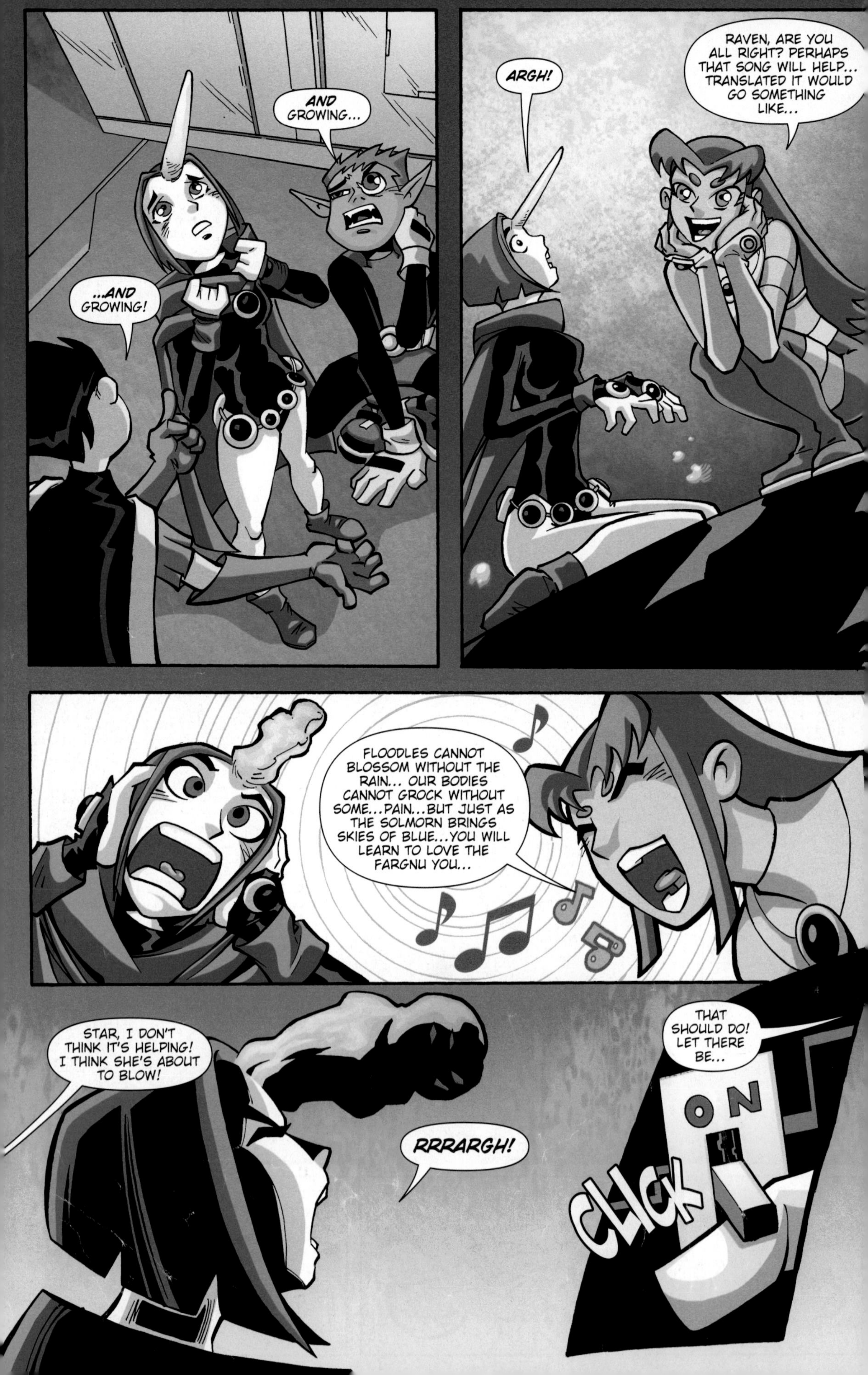
AND GROWING...
...AND GROWING!
ARGH!
RAVEN, ARE YOU ALL RIGHT? PERHAPS THAT SONG WILL HELP... TRANSLATED IT WOULD GO SOMETHING LIKE...
FLOODLES CANNOT BLOSSOM WITHOUT THE RAIN... OUR BODIES CANNOT GROCK WITHOUT SOME...PAIN...BUT JUST AS THE SOLMORN BRINGS SKIES OF BLUE...YOU WILL LEARN TO LOVE THE FARGNU YOU...
STAR, I DON'T THINK IT'S HELPING! I THINK SHE'S ABOUT TO BLOW!
RRRARGH!
THAT SHOULD DO! LET THERE BE...
ON
CLICK

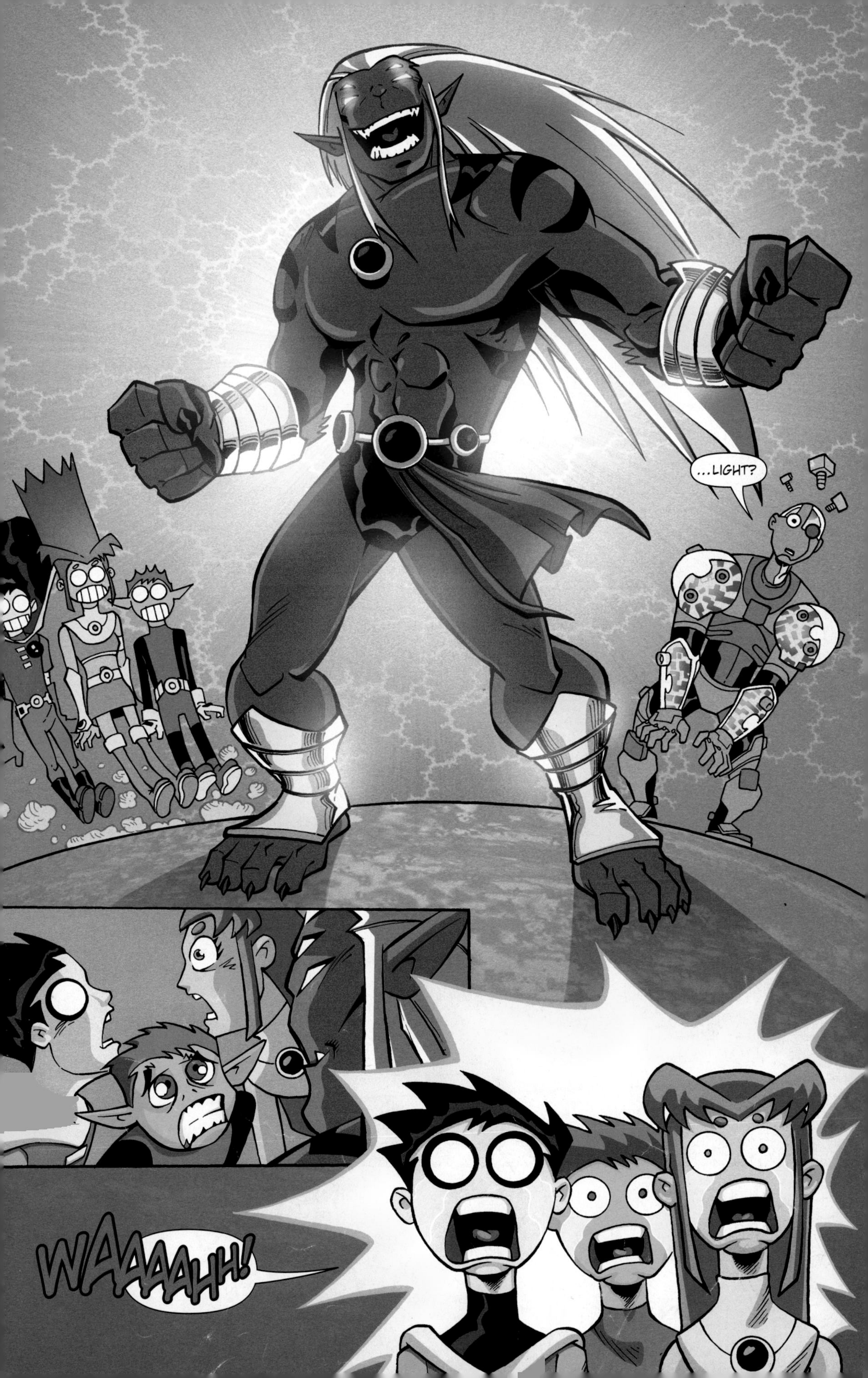
...LIGHT?
WAAAAHH!

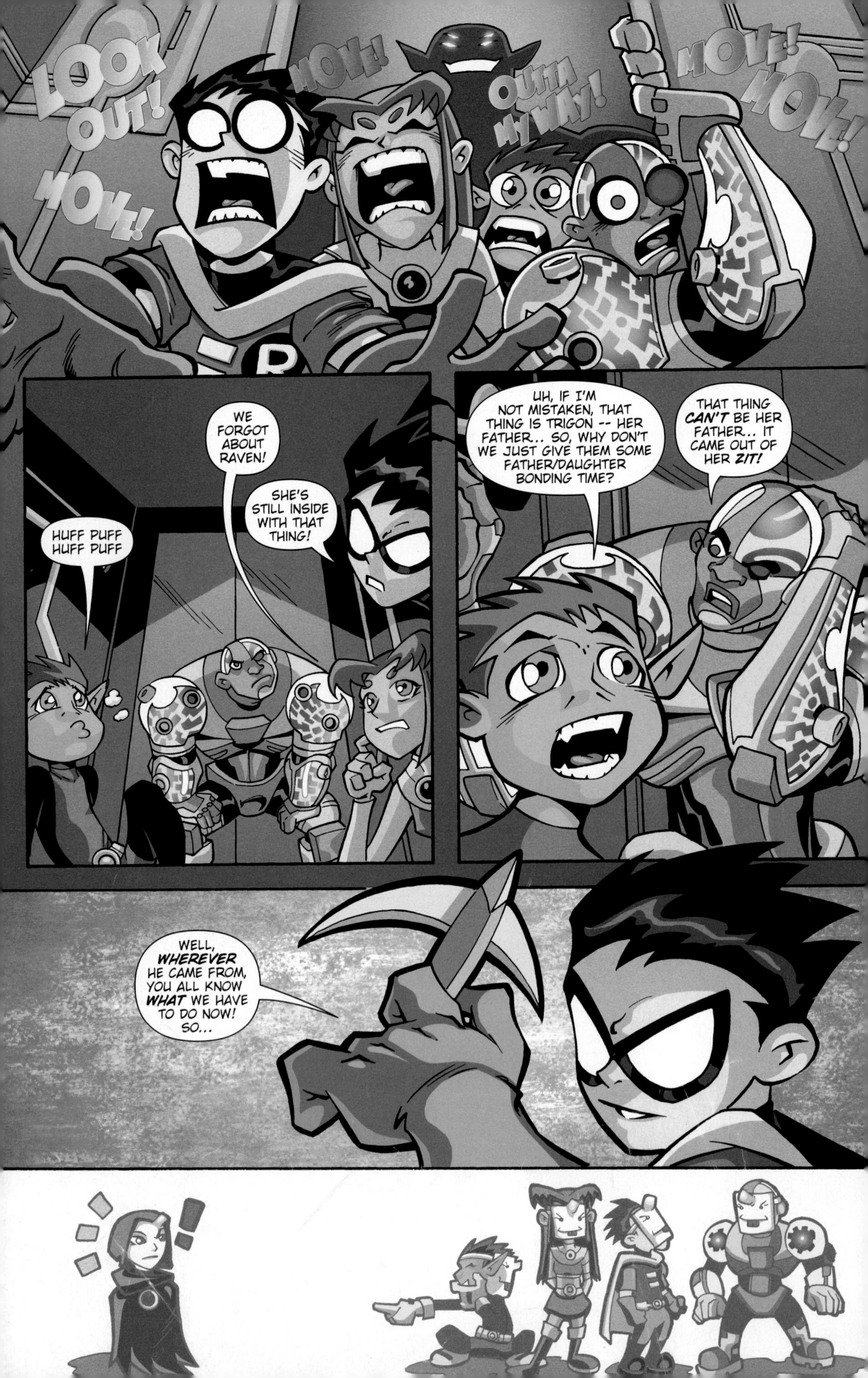
LOOK OUT!
MOVE!
MOVE!
OUTTA MY WAY!
MOVE! MOVE!
HUFF PUFF HUFF PUFF
WE FORGOT ABOUT RAVEN!
SHE'S STILL INSIDE WITH THAT THING!
UH, IF I'M NOT MISTAKEN, THAT THING IS TRIGON -- HER FATHER... SO, WHY DON'T WE JUST GIVE THEM SOME FATHER/DAUGHTER BONDING TIME?
THAT THING CAN'T BE HER FATHER... IT CAME OUT OF HER ZIT!
WELL, WHEREVER HE CAME FROM, YOU ALL KNOW WHAT WE HAVE TO DO NOW! SO...

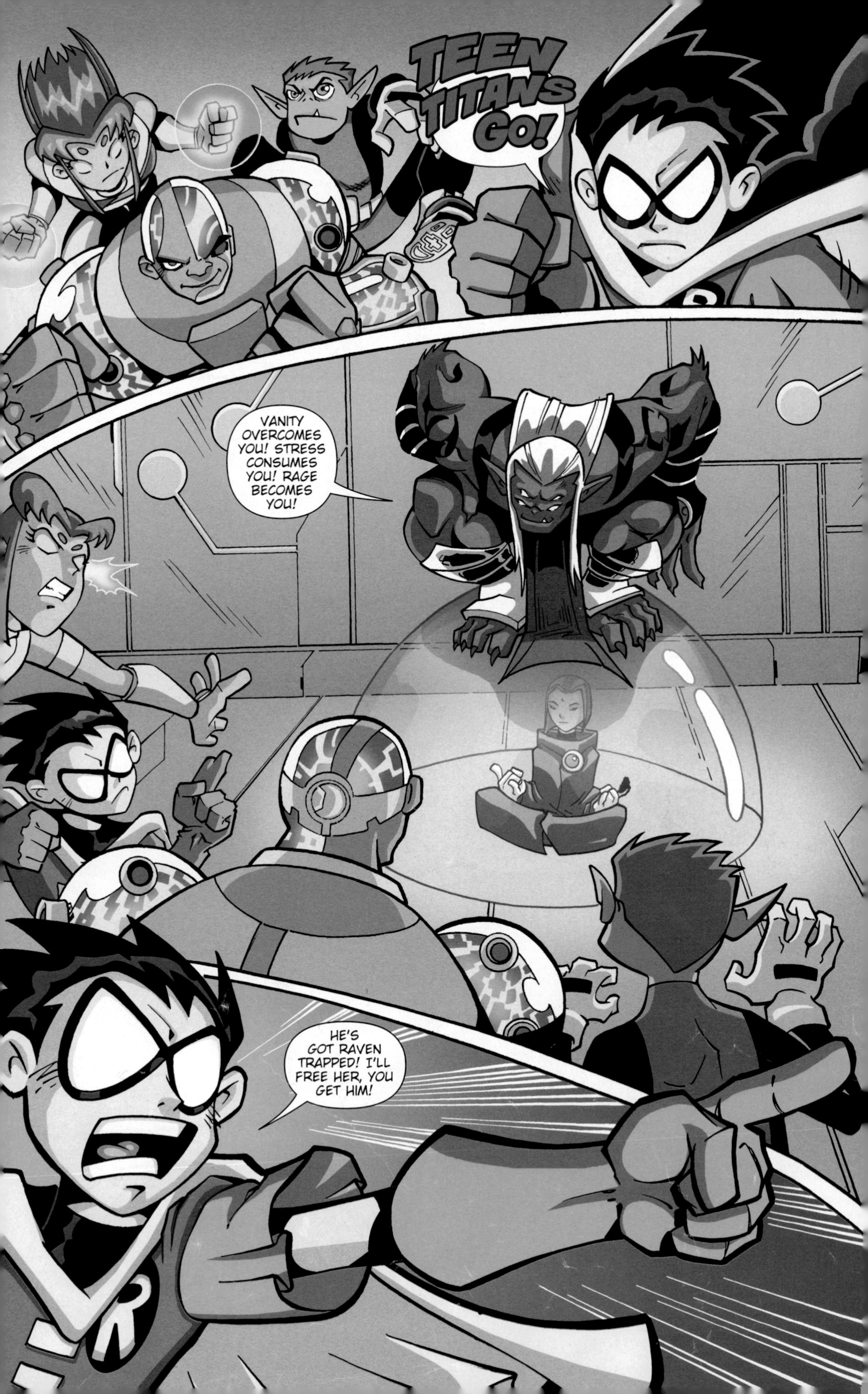
TEEN TITANS GO!
VANITY OVERCOMES YOU! STRESS CONSUMES YOU! RAGE BECOMES YOU!
HE'S GOT RAVEN TRAPPED! I'LL FREE HER, YOU GET HIM!

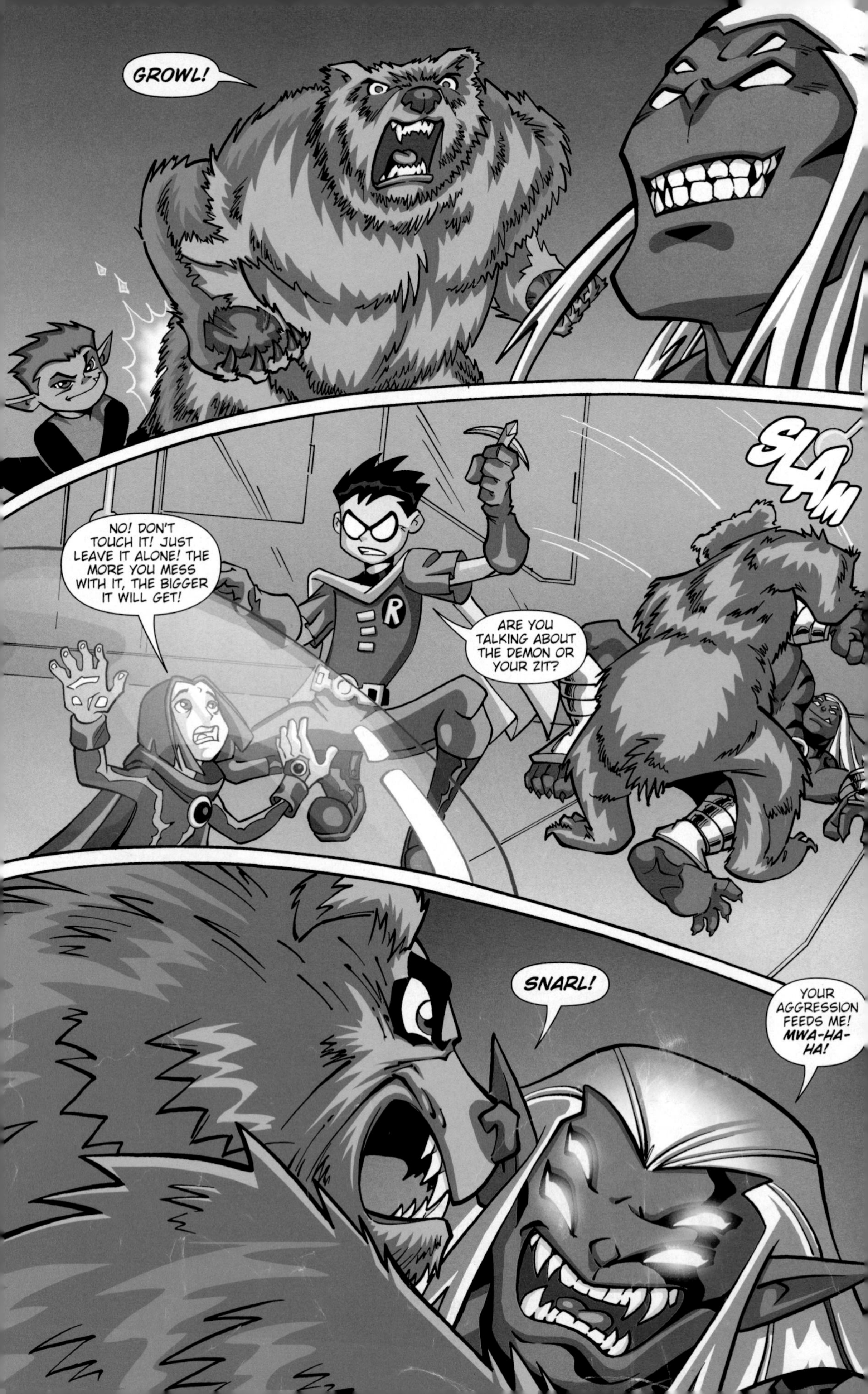
GROWL!
SLAM
NO! DON'T TOUCH IT! JUST LEAVE IT ALONE! THE MORE YOU MESS WITH IT, THE BIGGER IT WILL GET!
ARE YOU TALKING ABOUT THE DEMON OR YOUR ZIT?
SNARL!
YOUR AGGRESSION FEEDS ME! MWA-HA-HA!

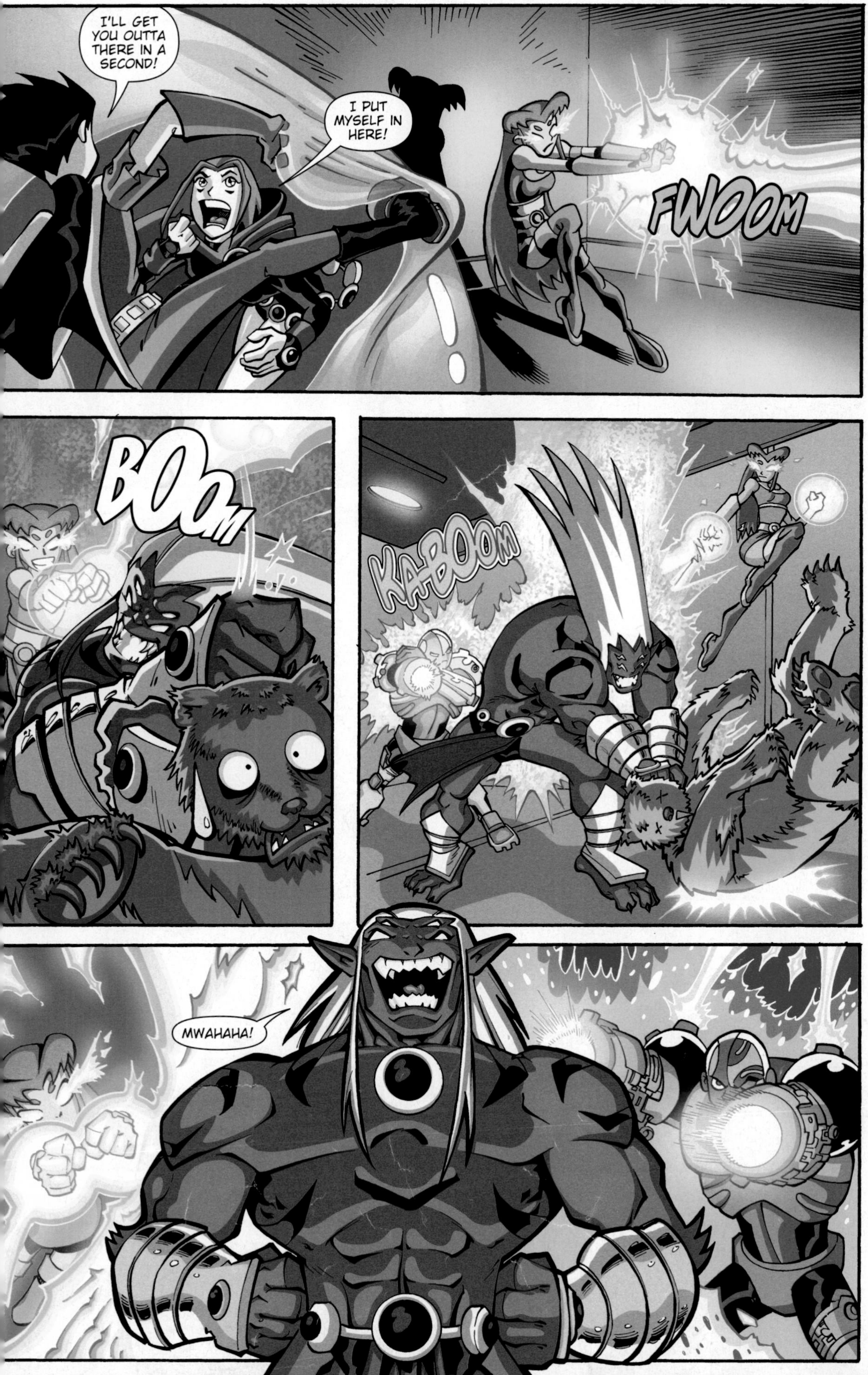
I'LL GET YOU OUTTA THERE IN A SECOND!
I PUT MYSELF IN HERE!
FWOOM
BOOM
KA-BOOM
MWAHAHA!

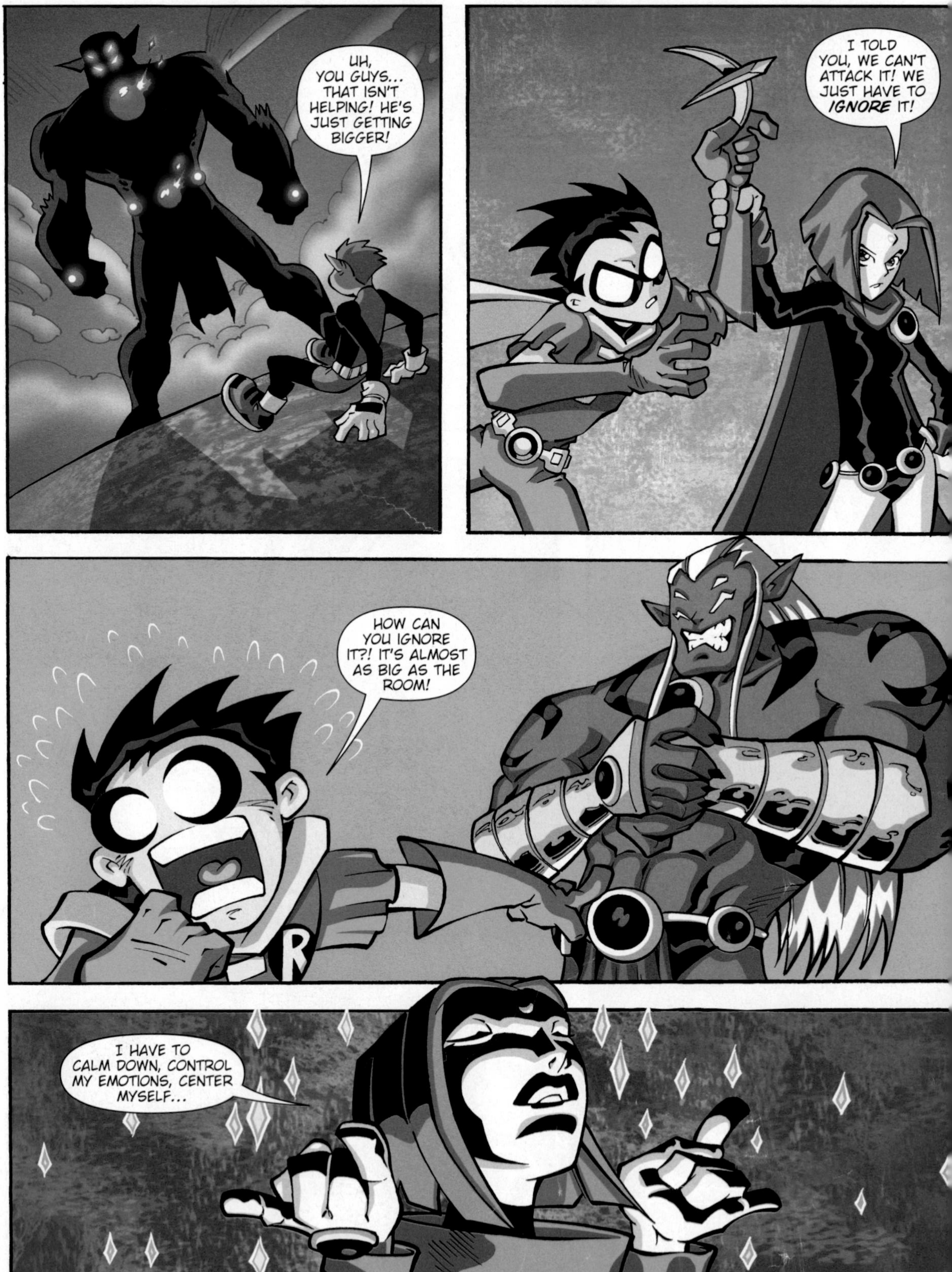
UH, YOU GUYS... THAT ISN'T HELPING! HE'S JUST GETTING BIGGER!
I TOLD YOU, WE CAN'T ATTACK IT! WE JUST HAVE TO IGNORE IT!
HOW CAN YOU IGNORE IT?! IT'S ALMOST AS BIG AS THE ROOM!
I HAVE TO CALM DOWN, CONTROL MY EMOTIONS, CENTER MYSELF...
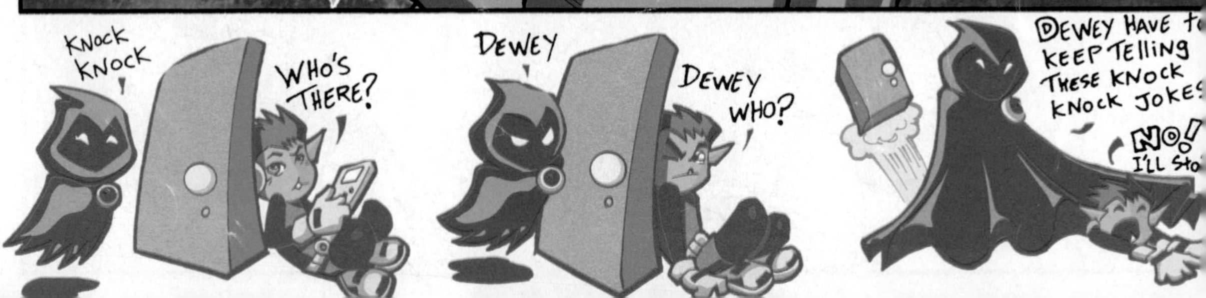
KNOCK KNOCK
WHO'S THERE?
DEWEY
DEWEY WHO?
DEWEY HAVE
KEEP TELLING
THESE KNOCK
KNOCK JOKE
NO!
I'LL

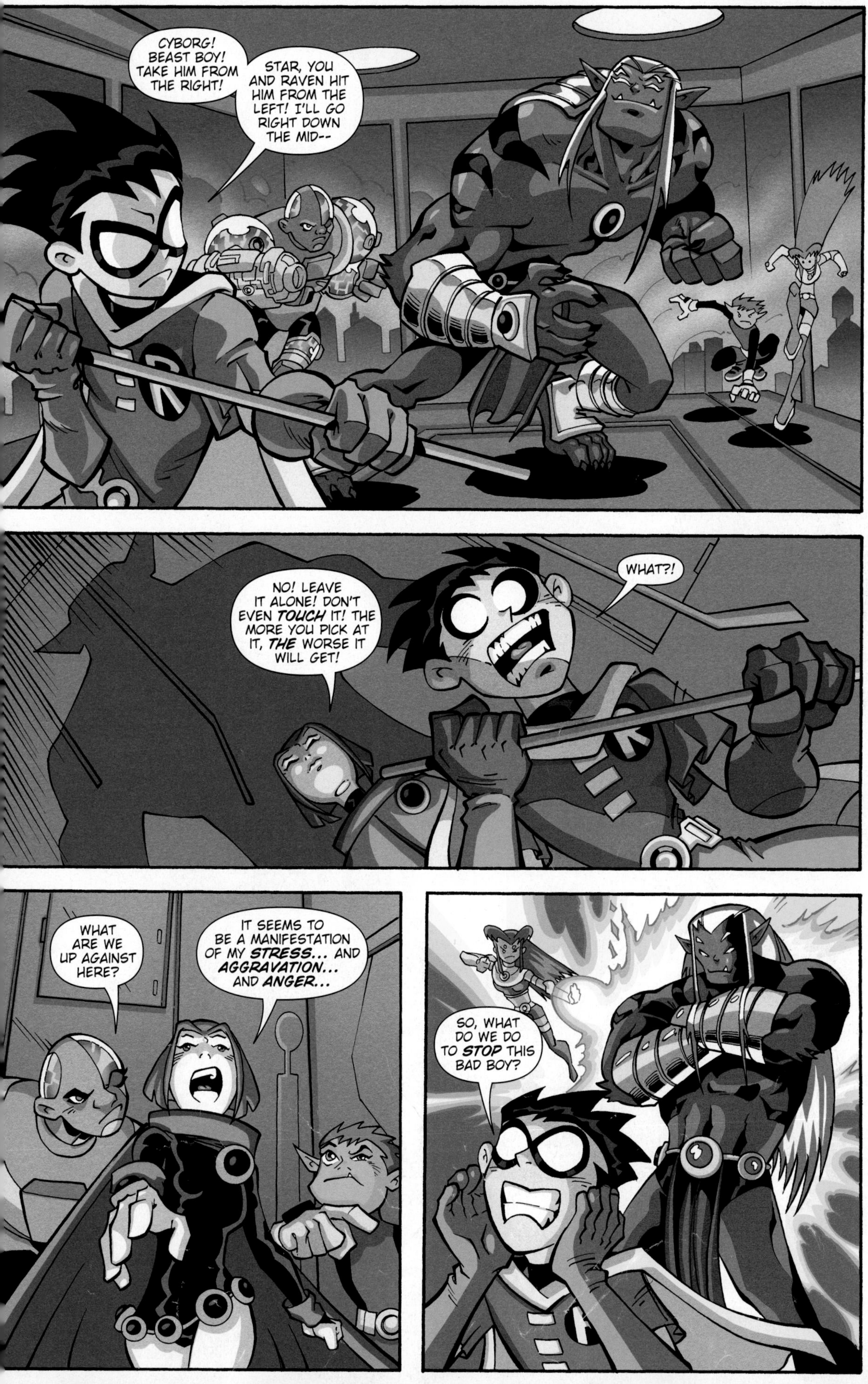
CYBORG! BEAST BOY! TAKE HIM FROM THE RIGHT!
STAR, YOU AND RAVEN HIT HIM FROM THE LEFT! I'LL GO RIGHT DOWN THE MID--
NO! LEAVE IT ALONE! DON'T EVEN *TOUCH* IT! THE MORE YOU PICK AT IT, *THE* WORSE IT WILL GET!
WHAT?!
WHAT ARE WE UP AGAINST HERE?
IT SEEMS TO BE A MANIFESTATION OF MY *STRESS*... AND *AGGRAVATION*... AND *ANGER*...
SO, WHAT DO WE DO TO *STOP* THIS BAD BOY?

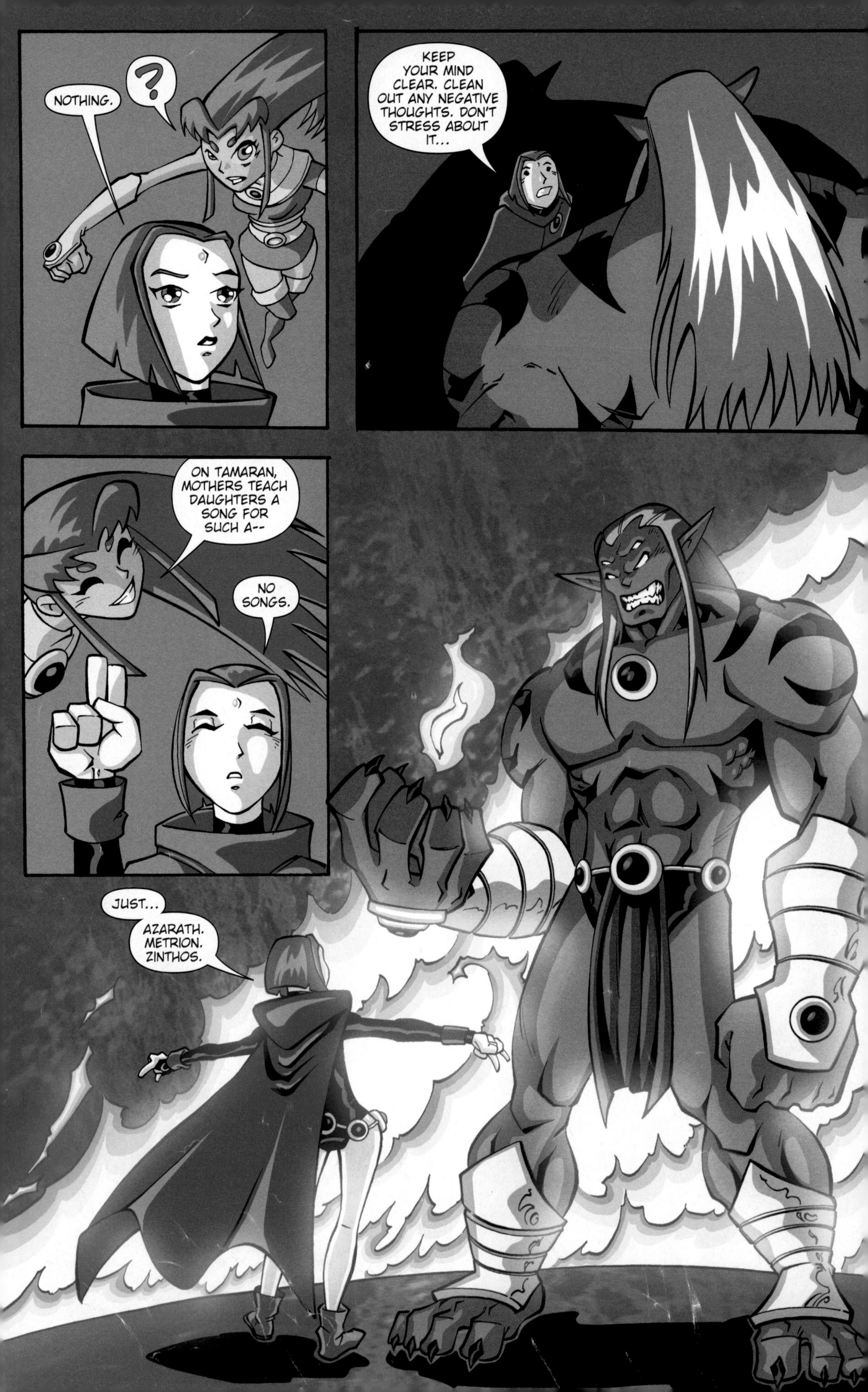
NOTHING.
?
KEEP YOUR MIND CLEAR. CLEAN OUT ANY NEGATIVE THOUGHTS. DON'T STRESS ABOUT IT...
ON TAMARAN, MOTHERS TEACH DAUGHTERS A SONG FOR SUCH A--
NO SONGS.
JUST...
AZARATH. METRION. ZINTHOS.

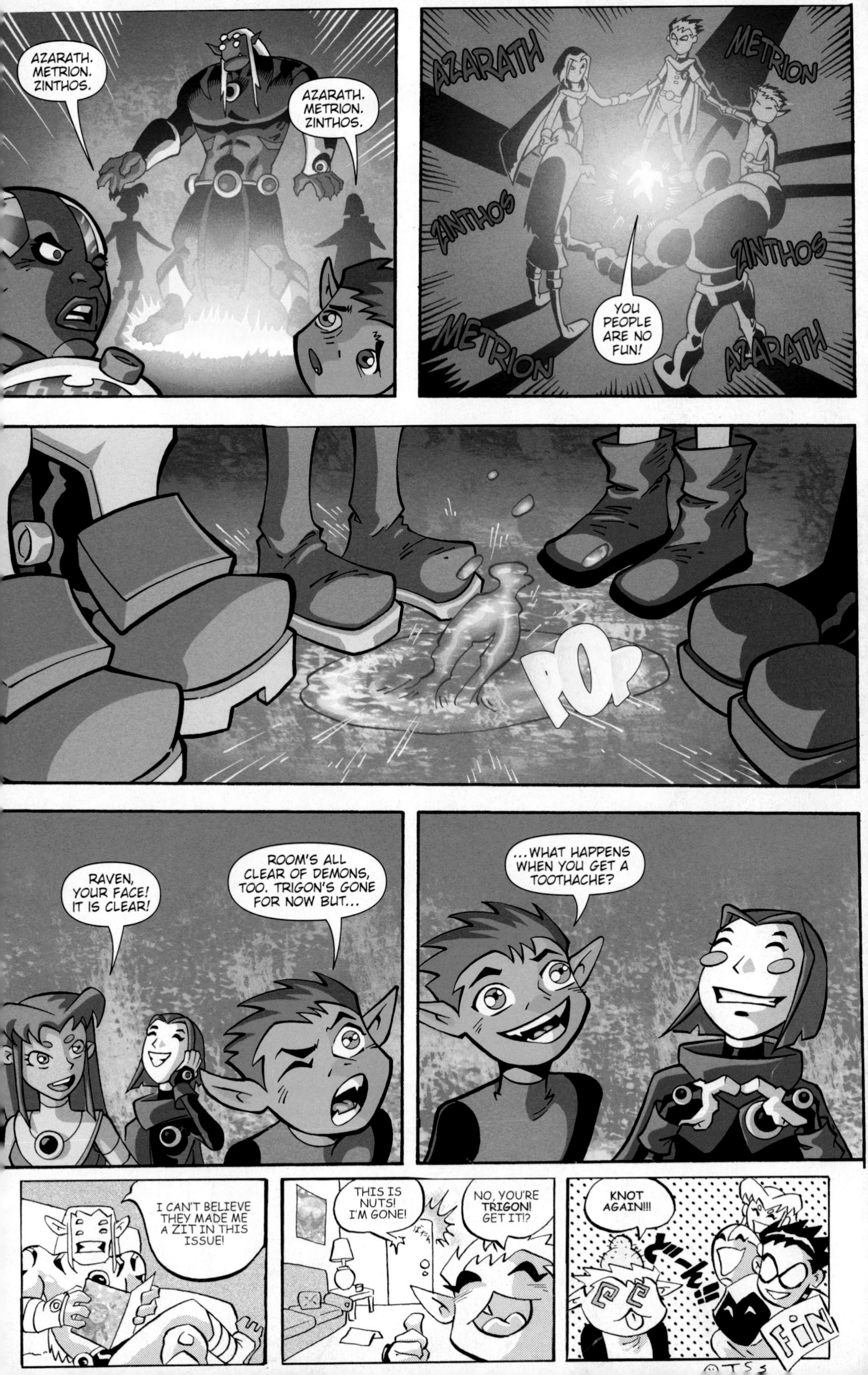

AZARATH. METRION. ZINTHOS.
AZARATH. METRION. ZINTHOS.
AZARATH
METRION
ZINTHOS
ZINTHOS
YOU PEOPLE ARE NO FUN!
METRION
AZARATH
POP
RAVEN, YOUR FACE! IT IS CLEAR!
ROOM'S ALL CLEAR OF DEMONS, TOO. TRIGON'S GONE FOR NOW BUT...
...WHAT HAPPENS WHEN YOU GET A TOOTHACHE?
I CAN'T BELIEVE THEY MADE ME A ZIT IN THIS ISSUE!
THIS IS NUTS! I'M GONE!
NO, YOU'RE TRIGON! GET IT!?
KNOT AGAIN!!!
FIN

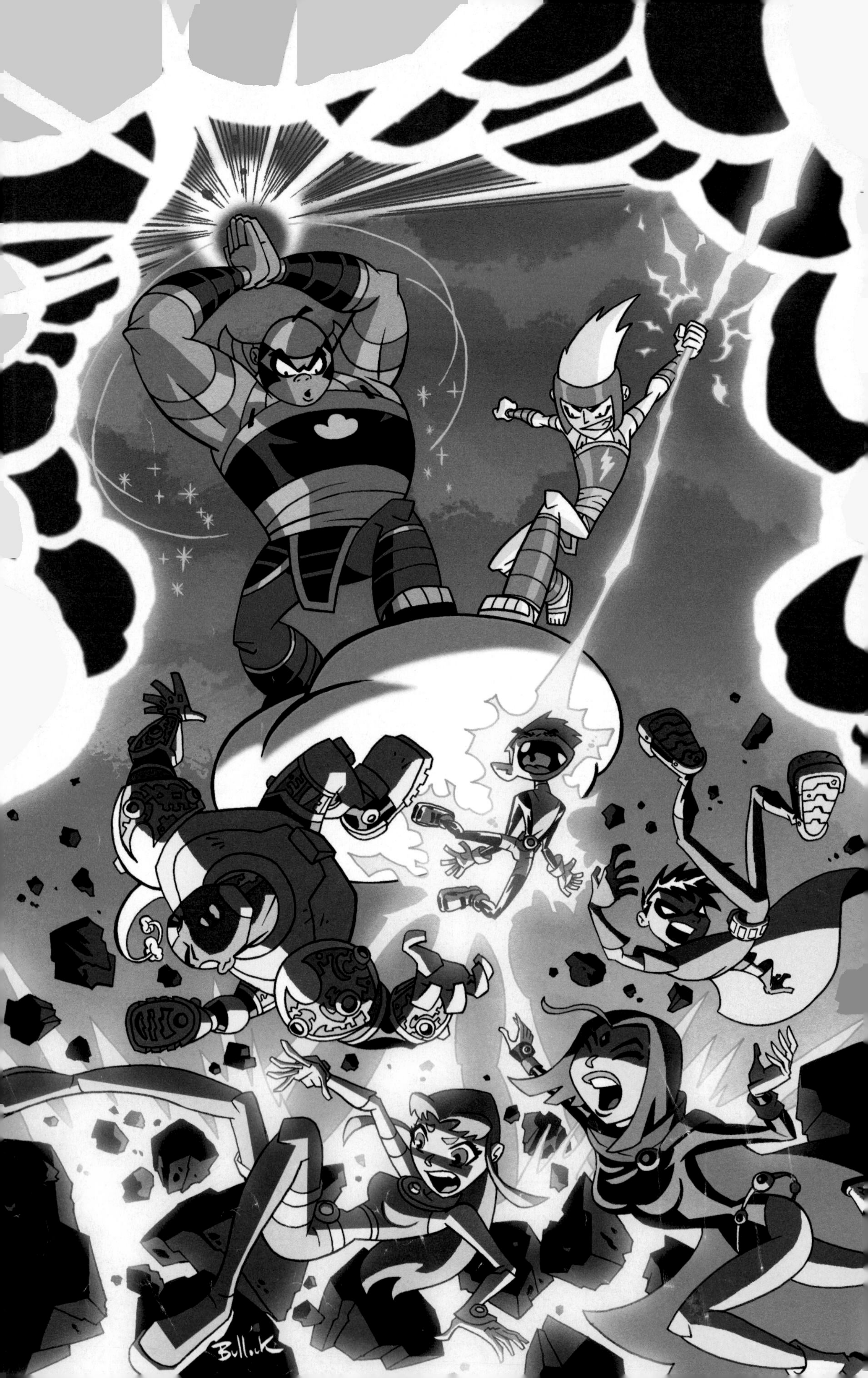
Bullock

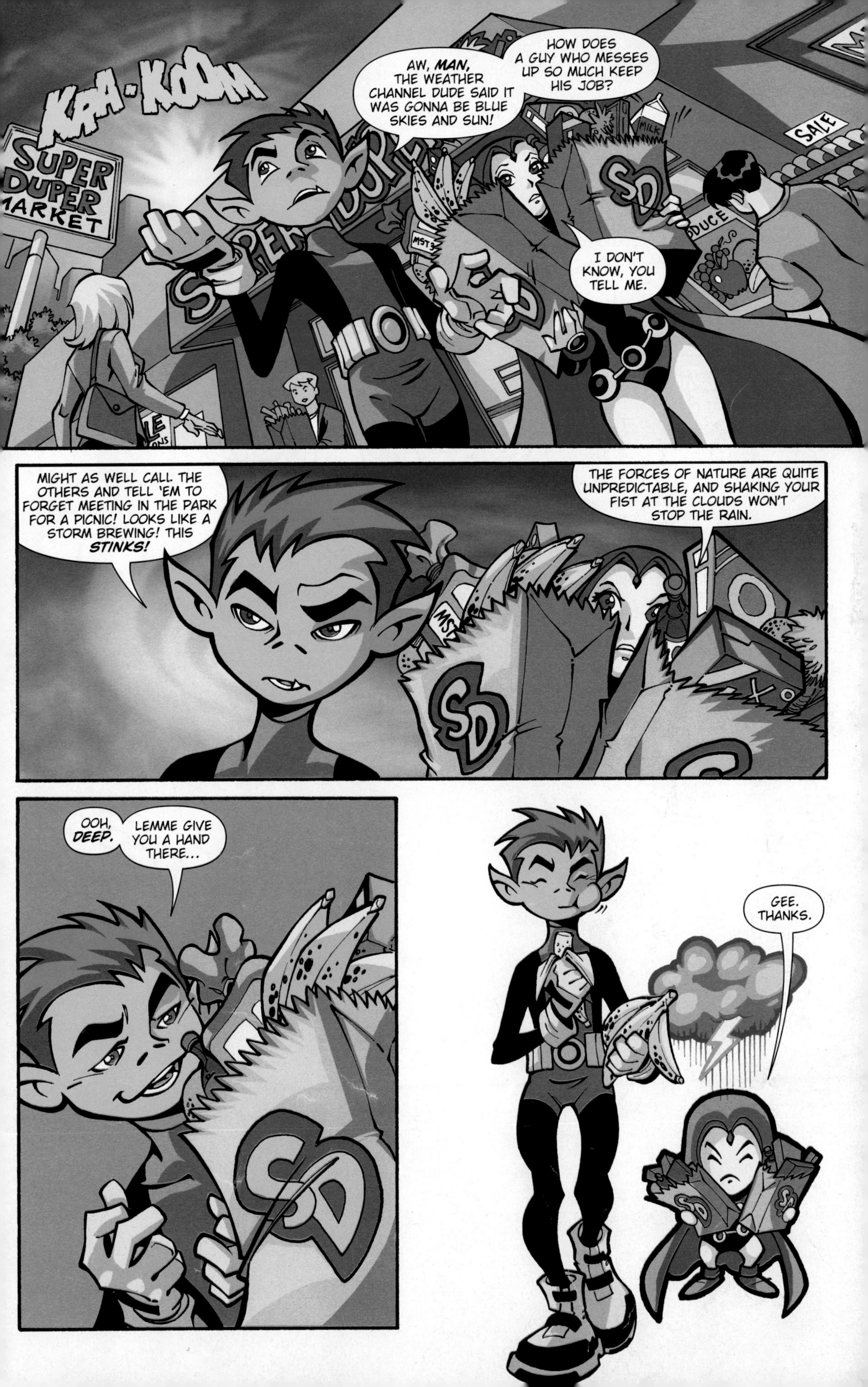
KRA-KOOM
SUPER DUPER MARKET
AW, MAN, THE WEATHER CHANNEL DUDE SAID IT WAS GONNA BE BLUE SKIES AND SUN!
HOW DOES A GUY WHO MESSES UP SO MUCH KEEP HIS JOB?
I DON'T KNOW, YOU TELL ME.
SALE
MILK
MIGHT AS WELL CALL THE OTHERS AND TELL 'EM TO FORGET MEETING IN THE PARK FOR A PICNIC! LOOKS LIKE A STORM BREWING! THIS STINKS!
THE FORCES OF NATURE ARE QUITE UNPREDICTABLE, AND SHAKING YOUR FIST AT THE CLOUDS WON'T STOP THE RAIN.
OOH, DEEP.
LEMME GIVE YOU A HAND THERE...
GEE. THANKS.

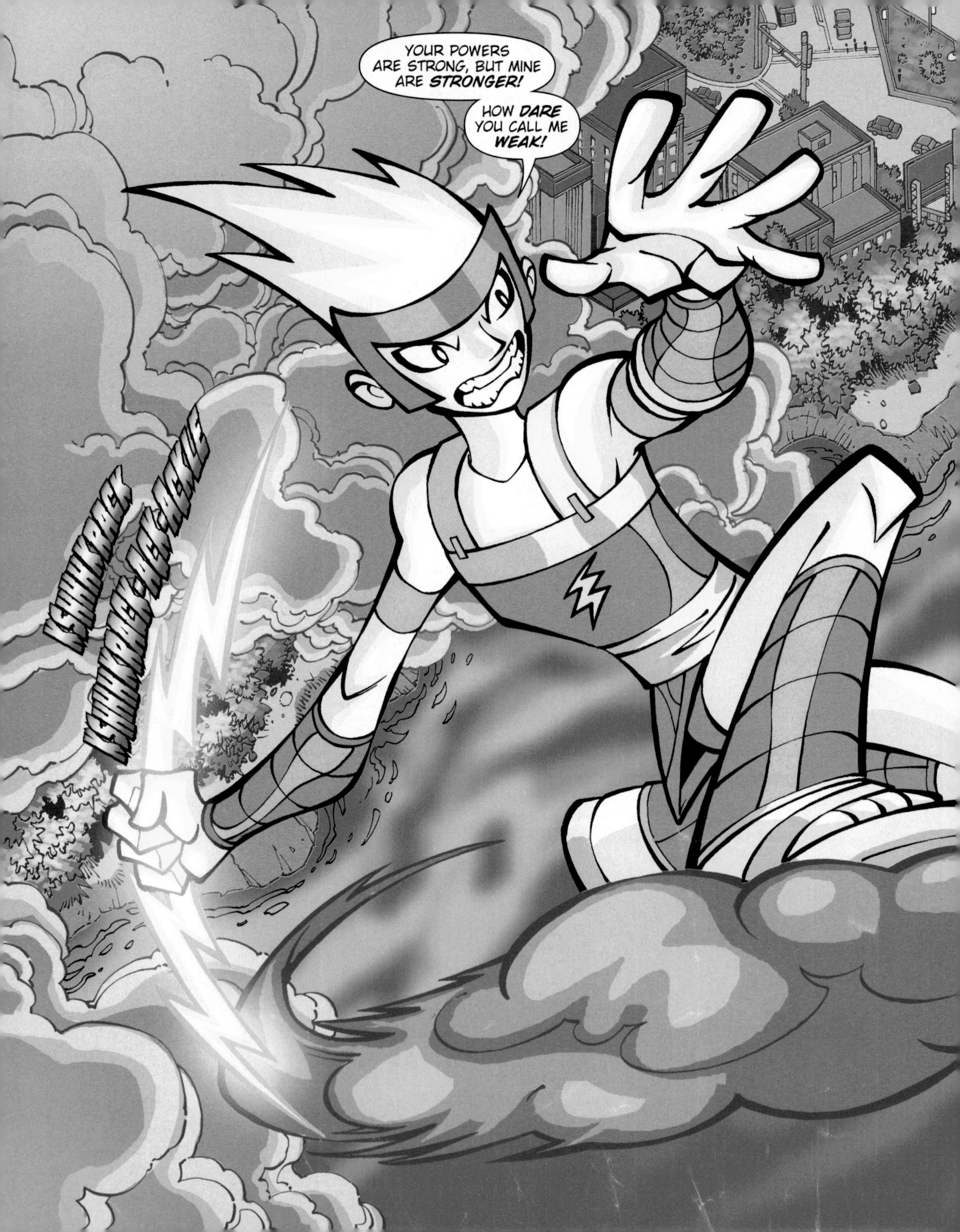
YOUR POWERS ARE STRONG, BUT MINE ARE STRONGER!
HOW DARE YOU CALL ME WEAK!
KSHHHRACK

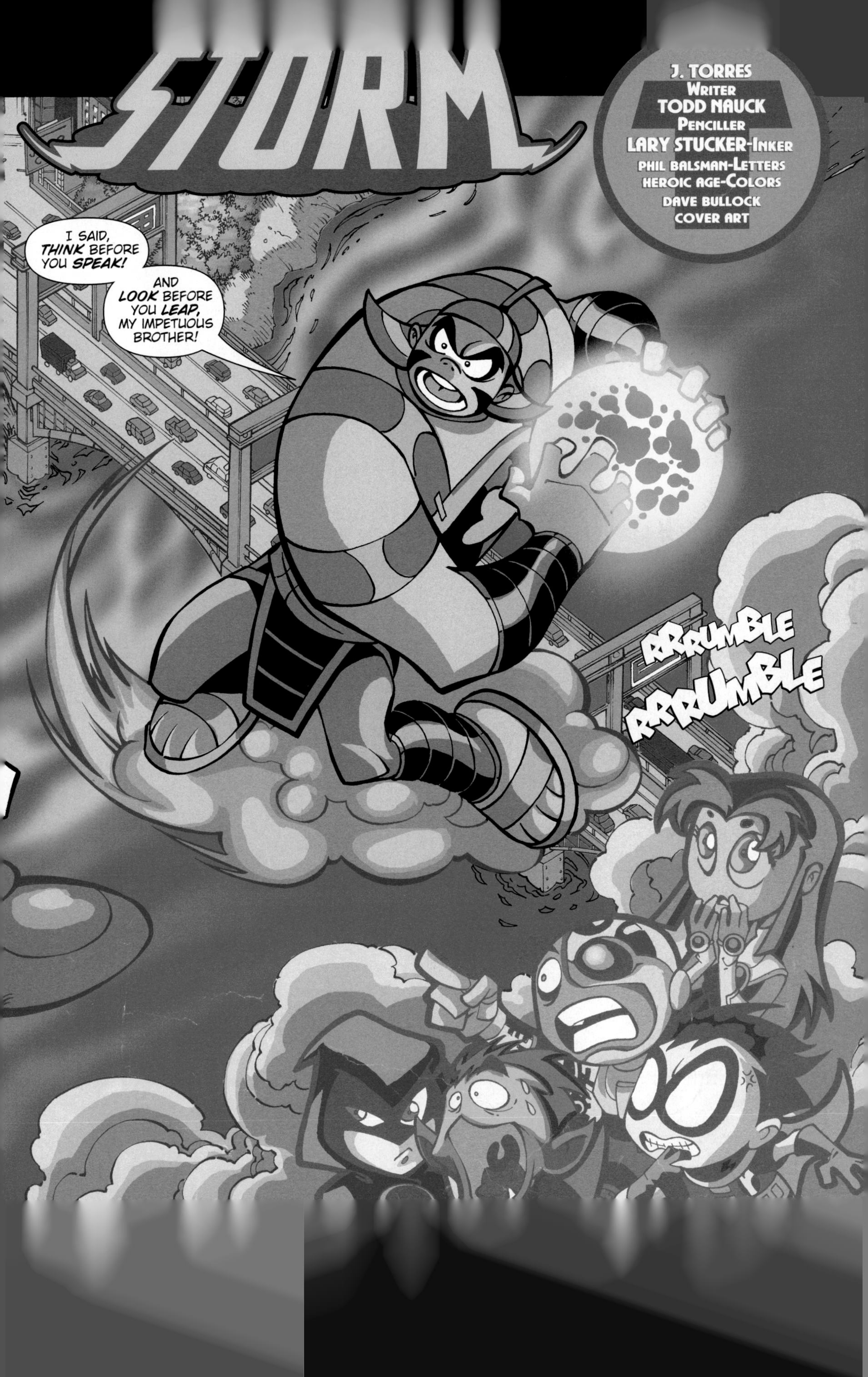
STORM
J. TORRES
Writer
TODD NAUCK
Penciller
LARY STUCKER-Inker
PHIL BALSMAN-Letters
HEROIC AGE-Colors
DAVE BULLOCK
COVER ART
I SAID, THINK BEFORE YOU SPEAK!
AND LOOK BEFORE YOU LEAP, MY IMPETUOUS BROTHER!
RRRUMBLE
RRRUMBLE

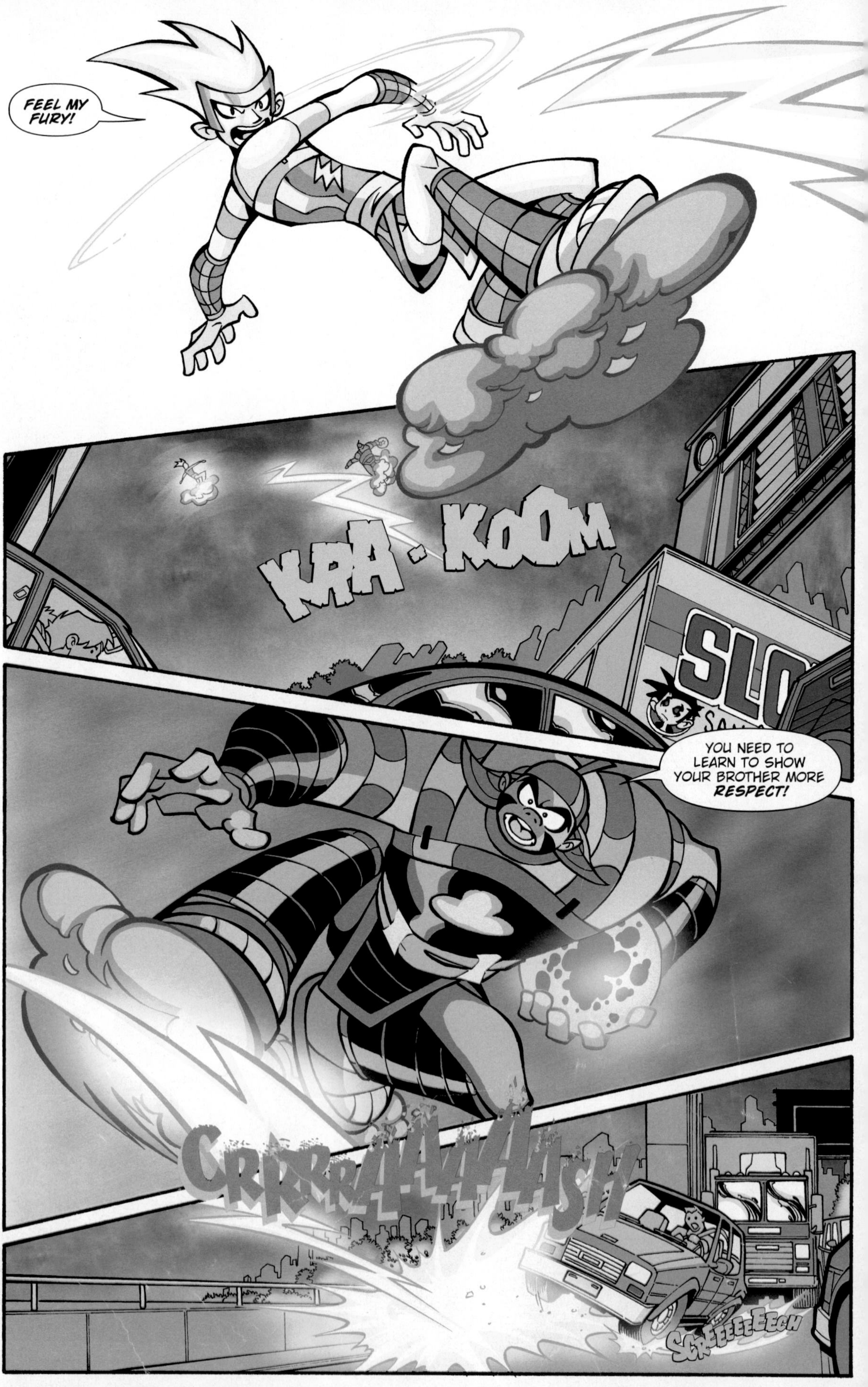
FEEL MY FURY!
KRA-KOOM
YOU NEED TO LEARN TO SHOW YOUR BROTHER MORE RESPECT!
CRRRRAAAAASH
SCREEEEEECH

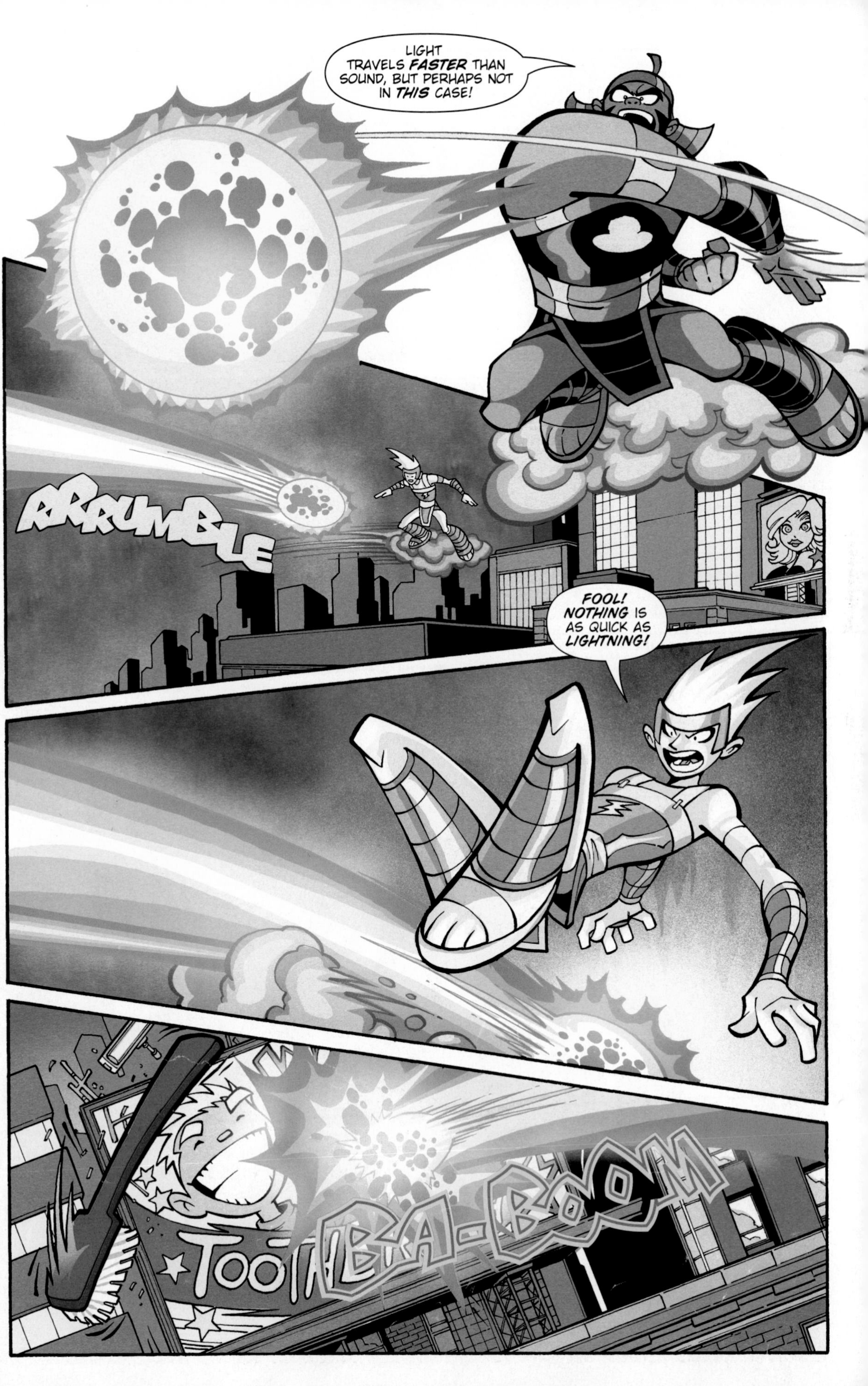
LIGHT TRAVELS FASTER THAN SOUND, BUT PERHAPS NOT IN THIS CASE!
RRRUMBLE
FOOL! NOTHING IS AS QUICK AS LIGHTNING!
TOOTH
BA-BOOM

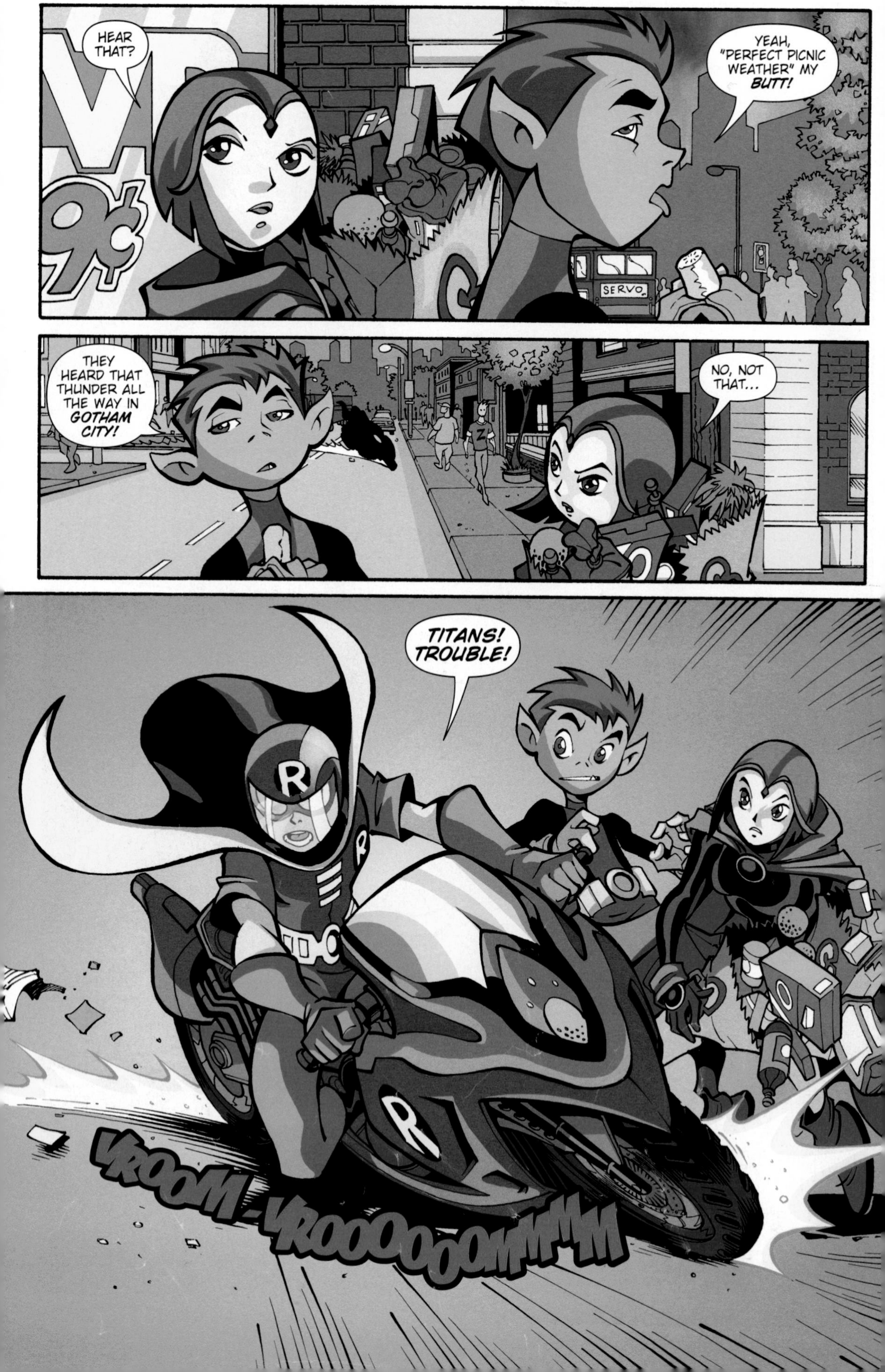
HEAR THAT?
YEAH, "PERFECT PICNIC WEATHER" MY BUTT!
SERVO
THEY HEARD THAT THUNDER ALL THE WAY IN GOTHAM CITY!
NO, NOT THAT...
TITANS! TROUBLE!
VROOM-VROOOOOOOMMMM

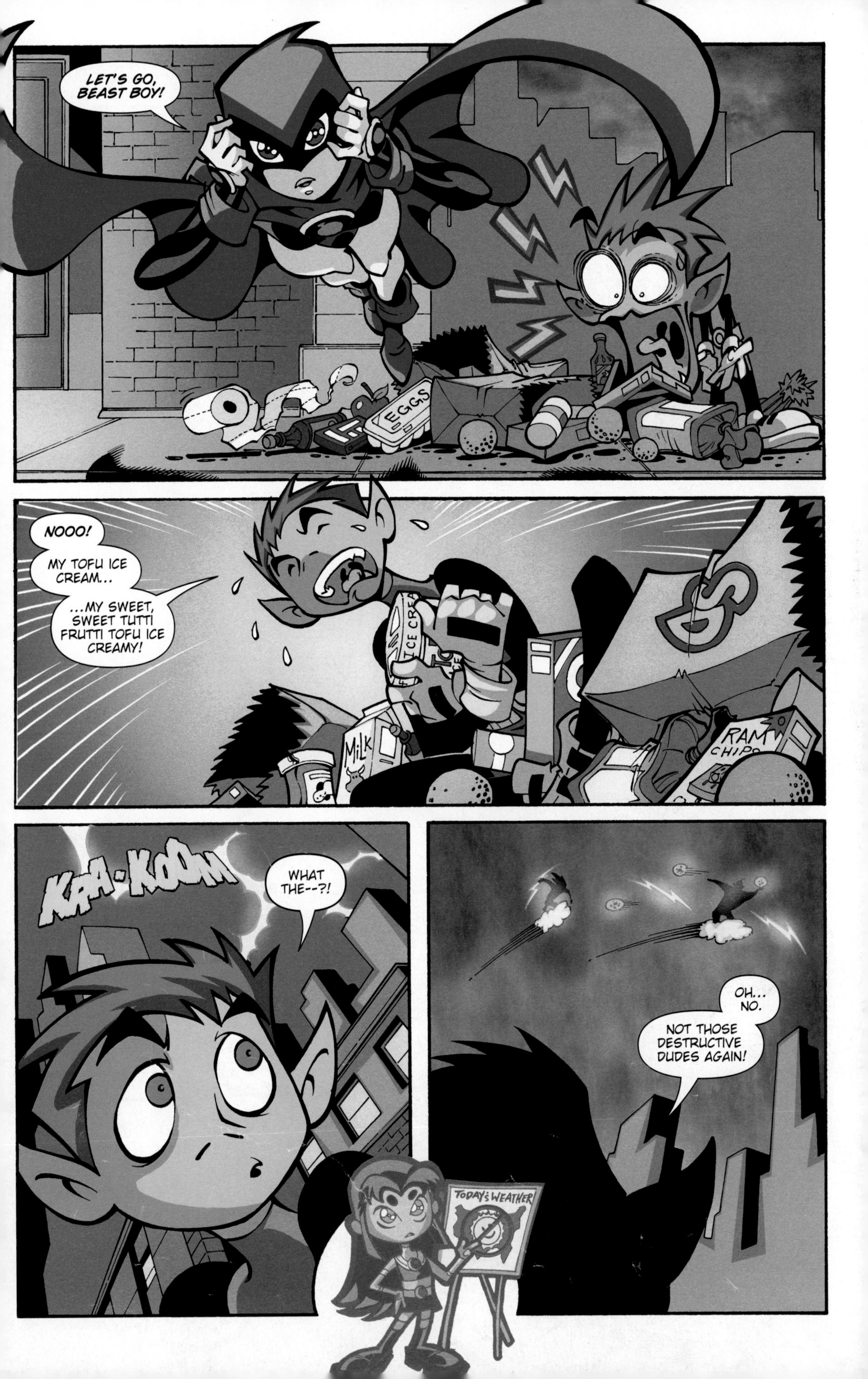
LET'S GO, BEAST BOY!
EGGS
NOOO!
MY TOFU ICE CREAM...
...MY SWEET, SWEET TUTTI FRUTTI TOFU ICE CREAMY!
ICE CREA
MILK
RAM CHIPS
KRA-KOOM
WHAT THE--?!
OH... NO.
NOT THOSE DESTRUCTIVE DUDES AGAIN!
TODAY'S WEATHER

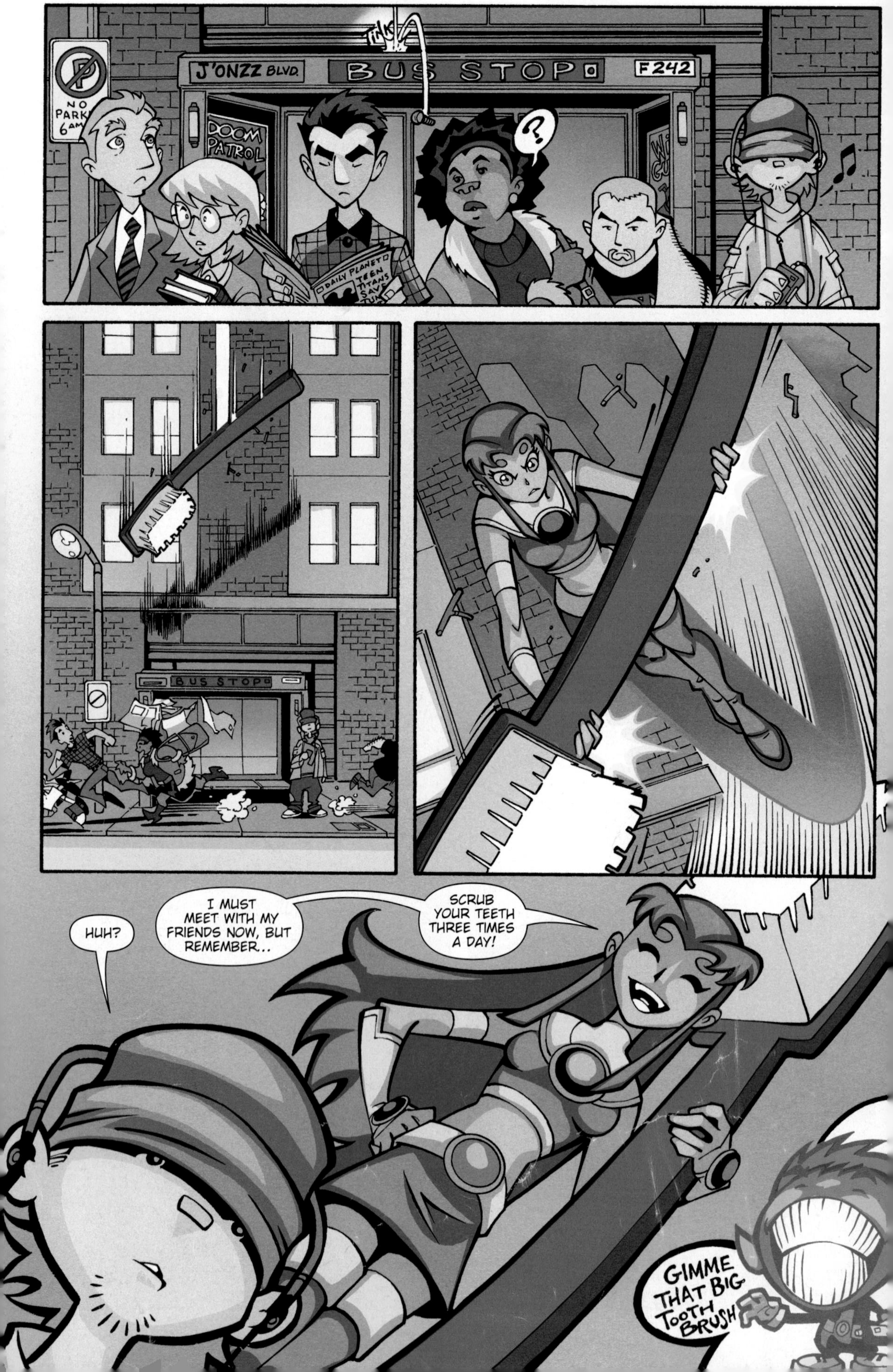
J'ONZZ BLVD.
BUS STOP
F242
NO PARK
6 AM
DOOM PATROL
?
DAILY PLANET
TEEN TITANS
BUS STOP
HUH?
I MUST MEET WITH MY FRIENDS NOW, BUT REMEMBER...
SCRUB YOUR TEETH THREE TIMES A DAY!
GIMME THAT BIG TOOTH BRUSH

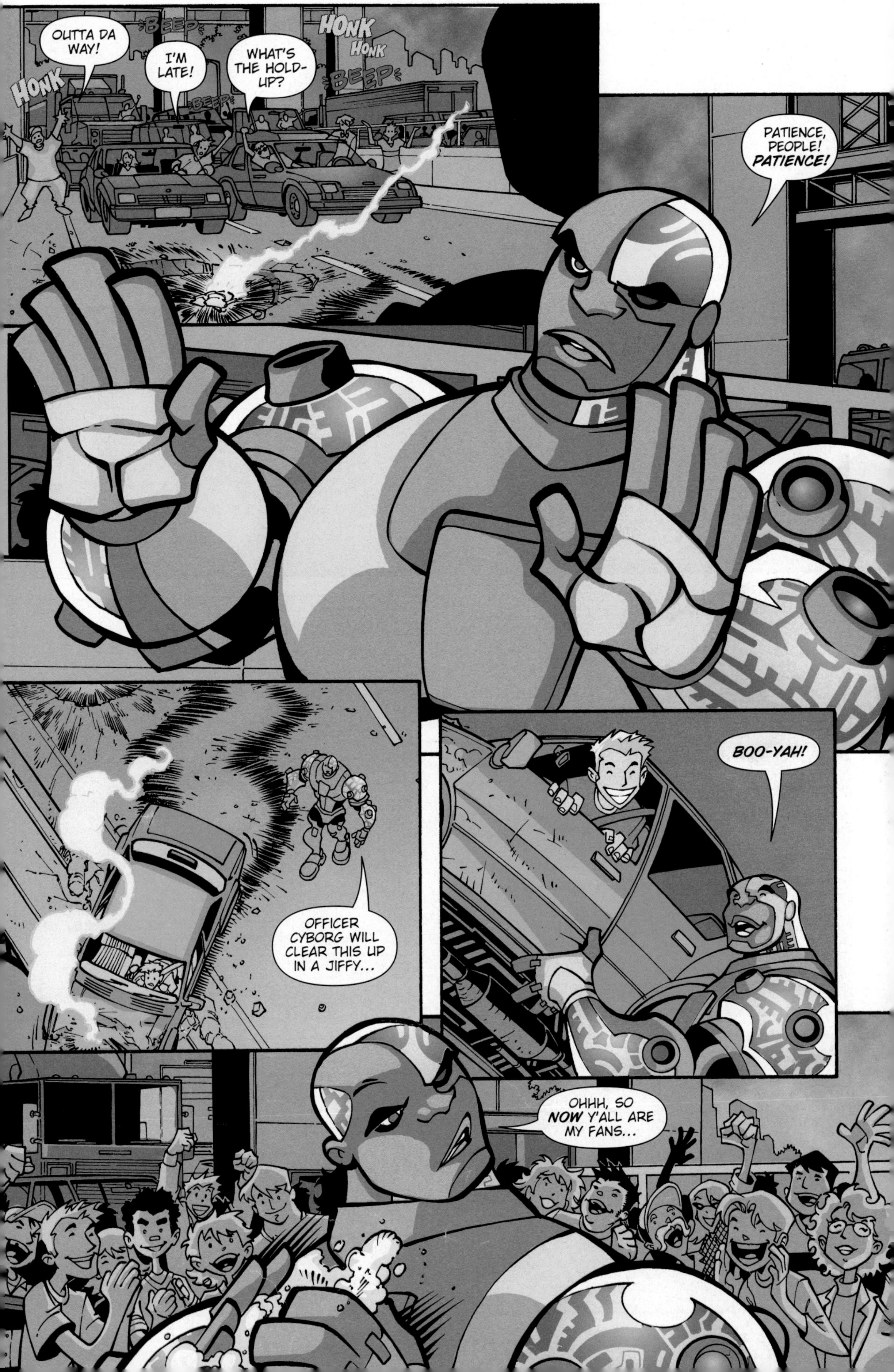
HONK
OUTTA DA WAY!
BEEP
I'M LATE!
BEEP
WHAT'S THE HOLD-UP?
HONK
HONK
BEEP
PATIENCE, PEOPLE! PATIENCE!
OFFICER CYBORG WILL CLEAR THIS UP IN A JIFFY...
BOO-YAH!
OHHH, SO NOW Y'ALL ARE MY FANS...

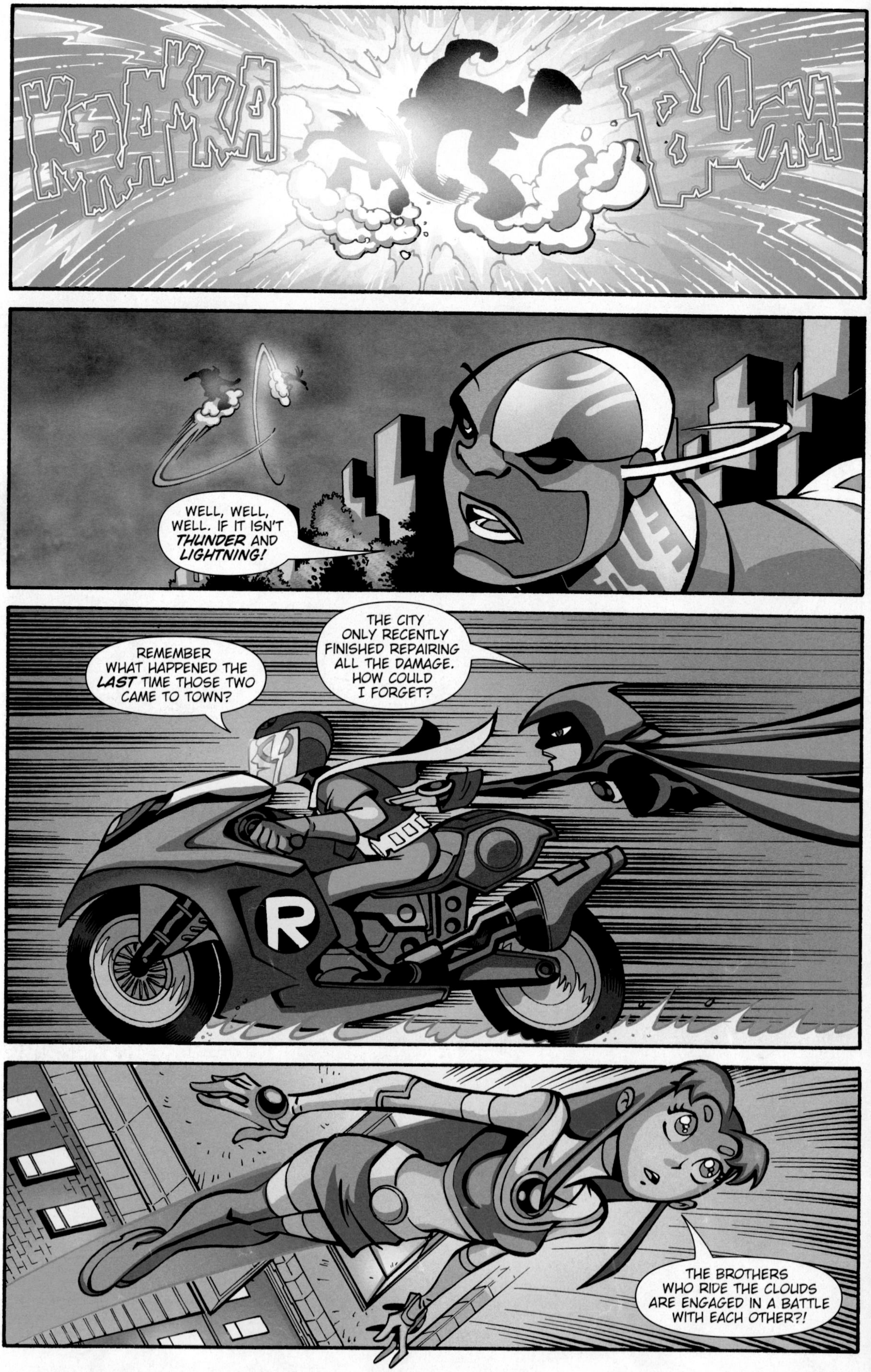
KRAKKA
BOOM
WELL, WELL, WELL. IF IT ISN'T *THUNDER* AND *LIGHTNING!*
REMEMBER WHAT HAPPENED THE *LAST* TIME THOSE TWO CAME TO TOWN?
THE CITY ONLY RECENTLY FINISHED REPAIRING ALL THE DAMAGE. HOW COULD I FORGET?
R
THE BROTHERS WHO RIDE THE CLOUDS ARE ENGAGED IN A BATTLE WITH EACH OTHER?!

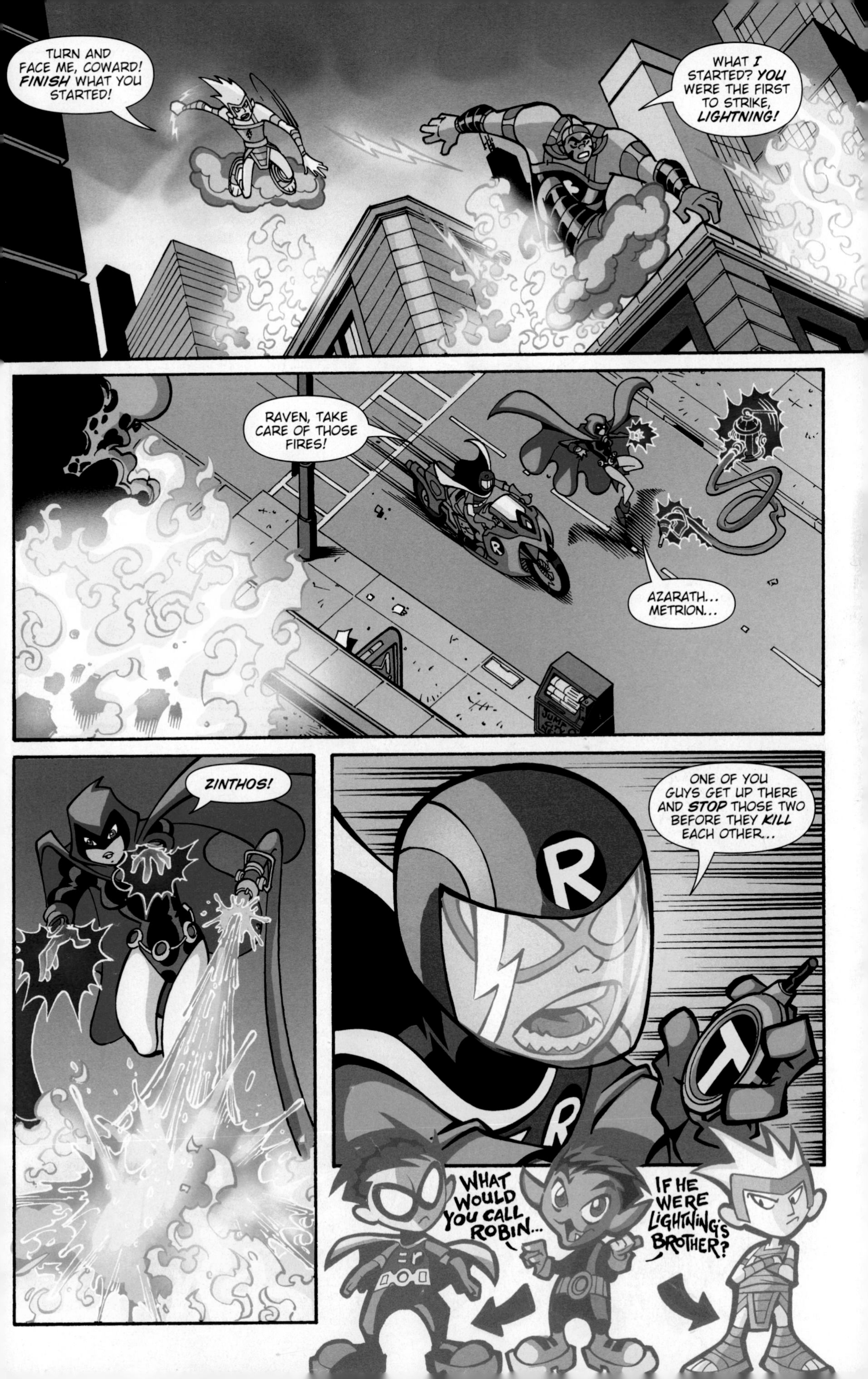
TURN AND FACE ME, COWARD! FINISH WHAT YOU STARTED!
WHAT I STARTED? YOU WERE THE FIRST TO STRIKE, LIGHTNING!
RAVEN, TAKE CARE OF THOSE FIRES!
AZARATH... METRION...
ZINTHOS!
ONE OF YOU GUYS GET UP THERE AND STOP THOSE TWO BEFORE THEY KILL EACH OTHER...
WHAT WOULD YOU CALL ROBIN...
IF HE WERE LIGHTNING'S BROTHER?

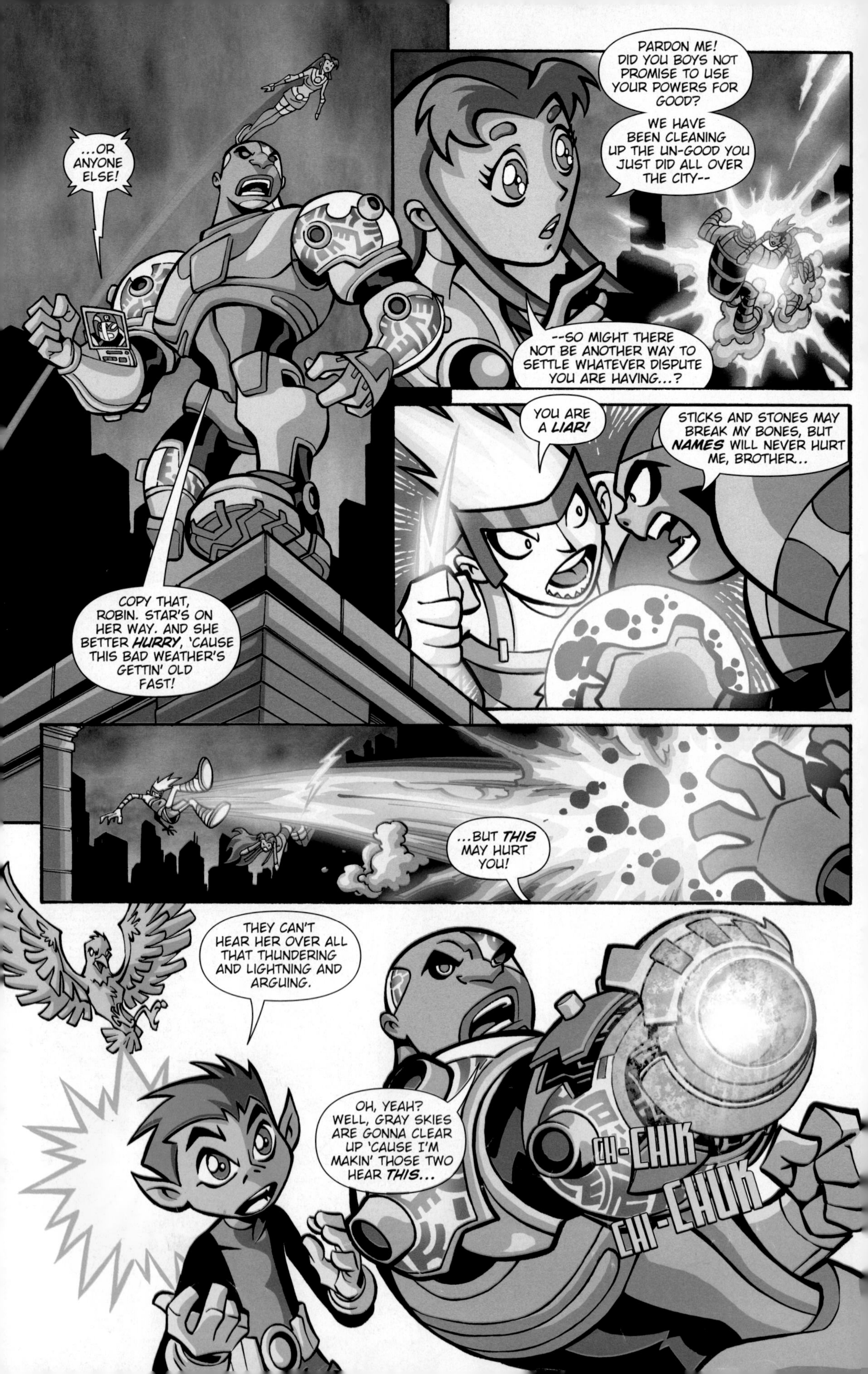
...OR ANYONE ELSE!
PARDON ME! DID YOU BOYS NOT PROMISE TO USE YOUR POWERS FOR GOOD?
WE HAVE BEEN CLEANING UP THE UN-GOOD YOU JUST DID ALL OVER THE CITY--
--SO MIGHT THERE NOT BE ANOTHER WAY TO SETTLE WHATEVER DISPUTE YOU ARE HAVING...?
COPY THAT, ROBIN. STAR'S ON HER WAY. AND SHE BETTER HURRY, 'CAUSE THIS BAD WEATHER'S GETTIN' OLD FAST!
YOU ARE A LIAR!
STICKS AND STONES MAY BREAK MY BONES, BUT NAMES WILL NEVER HURT ME, BROTHER...
...BUT THIS MAY HURT YOU!
THEY CAN'T HEAR HER OVER ALL THAT THUNDERING AND LIGHTNING AND ARGUING.
OH, YEAH? WELL, GRAY SKIES ARE GONNA CLEAR UP 'CAUSE I'M MAKIN' THOSE TWO HEAR THIS...
CH-CHIK
CHI-CHUK

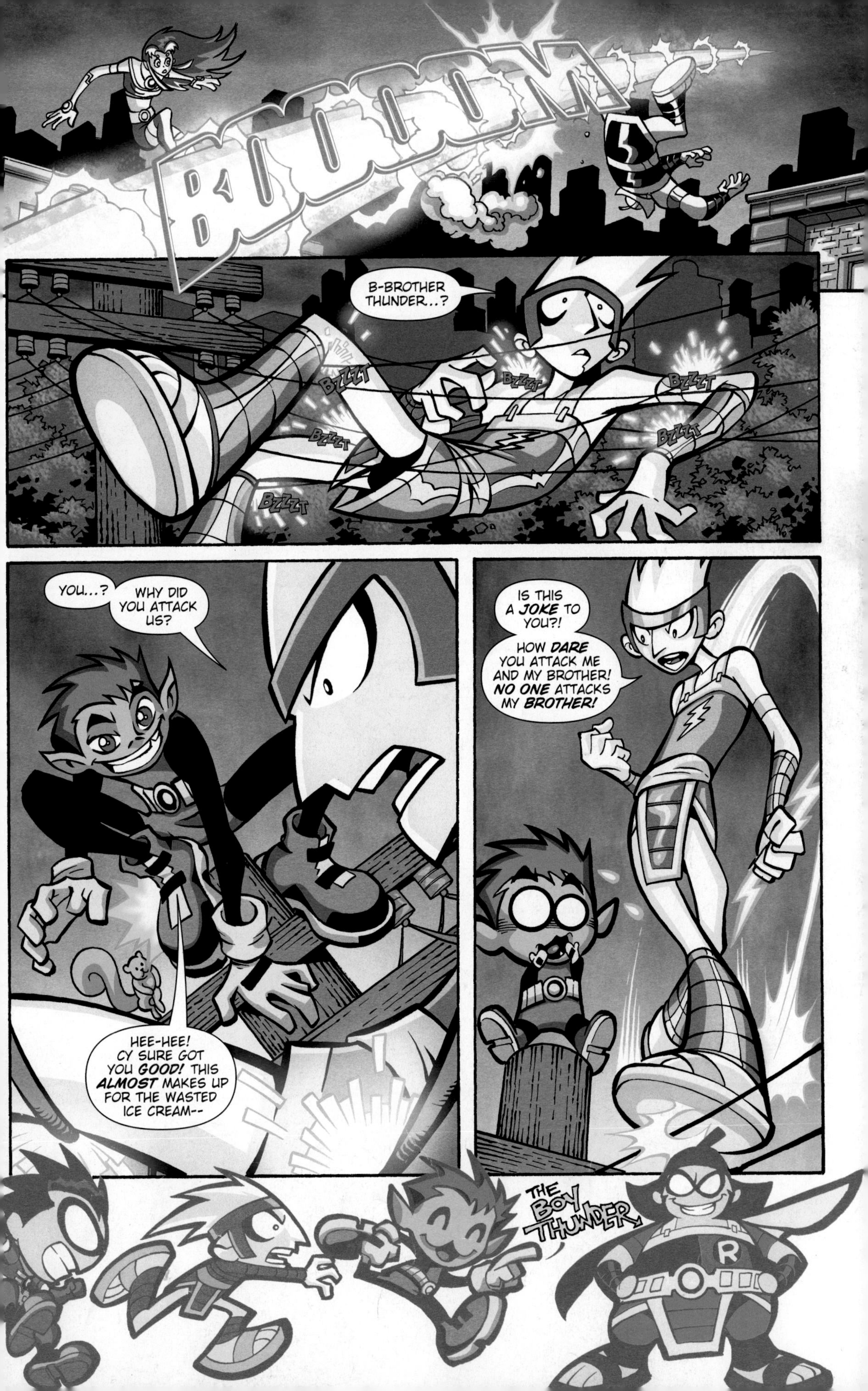
BOOOOM
B-BROTHER THUNDER...?
BZZZT
BZZZT
BZZZT
BZZZT
BZZZT
YOU...?
WHY DID YOU ATTACK US?
HEE-HEE! CY SURE GOT YOU GOOD! THIS ALMOST MAKES UP FOR THE WASTED ICE CREAM--
IS THIS A JOKE TO YOU?!
HOW DARE YOU ATTACK ME AND MY BROTHER! NO ONE ATTACKS MY BROTHER!
THE BOY THUNDER
R

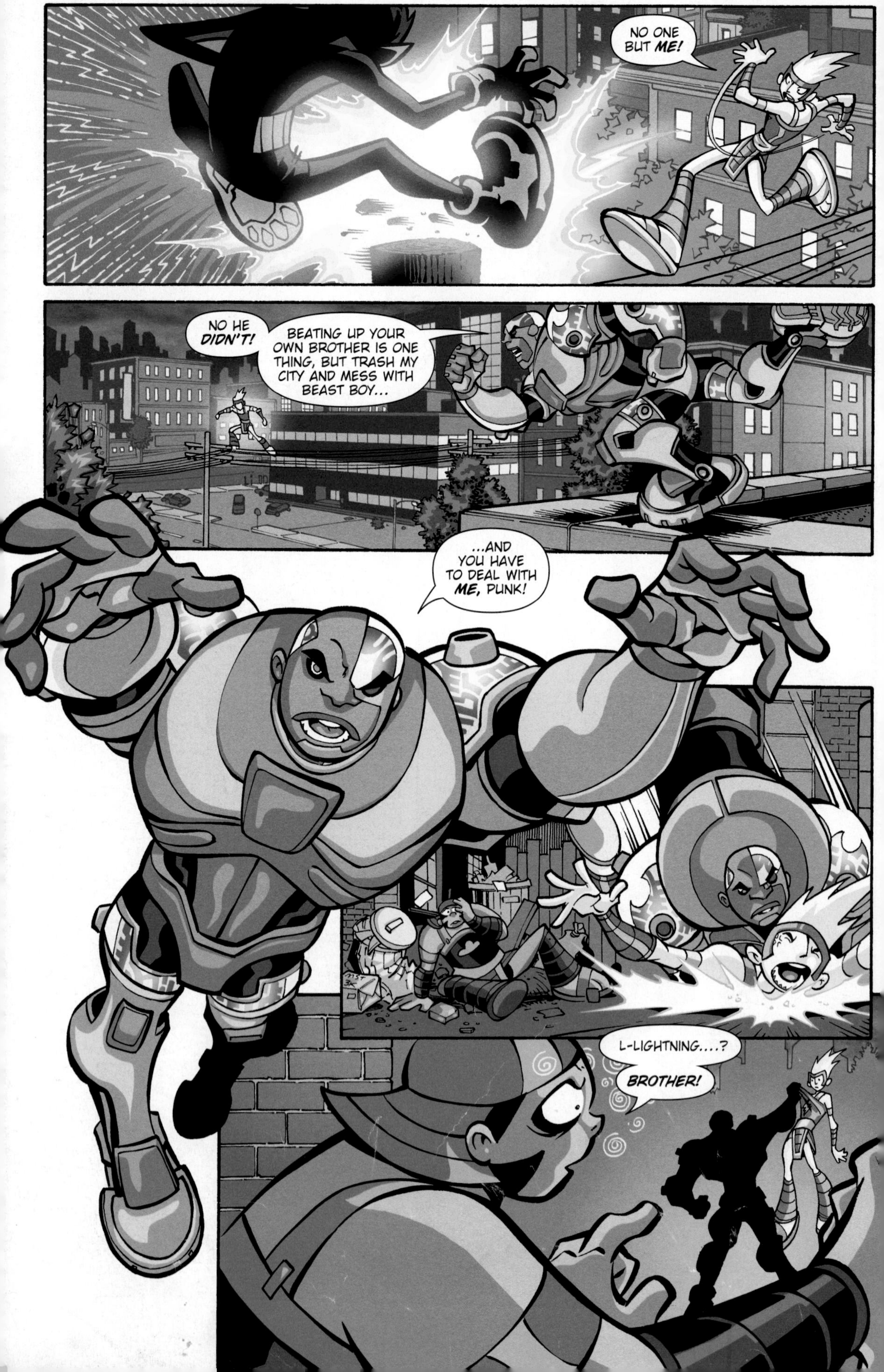
NO ONE BUT ME!
NO HE DIDN'T!
BEATING UP YOUR OWN BROTHER IS ONE THING, BUT TRASH MY CITY AND MESS WITH BEAST BOY...
...AND YOU HAVE TO DEAL WITH ME, PUNK!
L-LIGHTNING....?
BROTHER!

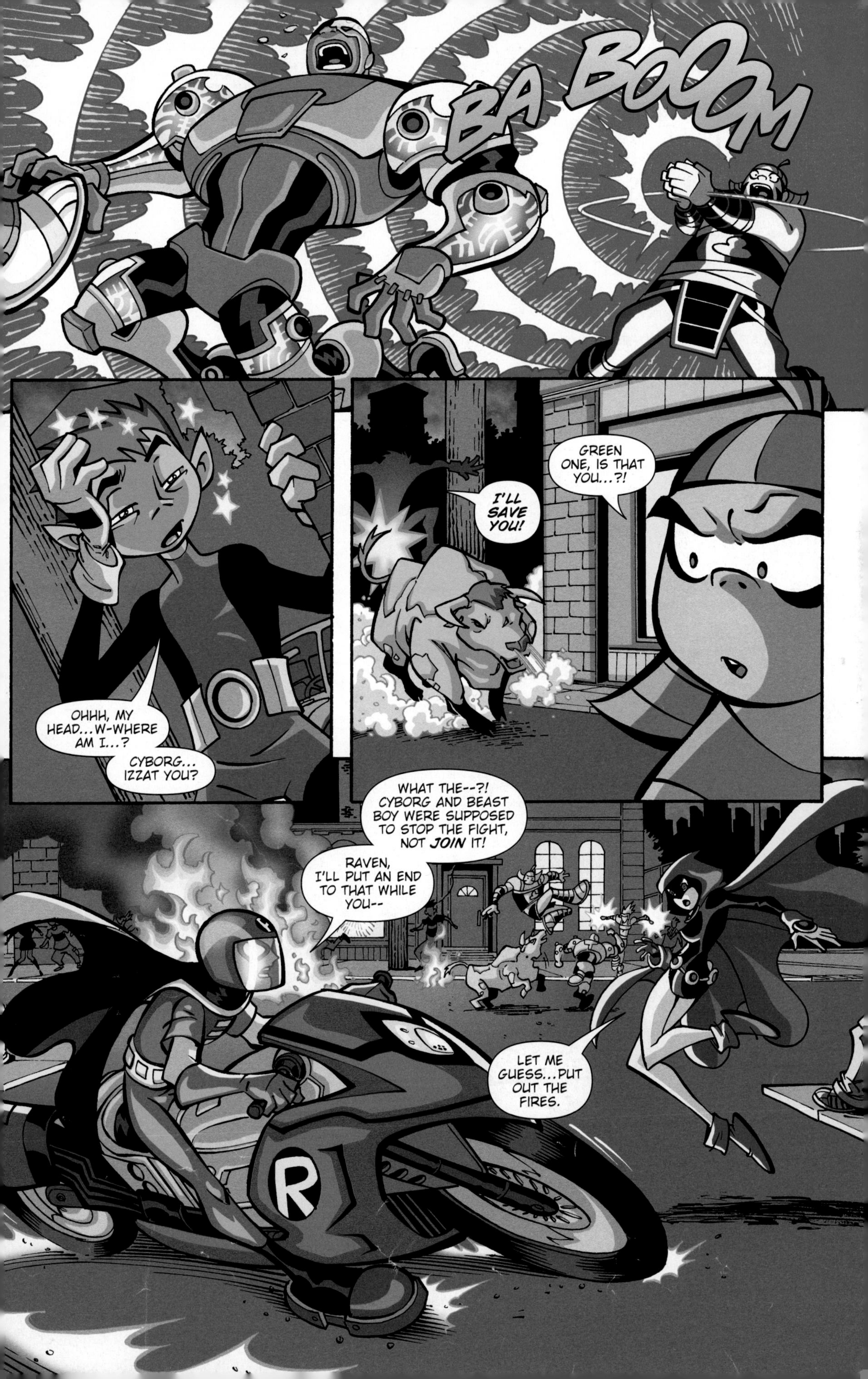
BA BOOOM
OHHH, MY HEAD...W-WHERE AM I...?
CYBORG... IZZAT YOU?
I'LL SAVE YOU!
GREEN ONE, IS THAT YOU...?!
WHAT THE--?! CYBORG AND BEAST BOY WERE SUPPOSED TO STOP THE FIGHT, NOT JOIN IT!
RAVEN, I'LL PUT AN END TO THAT WHILE YOU--
LET ME GUESS...PUT OUT THE FIRES.

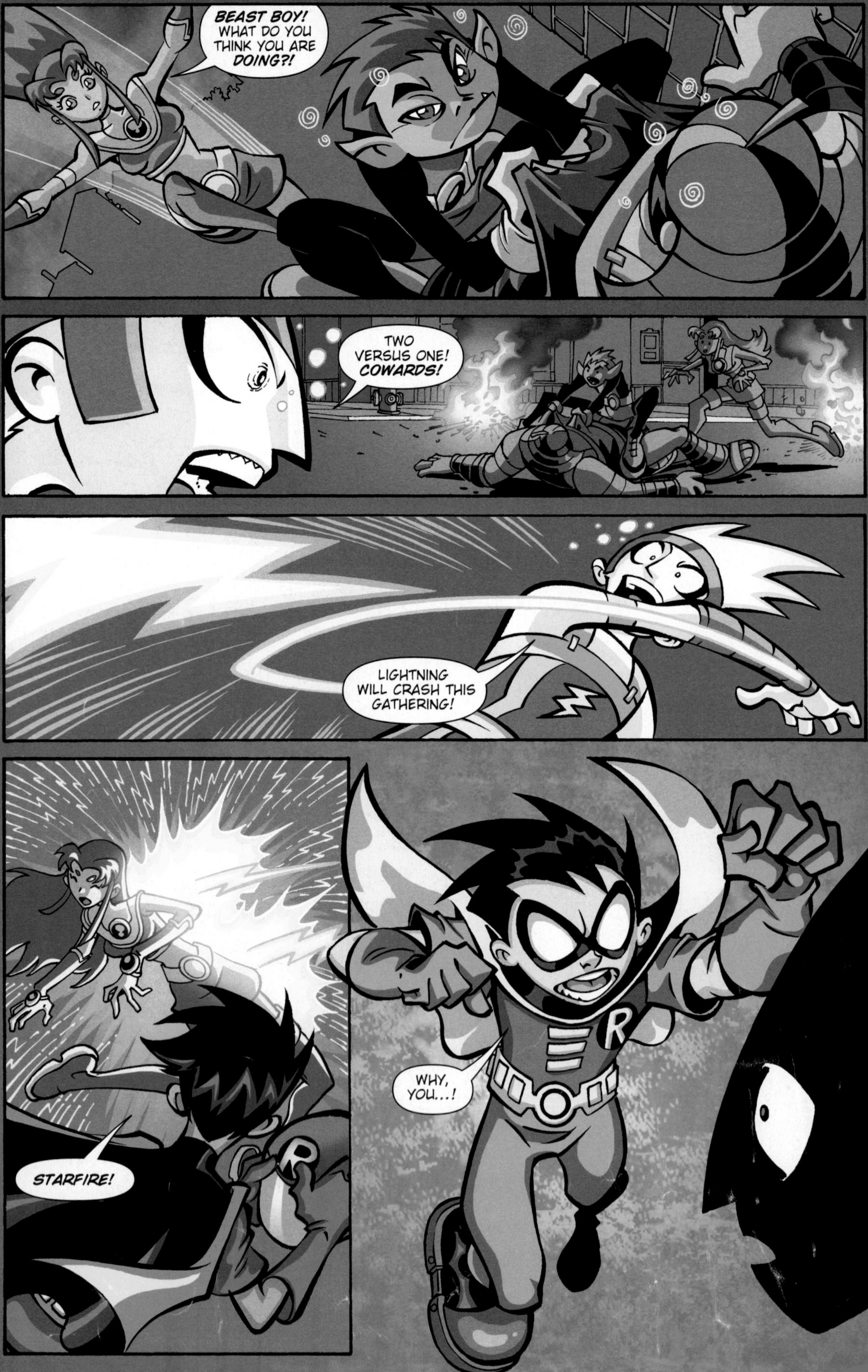
BEAST BOY! WHAT DO YOU THINK YOU ARE DOING?!
TWO VERSUS ONE! COWARDS!
LIGHTNING WILL CRASH THIS GATHERING!
STARFIRE!
WHY, YOU...!

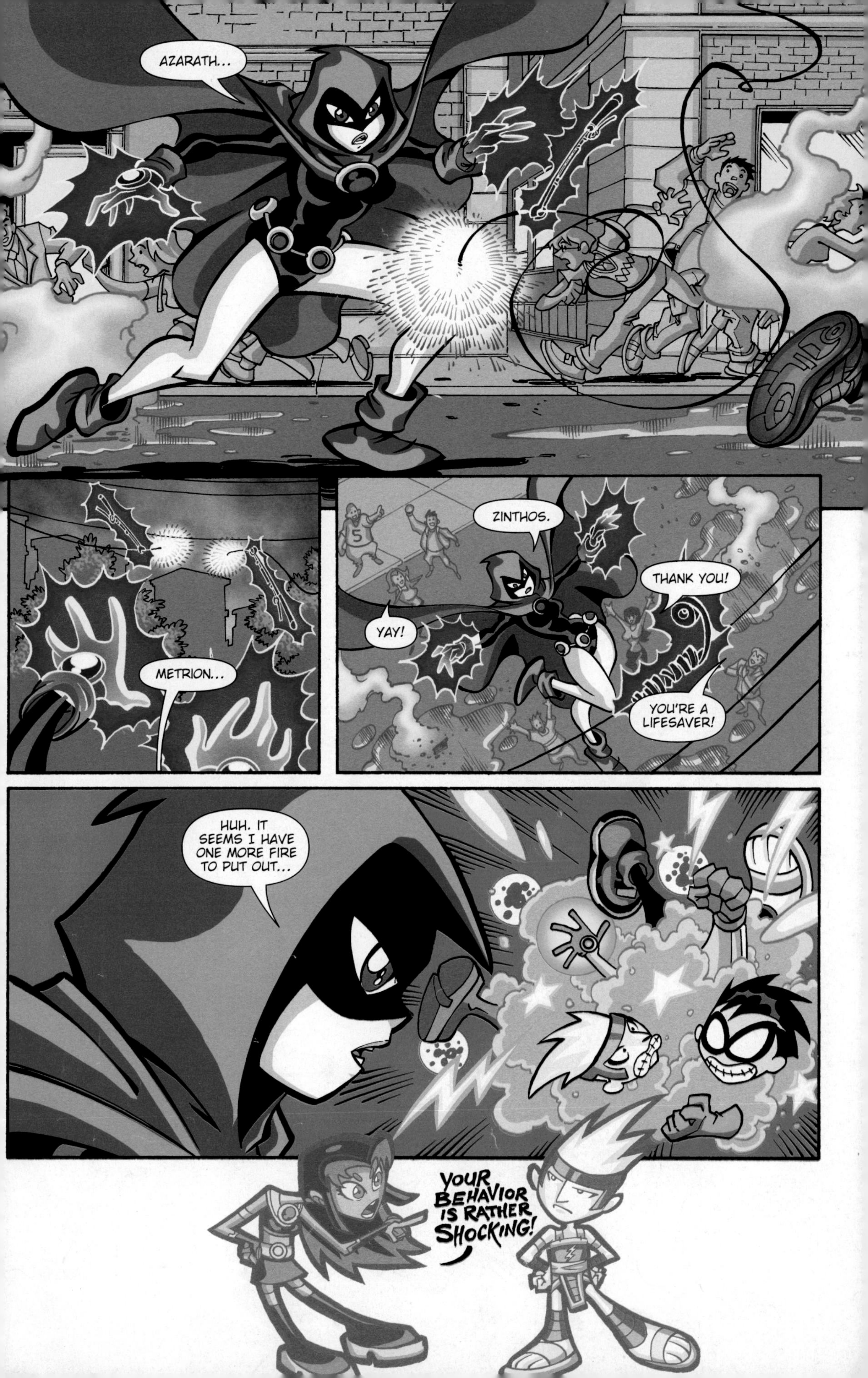

AZARATH...
METRION...
ZINTHOS.
YAY!
THANK YOU!
YOU'RE A LIFESAVER!
HUH. IT SEEMS I HAVE ONE MORE FIRE TO PUT OUT...
YOUR BEHAVIOR IS RATHER SHOCKING!

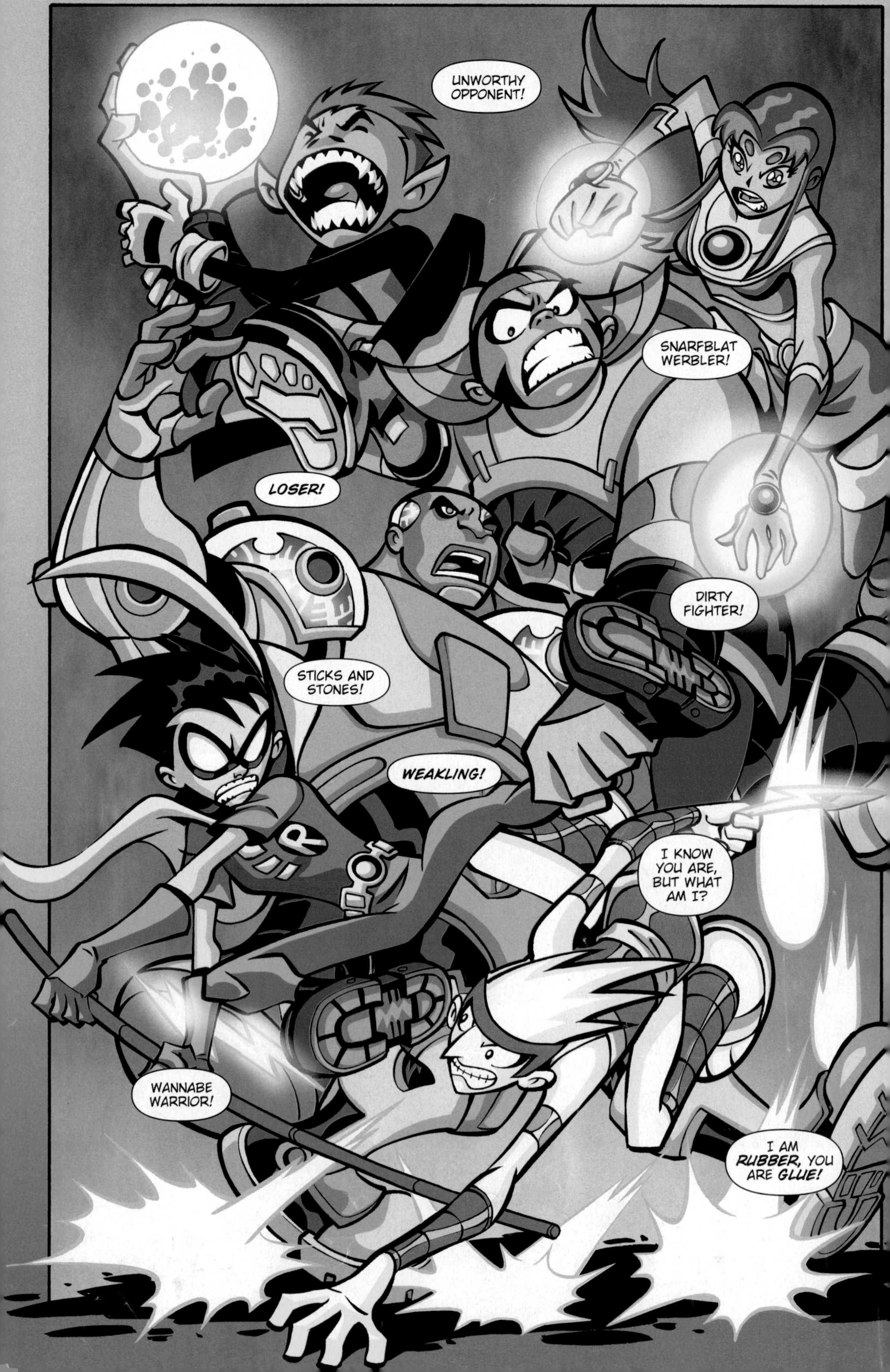
UNWORTHY OPPONENT!
SNARFBLAT WERBLER!
LOSER!
DIRTY FIGHTER!
STICKS AND STONES!
WEAKLING!
I KNOW YOU ARE, BUT WHAT AM I?
WANNABE WARRIOR!
I AM RUBBER, YOU ARE GLUE!

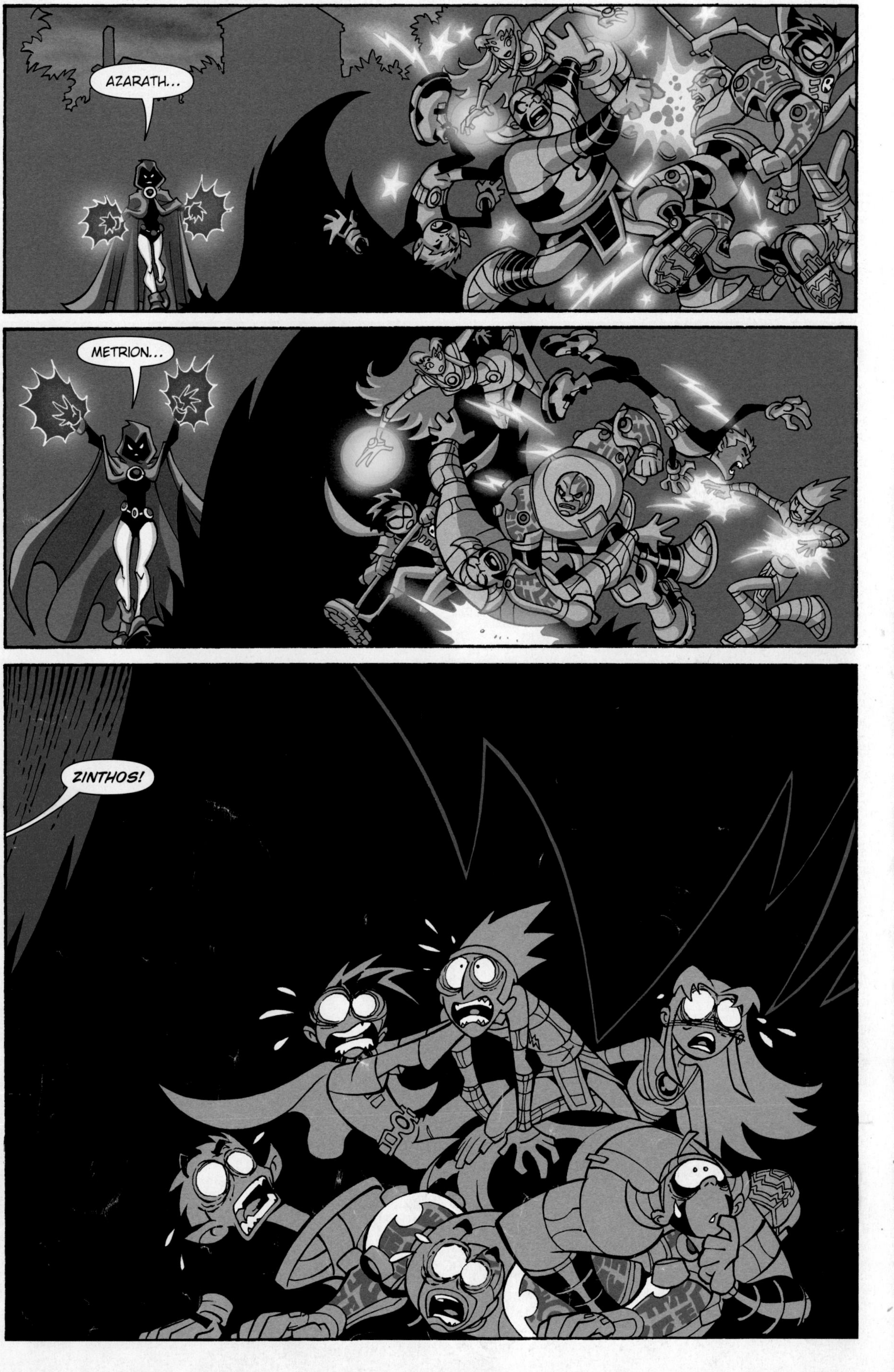
AZARATH...
METRION...
ZINTHOS!

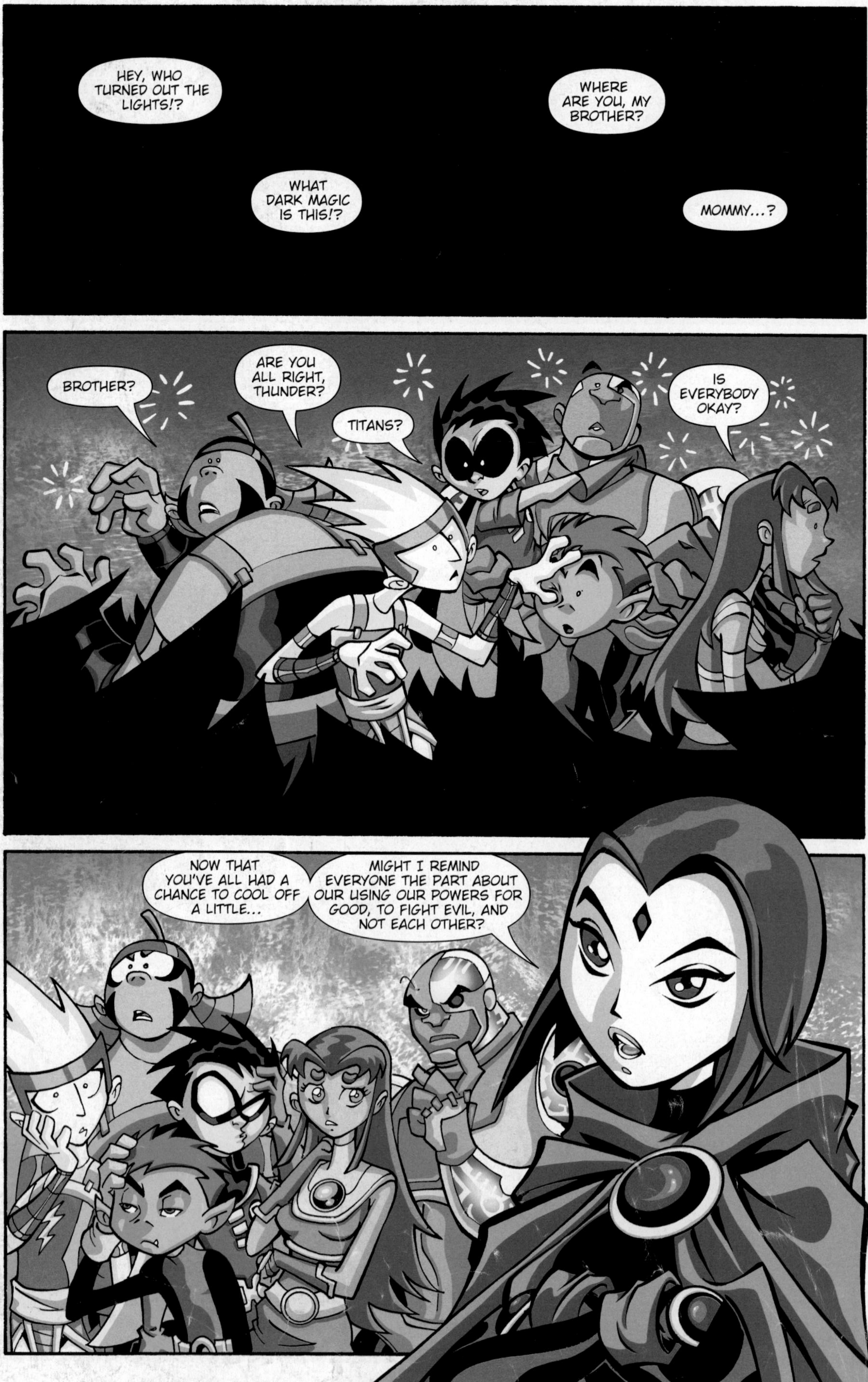
HEY, WHO TURNED OUT THE LIGHTS!?
WHERE ARE YOU, MY BROTHER?
WHAT DARK MAGIC IS THIS!?
MOMMY...?
BROTHER?
ARE YOU ALL RIGHT, THUNDER?
TITANS?
IS EVERYBODY OKAY?
NOW THAT YOU'VE ALL HAD A CHANCE TO COOL OFF A LITTLE...
MIGHT I REMIND EVERYONE THE PART ABOUT OUR USING OUR POWERS FOR GOOD, TO FIGHT EVIL, AND NOT EACH OTHER?

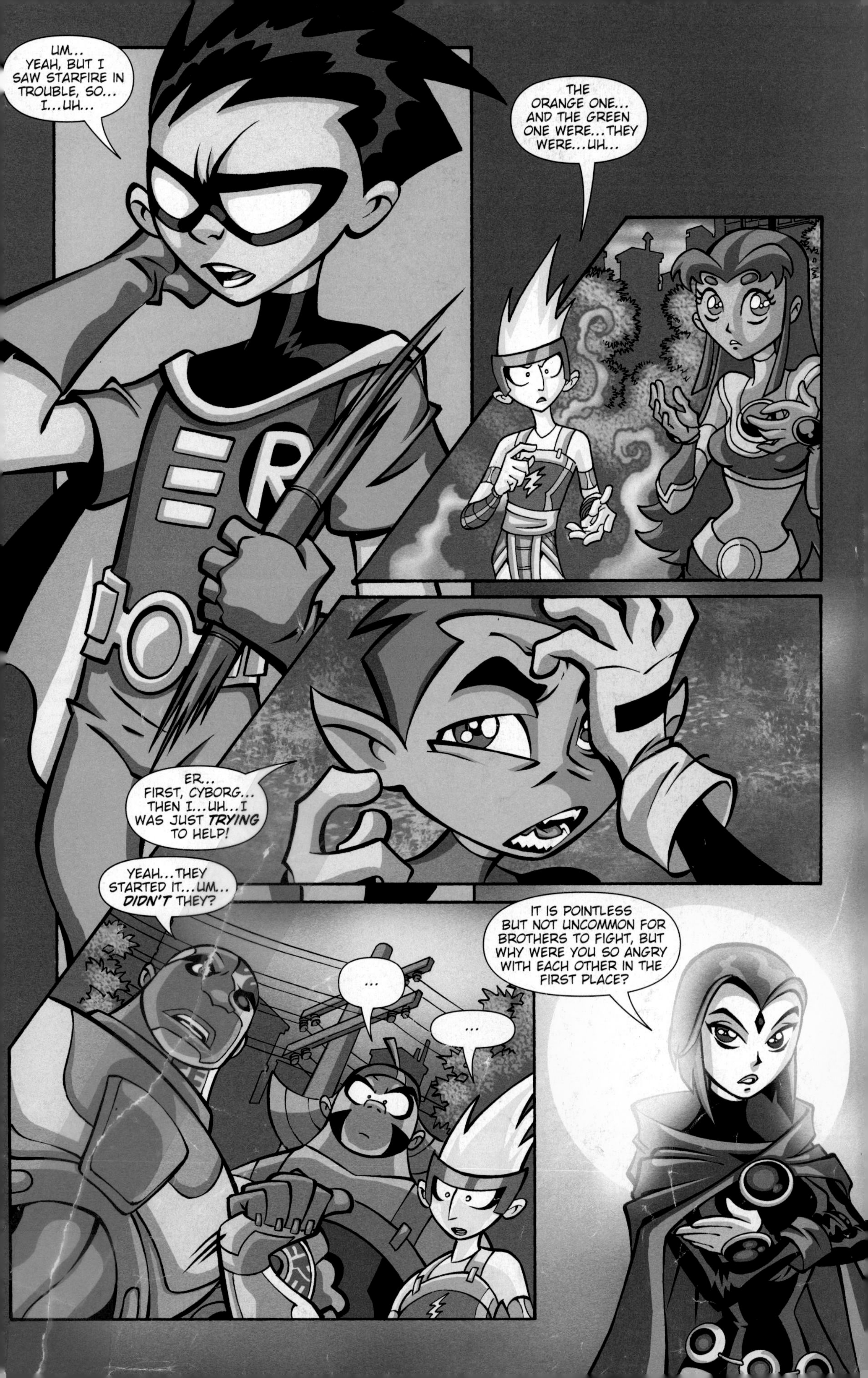
UM... YEAH, BUT I SAW STARFIRE IN TROUBLE, SO... I...UH...
THE ORANGE ONE... AND THE GREEN ONE WERE...THEY WERE...UH...
ER... FIRST, CYBORG... THEN I...UH...I WAS JUST *TRYING* TO HELP!
YEAH...THEY STARTED IT...UM... *DIDN'T* THEY?
...
...
IT IS POINTLESS BUT NOT UNCOMMON FOR BROTHERS TO FIGHT, BUT WHY WERE YOU SO ANGRY WITH EACH OTHER IN THE FIRST PLACE?

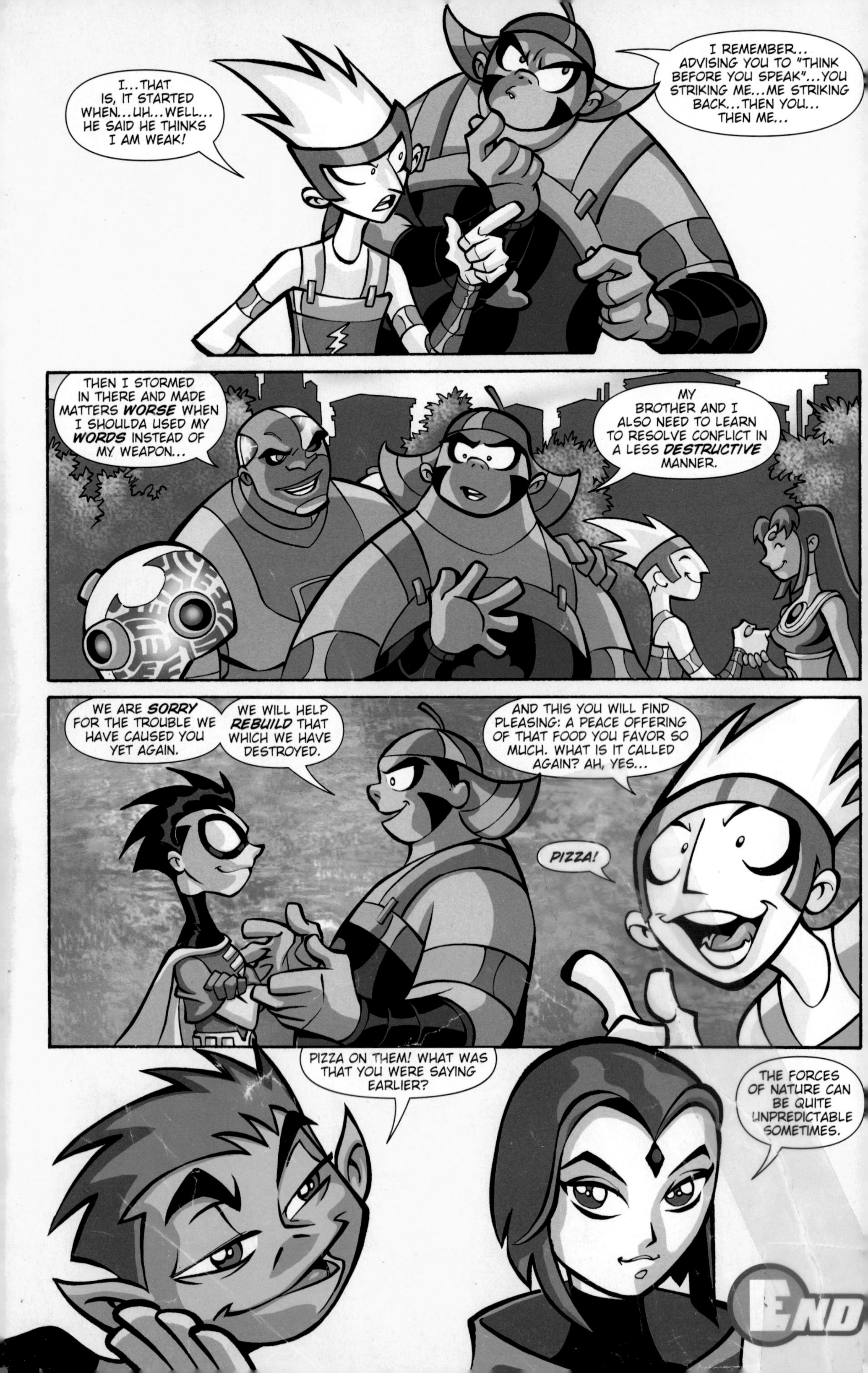

I...THAT IS, IT STARTED WHEN...UH...WELL... HE SAID HE THINKS I AM WEAK!
I REMEMBER... ADVISING YOU TO "THINK BEFORE YOU SPEAK"...YOU STRIKING ME...ME STRIKING BACK...THEN YOU... THEN ME...
THEN I STORMED IN THERE AND MADE MATTERS **WORSE** WHEN I SHOULDA USED MY **WORDS** INSTEAD OF MY WEAPON...
MY BROTHER AND I ALSO NEED TO LEARN TO RESOLVE CONFLICT IN A LESS **DESTRUCTIVE** MANNER.
WE ARE **SORRY** FOR THE TROUBLE WE HAVE CAUSED YOU YET AGAIN.
WE WILL HELP **REBUILD** THAT WHICH WE HAVE DESTROYED.
AND THIS YOU WILL FIND PLEASING: A PEACE OFFERING OF THAT FOOD YOU FAVOR SO MUCH. WHAT IS IT CALLED AGAIN? AH, YES...
PIZZA!
PIZZA ON THEM! WHAT WAS THAT YOU WERE SAYING EARLIER?
THE FORCES OF NATURE CAN BE QUITE UNPREDICTABLE SOMETIMES.
END